Praise for ELIZABETH WATASIN

The Dark Victorian: BONES

"Though I enjoyed the first book I just freaking adored this one."
— Goodreads

"Ms. Watasin's hasn't let down on the excitement of the plot or the rich tapestry of her world where the cold mechanical technology of Victorian England meets the glow of eldritch light. Pick this one up and give yourself a present... and here's hoping that book 3 will be out soon."
— My Ethereality

The Dark Victorian: RISEN

"There is a finely honed edge to The Dark Victorian: RISEN. Ms. Watasin's wit and imagination shine through the world of dark shadows and eldritch power and one quickly finds a home within the pages of this story."
— The Gilded Monocle

"I have no problem recommending this one, especially to fans of steampunk and other Victorian-era genres. I look forward to the next book in the series!"
— The Towering Pile

Books by Elizabeth Watasin

The Dark Victorian: RISEN
Charm School Volume One

Titles Upcoming:

The Dark Victorian: EVER LIFE
SUNDARK, an Elle Black Penny Dread

This BOOK belongs to:

Acknowledgements

The author would like to thank Jody Susskind and JoSelle Vanderhooft for their constant support. Such is *sine qua non* for making things happen.

The Dark Victorian:
BONES

Volume 2

By
Elizabeth Watasin

An A-Girl Studio book
published 2013 in the USA.

For additional information, please contact:
A-Girl Studio
P.O. Box 213, Burbank, CA 91503 U.S.A.
www.a-girlstudio.com

ISBN: 978-1-936622-03-0
Library of Congress Control Number: 2013933406
First paperback edition, 2013

❖

Cover Design and Illustrations by Elizabeth Watasin
Typography by Tom Orzechowski and Lois Buhalis
www.serifsup.com
Editing by JoSelle Vanderhooft
www.joselle-vanderhooft.com
"RISEN at the B-Ball Game", photograph by Paige Cavanaugh

*For
the
Rescued.*

CHAPTER ONE

"I Am Here."

A heavy fog rolled through London. Gaslights broke the dark as a hackney carriage drove down a deserted, cobbled street. Inside the carriage, Inspector Risk, a tall, dark-haired man with a thick moustache, sat and grimly regarded Dr. Speller, a bespectacled man with white mutton chop sideburns seated across from him. Dr. Speller moved his top hat around in his hands in excitement. The plainclothes sergeant, Barkley, took notes.

"It's Esther Stubbings, I'm sure of it," Dr. Speller said. "She is one of your victims."

"I've four bodies," Risk said. "Just skin and muscle. Full skeletons and organs entirely removed and no incisions made. Makes it hard to identify flattened faces. You're claiming that the organ almost sold to you tonight belonged to this Esther Stubbings, and therefore she's my victim."

"Well I've yet to identify the body, but the organ is unquestionably hers, Inspector, because I was the surgeon," Speller said. "Every woman's reproductive organs are different. I mean in shape. I recognized my own work, sir; I was the one who removed her second ovary. And Esther was alive and well just last week. The only way someone could harvest her organs is if she were murdered."

"And since we've her female vitals she has been," Risk said. "So this organ stealer, knowing you were a women's physician and vivisectionist, he comes to you for a sale."

"I vivisected only to learn," Speller said. "But for the most part I now merely dissect organs purchased solely from the Royal Surgical Sciences Academy."

"Indeed. The Academy. Which buys from men like the one you met tonight," Risk said. "Except this one knows to bring it directly to you. The dead woman I have is of the poor. We know it from her clothes. How can someone like that afford your services?"

"She can when she volunteers for the procedure," Speller said. "Like all members of the Academy, I'm a man of science and medicine. Not only do I use the skills learned, I practice new techniques that have successfully corrected female ailments. Esther Stubbings was on her way to becoming a fully healthy woman. And none of it, thankfully, by use of supernatural nonsense, claiming healing through organ transference and such!"

"But that's exactly what I have, doctor," Risk said. "Black arts surgery. Unless you can explain how four people have no skulls, eyes, or brains in their intact heads Without them having been pulled out of their nostrils."

"Not to mention," Sergeant Barkley said, "how His Royal Highness can be here with us today if not for supernatural medicine. Been nineteen years since he nearly died! We've a bunch of nonsense to thank."

Risk sighed while Speller glowered. The carriage came to a halt outside a lit station house.

"You stay here," Risk said to Speller. "We'll move on to the mortuary shortly for you to identify the woman. And you," he said to Barkley. "Stop talking. Let's go."

When Risk stepped down from the carriage he saw a young woman in an azure coat briskly leave the station entrance. Her brown hat was crooked, and wisps of dark hair escaped. Her skirts were cut high enough for the ankles of her boots to show. She wore a fitted leather mask on one side of her face. Helia Skycourt smiled at Risk and waved. She grabbed the penny-farthing resting against the station wall, took a running jump into the side-saddle seat, and hit the treadle. The lantern in front of her wheel suddenly lit. She sped away into the dark and fog.

Risk watched her depart, incredulous.

"Damn journalist," he said. "Does she never sleep?"

Barkley stifled a yawn. They entered the station building.

"Inspector," Barkley said in a low voice as they walked into the dimly lit room. A uniformed man was behind the desk. "This case . . . it being supernatural. When will the Secret Commission start helping?"

"When we ask for it," Risk said curtly. "And not before. What do you have?" he said to the policeman who rose to greet him.

"Sir," the policeman said. He led them down a narrow hall. "The fellow Dr. Speller had us arrest will be brought out of his cell shortly. He refuses to speak and has answered no questions. The doctor told us the man only spoke once during the negotiating of the price of the organ and his accent was German."

"Looks a foreigner, then?" Risk asked. He followed the policeman into a room with a desk and chairs. He took the seat behind the desk while Barkley went to stand near the small, barred window.

"No sir," the policeman answered. "Well dressed, clean-faced, trimmed hair, tidy, hands that haven't seen hard labor. I'm guessing he's of the medical profession."

"Organ stealers usually are," Risk said. "Especially those who work in mortuaries." They heard shuffling steps approach. Two policemen brought a shackled man into the room. He was a slim fellow, tight-lipped and with one, nervous eye. His other eye had been removed, leaving a gaping, black socket. He did not bother to shut his eyelid. The men escorting him sat him in front of Risk.

"*Wie ist dein name?*" Risk said.

The man looked at him in surprise.

"The sooner you answer our questions," Risk said. "The sooner we catch who's doing these black arts surgeries. Because it isn't you, is it? So if you don't want the blame, give us someone else's name."

The man's posture became stiffer.

"That's four dead," Risk said staring into the man's one eye.

"Is the gallows worth this surgeon? Give him up and you won't have to worry. Do your sentence and then get on with life, right?"

Risk watched the man; the prisoner seemed to grow even more frightened.

"Right," Risk said slowly. "Now who is he?"

A shot exploded, shattering the window behind the sergeant. Blood sprayed into Risk's face. The other men shouted and ran out the door. The prisoner sat slumped. Brain matter hung from the side of his forehead where the bullet had exited.

Shouts and running came from outside the station. Risk didn't bother looking out the broken window, knowing that all he'd see would be darkness and fog. He grimly pulled out his handkerchief and slowly wiped his face. Barkley touched the prisoner to see if he was still alive.

"Shall I send a message to the Secret Commission?" Barkley asked.

Risk stared at the dead man who'd just brought him an internal affairs nightmare.

"Do it," he said.

A hazy morning dawned in the East End of London, the fog and coal smoke lessening under the winds accompanying the rising sun. The street beneath The Vesta Club with its beggars, ragged boys, and costermongers was noisy with the clatter of hooves and wheels. Art stood before her third-storey window in the Vesta, the deep red curtains drawn open for sunlight. She was already fully dressed in her hat, gloves, and Secret Commission badge. Her dressmaker, Charlotte Thackery, had designed her new bodice with soft ruffles from throat to breast and a double row of tiny mother of pearl buttons down her chest. Two more buttons winked, iridescent, at her cuffs. Pinned at her throat was the skull cameo given her by the Secret Commission.

Art set her silver-handled, ironwood walking stick to the red carpet on the floor, her fingers upon the curved deer's head. At her full height she was well over six feet tall. She was well proportioned, broad of shoulder, and as was soon discovered by herself and others when she accidentally ripped her previous bodice during a fight, well-developed in muscle. Her first dress, shredded further by murderous reanimated children, hung on her armoire door. In a box stored on the closet shelf was the damaged corset, with its flexible, armour-like plates inserted between the boning that was Charlotte's patented design.

Upon inspection this morning, her boots' toes and heels appeared sturdy and whole, despite the various falls and jumps Art recalled taking on the last case to which she had been assigned. Even the singular silver caps tapped into the heel and toes remained unscratched. She had never seen their like on women's boots. The ornate heel caps were inscribed with the word "ART", which Art found odd because she had not read the inscription before naming herself. She hoped to ask Charlotte how the caps came to be enscribed.

While standing before the full-length mirror, she looked a very well-dressed lady except for her spectral glow. Perceptible even in morning light, the ephemeral aura bleached the colour from her garments, which, on this day, were a royal blue trimmed in Apollo-gold. Her skin and eyes were very pale.

This day marked her sixth day of life; her first was when she woke in eldritch fire and electricity in the Secret Commission's laboratory. Dr. Gatly Fall had resurrected her as an artificial ghost devoid of personal memories, though she understood that like the rest of the Secret Commission agents, she was formerly an executed criminal. She'd also been allowed to keep some elements of her identity. Why she was allowed to remain Quaker was a mystery. The name given her then was Artifice, and thanks to the papers this was how the people of London knew her. Jim Dastard, an animated skull and her partner, urged her to name herself, so she took the name Art. For the time being it seemed all the naming she needed.

Art thought she might make note of her first waking day once she purchased a diary. It would be useful for legal purposes to remember her new birth date.

She approached her red-curtained windows and gazed down at the street below. The club's short-haired and boyish-faced page, Alice, was purchasing a stack of newspapers for the members staying at the private club. The newsboy seemed unruffled by the fact that the young woman he was selling papers to was dressed in male uniform. No one on the street seemed to notice, and Art observed that it seemed to fit their present society to merely accept that male clothing meant the person was male without question, cross-dressing music hall performers aside.

The exclusive club Art was presently staying in, thanks to Jim, catered to upper-class deviants who had love of their own sex, though Jim would qualify that more as lust. As a Quaker, Art was uncertain a place suited for "trysts and treats", as Jim called it, was appropriate to live in, but for the moment she could not deny enjoying the convenience of it. She occupied the large, furnished "Rouge" room which had amenities such as a stove, carpets, gas-lights, and a tub. The club had services that, though in some ways pampering, lessened the more trying aspects of her work as a Secret Commission agent. Indulging in luxury was not Quaker, but Art couldn't deny that having such services as the Vesta provided had helped her when she sorely needed it.

Comfort, she thought, watching a worn-faced matchstick seller with her baby on the street. It was unfortunate that only the rich could afford it; Art was only staying at the Vesta by happenstance. Jim's first partner, Harold, had been son to the owner, Catherine Moore, and in gratitude she allowed Jim and Art to stay for free. Since Jim chose the Vesta as his haven and Art preferred to be near her partner for the time being, Art saw that it was practical to stay.

"As way opens," she said softly to herself.

She heard a muffled thump against her room wall. Were Art more prudish, as many of her Quaker brethren were, she might have changed her mind and consider leaving the Vesta right then. She moved swiftly in ghost form to poke her head into the wall. In the very narrow, secret passage between her room and the one beside hers, a maid was sweeping the strip of floor. With her back to Art in the darkness, the maid didn't notice Art looking in. Tiny beams of light from exposed peepholes lit the passage walls. The maid paused in sweeping to carefully close each one. She used a tiny key to lock their covers as she swept down the passage.

Art removed her head before she frightened the maid.

Earlier that morning Art recalled having discerned a peeper the night before. She discovered there were three peepholes into her room, all accessible by the one passage. She found it amusing that at each peephole a small seat could be let down for the peeper to sit upon. After some examination of the hole covers, she determined that the peepholes to her room required a different key than the ones peeping into the room next to hers. It also meant that the set of keys given her when she came to the Vesta did not include one to her own peephole. Therefore, she had no say or control over who could watch her.

She had argued with Jim that she thought the Vesta a brothel, no matter how reputable or exclusive. There were women in residence, Arlette and Manon, whose presence attested to the fact that indeed, the Vesta saw to sexual needs. But after meeting Catherine Moore and having benefited from the attentive service of the club's staff, Art was inclined to forgive the Vesta its more tawdry aspects.

Having a peeper whose identity was yet unknown to her did not bother her, surprisingly. She was not an exhibitionist, though as a former physical culturist—as evidenced by her developed musculature—she didn't mind being nude and having others see her thus. She was more intrigued that someone would want to spy on her. With her superior hearing she noted the maid's final exit from the passage. Art put her stick aside. Laid on her red bedspread were different objects of size and material.

During the time between night and daybreak, a thought had occurred to her to test what could accompany her while in ghost form. The spectacular accident where she had tried to take Jim with her through a wall proved that at least something of bone could not travel with her. She perused what she'd laid out and decided on a very simple test first. She picked up Helia Skycourt's silver-engraved card from her dresser. It passed swiftly with her as she ghosted into the secret passage and then out again. Art smiled, looking at the card. It was no substitute for the actual woman but it gladdened Art to have this little token of Helia. She picked up the iron poker.

Art walked through the wall in ghost form and heard the iron poker she carried fall with a dull thud to her room's floor. Art poked her head back into her room, perplexed. She tried again with a water glass, though this time by crouching in the secret passage and reaching for the glass on her bedroom floor. When she slid it towards her, it hit the wall.

There was a knock at her door while Art was still in the passage, coaxing her hand through the wall while holding a box of matches. Art decided not to answer; she had already spied in the room next to hers that the Vesta maids were busy cleaning and making up beds. She felt she might be close to getting the match-box through the wall if she worked on varying her solidity.

∼

Alice entered Art's room with a second female page, pushing a serving cart laden with covered silver dishes. Arlette breezily followed, leading Manon by the hand. Both young women were of the same height and build, their bodices loosely fastened. Arlette was dark-haired while Manon was blonde. They were barefoot and had their hair down. The pages arranged breakfast by the bright windows. Arlette and Manon looked curiously about for Art. Arlette spied Art's gloved hand moving against the wall, holding the box of matches. Stifling a giggle, she pointed it out to Manon. Then she approached and with deft fingers, plucked the box from Art's hand.

∼

Art poked her head through the wall in surprise. The second page shrieked and upset one of the plates.

"*Bonjour,*" Arlette said with a smile, looking up at Art.

"*Bonjour,*" Art said kindly. "How is the Spirit with thee, Friend?"

"*Bien*," Arlette said, sounding amused. She moved for the breakfast table. "Remain there," she added when Art was about to step out of the wall. "You are trying something, I see. Try this." She picked an orange from a small basket of fruit and tossed it to Art.

Art caught it and realised Manon was near, studying her ghost state. Manon reached out and passed her fingers through Art's phantom hand that held the orange. The touch gave Art a thrill. Perhaps Manon was only curious, but the gesture seemed friendly.

Art withdrew completely into the wall, and then reemerged, stepping back into her room. The orange had traveled successfully with her. Manon placed her hand on top of Art's then solid hand, her fingers warm.

"How did thee know?" Art said to Arlette.

"I didn't," Arlette said. "But among the objects on your bed there was no food. It seemed the thing to try. Now that is done, come have breakfast with us! We have brought you something to eat too."

Alice pulled out a chair for Arlette, who promptly sat down. Manon grasped the orange in Art's hand.

"*Bonjour*," Art whispered to Manon, who stared quietly into her eyes. Art felt she might fall into Manon's green-eyed gaze again, lost in the sensation of standing in an ancient forest. She didn't understand why Manon sought to beguile her; Arlette seemed wholly unaffected in Manon's company. Art thought it might be a test to discern her reactions to Manon's otherworldly nature. So far, Art hoped she pleased.

"Is thee happy with the staff I gifted thee?" Art asked softly. She was referring to the powerful wood staff she and Jim had retrieved from a medium on their last case. It was in Manon's safekeeping. The sudden smile of delight that lit Manon's face was enough answer. Art smiled in relief.

She felt a tingling in her palm. The orange trembled slightly, as if it would sprout right then. It pulled itself out of Art's hand and into Manon's. Manon looked back and slowly walked to the table. Art quickly pulled out the pin securing her hat. She took it off and then her gloves. She wasn't sure why Arlette and Manon were visiting when they should be sleeping, having worked the night but she was not about to complain. Since discussing Manon's possible true nature with Jim, who would only lead the topic to that of dryads, nymphs, and imps, Art looked forward to more of her company.

Arlette and Manon seemed unperturbed by her ghost nature, so she sailed up to the table and solidified. Alice, standing by the serving cart, maintained her composure, but her fellow page turned white as a sheet. Alice went to Art's armoire to take the shredded dress and the box with the ruined undergarments and corset. The pages discreetly left with the cart while Art seated Manon.

"I thank thee for breaking fast with me," Art said, taking the chair between the women. "Should we fetch Jim?"

"This is not for Monsieur Dastard," Arlette said, her gaze mischievous. She retrieved a sausage from a plate and ate it.

"As I thought," Art said, smiling. "By whose generosity do I have the pleasure of thy company?"

"A benefactor who shall remain nameless, and who likes to see you happy," Arlette said. "To begin." She removed the cover of the center dish. "Your food."

On the plate was an artful pyramid of raw, whole herring, the fishes' blank eyes bright and clear. Art felt a stirring within her that she recognized as hunger.

"Art approves," Arlette said to Manon, laughing. She removed the cover of another dish. "And this?" A bundle of fresh watercress was spread upon the plate.

The vegetable was a staple for the working class and it gladdened Art to see the familiar leaves included in this repast, courtesy of the Vesta.

"Aye, I eat greens," she said.

Manon reached across and picked a watercress sprig. She slowly ate it, watching Art.

"*Coquine!*" Arlette lightly admonished. "You have your own food!"

Manon ignored her. She picked up dill. The herb waved in her grasp. She touched it with her tongue before biting it.

Dill? Art thought. She looked down. She then noticed the food of the other women. While Arlette's side of the table contained the dishes of a typical upper-class breakfast—sausage, bacon, eggs, toast, and broiled fish—Manon's had fruit, a selection of fresh herbs—basil, dill, mint, and thyme—and a pile of various flowers. After all of Jim's circumvention of what manner of creature Manon might be, Art felt honored to be allowed to witness her eating habits. The staff of the Vesta was apparently also aware of her difference. Manon picked up a purple violet.

"*C'est vous*," Manon whispered to Art. She pulled off the fragrant, purple petals. Art recalled the color's meaning as she watched Manon eat each petal.

"I am more the blue," she said to Manon.

"Flower talk," Arlette said dismissively, eating her eggs. "Won't you eat, Art?"

Manon broke her hypnotic gaze with Art to narrow eyes at Arlette. Art shook herself. Arlette merely raised an eyebrow at Manon and put more pepper on her eggs. Art sensed the conflict between the two. It was not antagonistic, simply Arlette asserting dominance. Art thought perhaps this was why Manon was with Arlette. Arlette could not be bothered with being beguiled.

"My manner of eating is unnatural," Art said apologetically.

"And Manon eats weeds," Arlette said. Manon threw a flower stalk at her. Arlette chuckled, but when she looked at Art it was meaningful. "She does not eat her flowers so openly."

"I understand," Art said.

"And she is very particular, to whom she gives company," Arlette said. "For pleasure or otherwise."

Art pondered that. Was Arlette saying that Manon was very exclusive? This breakfast, then, was very well paid for.

"We perform together because Manon will only have pleasure with me," Arlette said.

Art blinked.

"But when the client pays the Vesta's price," Arlette said, "Manon will allow touching. And when more is paid . . . then the client may do more."

"Oh," Art said. She looked at Manon, who merely watched her, her eyes deep and calm. Art felt odd with this talk of prices. Arlette tapped Art for her attention.

"You," Arlette said to Art, "may do more."

"Oh," Art said again. She wondered if it were possible to blush, pale as she was. She felt unaccountably self-conscious and had the silly feminine desire to hide behind her napkin. Who was this odd benefactor of hers, gifting her with . . . Manon? Art doubted she'd been in the company of the living long enough to have a secret admirer, much less a doting patron — if this situation could be called an example of doting.

"I thank thee . . . for this understanding," Art finally said. Her cheeks were warm.

"*Bon*," Arlette said, smiling. "Won't you eat now, Art?"

"Aye," Art said, relieved. She beheld both of them with gratitude. "My thanks for sharing this meal with me." She closed her eyes to make that thanks known silently. Then she raised her palm. The herring on the table began to tremble. They flew into Art's body en masse, and she swiftly absorbed them.

Arlette's eyes grew wide. "*Extraordinaire*. . . . and you are finished?" she asked.

"Aye. Unless they were living, then they might wiggle."

"The cook was told you take no animal of hoof or feather," Arlette said.

"I have eaten eel and whelk. It seems I tend to the water creatures." Art laid a hand over the watercress. She drew them in, leaving a few for Manon. The greens had a spicy bite she enjoyed.

"Did you sleep?" Arlette suddenly asked. "Your bed is still made."

"Jim told me to sleep," Art admitted, looking chastised. "I tried a short while. I've not taken rest in nearly six days."

Arlette exclaimed and Manon merely munched, listening quietly. Arlette spread butter on her toast, deep in thought. She also spread blueberry jam on a second slice and marmalade on another.

"*Pourquoi elle dit biche 'thee'?*" Manon asked Arlette.

Arlette shrugged.

"*Elle est un Puritain*," Arlette said.

"I am not a Puritan," Art said. "I am Quaker."

"*Qua qua*," Arlette said to Manon, who briefly laughed. Art's heart lightened to hear it.

"For thee I would be a duck," Art said in amusement.

"Again," Arlette said, "you say 'thee'. I know my English. Why do you not say 'thou'?"

"For myself, 'thou' is like 'you'. To speak thus is an address of class. It is title and flattery and unlike the Friends," Art explained. "By my address of 'thee' is our equality assured."

"'Equality'," Arlette repeated. She gave Art a sceptical look. "*C'est incroyable.*"

Arlette ate her toast, apparently lost in thought. Art then noticed that all the watercress on the plate was gone; in their place were blue violets. She looked at Manon, who merely waited. Art placed her hand over the violets and absorbed them. They were fragrant and sweet, like nectar.

Art shivered. It was her first taste of such purity. She felt as a child might, tasting sweets for the first time.

Manon slowly blinked. Her eyes seemed to give approval.

"And it is not easy for you to die?" Arlette asked. "Like Monsieur Harold, before you. He ate many, many things, in the manner we do, and it helped him remain whole."

"'Tis true," Art said. "I do the same."

"Ah. As long as you have your fish and snails. You are not like Manon," Arlette said. "She can hurt and die like me. And she only talks to grass and dirt. What good is that? You can do things no one can. You do not have to live like us. You can. . ." She gestured with her knife, searching for words. "Live in the sky, or in the water. Go to the seaside, the coast faraway, eat as much fish as you want, and merely pull them from the ocean. We mortal women, we need money. You do not need it. You may not need clothes, this room, someone to marry. You do not need to marry. You are a ghost! You can go wherever you want, do what you want. No one can stop you. You are free to be anything."

"What would that be?" Manon asked softly. Art was surprised to hear her speak English.

"Queen of the sea," Arlette said.

They sat in contemplation while Arlette ate the remainder of her breakfast. Art thought of Helia, then of Manon. She very much wanted to know both women better. She could not do that living solely among God's animals.

"I cannot talk to fish," Art finally said. Orange scented the air. Manon was breaking her orange into a perfect half, rind included. She raised one half to Art.

Art leaned in, her eyes nearly closing from the smell of the fruit. The orange shook slightly in Manon's hand, and then disappeared into Art. It was deliciously sweet and also had a sour tang, much like the berries she had when Jim treated her to tea. Arlette chuckled around the piece of toast in her mouth.

"She is not your pony," Arlette said to Manon.

"Hello, hello!" Jim cried from the adjacent study. "I'm awake! Is anyone there?"

Arlette quickly wiped her mouth with her napkin. "Oh, he knows we are here! He has the hearing of a fox. I will see to Monsieur Dastard." When she rose, she suddenly stayed Manon's hand with its slice of orange. "Do you really want to eat that? It has been to the Fourth Dimension," she teased.

Arlette left for the adjoining room. Art had thought the door to the study was for a closet until Jim requested she help him retire for the night. The adjacent study was a nook with its own windows facing the street. It held books, a leather chair, and the cabinet in which Jim slept. Art had left the door ajar, not wishing to isolate Jim though he was behind the doors of his cabinet. She could hear Arlette open the curtains as she greeted him.

"What is the Fourth Dimension?" Art asked Manon.

"The place of phantoms," Manon said. "It is new. Arlette reads many things." She blithely ate the last of the orange.

"I have not seen others like me," Art said in a low voice. "If I am indeed like them." Manon looked at her, and then grasped her hand. Her hand was warm and delicate in Art's.

"I have not either," she said.

Art held her hand, recalling when Manon had asked if she could see Manon's dead sister, and felt sorrow. Arlette and Jim were conversing. Art caught the sound of a body's soft shift behind the wall. She knew that the table they were sitting at was in direct view of one of the peepholes.

"I must ask a question," Art said apologetically. "Thee gave me my keys to the Vesta, but one key was missing. Who possesses the key for peeping into my room?"

Manon smiled, looking quietly amused. Her fingers rubbed Art's.

"I see," Art said warmly. "No harm if it makes thee smile."

"Good morning!" Jim heartily greeted as Arlette carried him in. "If you'll excuse me, Art, I must use your basin for a bath, since Arlette is so kind to do the honour!"

"Please, Friend. And good morning," Art bade, smiling. Arlette took Jim into the closet with the water basin.

"Another question," Art said softly to Manon. "This talk of . . . the price of thy company. Thee is here for more than breaking fast?"

"*Oui*," Manon said, gazing at Art. "And Arlette is correct. I am particular. But for you, I am well paid for. Arlette will take Monsieur Jim away if you wish."

Art found her throat dry. The fantasy that came unbidden to her mind was soon chased away by her heart's sense.

"I know not how 'tis done, but," Art said, "somehow Arlette's leaving does not seem . . . as thee would like."

"Arlette never leaves," Manon said. "It is my rule. But the Vesta also gives that a price."

Art felt dismay. Though this was Manon and Arlette's work and she wished to respect it, she could only see it differently. They were not independent women; they were held by contract.

"Thee is not chattel to me," Art said. "I am not thy better, no matter the payment. 'Tis thy time we are spending. Thee will have me at thy choosing."

Manon stared at her with intensity, her eyes dark and enigmatic.

"If," Art added nervously, "if thee choose."

After a moment, Art let go of Manon's hand.

"Or not choose," Art said. "Thee must do as thee likes. With Arlette. Or . . . thee may sleep. Or play cards—"

Manon took Art by the ruffles of her bodice and pulled her forwards. She kissed her deeply.

"Oops!" Jim said. Arlette was emerging with Jim in hand, one foot out of the basin closet door. "Back in the closet!"

Manon broke her kiss with Art.

"Only if Manon wishes," Art said raggedly.

Manon slowly let go of Art's bodice front. Her smile was fierce.

"This is different," Arlette said slowly, looking at them. Manon beckoned to her.

"*Viens!*" Manon bade in a hushed tone. Arlette set Jim upon the table and went to Manon's side. She bent so that Manon could whisper in her ear.

"Well, my young friend!" Jim said. Had he eyebrows, Art was certain they would be wagging. His black top hat was at a rakish angle on his pate. His eye sockets and teeth gleamed from his washing.

"Good morning, Friend," Art said, smiling.

"I was surprised to see Arlette still awake but it seems her time and Manon's are accounted for," Jim said.

"'Tis," Art said. "Generously."

"Ho, ho! Lucky you. My dears!" Jim called. "Will you be staying a while longer?"

"For Art, *oui*," Arlette said. She straightened and looked at Art. Her perusal was several parts incredulity, approval, and bemusement. Art fussed with her napkin.

"Oh good! Because I want to read the paper," Jim said as Arlette sat down.

Arlette sighed. She reached for the side table where Art's copy of the morning paper lay folded. She placed it on the breakfast table. "He insisted I show him the front page right away," she told the other women. "Monsieur Dastard, if Art would like to read it, then we will read it."

Art turned the folded paper to see. "BONE STEALER KILLS FOUR: WILL THERE BE MORE?" read one title. The article was by Helia Skycourt.

Manon took Art's free hand. She stifled a yawn with it. She then leaned back in her chair and brought Art's hand into her lap.

"That Skycourt! Always on the ball, isn't she? Art, do read it to us!" Jim said.

Art turned her attention from Manon to Jim; once again he used a phrase that baffled her. Arlette gave a minute shrug behind him, apparently used to his queer utterances. Art decided to not ask what 'ball' Jim was referring to, though it made her think of Helia balancing like a circus bear. However, she could not open the paper right then because her other hand was trapped between Manon's, and Manon did not seem ready to relinquish it.

"Art is busy," Arlette said in humour. She took the paper from Art. "I will read."

CHAPTER TWO

"The Times
"Friday, 11 March, of this year 1880
"Bone Stealer Kills Four: Will There Be More?
"Helia Skycourt

"Spring-tide brought an unwelcomed visitation to the unsuspecting mudlarks who scavenged the Thames. In the early morning of 10 March, beneath Vauxhall Bridge, four burlap bags were found floating in the water and leaking blood. The mudlarks knew this was no gift of slaughtered meat, fallen off a coal barge. As one Hart Loxton said, nothing but grave misgiving was felt upon sight of the bleeding bags. When opened, each sack contained a murder victim in a grisly condition never before seen. Those mudlarks who saw them thought they were gazing upon the skins of people who had been flayed whole.

"Yet the human skins, with scalps and digits completely intact, were never peeled from the body! Like rag dolls without stuffing, only the organs and bones were missing from these poor murdered victims. Formal examination could discern no sign of incision or violation. The skin and muscle tissue were whole. Even more mystifying, the victims were still fully clothed, down to laced shoes and buttoned coats. After the snatching of all organs and bones, the blood left behind had continued to slowly drain from the bodies' orifices.

"Each victim was of adult age, and upon examination of his or her muscle tissue and quality of skin, in the full vigor of life; none were aged or decrepit. Though their garb gave evidence that the victims were poor or working class, they were of hearty constitution before their deaths. Personal effects found in the pockets might give clues to identity, but what is assumed is that the victims were not related in kin or in personal association. The killers of these unfortunates targeted healthy victims specifically, as one would when hunting the best and biggest of a herd.

"The woman in particular, Esther Stubbings, had recently survived successful female surgery, and was identified when her female organs were offered for dissection to the very doctor who performed her operation. It is clear that each of these unfortunates was chosen for the health of his or her bodies. None stood a chance once targeted, having been thoroughly harvested.

"Never have organs and the full set of one's bones, right down to fingers, toes, and skull been completely ripped away in so clean and efficiently a manner. The coroner attested that the muscle tissues showed no sign of cut or tear. This writer had viewed Esther Stubbings' face while her doctor identified her. She laid there a lumpy emptied vessel, her skull, brain, eyes, and tongue stolen. What manner of organ thieves were these, except of the sort capable of the most violating of black arts harvesting? The question most urgent to consider: who bought these organs and bones?

"As proven by the attempted sale of Esther's female organs, her eyes and other vitals may already be scattered amongst many anatomy enthusiasts. The scarcity of executed criminals and fresh cadavers from natural death has raised demand in the medical profession for human organ specimens. Most prized would be a skeleton, fully intact.

"However, nothing can fetch a princelier sum than what is desired by the sick who can afford the doctor, not of science, but of the black arts. Supernatural medicine has flourished alongside legitimate science, but only in those dark places where currency can purchase further life; in this case, the stolen lives which once belonged to poor yet healthy individuals. Will more good men and women lose their vitals because those with means and money can forcibly take them? Four sets of bones have been stolen and the organs possibly scattered. Find the bones of Esther Stubbings and there may her killers be found."

Arlette finished reading aloud and closed the paper.

"That's it?" Jim said. "I liked her re-animationist story better. And not just because Art and I were in it. Skycourt was dozing, writing this one."

"Not enough gore, monsieur?" Arlette asked.

"Was there an illustration at least?" Jim said.

Arlette sighed and unfolded the paper in order to show Jim.

"Horrifying," Jim said. "Show Art!"

"I've no need," Art said. She was contentedly caught in Manon's sleepy-lidded gaze. Art's thoughts drifted amid ancient trees and deep meadows.

"Perhaps you'll receive this case, Monsieur Dastard," Arlette said.

"Depends, Metropolitan Police might have this well in hand. Though once the Surgical Sciences Academy puts the pressure on, ha ha! Those men of science hate this kind of attention."

They heard a knock at the door. Alice entered with the second page and the serving cart. They headed for the table to clear the dishes. A maid followed, carrying clothes. She went to Art's armoire and hung a new dress up.

Arlette rose with Jim from the table. Art also stood. Manon released Art's hand and walked away. When Arlette turned, Jim spied the new outfit.

"Art, that dressmaker of yours, she's quite excellent!" he said, admiring the garment. It was a dark garnet with a trim in claret. The skirt was edged in deep grey-black.

"No frills or froufrou," Jim said. "Just good clean tailoring with smart accents. Look at the lapels on this one, it'll really show off that chest of yours. And I can't believe I'm discussing fashion. I'm just thankful I'm being carried around by someone dressed in someone else's good taste."

"I had requested the 'no frills'," Art said. Arlette stepped near Art and touched the cascading ruffles on her bodice.

"*C'est belle*," she said in admiration. "I love these. And these." She ran fingers along the rows of mother-of-pearl buttons adorning Art's chest.

"'Tis worldly," Art said, smiling at Arlette's touch. "But I wonder at the cost."

"No matter the cost, no bonnets," Jim said. "Which reminds me, you still yearn for that Quaker meeting amongst your bonneted brethren?"

"I do." Art caught Manon's gaze. "I must leave," she said with regret.

"How unexpected! We must schedule another time," Arlette said.

"Whenever Manon wishes," Art said. "If she wishes."

"The time is paid for. Therefore Manon must," Arlette said. "And if she wishes . . . we will play cards." Her face was mirthful.

Art felt her cheeks warm again.

"Before you go, show the girls what you showed me yesterday," Jim said. "You must see this, dears, it's a testimony to her dressmaker. No more bodice-ripping for Art!"

"Why does that sound disappointing?" Arlette said.

"'Tis a simple trick," Art said.

"Show, show!" Jim said.

Art looked at Manon.

"This requires another," she said with a smile. "Take this arm."

Manon stepped forwards and did, appearing curious. Art stood to her full height, placing an arm behind her. She then raised the arm Manon held and flexed it, causing her bicep to bulge and stretch the fabric of her sleeve.

"Ho ho!" Jim said while Arlette laughed in glee. The second page and the maid stopped to stare. Alice grinned widely.

"Lift thy feet," Art said to Manon. Manon took hold of Art's flexed arm and did as instructed. Art adjusted for Manon's weight and stood firmly. Her onlookers applauded.

"Sideshow!" Jim exclaimed. "I didn't expect that!"

Art let Manon down gently. "Aye. Nor did I. I can guess thy weight. Thee is eight stone."

"Eight! Which measure? She weighs the same as myself!" Arlette said.

"The fourteen pound," Art said. Manon smiled. Her hand slowly ran up Art's arm in delight.

"Then you are correct. That is our weight. *Ah, allons, ma fleur,*" Arlette said to Manon. "We should leave Art so that she may depart." She raised her hand and Manon took it.

"I'll tuck you girls in. Then Alice will fetch me," Jim said.

"Yes sir, I will," Alice said. They cleared the table and she and the second page rolled their laden cart for the doors. The maid, finding nothing more to do in Art's room, took her feather duster into Jim's study.

Arlette touched Art's shoulder for a kiss. Art obliged. When she straightened, Manon merely watched her. Art stood awkwardly. Manon took Art by the ruffles of her bodice again and urged her down. She kissed her.

When Manon finally pulled away, Art slowly straightened. She grinned.

"Once you return from your pacifist, silence-filled meeting, remember Art," Jim said. "We like you violent!"

Arlette carried him through the door.

Manon's gaze lingered on Art as she followed Arlette.

The door closed, and Art thanked herself for listening to her heart, though her decision also left her feeling very flustered. She took a deep breath to rid herself of agitation and went to her dresser to fetch her hat and gloves. She put them on. Unlike her first outfit, her hat had survived intact, and she enjoyed the formed slope of the brim. Her fingers ran briefly along it. The crown was low, and the band sported a thick ostrich-tail feather and plume. She took personal pride in the fact that despite odds, she had preserved her hat's respectability.

Jim needn't fear her returning to Quaker garb, she thought. Charlotte's beautiful clothing may have ruined her for plain dress and bonnets. While looking again at Helia Skycourt's silver-engraved card upon her dresser, she heard the soft snore of her peeper behind the wall.

She deliberately dropped her walking stick against the wall. The peeper woke with a start. The person rose. Art heard the rustle of a skirt and then fabric brushing along the wall. The peeper departed.

Art picked up her stick, not at all surprised to learn that her peeper was a woman. She made certain that she had her keys to the Vesta and exited.

Art stepped through the Vesta's iris portal for the cobbled street, and the metal door spun shut behind her. In this bustling yet impoverished section of the East End, Whitechapel, the Vesta was easily discerned by its fashionable entrance, which imitated the round entrance portals of airships. It was a prosperous establishment tucked between the poorer buildings. Considering the deviant interests of the Vesta's clientele, Art could understand why the club was not located on a wealthier street and amid the other exclusive clubs. She moved from beneath the Vesta's portico and set her stick to the walk. The hurrying passersby kept a wide berth from her glowing form. She headed for an address where the Society of Friends held their meetings.

On her first case with Jim, Art accidentally killed a bewitched slaughter man, Dennis Bell, unknowing of her own true strength at the time. She pledged to take care of his widow Fiona and their two small children. She also slew all the murderous undead children who had been wrongfully reanimated. Had she chosen not to, more people would have died. Her duty as an agent of the Secret Commission meant being involved in fatal matters, and she accepted the responsibility. Since the Secret Commission had resurrected her, she had no choice. However, her personal values were sorely tested. She desired the counsel of others who followed the way of non-violence.

She stopped to buy matches from the matchstick-seller holding her baby. The tired woman didn't seem to mind, or perhaps even notice, Art's unearthly appearance. A gang of ragged boys ran down the street and surrounded them.

"Secret Policeman! Secret Policeman!" the boys cried. Art smiled and resumed her walk down the street, leading them away from the matchstick seller.

"You're the Secret Inspector who smashed all the undead children!" one said. Art tamped down the horror she felt from those words. The eager faces looking up at her were a sharp contrast to her sudden recollection of the reanimated children.

"Look! There's her stick!" The boy pointed eagerly at her silver-handled cane and the deer's head on the end. Art mustered a smile.

"Aye," she said.

"Someone's stealin' innards!" another boy said. "With black magic! 'Ave you fought 'im yet?" Before Art could answer, one small child posed menacingly.

"I'm the Blackheart, I'll get the Bone-Stealer!" he said in a deep voice and roughed up one of his companions. The other boys laughed. Art smiled to hear him play the part of the legendary monster fighter, Nick Blackheart. She wondered briefly if she would someday meet the present incarnation.

"The Blackheart's a woman!" a boy in a cap said.

"I'm not 'er, I'm the fourth Blackheart. He was a man!" the small boy said.

"He's dead!" his friend replied. "And so's the Blackheart before 'im! And the Blackheart before 'im too!"

"I'm the, um," the small boy said.

"Sixth," Art prompted him.

"I'm the *sixth* Blackheart, because the fifth, she's gone to France!" the small boy cried. He waved an imaginary sword at his fellows and attacked them. He swung to lop off their heads.

"She's been in France a long time!" one boy cried amid more laughter.

Art felt her skirt tugged. A little ragged girl looked up at her.

"Is you an' the Blackheart fightin' together?" she asked.

"If we meet, aye," Art said. "Where is thy home?" The little girl pointed to a doorway. Art picked her up and brought her back. Her older sister was busy carrying a baby and corralling other smaller siblings. An old woman sat outside calmly shelling peas. She only briefly acknowledged Art's presence. Within the small room, the mother and another older child were pasting together matchboxes. The mother glanced at Art and her littler girl and after a fleeting look of concern, seemed to calm down. She clucked at the child when Art put her down. Art chatted with the woman as the family tended to their piecework. Feeling that the mother would not accept charity, Art helped paste matchboxes with supernatural speed until a decent pile grew upon the table. She then bade the family farewell. As she exited, the boys ran by again.

"I'm on me big 'orse! *Arr!* Beware the Blackheart! I've your 'eads!" the small boy roared at his friends. They ran laughing. Art continued down the street.

After a few blocks, she found the tenement where the meeting place was located. She waited outside, looking down the steps that led to the door of the basement room. On the door was the sign: SOCIETY OF FRIENDS. No one had answered when she knocked. She was early. The tenement building was as poor as those around it, though Art noted it was better maintained and its windows thick and whole.

She heard a door slam and footsteps descend the stairs from the room above the meeting place. Art looked up. Helene Skycourt stood on the steps and stared back at her in surprise.

Lady Helene Skycourt, twin sister to the journalist Helia, wore the same long, black high-collared coat Art had seen the last time they met. Helene had spectacles, though the frames did little to lessen her intense blue-eyed gaze. She wore no hat or gloves. She held a black book to her breast. Standing on the steps, Helene could look Art right in the eye.

Art recalled Helia's untidy locks beneath her hat and compared them to her sister's neat and pin-backed hairstyle. She wondered how a face she knew as lively in one person could look so stern in another.

"How prospers truth in thy parts, Friend?" Art greeted.

"My parts are well," Helene said. "What are you doing here?"

Art swallowed. Helene's usual manner, it seemed, was to invoke challenge.

"'Tis not to see thee," Art said. "Though thy sister says she knows me. Therefore, by same reasoning thee must know me too."

Helene stared at her. Her demeanor softened.

"I've been insulting," Helene said. "My being unused to what you are now is no good excuse." She stepped down to the walk and looked up at Art. "Welcome back to the living," she said.

Art stood in uncertainty. Though Helene was respectful in her well-wishes, Art sensed a touch of sadness.

"My thanks," she said. "Thee resides here?"

"Yes."

"Yet thee is a lady," Art said. She looked at the austerity of Helene's clothes. She was entirely in black, and her skirts were cut high enough to show her boots.

"Yes, I'm heir to an earldom. I still manage Skycourt Industries," Helene said. "And I've my reasons."

"Adventuring," Art said cautiously, not wishing to insult. The aristocracy was known to slum among the poor for the thrill and freedom. Helene smiled.

"No, not like that," she said. She nodded to the closed door below. "I've just realised. You're here for a meeting."

"Aye."

"Enjoying your stay at the Vesta?" Helene asked.

Art was surprised. Helia had seen Art enter the Vesta after the fateful re-animationist encounter; perhaps she had told her sister.

"Aye," Art said.

"Did you breakfast? Well of course you did. I hope enjoyably." She laughed to herself, the sound short and rueful. "Have a good meeting," she abruptly said. She turned and walked away. Art watched in bafflement.

Was Helene her peeper? she thought. It was very doubtful. Helene looked well rested.

"Friend, has thee been to the Vesta?" Art called after her.

"This morning?"

Helene stopped and looked at her in surprise.

"No," Helene said. "Whoever you saw wasn't me. And it wouldn't have been Helia because she's banned."

Art joined Helene.

"I only wondered," Art said. "Aye, I had an enjoyable breakfast."

"Catherine Moore runs a very good club," Helene said. "There's a vulgar element; can't be helped with some of those members, but overall it's meant to be safe. I suppose you may see me there on some occasion. For God knows what reason. I've a membership."

"Thee likes women," Art said in wonderment.

"You are still forthright," Helene said, smiling. "How do you know I don't like the men who like men?"

Art stared at Helene. She tried to imagine it. Helene chuckled.

"I fancy both," she gently said. "But I didn't become a member for that. I understand that agents are resurrected with no memories. So while at the Vesta have you learned something about yourself?"

"I learned well before the Vesta. I've love of women," Art said. She recalled when she first saw Helia. The thought warmed her. "Why dost thee have a membership?"

"It's convenient," Helene said. Then she shook her head and laughed again.

"Give me the jest, Friend," Art urged.

"It's nothing. Just something Helia had said." Helene then looked at Art thoughtfully.

"We're doing it to you again," she said. "Even if it's not really you. You deserve to know what's going on. I'll tell Helia to tell you."

"Canst thee tell me?" Art asked. Helene was already walking away.

"I only pay the bills," Helene replied. Art watched her retreating back.

Art stood on the walk and wondered what she'd just learned. None of it would make sense until she talked to Helia again. She turned her attention to the meeting she meant to attend. When she walked back, she saw that the door was propped open.

A Quaker couple in plain dress was entering. Art thought the woman's bonnet rather large. She chastised herself for judging. She followed them in.

It was a simple large room with rows of benches. The basement windows were sunlit. When she stepped inside, other Friends— men of various ages and some women—were standing or sitting. All were in plain garb and the women in bonnets. Art felt at ease; she sensed the calm and practical nature that Friends carried within. She hoped that when she stood in meeting they would forgive her for talking overly much when introducing herself.

Then the Friends noticed her.

At her presence they stilled. Art knew she looked otherworldly, but their gazes, varying in shock and fright, told her more. She was recognized.

"Dost thee know me . . . Friends?" Art said. She remembered how Helene first reacted upon recognising her: with fury. The sinking dread in her stomach deepened as the fear in the room heightened. The couple she had followed in clung to each other. One woman rose slowly from her seat, her eyes stark.

"Thee . . . was executed," she said in a hushed voice.

Art felt the words like a blow. The question of why she had deserved the gallows returned. What sort of criminal had she been? Was she right then, a murderer in their midst—perhaps one who had harmed her own brethren? She'd learned that despite being Quaker she fought well—far too well. There she stood, and the Friends present were so affected that they could not overcome her past deeds and witness her.

Her Light, then, was not enough to surmount what she had done.

Art could no longer take their gaze. She fled up the steps.

Once on the street, she set her stick to the ground and walked rapidly away. In her upset she had gone the wrong direction but she didn't want to turn back and run into a Friend. She would go around the warren; she would forget she had tried attending.

Steam whistled among the tenements she hurried by, the white mist escaping leaky pipes that tapped the pumping engines beneath the ground. Three washerwomen took the heated water down by buckets. Art avoided the debris in the street and ignored the children and chickens that suddenly trotted by. She walked past shacks, one of which was a blacksmith's, the space next to it opening into a yard for horses. A stable lay beyond it. Helene was there, talking to a wiry Asian man in tie, waistcoat, and shirtsleeves. Art continued walking. Helene noticed her and moved quickly across the yard to come by her side.

"What has happened?" Helene said. Her hand caught Art's arm. The authority of the grip surprised Art; it did not impose brute strength as much as convey in its firmness Helene's wish that Art would halt. She did. She found she was still too hurt for words.

Helene looked up at her, her eyes searching. With surprising gentleness, she wiped the tears from Art's face. Art hadn't realised she'd been crying. Art fumbled at her cuff. She'd forgotten to store a handkerchief.

"Follow me," Helene bade. She turned and walked back to the stable. She went inside. Art wiped the last of her tears with the back of her glove and followed Helene.

When she stepped within the stable, she saw Helene stroking the head of a huge black horse. The Asian man stood nearby and smiled warmly at Art. His short, black hair was thick and though combed back, stuck out impressively. He wore a broad leather belt with a large, ornate silver buckle, illustrated with a snake-and-scroll pattern. He had a bearing to his chest and shoulders, upright and square, that reminded Art of a soldier.

"You knew both before, but I'll introduce them again," Helene said to her. She motioned to the man. "This is Ganju Rana, he assists me. And no, he's not Chinese, he's Nepalese. He's also a Gurhka, which I'll probably have to explain to you later. And this is Rama, my boy." Helene caressed her horse fondly. "Just don't get the two mixed up."

"*Namastae*, Miss Art. It's good to see you," Ganju said, beaming. Art cleared her throat.

"My thanks, Friend. . . I am happy to know thee again," she

said. "Please, call me 'Art', no title needed."

Ganju nodded, quietly chuckling. Art thought it was very probable she'd said the same to him in her previous life. She came closer, but Rama started, snorting loudly. Helene looked at her.

"Come. Give me your hand," Helene said, extending hers.

"I'm a ghost, he likes me not."

"Let him be the judge. Slowly then, hm?" Helene said with a smile. Art acquiesced. Helene took her gloved hand and brought Art around so that she could touch Rama's neck. Art stilled her nervousness and Helene guided her to stroke his neck and shoulder. His ears pricked forwards as he watched Art. Helene then moved Art's hand to touch his face. He began to nibble at Art's fingers. When Helene turned Art's hand, Art discovered that she had placed sugar cubes in her palm. Rama ate them.

Art gave a sound of relief and smiled. With Helene's encouragement she continued to pet the horse.

"Now, what has upset you?" Helene asked.

"I'm . . . I'm not welcomed amongst the Friends," Art said.

"They said so?"

"No," Art said. "But I frightened them, and I know I was a criminal and executed. I'm too evil even for their benevolence," she whispered.

"That's not true," Helene said. She stood facing Art, her aspect stern.

"I've done evil."

"No."

Art was confounded. "I was imprisoned."

"You ended up dead because others wanted you dead," Helene said. "Imprisonment was an easy way to torment those who loved you. And I know, for I was one of them," her voice grew rough. Art saw the pain and anger in her eyes. "Believe me when I say that you have never done wrong. You died a victim, a cruel joke. And whatever Helia thinks she's doing now is her idea of penance for it."

Doubt still resided in Art, but Helene's words lightened her heart. These new revelations made her wonder. Her death was somehow a mistake? Yet why the Friends' reaction?

"I don't understand thy words, but I take them to heart," Art said gratefully. She was about to ask more when her badge glowed. It stopped, and then glowed again. The pattern repeated. Art tapped it as Jim had taught her. Nothing happened. She pressed it. The badge continued its glow pattern.

"I . . . must return to my partner," Art said. "My thanks for letting me meet Rama and Ganju again." Ganju, who stood away from the two, nodded at Art's words and smiled.

"Art," Helene said when Art turned to go. "One more thing."

Art turned. "Yes, Friend?"

"You tried to attend a Quaker meeting. I hope you're not trying to confuse things. Because you're a fighter now. And if you want to live you fight to win, understand?"

Art held her stick. The intensity of Helene's gaze seemed to bore into her.

"Yes, Friend."

"Good. Be safe." Helene returned her attention to her horse. Ganju picked up a bucket with brushes and set to work brushing Rama. Art turned slowly and left. Once she stepped out of the stable into the sunshine, she took ghost form and flew.

CHAPTER THREE

Art flew directly into her third-storey room at the Vesta and took solid form. She was about to exit to find Jim when she heard his voice from his study. The door was ajar. There was the smell of cigarette smoke, and Art heard a woman speaking.

"Well it's good to know you'll be on it," the woman said. Her voice was cultured. "God knows what the Blaggard would have done to solve this nuisance. Probably sweep by taking off reputable doctors' heads with a scimitar."

"I've always liked that woman's style. Wish she'd come out of hiding—or her coffin if dead. With the Blackheart back on duty I can finally take that seaside holiday," Jim said.

Art rapped lightly on his door with her stick.

"Art is that you? Come in!" She entered. "Sorry I had to interrupt your meeting," Jim said. "Milly, if you'll be a dear, just tap my pin four times."

Jim sat on his table with its pile of newspapers. He had a cigarette between his teeth. The woman, Milly, was in full gentleman's attire wearing a black coat and with a cigarette in hand. She leaned forwards from the leather chair and tapped Jim's Secret Commission pin on the table. Art's badge stopped glowing.

Milly was middle-aged, with a face slightly lined and a body with a thickened middle. Her hair was not cut short, but to complete her garb she wore men's jewelry. She had a large onyx ring on her hand, a jeweled pin at her tie, and jeweled cufflinks that flashed when the sunlight hit them. She leaned back and smiled at Art. Her gaze was warmly assessing, though Art thought it lingered on her bosom overly long.

"Art, this is Baroness Millicent Sedgewick," Jim said. "And Milly, my partner, Art. We were just discussing the Bone Stealer. We've the case, Art, which is why I called you back."

"I understand, Friend," Art said.

"'Friend'?" Milly said, looking amused. "Well this is news to me."

"Isn't it common knowledge that my new partner is Quaker?" Jim said. "Rather remiss of you, Milly."

"Oh, I just find it odd that your Commission would bother to resurrect her as such," Milly said. "Though her exploits since rising have been the talk of the drawing rooms." She inhaled, blew smoke, and then grinned. "How was your breakfast, Art? Enjoyed the company?"

"Aye, 'twas good fare," she said.

"Do join us in the dining room sometime. We've a nice buffet. And come down to the drawing rooms. We're looking forward to meeting you." She grinned more. "We don't bite."

"Thy invitation is most kind," Art said. "When I've time, I'll grace the rooms with the latest sermons."

Jim coughed on his smoke. It blew out his eye sockets. Milly's grin grew incredulous.

"Well," she said, putting her cigarette out in the ashtray. "You've the case to discuss, I'm sure." She rose and picked up a stick and top hat laid at the side table. She took her gloves out of the hat. "And I was just on my way out when asked to chat, Jim."

"So good of you to spend time, Milly," he said. "You know how greatly I value the things you learn."

"Whatever helps. In this case, to catch a thief." Milly smiled at Art. "When you grace us with your lovely presence below, no need to bring the sermons."

"If thee insists," Art said, offering her hand. Milly accepted, but instead of grasping it in a handshake, she turned Art's hand and held the fingers.

"Perhaps I'll bring the latest hymns," Art said.

Milly stifled her guffaw in her attempt to kiss Art's hand, abandoned the attempt, and released her hand gracefully.

"A treasure," Milly said to Jim. She placed her hat upon her head, gave Art a parting grin, and left using the door leading into the hallway.

Once the door was firmly closed, Jim hopped to look at Art.

"Do Quakers sing?" he asked.

"Not I," Art said. "And I know no sermons."

"You didn't just commit your first fibs, you once-pious young friend of mine?" Jim said in humour.

"No, Friend, truly I would have brought hymns," she said. "I never said I would sing them."

"And sermons you wouldn't have known the words to," Jim said. "Art, she wasn't that bad. For a toff, anyway. "

"Is she in residence?" Art asked.

"No, Milly doesn't stay at the Vesta. She meets her lover here, who is a very rich widow. Milly's vice is gambling. She's most often broke. But you'll see her frequently because her lover pays her membership. I've found that she can be quite valuable for certain kinds of information. However." He inhaled on his cigarette until it all burned and disappeared. He absorbed the ash.

"She's aristo," he continued. "A baroness by a dead husband's right, and she's as hoity-toity as they get. What makes her different is she loves to slum. She doesn't mind the company of the poor as long as it's entertaining. A toff like that can easily talk to we resurrected, for example."

"We are not of class," Art said.

"Correct. Though to an aristo, classless creatures like ourselves are merely lumped with the rest who are beneath them. The upper class protects itself in a manner that elevates all who belong to untouchable—and in this case, above crime. Barreling in like Inspector Risk with our badges does not catch the fly as much as honey. Therefore, Milly. Her other weakness is that she's a gossip. Notorious. She likes dirt, and she likes to share dirt. She doesn't mind spilling the beans on her fellow gentry."

"Thee has learnt from these spilt beans," Art said. She thought the queer phrase sounded American.

"I have. And I'll share," Jim said. "On our way to our next destination. Though I love the manner in which you run through our London streets like the wild spectre you are, we must forsake your powerful gait for a hackney carriage. In that way I can converse with you civilly."

"Very well," Art said. She picked Jim up. "Did thee ingest enough smoke and ash?"

"I'd a good meal, thank you," Jim said. "Risk dropped by earlier and we had cheroots."

She picked up his pin and put it between Jim's teeth. He gulped it, storing it with the other possessions inside of him.

"One moment, Friend, I must retrieve something," Art said.

While in her room she placed Jim on her bedspread and went to her dresser. She hadn't looked yet if Charlotte had ordered the handkerchiefs promised. She searched the drawers.

"Art, your bed was still made when I woke," Jim said. "How long did you take rest?"

"Not more than an hour, I think, Friend," Art said. She found the folded handkerchiefs. They were plain, not embroidered, and edged with soft lace. She picked one and tucked it into her left cuff.

"It's always the same with newborn partners," Jim complained. "So carried away by their shiny new supernatural states. You feel that you can go on and on and on forever, without food or rest, and then poof! You're a heap of jelly."

"Jelly?" Art said apprehensively.

"Damn it, Art, you should have slept more," Jim chastised. Art went to pick him up. "Was that your eldritch presence I felt wandering during the night? Either that or another ghost has taken residence."

"Aye, 'twas me. I'll try sleep again tonight," she promised.

"We might be working through, like we did with the re-animationist case," Jim said. "For evil never rests. And they do their worst at night. Whenever you tire you must say so. Or you're jelly."

"Yes, Friend," Art said. "I do not wish to be that." She straightened Jim's hat. She nearly walked through her doors and remembered that Jim could not. She opened one of the doors and shut it behind them.

Art had wandered the Vesta when she couldn't sleep. She and Jim had discovered that when she fully ghosted she became invisible. Bored with the confines of her room, Art drifted about the club unseen. The third and fourth floor had rooms let to members. On the fourth she followed the night page as she rolled a dinner cart to one room. Before the door was the wax-mustached, bald, and muscled Russian, Oleg, Manon and Arlette's protector. Curiousity got the better of her and she watched Oleg open the door for the page. Inside, Art spied Manon and Arlette naked upon the bed, tangled in a languid, intimate embrace. A man was seated before them with an easel, sketching rapidly. The floor was littered with drawings. When Oleg shut the door and turned, Art solidified. He stood stock-still before her. She admired his composure.

"Are his drawings very good?" she asked. She wished she could see. Oleg smiled, his dark eyes twinkling. He reached beneath his chair and showed Art a very beautiful head sketch of Arlette.

On the second floor Art resumed invisibility and found the Vesta staff cleaning up a formal dining room that had just hosted a dinner party. She looked at the china and silver finery being gathered and watched the servants summon swift dumbwaiters hidden behind wall panels. The waiters operated like the ascension chambers Art rode at the Secret Commission, by steam mechanism. The Vesta's housekeeper supervised as the remains of dinner were whisked away. Art had never met her but assumed that an older, authoritative woman wearing a silver chatelaine with keys had to be head of staff.

Two other rooms on the second floor were large enough for gatherings or dancing. That night there were themed parties in fancy dress; at least Art could only describe them as such.   She caught a glimpse into one when the door was opened and, in alarm, quickly decided she needed to know more.

She flew in. The party's setting was Orientalist; women and a few men were dressed in turbans, silk robes, and sashes, some smoking water pipes. They lounged on cushions and animal skins while naked young women were displayed on a stage for their perusal. A man beat a drum, lending a hypnotic air to the sweet-smelling smoke curling about the hung silk and diaphanous curtains. The women were being silently auctioned. The seller's eyes were darkened with makeup to look exotic and sinister.

What had alarmed Art into mistaking the scenario for an authentic scene were the iron manacles and despondent faces the enslaved women wore, but one girl giggled when her new owner received her key from the auctioneer, and Art realised it was an act. In relief, she forgave herself her silly reaction but even she was aware of the unfortunate kidnap and sexual trade of girls in London — especially virgins.

When Art looked at the girls and then the turbaned gentry pretending to be buyers, she finally deduced that the girls were not upper-class women playing along but were hired. She drifted out of the room, deep in thought. She saw two gentlemen dressed in Grecian togas enter the large room opposite.

Inside, more men in togas and wearing laurels lounged on divans in an ancient, marble temple setting. Slave boys served wine. There was another slave auction, this one of young nude men. One naked young man was chained to an Ionic column. He was being flagellated.

Art let the door close without her investigating further. She stood in the hall of the second floor and contemplated the gentry's sexual fascination for the enslaved. She doubted the poor or working class person had similar erotic interest . . . unless they were well paid for it.

Art stepped on the second-floor landing with Jim just as Mrs. Catherine Moore was about to ascend. She wore a black dress and her blue sapphire at her breast. The older woman smiled at Art and Jim, and they bade "good morning" all around.

"Did you have a good breakfast, Art?"she asked. "And was it enjoyable?"

"Aye, very much," Art said. "My thanks."

"You needn't thank me," Catherine said. "I'm to make sure you had a very good breakfast." She stifled a yawn. "My apologies."

Art looked at her curiously and wondered if Catherine was her peeper.

"Mrs. Moore," Jim said. "Late night for you?"

"Oh, a very late one for me, Mr. Dastard," Catherine said. "It was exciting to host Olivia Hill here last night. I had to oversee everything."

"Your fondness for the male impersonators of the stage rivals my own," Jim said. "I'd gotten Miss Hill's autograph when she appeared at the Egyptian. I felt I could not top the experience. Nor did I want to deprive a young lady of her autograph ticket when I learned Miss Hill was to appear here."

"The engagement was a perfect success!" Catherine said. "Fourteen lucky women and one gentleman were very pleased to be in Miss Hill's company for an hour, listening to her stories. Weren't they, Art? Art was there for when it ended."

"Art," Jim said. "You were haunting below?"

"Aye," Art said. After exploring the second floor she'd taken solid form when descending to the first. There she saw that the drawing room for female members had an intimate engagement. An illustrated signboard had read: "An Evening with Olivia Hill". When she glanced in, she saw a very handsome woman in finely tailored male dress and shoes engaging an enrapt small audience. A beautiful white carnation was in the black lapel of her long tan coat. She wore red ribbons in her cuffs. The masculine attitude in which she stood and spoke had a sensual ease. Olivia Hill's presence was warm and magnetic; Art immediately became fond of her genial manner, smile, and tone of voice.

When Catherine Moore noticed Art watching, she pointed out a young dark-haired woman who sat behind Miss Hill. The young woman observed Miss Hill with quiet pride and love.

"The young lady there is her wife," Catherine whispered to her.

Art was impressed to witness her first couple in female marriage.

"Art, did you meet her?" Jim asked. "Perhaps I should have obtained an autograph ticket for you."

"I'd not known of her," Art said. "And her beauty would have tied my tongue." When the engagement ended with much polite applause, Art had seen the long line of autograph purchasers in the hall, patiently waiting. All were women of various ages and nearly all held gifts as well as programmes. The gifts were handmade and many were embroidered with messages.

"Tied your tongue, yes, but that Quaker silence might have seduced her!" Jim said.

"Art, Miss Hill is most kind with her admirers," Catherine said, smiling. "Had you waited until the signing ended, I would have introduced you."

"I did not want to weary her," Art said. "But she is impressed upon me."

"No future gifts of sermons or hymns, then?" Jim said jovially.

"'Twould have never come to mind," Art said, smiling.

They bade Catherine farewell and exited the Vesta. Art saw the many hansom cabs making their way in the traffic of the street.

"Thee would not prefer a hansom cab instead?" Art asked. She spied a hackney carriage and raised her stick for it. The four-wheeled carriage looked worn, an old crest painted over on the door, but Art thought that overall, horse, vehicle, and driver appeared well maintained.

"I love cabs! So smart they are, with their two wheels and open front! Art, I know that you are only a few days living, but don't you remember that it's improper for a lady to ride in an open cab?"

"I am more creature than lady," Art said as the carriage rolled to a stop beside them. "And the hansom cab looks adventurous."

"True, but right now, a hackney can ensure privacy," Jim said. "To the Royal Surgical Sciences Academy!" he called up to the driver.

Before the driver could pull his lever to open the door, Art passed Jim through the carriage's window and entered in ghost form. Once seated the driver prompted his horse and moved the carriage into the street's traffic. Art put her stick to the carriage floor and held Jim up.

"Now! Recall those harvested skeletons and whatnot," Jim said.

"Aye," Art said, "I am in recall."

"Nasty business. But I'll tell you. Whenever something like that is stolen the wealthy are always involved, because who else can afford such prizes? Then when it's time to interrogate, the doors are barred, curtains drawn, and the maid left as the sole soul to talk to. Hopefully she's a comely one."

"Yet I can enter any door. Nor can I easily be thrown out."

"True. But boring them with your Quaker silence will take too long. Thus, I smoke with Milly, and receive the beans requested. But to cut to the chase: four deaths we know of so far. Three men, one woman. All tough-luck characters of once hearty constitution. But guess what's happened on the other side of the tracks? A formerly bedridden, arthritic viscount is miraculously walking again. Even climbed on to a horse for a hunt. A hunchback baron has straightened up. And a certain debutante's clubfoot is, to the delight of dance partners, clubbed no more. Each attributes steadfast Christian piety awarding them a miracle. "

Art remained silent.

"Yes, I agree. And there, see, that thoughtful silence again."

"I like this not," Art said. "What chase are we to cut?"

"Keystone cops! How the hell should I know?!" Jim exclaimed.

"Peace, Friend, I only asked," Art soothed. She should have known to leave Jim's queer phrases alone. He had already told her that the strange words that came from his teeth confounded him as well, and might even be Americanisms.

"'Tis three accounted for," Art said. "What of the fourth?"

"The fourth has not shown off. Smart of him," Jim said. "His identity is not needed. Our viscount has suddenly partaken of Paris and the courtesans therein. The baron has ridden his newly straightened spine to Scotland, perchance to enjoy his new wife. And our lovely debutante is right now on a ship headed for the bachelors of America. So you see, though we know of them and of what they stole, they are of no use to us. We must go directly to their provider."

"Aye, what thoughts, Friend?" Art asked.

"It's not a gang," Jim said. "Of the grave-robbing or mortuary student type. The harvesting is too sophisticated. Our revitalised bluebloods are proof that a very learned black arts surgeon is in practice, probably for exorbitant sums, and we must stop him before more of the rich may use him."

"He is at the Surgical Academy?" Art said.

"That would be too easy," Jim said. "No, there are only men of *science* at the Academy. We are doing what Skycourt had noted astutely: we are following the bones."

"To the Academy," Art said.

"Yes, for they are collectors, these men of science. They like peculiar things," he said. "Maladies, disfigurements, freak births, and afflictions. They like to put it under light and knife and dissect. Strip it, peel it, sauté it, stew it, and have it floating in a jar to admire and hand down to students to also admire. Think: you are a hunchback. A black arts surgeon snatches a healthy, erect skeleton out of one man and puts it inside you. Your old crippled bones, then, are displaced. Whatever happened to them?"

"They are sold," Art answered thoughtfully.

"Yes, to the crippled-bone lovers," Jim said. "How excited the Academy must be! Positively perverted."

"By query we may find the seller and thus the surgeon," Art said.

"One hopes. Risk had the seller of Esther Stubbings' female vitals in hand. Guess what happened to the fellow before he could confess? Shot in the head by an assassin, right inside the police station. Risk is in deep having to account for the event to his superiors, but it does tell us one thing."

"They've guns?"

"They've someone very, very important to protect. Or scary. Same thing."

"They've yet to meet us."

"Ha! If I'm shot, just pick up all my pieces. Reminds me of a case Harold and I had," Jim said. "Again, scientists and their cadavers. How unhappy we were when we discovered it involved a deviant with a mania for corpses."

"A . . . mania?" Art said.

"Oh dear. Do you need it explained?"

"No need," Art said quickly. "I've the gist."

She thought a moment, remembering her witness of flagellation.

"Friend," she said. "If I may change subject, when I wandered the Vesta last night I saw vulgar aspects, and also aspects which gladdened me. It seems the Vesta is of two natures, both haven and . . . "

"Vulgar playground?" Jim said. "There are more coupled members now. Notable are the females in marital contract with each other. You've probably noticed them in the library, Curiosities and Mechanical Room, card room . . . they like the Vesta for these distractions. You'll see them at the dances and talks and engagements. Such intimate friendships, shall we say, are not interested in the trysts and treats. We have Catherine and her sterner hand to thank, after she took ownership of the Vesta from her husband."

"Catherine does not introduce herself by her husband's name," Art said.

"Yes. She likes to be clear about that, doesn't she? They are divorced. He is presently in Sweden, maintaining contractual, marital bliss with the very reason for their amicable dissolution: his gallant husband."

"He lives his Light," Art said approvingly. "Yet, Friend. Thee is saying that the Vesta was once less respectable . . . and more pleasurable?"

"Delicately put! Those who were ruder and highly deviant have long moved on to other clubs that would have them. In their absence, Catherine has built up a most intriguing and surprising membership."

"I am glad to have taken that walk," Art said.

"You should have slept. Don't poop out on me," Jim said.

Art had no understanding of how she might be a ship's deck.

"Aye," she simply said. The carriage's wheels slowed. Jim hopped in her hand to look out the bright window.

"Hello! He's taking London Bridge, isn't he," Jim said. Art put her head out the window. The bridge was before them, crowded with pedestrians, laden wagons, hansom cabs, and horses. All moved at a very slow pace, if at all.

Art brought her head back in. "We can leave and I can run. Where is the Academy?"

"In Southwark. But this is a good time to make you take rest. And then I can look out at our sparkly river! I like the Thames when the sun's out."

"Friend, I am well," Art protested.

"Those bones aren't going anywhere," Jim said. "Rest! *Rest!*"

Art sighed. She leaned back. With one hand on her stick, she placed her hand with Jim on the seat next to her.

"I'll speak to you a lullaby. Close your eyes," he said.

Art did. Jim began to speak.

"Acacia. Acacia rosea. Acanthus. Amygdalus, amaranthus, angelica, arum vulgare. Bellis perennis; betonica officinalis. Biscutella laevigata; botrychium lunaria. Buglossoides purpurocaerulea. Buphthalmum salicifolium. Bupleurum praealtum . . . "

Art fell asleep before Jim finished all the Latin names for daisies.

～

"Art! Wake up!"

Art stood up immediately, stick in hand and rammed her head into the carriage's ceiling. With her hat in her eyes she tried to look about her; they were in no danger.

"Art, straighten your hat!" Jim said in her hand. "We're here!"

The carriage door was open. Art stepped out. She paid the driver, straightened her hat, and looked around as the hackney carriage drove away.

In what would have been a sedate, well-to-do neighborhood of quiet homes and businesses, a large gathering had assembled in a small square before the fenced and gated grounds of the Royal Surgical Sciences Academy. Most of the demonstrators were working-class women and men, though Art could spy among them the independent spinsters dedicated to social causes. One in spectacles and a jaunty hat was standing on a box and speaking via megaphone, a pointed finger raised. Many in the gathering carried signs protesting vivisection. A woman's sign said: ANIMAL EXPERIMENTATION IS LIKE WOMEN'S OPPRESSION.

"The papers have brought the anti-vivisectionists out again," Jim said. "Perhaps this bone stealing will be the last straw and finally result in change. That is, if they'd just focus upon the animals for once."

"Living animals," Art said soberly. "Made to suffer and die."

"Yes," Jim said.

As Art and Jim moved closer she saw the smaller groups within the gathering. There were pastors and their followers. One group held signs that said: SCIENCE IS FORBIDDEN FRUIT, and IDLE CURIOUSITY IS DEVIL'S CRUELTY. Several older girls in factory uniforms stood together. They chatted animatedly among themselves as the woman on the box continued to lecture. All the girls held up copies of a book. Art read the title: *Black Beauty*.

"Friend, the book, *Black Beauty*. What is it?" Art asked. Jim hopped in her hand so that she'd look at him.

"When you couldn't recall the Blackheart, who is in the lexicon of our present culture, I could understand," Jim said. "Fall made a mistake in the excising of your memories. He was only supposed to remove your personal ones. Personal! And I can only think that you don't know what *Black Beauty* is because you must have loved the book. As any young girl would. It's a very beloved, empathic story about a black horse and animal cruelty, and written by one of your brethren, Anna Sewell."

"'Twas Quaker?" Art said. She took a shaky breath. The knowledge was a sudden hurt, deep in her chest. "I . . . I am only now understanding what has been taken from me!"

"Hush, hush now," Jim soothed. "Take a breath, let this upset slide away. Revelations are a bother, aren't they? Remember, you've a new life now. You've come toddling into the world and learned quite a few things about yourself already, true? The important things. The necessary ones. Liking women, for example. Now that's important. These all come in good time. Think of *Black Beauty* as yet another fond rediscovery, waiting for you."

Art looked at the girls again, some bored and some casting proud glances about as they held their books up.

"Thee is my weighty Friend," Art finally said. "And speaks the heart to my mind. I will think on this . . . another time."

"Good girl. As soon as this case is solved, we'll hie thee to the library. Now! Let's find a way in," he said eagerly. "If they're nervous inside it'll be a good time to say, 'Boo!'."

Art approached the wrought-iron fence surrounding the Academy complex. When she turned her head to look down the walk, she suddenly saw the same Friends from the meeting standing in a group. They stared at her in surprise. The sign they held said: VIOLENCE UPON NONE.

"Art, let's try going around so we don't draw attention," Jim said. "There must be a wa—WOO-OOP!"

Art tossed Jim high in the air over the fence's iron spear points. She passed through as a ghost and caught him on the other side. She crossed the lawn and hurried away.

"*Art!* What was that?! I nearly lost all my cigarettes!"

"Sorry Friend, I—I needed to get away," Art said. "Where are we to go?"

The grounds appeared deserted. Art stood before the main building, a stone-and-columned edifice, while the protest continued outside the gates.

"The building we want is at the other end of this campus," Jim said. "Perhaps you can't warn me when you need to toss me about Art, but that seemed unnecessary!"

"My apologies again, Friend. I wish thee could travel with me." Art dismissed her feelings of shame at the sight of the Friends. She took a breath and proceeded down a path that followed the outskirts of the Academy's buildings.

"It's something I wouldn't mind," Jim said. "Flying with you. Turning invisible with you. Now that I'd like to do."

"Since dropping thee that last time, I thought to test my gift," Art added. "I can carry an orange as a ghost."

"Well, it's of nature and not by the hand of man," Jim said. "Good to know you can carry food around, yes?"

"And my own hat, stick, keys, and the coin put in my purse. And a card. Yet not things I've taken in hand, as small as a matchbox. I've a handkerchief just picked before leaving the Vesta. I've ghosted twice yet still have it."

"You've marked yourself on those things," Jim said. "Not sure how. Let's put it this way, and pardon my saying, but like a dog pissing."

"Thee is pardoned," Art said. "Though I prefer more like a cat rubbing."

"Mine's better. It's enough of a taint that these objects seem a part of you. Which you should be glad of, or you'd lose all your garments and not just your kerchief whilst ghosting around. London would be well learned on your Grecian proportions!" Jim laughed.

Art thought of the artist who sketched Manon and Arlette and smiled.

"Thee is natural and I've carried thee often," Art said. "Yet thee cannot pass with me when I ghost."

"Well it's because I'm living, Art. Have you done any reading at all on what it might mean to be an apparition?"

"No, Friend, I've yet to find that time since being reborn six days before."

"Sad excuse! The spiritualist movement has brought many aspects of faith to scientific speculation," Jim said. "One, what is a soul? Two, where in hell's name might it reside? So far the theory is that there is a Fourth Dimension, one where spirits of our loved ones or of our haunting spectres tarry. We bodies — well, I a skull — must remain here in the Third. Our souls, however, can apparently move into other places. The only way you could take me through walls in your Fourth Dimensional state is probably when I am entirely dead."

Art stopped in her circuit around the academy's buildings. Beyond the garden path on which she stood was a small side-entrance gate. Helia Skycourt knelt at the lock, attempting to pick it. She wore an azure coat. She had a bespectacled woman by her side, short and plump and with a leather satchel hanging across her body. The woman was watching the street and looked from side to side.

Art and Jim stood awhile, watching Helia fiddle with the gate's lock.

"It amazes me that in my five years as an agent I hadn't the privilege of running into Miss Skycourt during any of my cases, and here I've seen her again, and within the span of a day! What odds are those?" Jim said.

Art walked forwards. "I will see her more, she knows me," she said.

"Serendipity," Jim said. "What? Knows, as from before? Really? But she's a madwoman!"

"Aye." She stood before the gate and looked down at Helia. Helia's dark locks strayed from beneath her petite, brown cavalier hat. She blew at the one that fell over the masked side of her face.

Art studied the striped, brown tail feathers fanning in the band of Helia's hat and determined that they were of an owl.

Art saw Helia notice her skirt, raise her gaze, and then leap up.

"Oh!" she said. Art smiled, delighting in Helia's blue eyes. The three, tiny forget-me-nots painted beneath Helia's masked eye complimented the blue. Helia's friend abruptly turned and raised her fists at the sight of Art and Jim. Her thick spectacles magnified her eyes.

"Not vivisectionists, *no*, though she is carrying a skull," Helia said, laying a hand on her friend who was waving her fists. Helia pocketed her tools and turned to the agents, smiling. "Dear Art and Mr. Dastard, agents of the Secret Commission! My heroic friend here is Aldosia Stropps, illustrator for *The Strand*, and you know myself."

"How can we not, Miss Skycourt?" Jim said. "Or should we

address M'Lady'?"

"That won't be necessary, Mr. Dastard," Helia said, smiling.

"Then let me just say that you are singular in your fashionable wearing of that pretty leather half-mask!"

"Oh if curses were fashionable," Helia said. "All the women would be wearing them. Stalwart agents! We've found ourselves in the embarrassing situation of being on the wrong side of the gate. Won't you let us in?"

Art tested the locked gate as Jim spoke. "We'll certainly try! Perhaps we seek the same, Miss Skycourt. Might I ask your business?"

"Vote for all! Equal rights! Bloomers damn your pants!" Aldosia said. Helia laughed.

"Pants pants pants!" Aldosia said.

"Stropps has a condition, mouth to brain, mouth to brain," Helia said, demonstrating with her hands. "She's also a suffragette, so it comes out all mixed-up. But she's an exceptional draftsman. Needs only see something once and can draw the whole thing! Peculiar mind! Wonderful!"

"And what do you hope to see but the once?" Jim asked. Art placed him on a stone post and laid her stick against it. She took hold of the gate's bars, one in each hand.

"Nicked bloomers," Aldosia said.

"Bones, bones," Helia corrected.

"Bombs in yer bloomers," Aldosia said.

"Ah, nicked," Jim said. "Well now . . . like a former hunchback's crooked spine, perhaps? Or the unfortunate malformation once belonging to a clubfooted young woman?"

"Such words!" Helia said. "Easily taken for mine, or yours, or mine!" The metal bars loudly protested as Art slowly pulled them apart. Helia gleefully squeezed through and pulled in Aldosia, whose plumper mass made passage difficult. Art pulled the bars more.

Once Aldosia had wiggled through, she held her hat and ran down the path for the Academy proper. Helia looked up at Art, her eyes bright and cheek flushed.

"Did you have a very pleasant breakfast? But of course you did!" she said. Art smiled in surprise.

First Helene, and now Helia enquiring? she thought. It was a very odd coincidence. But she promptly lost the thought at the sight of Helia's stray locks in need of tucking. Art was tempted.

Aldosia whistled and waved franticly. Helia jumped and ran after her.

Art picked up Jim and set her stick to the walk. They watched the two women disappear into a wing of one of the buildings.

"So you knew Helia Skycourt—Lady Helia, from before?" Jim said.

"I've been told, and her sister confirms," Art said. She walked in the direction Helia and Aldosia had disappeared to.

"Lady Helene, the adventuress? Their family has an earldom! And they make airships, you know! My, my," Jim said. "Had I known you were a Clydesdale who'd run amongst Arabians, I'd have put a notice in the paper of your rebirth. Might have snagged you nice gifts."

"Joy and love are all the celebration needed," Art said. "But Friend, do I not deserve the same notice had I been a mere Clydesdale?"

"Ah," Jim said.

"All babes are of the same Light; in God there are no breeds."

"Tell that to the breeds with money. I'll smoke a cigar later for the occasion," Jim said. "Your having sprung from the head of Zeus, fully formed. And how. Ah! Looks like our intrepid ladies found an unlocked door."

A door had been left ajar within the portico of a building. Art went up the steps and walked in.

CHAPTER FOUR

In the building's atrium, Art and Jim read a notice posted within the glass of a signboard. It read:

To all Colleagues, Members, Students, and Visitors,

We regret to inform that on 11 March, this year 1880, the Royal Surgical Sciences Academy will be closed in anticipation of further public demonstrations outside our gates. In light of this emergency decision, all offices, classes, and buildings will be inactive. It is encouraged that no one remain on the grounds during the closing, for we would not be responsible for any incidents resulting.

Sincerely Yours,

The Royal Surgical Sciences Academy"

"How dare they not be here for us to scare them?" Jim said.

"Should we view the bones, as Helia and Aldosia are doing?" Art asked.

"That would just confirm the gossip and not give more," Jim said. "But on the off chance one of those men of science couldn't keep away from a precious new acquisition . . . let's look."

Jim knew the way; Art assumed his familiarity came from his previous cadavers case. They headed for the Academy's Artifacts and Remains Collections. As Art walked down the deserted hall, her stick's rhythmic tap echoed. They heard Helia's distant voice speaking.

"Arr," Jim said. He sniffed. "Salt in the air. Like the sea, but more sickly. Perhaps they're storing a captured mermaid."

"Aye, 'tisn't a fresh scent."

Art cocked her head, aware of a subdued sound. She paused in her walk to still her stick. She discerned a very faint tapping. She looked back down the hall they'd just walked and saw no one.

"Heard it too? Odd, that," Jim said. "Not quite the tap of a walking stick. Perhaps someone is working on something. On something being trepanned," he added in a dark tone.

Art resumed walking. She glanced briefly at a large glass case displaying human skulls, from adult to child. Some were drilled into, or cut open around the cranium. Many had diagrams drawn on them.

"*Objets d'art*," Jim said in sarcasm. The venom in his voice surprised Art.

"Here, the fifth door," he then said. "This is a back way that leads into the collections' workroom."

Art opened the door and entered a still and musty storage room. Helia's voice grew louder. She passed shelves bearing labeled boxes. She stepped into the next room. Helia was by the window and browbeating a seated short man with a thin moustache. He was dressed in waistcoat and shirtsleeves. Helia had him trapped in a wheeled swivel chair while she waved her arms at him. Aldosia stood at the front of the room, slowly looking about. She saw Art and Jim but gave them no more attention than a person would to furniture.

Art looked around as well and saw the stored contents; there were strung human skeletons, boxes full of bones, more skulls, plaster molds, display boards, and hung diagrams. When she returned her attention to Aldosia, she thought the woman's attitude casual and hardly studious, but she didn't doubt that Aldosia was committing every artifact in the room to memory with the peculiar power of her mind.

Aldosia stepped forwards to where human bones lay upon a large worktable. The deformed spinal bones were meticulously laid out in a pattern denoting an abnormal curvature. Aldosia retrieved a large sketchbook and wood pencil box from her leather satchel. She opened the box, which contained a steel-point dip pen and brass, portable inkwell. After clicking open the lid of the inkwell and dipping her pen, she began rapidly sketching. Art heard the man protest loudly. She turned to look at him.

"I know nothing more, truly!" he cried. "I've no idea where the seller came from or even his name! The German only dropped off the bones and accepted the money. That is all!"

"A German, you say?" Helia went to Aldosia's satchel and pulled out a sketchbook. The man tried to escape.

"Ah-ah! *Back!* Back in the chair!" Helia ordered. He reluctantly obliged. "Now look at this." She opened the sketchbook to a page and brandished it before him. "Did your German look like this?"

"Good Lord, dead?! No!" the man said. "He was bigger, had both eyes, and was scarred! Oh my, is that his brain come out the side of his head? Fascinating! Shot, was he?"

"Do you have a mania for cadavers, sir?" Helia cried. "Do you?"

"What?! No, never! Oh don't write about me, please!" He covered his eyes as if that would make her disappear.

Jim chuckled.

"Pleasure to see how the woman works," he murmured to Art. "She's only distracting him now, so that Stropps there can do her work. The fool knows nothing. Let us away, Art. The Academy's a belly-up for us. We must journey to another destination."

Art was about to withdraw when the man spun in his swivel chair and dashed for the back exit Art stood in. He abruptly halted and gaped at the sight of them.

"Oh!" the man said in fright. He dropped his hands when he gave Jim a close look. "Oh! Have you brought us something new? That looks a fine specimen!"

"Keep your hands off me!" Jim said brusquely when the man reached for him. Art moved Jim away, and the man quickly withdrew his hands.

"Oh!" he cried. "It talks!"

Helia pushed the swivel chair into him, the wheels squeaking. In surprise, he fell back into it. She looked at Art and winked, eyes twinkling.

"Stop talking to that skull and ghost!" Helia said. "I'm not done with you!"

The man loudly lamented as Helia wheeled him away.

Art stepped back from the room as Helia spun the man to face her and resumed her verbal barrage. Art glanced at Helia one last time, admiring how freely she gesticulated with no concern for propriety or feminine decorum. The man attempted one more escape, and this time Helia chased him out the front door.

Art exited the back storage room and proceeded down the empty hall. They passed the glass display again with its collection of dissected and diagrammed skulls.

"That fool," Jim muttered in anger. "He'll end up the same sooner or later, but these science men never think on that."

Art looked at the skulls and then at Jim.

"Friend, I apologise that thee should see these."

"Well. I've been shown worse. While we're here you should witness something. Continue down."

Art heard the scurry and skid of boots. Looking behind her, she saw Aldosia and Helia run out of the collections room's back door. Aldosia waved her sketchbook to dry the pages. Helia pointed in the direction of the building's exit. Holding their hats, the women ran for it.

"Art, eyes forwards," Jim said in humour. "Must you be distracted by skirts?"

"Only certain ones," Art said, turning back again. She approached the end of the hall. There were large double doors. A sign above read: SURGICAL THEATRE.

Art pushed the doors open.

The Academy's Surgical Theatre had a large skylight. Sunlight shown upon a wood stage platform with two mechanised tables sheeted in metal. They were set at a distance from each other. One had been left at a tilt. Lamps hung from long armatures.

Wooden tiers surrounded the front of the stage in a semi-circle. All the rows of chairs were in disarray. The place smelled of wood rot, sawdust, and dried blood. Art looked down and saw the old stains, dark and numerous, on the floor.

"Their pride, their Coliseum," Jim said. "Where many a scientific spectacle of the body has been explored. To self-congratulation and accolades. I'm sure you know at what price."

"They should not harm animals," Art said.

"It's not too much to ask that they be humanist. I agree," Jim said. "But I wanted to show you the setting of surgery. Most procedures are done on people's kitchen tables, but I think for the one we are seeking, our black arts man, he will need a good amount of space."

"A barn?" Art said.

"In London? But it has to be somewhere of significant size. Hopefully not with victim number five in it. Off we go, then."

Art emerged from the theatre and headed for the exit Helia and Aldosia had used. She paused, finally recognizing a vague feeling of unease that she felt since coming into the corridor. The scent of salty dankness grew stronger, and the odd, faint tapping continued. The sound was muted, as if deep inside something, faraway. She looked down the hall's end at another set of double doors. They were thick and padlocked.

What she felt had nothing to do with eldritch presence. It was the simple matter of recognising the very subtle, nearly indiscernible sign that something was wrong.

It was the faint sound of animals crying behind the locked double doors.

"Art we must go," Jim said. "I know what you are looking at. And I would let you look, truly. But it would not help for you to see it."

Art stood, clutching her stick.

"Art. We do have to go."

With great reluctance, she stepped out the door.

Art remained silent as Jim directed her down a street from the Academy and its protesters, her thoughts on the captive animals left behind. When she came to the shop Jim told her to enter, the store sign said: ANATOMY & MEDICAL CURIOSITIES SHOPPE.

"We've visited the reputable men of science, now we must gain passage into the place dark arts men dwell," he said. "And what we require is an invitation. I will get us one, here."

"Friend, what place of business is this?" Art said. The windows had anatomy plasters, luridly painted to show the organs, as well as stuffed, strange animals. Art stared at the armadillo, mounted askew on its stand. Shrunken heads dangled by it.

"Its goods are meant for student anatomists and anatomy collectors," Jim said. "And collectors of the odd and eccentric. Oh what the hell, it's a place for weirdos. But quite a few of the middle class have a shrunken head in their curiousity cabinets. It's fashionable."

"And giant . . . dried spiders?" Art asked.

"Pah! The tarantulas? I'm not one for fashion; I'm the only dead thing in my cabinet. I'd rather a glass eyeball. Prettier."

Art smiled at Jim and pushed the door open, its bell tinkling. She went in.

When the odor of the shop hit her she nearly pulled out her kerchief. It was the overall flat scent of dead organic matter, tainted with chemicals and strongly tinged with decay. It was not overly offensive, but Art could not help thinking of the reanimated children. The anatomy shop shelves were stuffed to the ceiling with jars of preserved organs, dissection models, bones, scientific instruments, petrified specimens, and molds. There were mummified animal paws and some jars holding two-headed fetuses. There were death masks. Small hand-lettered signs were set everywhere admonishing: Do Not Touch. Art's gaze fell upon a wizened white-haired man behind the counter, bent and with a crooked mouth. He stared through thick spectacles, his small, sharp eyes calculative.

"Here to sell yourself, Mr. Dastard?" he said.

"Horfinch, take an acid bath," Jim said caustically.

"I've told you time and again, whenever you want to forsake this silly inspector business I can find a very good home for you."

Art sidestepped a stuffed and snarling wolverine while Horfinch grinned. She slowly approached the counter.

"A new partner, I see?" Horfinch said, adjusting his glasses. "My, what an Amazon! How is it that you always survive, Mr. Dastard, having no legs or arms, and yet all your hardy partners lose their lives? What did they do? Lose them for you?"

"How is it you haven't been eaten yet?" Jim said.

"Too stringy." Horfinch grinned. "Now, what business do you bring me? Because there's a sultan in Arabia still waiting for a talking skull."

"Horfinch," Jim said warningly.

"I've told him he can cut your cranium off to make into a snuffbox. Or an ashtray. You can function perfectly well without the top of your head. Then he may use you as a wine cup."

Art's stick knocked into a hung ape skeleton. The strung bones clattered musically.

"Watch yourself!" Horfinch said severely. "Can't you read the signs? Do not touch!"

"My apologies, Friend," Art said. "There's just so much around—"

She turned and accidentally hit a display case with frogs and giant worms floating in jars. The entire case rattled.

"*Careful!*" Horfinch cried.

"Oh," Art said. Her hand with the stick came around and across the glass counter. She bumped the tray full of glass eyeballs. Several fell loose and rolled across the countertop.

"*No*, you stupid bitch!" Horfinch yelled. He hurried to pick them up before they fell to the floor.

"Oh, you shouldn't have said that," Jim said in a dark tone.

Art looked at Horfinch. With her finger, she touched the petrified piranhas mounted on stands. Like dominoes, they fell over.

"What is it?!" Horfinch cried. "Just ask for it and *go!*"

"Very well," Jim said. "Bone Stealer. Who is it?"

"I don't know!" Horfinch said. "For he's too exclusive for the likes of me!"

"Then tell us what you do know," Jim said.

Horfinch's mouth shut.

"Before my partner should stumble," Jim said, "having not had her beauty rest. Let me inform you that those who buy certain bones of a crippled nature are sought by the police."

Horfinch opened and closed his mouth in surprise.

"I see," Jim said. "Which did you buy? The clubfoot? Never mind. Time to signal Inspector Risk."

"Wait!" Horfinch said. "The surgeon is about to share his technique. After those . . . what has happened, there are black arts doctors who dearly want to know how he did it. There's going to be a demonstration. A very exclusive one."

"Where and when?" Jim demanded.

"I don't know, I—truly I don't!" Horfinch cried as Art brought her hand with the stick up. She looked at him in mild surprise and scratched her nose.

"I told you, the man is beyond my circle," Horfinch said. "This is all I've heard."

"Right, then. Now give us an invitation to the Black Market," Jim said. "Show all of them. Or I release my bull in your stupid china shop."

"Here." Horfinch hurriedly reached beneath his counter for a box. He opened it and brought out wooden cards, each illustrated with a different body part: an eye, a mouth, a hand, female genitalia, male genitalia, a head, and an ear. Each had a black mark above.

"Art, take the one of a body," Jim said. Art picked up the card of a headless body.

"Now go, damn you—" Horfinch cried.

"Ah-ah," Jim said. "Do you really want to further offend my lady friend?"

Art and Jim stood there while Horfinch said no more. He glowered at them.

"Never a pleasure, Horfinch," Jim said. Art turned and walked out. The door's bell tinkled.

"There were police and plainclothes men at that demonstration," Jim said once the shop door shut behind them. "Let's hurry and send them to Horfinch. He'll rush right now to hide his purchase or at least try to dispose of it. Either way, he needs a good searching."

After informing the police of what to look for at the Anatomy & Medical Curiosities Shoppe, Art hailed another hackney carriage. Jim grumbled in her hand.

"If you weren't Quaker I'd have asked you to punch that odious man for me," he said as a carriage approached them. It stopped and the driver pulled the lever for the door.

"To Billingsgate Market!" Jim cried to the driver.

Art boarded the carriage and seated them.

"Thee would need to goad him into punching me first, but aye, he was a cruel one," she said.

"I hope the police seize many things. Or break 'em. My young friend, you were most naughty back there," he said in good humour.

"I disrupted that skeleton on accident," Art said. "But that man's manner only worsened my composure."

"And the petrified piranhas?" Jim asked.

"The fanged fish?" Art said. "I must ask for God's forgiveness." Jim chuckled.

"Had it come to my asking you to ruin his shop it would have been a failed bluff," he said ruefully.

"'Tis true," she said. "Unless thee agreed to pay for all that was broken."

"Arr," he growled.

Art brought the wooden card out of her pocket. She looked at the drawing of the headless body.

"What dost this signify, Friend?" she asked, showing Jim.

Jim sighed. "A wish needing fulfillment. Those invitations are usually bartered for. And then the sick must barter again, once admitted. But sometimes an ailment is beyond supernatural cure. We're off to the place that trades in futility and last hope.

The Black Market. A necessary underbelly I must expose you to"

Art pondered the Americanism. '*Under*', '*belly*', she thought. She could imagine it.

"And there, may we find the black arts surgeon?" she asked.

"I doubt it," Jim said. "He sounds more and more of the hoity-toity set. I believe he personally approached each of those clients, the viscount, baron, and debutante. If Risk delves further he'll probably find that each traveled to London on a specific date for their God-granted miracle. Whoever this fellow is, he's been building up to this exclusive engagement."

"The demonstration," Art said.

"Yes. I'm just not sure why. Selling tickets does not seem a proper motivation."

"We shall find a ticket purchaser?" Art said.

"That's the idea. Or better yet, we might win a seat for ourselves. Better hide your badge. Though we've been in the papers thanks to Miss Skycourt, it's known amongst the underbelly that I've history with the Black Market."

Art set Jim down in order to unfasten her Secret Commission badge.

"If I'm to understand correctly," she said when she'd pocketed her badge and the card, "we are to act as officers corrupted."

"Yes," Jim said darkly. He fell silent.

"I am thy junior and very new," Art said. "The sham is believable."

"As long as it stays a sham," he said. "You're not going to ask about my sordid past, are you?"

"I was biding my time," she said.

"Well, the simple version is, I'd an offer. I . . . accepted it," Jim said. "And never concluded it."

"Was it a very evil offer?"

"Not really. No. No harm to it or to anyone. Unless to the dead. But the sordid part was that it meant a bargain. Being beholden to someone like, say Horfinch. That's the evil part."

Art thought awhile as the carriage lurched and rolled.

"I've been curious as to the unknown sponsor of my breakfast," she said at last.

"Oh yes, and of Manon," Jim said. He laughed merrily.

"If thee is laughing and Manon is not upset, then I've no worry," Art said.

"Well, I asked the girls in order to make certain, but where we are concerned Catherine Moore would evaluate any such offer," Jim said. "She *is* a businesswoman. However, Harold's memory makes her our ally. Believe me, she would have turned down the transaction if it smelt the slightest bit bad. What you are given through the Vesta I would not worry about."

"Then I shan't," Art said. She thought about the identity of her unknown benefactor again.

"Is that why you didn't partake of Manon's company?" Jim asked curiously. "I was surprised you chose to leave. There are always Quaker meetings."

Art felt her cheeks warm.

"Was it your thinking she's younger? Because she isn't, far from it," Jim said.

"No, no," Art said. "I believe more, she is not so young."

"This is not some pious Quaker thing, then? You hardly seem the chaste type with all that skirt-chasing you do."

"Well, I — 'skirts-chasing?'" Art said.

"So far you've chased with your eyes, but oh I see the charming, Quaker wooing coming —"

"I wish to give Manon choice," Art hurriedly said.

"Really? But she's an owned — really? My! How interesting!" Jim said. "Such a concept!"

"Thee needn't be so amazed," Art muttered.

"Of course I'm amazed. I'm a man, and for all the work of suffragettes and humanists, women are still property," Jim said. "If Manon were offered to your Quaker males I doubt they would be that understanding. Come now, would they? Abolitionists they may be! No, a prostitute is a prostitute! They wouldn't give her choice, they'd make her pray!"

Art did not answer.

"And if you just needed time being new to corporal pleasure,"

Jim said, "that's unders—"

"'Twasn't that!" Art said.

"I've seen you kiss very well, Art," Jim said. "But woman to woman requires some—"

The carriage had stopped moving. It had entered the thick congestion of London Bridge. Art hurriedly exited it in ghost form. She reached in and retrieved Jim.

"—and I've a book. With pictures! But Art, I'd like to talk more!" Jim protested as she paid the driver.

"We've no time," Art said. She weaved quickly through the throng of pedestrians and vehicles. She jumped up to the parapet where she held her arms out for balance. A boat sailed below.

"Art! I'm over the water!" Jim yelled.

"I'll not drop thee, and thee likes the Thames."

"You can't walk the parapet! The lamps are in the way!" Jim said. "And why the hurry?"

"Thee forgets. Billingsgate is a fish market," Art said, smiling. "And the thought gives me hunger." She began to run. She swung around every lamppost.

"I shall lose all *my cigarettes*—Ah ha ha ha!" Jim cried. He flew over the bright water as Art sped them both back to central London.

CHAPTER FIVE

Art smelled Billingsgate Market long before she slowed in her run to pick her way through the swarm of costermonger barrows and delivery wagons come to haul their hard-won lots for the day. She avoided the teetering stacks of crates and kegs being loaded and followed the lingering sea scent wafting from freshly caught fish. She passed men and women exiting the market courtyard before the Italianate façade of the building. They carried baskets, hampers, and boxes full of cod, mackerel, herring, and sole. A man hurried by balancing a tray of live lobsters on his head. The lobsters snapped for her hat. A large fish in one man's arms suddenly slapped its tail, and Art raised Jim out of its way. Along the sides of the narrow street that faced the river were stalls selling fruit and vegetables. Art saw crates of oranges. She stepped out of the muddy walk for the courtyard.

More costermen, women, and fishmongers milled before the great, enclosed arcade of Billingsgate, trading on dried fish. She passed them and walked inside the building. The glass-roofed arcade stood several stories high. Huge lots of fish were laid out for auction on its expansive floor. Salmon, turbot, brill, and sole were being bid on by fishmongers and restaurant suppliers. Plaice, haddock, and skate were the focus of poorer costermongers and enterprising boys.

"Fancy a salmon, Art?" Jim asked above the cries of the auctioneers. "Or a handsome Welsh trout? Perhaps you should snare that noblest of fish, the royal turbot! The price won't be so exaggerated!"

"I like haddock," Art said. "'Tis satisfying. But while here, I would like a shellfish." As she walked she saw water tanks filled with wriggling eels. She stopped to stare at them, remembering when Helia had brought her a barrowful of the creatures.

"Shell animals are steamed and boiled in the caverns beneath our feet," Jim said. "Light me a cheroot, if you would? Then on to your cockles and mussels!"

Art looked down and saw that the floor had round glass inserts, meant to allow natural light into below. She set Jim on a pile of empty crates and removed a small, short cigar and a brass figural match safe shaped like a dancing, German folk woman, stored in his top hat. She used the figure's legs to clip the cheroot and then lit it.

Once Jim was puffing away, Art found the entrance to the basement. Costerwomen walked in and out, carrying their baskets of whelks, shrimp, prawns, cockles, and mussels. All the shellfish were freshly cooked. Art watched them pass and discerned what she wanted. She gently accosted one old woman with her basket, about to enter below. Art gave her money, and the woman descended. Jim smoked and chuckled as he observed the bidding activity around them. When the old woman returned, her basket was filled with tiny periwinkles, their shells still smelling of seawater.

"Ha ha!" Jim laughed. "Snails! All crawly-wally! You could have turbot, you could have oysters, but no, you chose—"

"Winkles," Art said, smiling. She and the old woman went to stand aside from the activity. Art raised a hand, and the sea snails flew from the basket into her body. She swiftly harvested the creatures. Their empty hard shells fell from her to the ground, and Art's spectral glow brightened. The old woman nodded with a satisfied smile and left again for the basement below, her purse carrying extra earnings for the day.

"Now that you've your treat, let us enter the Black Market," Jim said.

"Very well," Art said. She picked Jim up and waited for him to further direct her.

"Tut, tut. This paradise of food has beguiled you. Same always happened to Billy, my coal-eating partner. And you know how much coal is lying around London."

"Thee is saying . . . " Art said.

"Yes. Go look for it."

Jim smoked more, the white plumes rising from his eye sockets while Art looked around. Unlike with the re-animationist and his reanimations, she felt no eldritch activity. With her senses opened she sought a signal or the slightest flicker of otherworldly presence. She felt nothing. In the midst of all the cacophony of the market floor, she was aware of only the layers of normalcy.

Layers, she thought.

"There's a blanket," she suddenly said.

"Now you're on to something," Jim said. He puffed and managed to blow double smoke ringlets out of his eye sockets.

Art left Billingsgate's bustling arcade. Once outside she walked past the dried-fish sellers and their hampers. Near the pavilion tavern that flanked the arcade proper stood a plain, two-story storage house with shut lofts and a lone entrance door. It had the 'blanket' she'd become aware of. To her supernatural perceptions, it hung like a painted canvas, showing the world outside an unassuming, inactive building. Art wondered what the warehouse's real appearance was. She felt the wooden card in her pocket suddenly warm. She pulled it out. It was glowing.

"Those who seek the Black Market can't find it without an invitation," Jim said. "Unless they also practice black arts or are creatures like ourselves. Now remember our roles. Just follow my lead."

"Aye," Art said. "I trust thee." She left the busy crowd behind, the people seemingly oblivious to the building next to them. She approached the closed door. Instead of knocking, she decided to simply turn the knob. The door opened; the interior was black.

She stepped inside. Jim's cheroot gave a small, red glow. Her superior eyesight adjusted to the darkness.

They were in a small waiting room with extinguished gas lamps and a curtained exit. A tall, reedy woman with a narrow face sat erect on a high stool before a podium. She wore her hat nearly sloped over her distinct and prominent nose, her chin raised as if she were regarding the ceiling. Two long pheasant feathers with plumes arched stiffly from the front of her hat. The round lenses of her spectacles were opaque black. She was reading a small open book with the long fingers of her bare hand. Her fingertips slowly ran across the page. All the while she smiled a strange half smile.

"Ellie Hench!" Jim exclaimed. "Working the door of the Black Market?"

"Mr. Dastard," Ellie said, turning her head. Her fingers continued to read the book. She didn't look directly, only up. Art wondered why a blind woman was watching the entrance. Though Ellie gave no eldritch signal, Art felt wary.

"Just makin' a shilling while I wait on someone," Ellie said, smiling her peculiar smile.

"Well, work on, then! Ellie, this is my new partner, Art."

"How d'ye do," Ellie said.

"Friend," Art said.

"Art, if you would show Ellie our invitation."

Art pulled out the wooden card, which no longer glowed. Ellie turned her head in Art's direction but again did not look directly. She smoothly pulled a walking stick out from behind her. She was not as tall as Art yet her stick's length rivaled Art's. It was a blackthorn with slugs of silver embedded between the thorny knobs of the wood.

Ellie flipped the long stick so that she held the end, with its battered, brass ferrule. Art saw the silver snake wound tightly near the handle.

Art held her ironwood stick firmly.

"May you find what yer looking for, Mr. Dastard," Ellie said with a grin. She hooked the curtain with her stick's crooked handle and pulled it aside. Noise and light became apparent through the opening. Art gave Ellie one last look, bent under the curtain, and exited the small dark room with Jim.

Before her was the large floor of the warehouse. A settlement of makeshift, two-storey shacks and shops ran in narrow rows down the length of the building. Gaslights brightened the dimness while shop fronts glowed with more light. People holding invitation cards slowly picked their way among the shop fronts or stood bartering with proprietors. Painted shingles hung from every doorway, displaying boldly lettered words or cartoons of body parts. Several said, DENTISTRY, with more signs reading: PAINLESS EXTRACTION, and COMPLETE TEETH, 1 GUINEA. Others read: WOMEN'S PHYSICIAN and OBSTETRICIAN. Art saw gaudily dressed women waiting within one shop, either reading, chatting, or dozing.

"You can bet most physicians here are struck off the medical register," Jim said as Art approached the row with dentists. "It's the hocus pocus bunch versus the men of science. If black arts medicine should ever become completely legitimate, well. I'm sure the sick would overwhelmingly favor the knifeless cure rather than the scientific approach."

One dentist shop had no front wall, only a counter and drawn curtains. Art saw a patient seated in a brass dentist chair upholstered in red leather. The man wore a metal inhaler strapped to his face with a fixed ampoule of chloroform slowly dripping a measured dose into the inhaler's stored cotton. The dentist pulled a floor lever. The chair jumped higher, steam shooting from beneath. With the patient carefully positioned before him the dentist placed both bare hands over the man's slack mouth. He planted his feet firmly and concentrated. He shook. With great exertion he suddenly flung a bloody rotten tooth into the porcelain bowl beside him. His hands were coated in blood.

Art walked farther and approached another storefront with more seated women waiting within. The picture window had thick, drawn drapes, and the cozy waiting room was pleasantly wallpapered and furnished. The full-sized wax figure of a naked woman in sleepy-eyed repose lay on display before the window.

She was recumbent on silk sheets with a silk-covered pillow. Her arms were slightly bent, as if she were attempting either to rise or resign herself to languid stupor. Her skin tone was milky, and her long, wavy hair was splayed upon the silk. A string of pearls was around her neck. She had pubic hair, dark and curly. Her front torso fitting, with its soft breasts and belly, was removed and set aside, displaying her organs.

Art stood close to the glass and stared.

"This learned doctor," Jim said. "He was expelled from the London Obstetrical Society. But he's very successful with disease and female surgery, and therefore is a popular healer with prostitutes. Why hello, Bessie! Yes, I see you! Please wave for me, Art."

Art raised her hand with the stick to the smiling woman waving within.

"Having a Medical Venus on display rather adds to this doctor's mystique, doesn't it?" Jim said. "As if it were evidence of his sympathetic understanding of your sex."

Art returned her scrutiny to the wax figure's beautiful features, her parted lips, and her heavy lids. The figure's arched neck was long and graceful. Her eyelids barely lifted to reveal the glass irises behind them.

"Lungs and intestines are removed so we can see the vitals beneath," Jim said. "There her heart, stomach, liver, kidneys . . . and of course her female organs. Tucked all neatly inside her."

"I don't know, Friend," Art finally said. "If the presence of this Venus inspires thought of sympathy towards my sex. She is beautiful, yes, yet she lies not dead or in sleep but as one alive, her body sensitive and with feeling, and by her expression I think her in surrendered emotion."

"Yes, that is the pose," Jim said.

"To ecstatic pleasure," Art said.

"I more thought 'anesthetized'."

"And yet she feels so while being vivisected."

"I was hoping you would notice instead her uterus and the tiny, funny baby within," Jim said. "But yes, my young friend. She is as you say she is."

Art left the window and walked farther down the row.

"I am a mere skull, so I may not explain this very well," Jim said, "for it is only those of flesh who can know this. Harold discussed it with me once, since he was an avid participant in, shall we bluntly say, pleasure received through pain."

"I have seen it, ghosting at the Vesta," Art said. "Please explain if thee can."

"Well, perhaps you've experienced something of the like as a once-physical culturist. I can only think that such avid exercise as you body enthusiasts indulge in would be painful, and yet you bear it and somehow derive pleasure from the activity. Harold thought that the body, when made to endure extremes, reached states of euphoria."

"'Tis no excuse to vivisect another," Art said.

"Yes," Jim said. "That is mere cruelty."

Art avoided a large woman, heavily pregnant, headed purposefully for a small storefront that had the sign DOCTRESS. The woman passed through the curtained door and disappeared.

"I should confess that I've a very wee Medical Venus in my cabinet," Jim said. "She's ivory with hinged limbs and a crystal glass belly, and inside her belly besides the removable organs is a very tiny ivory I swear is of a kitten. Oh, it amuses me so when Arlette moves the little legs and my Venus births a kitten."

"Thee has a doll," Art said, smiling.

"A figure, Art! A medical figure."

"Friend, I should have asked thee for direction. I am merely wandering, and know not our destination." She saw an eye doctor receive a woman carrying a child with an enlarged left eye, his little head lolling. The case in the window held glowing glass jars with floating eyeballs. Black cables emerged from the side of the building and ran along the edge of the shop.

Electricity, she thought.

"The way you've picked is fine," Jim said. "This happens to be Sawbones Row. For a card like ours, we must go to the end of the line."

"I also want to ask about Ellie," Art said. "For I feel I should take her measure."

"No doubt, she has already taken yours," Jim said. "She's a stick for hire."

"A blind woman?" Art said. She glanced back at the shop with jarred eyeballs.

Could Ellie have working eyes after all? She thought.

"Ellie once drubbed my partner Deck well and good," Jim said. "Deck, that thrice-times ox of a man. I wasn't there to see the fight, and Deck's pride prevented him from speaking of it. She's gifts, that one, I suspect a combination of science and that thing clairvoyants have. She keeps it quiet, you see. That's why you can't read her. Then you don't sense her ability until it's too late."

"Thee seemed on friendly terms," Art said.

"Well, she only takes her formidable shillelagh to the likes of us if hired to," Jim said. "Otherwise, we could have tea, no hard feelings. She's really quite fun. Oh, you should see her dance. I think she prefers uncomplicated men." Jim sighed.

"'Tis her loss, Friend," Art said.

"Seeing her makes me wonder what it would be like, being a free agent. Though she is quite the *condottiere*."

"I would not choose the mercenary profession."

"'Ghost and Skull for hire', it has a nice ring."

"Services offered with discretion and piety."

"Oh, most piously! Well, we're venturing into the zoo exotic. You will probably spy whole bodies at this point," Jim murmured. "And I don't mean of wax. No matter what you see, don't judge. And don't rescue. A corpse, at this point, is nothing but a bag of meat to be harvested."

"I hear thee, Friend," Art said softly. Jim gulped the end of his cheroot and blew one last puff of smoke from his eye sockets. More bundles of electrical cables snaked at the foot of shops and up the walls. The air above their heads became crisscrossed with power lines. Storefront shingles read: SAWBONES.

Art heard a mechanised saw start within a shop. If she allowed her nose's superior sense its range, she was certain she'd detect the scent of burning bone and freshly bleeding flesh being sliced.

Two thugs in slouched caps suddenly rolled an older man, white haired, corpulent, and fully clothed, onto a table. The shop's sign bore an illustration similar to the one on Art's card. The man's still face, though ashen, had the ruddy aspects of one who indulged in drink. Several men in top hats and overcoats stepped up to the table and began bidding on his body. The man on the table was dead.

Art turned her gaze away.

Across from the bidding, a neatly dressed, smooth-faced, middle-aged man stood in a shop door. A jeweled watch chain hung across the prominent belly of his waistcoat. He wore spats. His round eyes stared from the side, as if he had a thought worth hiding. Art felt that the upturned corners of his mouth were less a smile and more a smug expression of assessment.

He gestured to Art to come forward and stepped back inside his storefront.

"His name is Livus," Jim murmured. "And if anyone knows what we want, it's he. Well, to it, then."

Art entered Livus' shop. Behind her, the auctioneer's hands came together in a loud clap, finalizing the dead man's price.

The interior was a small showroom; glass coffins lay on tables, glowing from the electricity fed by black cables and which snaked on the floor. Each coffin had a label holder with a list of precisely written measurements. Within lay naked dead men.

Art looked at them. One man's cranium had been bludgeoned, and his hair was matted with dried blood. Another had stab wounds to his pale chest, all cleansed. She suddenly bristled; the men had been murdered.

"Oh, Art, come now!" Jim exclaimed loudly. "It's merely male nudity!"

"Is your lady friend upset by the displays? I am sorry," Livus said. He drew up the black clothes used to cover the coffins and concealed the offending body regions in question. "Is that better?"

"Aye," Art said stiffly. "Though damage has been done to my sensibilities."

Livus apologised profusely. Nudity did not bother her, but Jim's exclamation successfully excused Art's outrage for feminine propriety. If their sham was to succeed, she grimly realised, she needed to better control her reactions.

"Mr. Dastard has yet to introduce us, so if you'll forgive me," Livus said to Art. "I am—"

"We know who you are," Jim said. "And you can easily guess why I'm here, in this Godforsaken hellhole again."

"Oh, I don't know, Mr. Dastard, it's been a while since you last haunted the Black Market," Livus said with a smile. "Can it really be that keen desire of yours, come again?"

"The time seems right for it," Jim said. "Right circumstances . . . right surgeon."

"Really," Livus said.

"Yes. Perhaps now I can get what I really want. Transference. My bony pate switched into a living body. Myself with a set of eyeballs, nose, ears, and tongue. Body, limbs, everything. Though I could probably do without the other fellow's brain. I believe a man has finally come who can do this for me."

"Mr. Dastard," Livus exclaimed. "This is beyond what you once sought. And such an extraordinary idea." He took out a small leather-covered notebook from his waistcoat pocket, removed a pencil from the book's holder, and began to write delicately in it.

"Are you taking my measure, Livus?" Jim said. "Because to me that means you think it possible."

"I am noting certain measures, most assuredly, Mr. Dastard," Livus said. He glanced up at Art, smiling. He then looked at Jim. "But that is a powerful and uniquely learned surgeon you've imagined. Very powerful. However, should I participate in your fantasy, I too can imagine, and what I see is a very profitable enterprise for such a surgeon, and the humble man who aids him. You're six foot two, aren't you?" he said, addressing Art.

"Aye," she said, surprised. She knew this from reading one of Dr. Fall's notes.

"With two more inches added by your shoes. Yes, lovely height," Livus said. He returned his attention to Dastard. "That's rare.

Rare is good."

"Nice sideshow talent. So who's making use of your eyes?" Jim said. "What powerful surgeon have you been measuring poor wretches for?"

"Now, now, Mr. Dastard. Anyone who enters my place does so willingly," Livus said. "And they give willingly. Whether of themselves or, well, someone in their possession, most recently perished. No business is conducted that's not desired."

"Yes, and business requires two, Livus. I'm interested in the side that has bought your expertise. Let's talk. For what I want, a tidy sum might await you. Consider that good business."

Livus smiled. He reached for a bell on a table and rang it. "I'm sorry, Mr. Dastard. I'd four very happy customers recently," he said. "And that was better business."

Art stepped forwards.

"Speak plainly, Friend," she said, her tone cold. The curtains of the back entrance behind Livus parted, revealing several menacing thugs.

"I just did," Livus said.

~

Delphia Bloom walked down the Black Market's Medicines Row where the chemists, dispensaries, and apothecaries resided. A tall, lanky girl of seventeen, blonde and grey-eyed, she still wore her long hair down and her skirts short. She was dressed in a grey apron over her long-sleeved blouse and skirt, the front of which had speckles of blood. A worn shawl was pinned over her shoulders. Her bottom lip sported a small, fresh gash. She held a wooden card with a drawing of a leech.

Delphia was determined to reach the end of the row where the blood-letters kept shop. She'd learned that one's healthy blood could be used in a medical process called transfusion, which benefited those who hemorrhaged when delivering babies and such. Therefore, a bit of coin could be made by selling her blood. Thanks to Hettie O'Taggart's vengeful fist, a far too beautiful delivery boy named Tom Frye, and their employer witnessing her unfortunate altercation with Hettie, Delphia had lost her position at the green nursery that day.

Delphia's mouth still stung. But she was also of the mind that if a boy hadn't already confessed that he had a new sweetheart, namely Hettie, then her conversing rather enjoyably with such a boy shouldn't be construed as her trying to steal what Hettie thought was hers. She did understand, however, that socialising while working had been a grave mistake, and she needed to rectify the loss of yet another position, if a little poorly, with some needed coin earned before trudging back home to Mother.

She gazed at the strange contents of dusty apothecary jars as she passed a stall and mused on how she'd never imagined venturing so far from her Bethnal Green street, but she tended to be as adventurous as her brothers. The only reason she became aware of the Black Market was because of Elsepeth Fidd, a fellow worker Delphia had befriended right after she'd lost her position at the boot-making factory. Like Delphia, Elsepeth was well-spoken and well-mannered, which was unlike the other factory girls. A black-haired girl, with bird-like bones and chalk-white skin, Elsepeth had given Delphia her first invitation to the Black Market.

"See the blood-letter named Von Fitz," Elsepeth had urged. "Now that I've explained what 'transfusion' is, surely you'd like to help those birthing women who might die from so much blood loss, and be paid too?"

Delphia did want to help, but since this was the Black Market, she wondered if her blood might be used for other, darker purposes. Transfusions were a very new science and leeching to cure ailments was still a common practice, but Elsepeth was adamant that blood-selling helped others. So Delphia visited the market and found the experience not so very unpleasant, especially when she was allowed to rest in the shop after the procedure. The only hard thing was explaining to Mother how she came by the money, and especially assure her, much to Mother's deep relief, that no, Delphia had not resorted to prostitution.

When Delphia inexplicably lost her next position at the chocolates factory, Elsepeth happened by again, this time with several invitations held in her slender, white hand.

"I went to the Medical Academy to see if I might read more about transfusions in their library," Delphia said to her. "Since you are so disproving of the science of humours. But I wasn't allowed in due to my sex."

"Really," Elsepeth said. "What an odd thing for you to do."

"But I did go to the secondhand booksellers nearby and found the latest medical journals. Did you know that transfusions are outlawed in France?" Delphia said. "And yet the origin of disease may be caused by matter invisible to our eye called 'bacterium'! This can explain a great many things, but it does make our understanding of humours quite unreliable."

"You're so very smart, Delphia," Elsepeth said admiringly. "Such a pity your family fell upon misfortune, you don't belong in factories. Now do you understand why blood is transacted in the Black Market?"

"I do," Delphia said.

Thus, to aid her family, Delphia braved the Black Market, and though she found aspects of it unsavory, she also saw that supernatural medicines benefitted those who sought healing. Von Fitz, the blood-letter, was always polite, and though Delphia knew she was a mere girl traveling alone, she had yet to come to any direct threat or harm within the market.

And Father didn't mind such adventuring, as long as she returned with descriptions and anecdotes about her visits. She especially made note of apothecary jars and bins that claimed to have the powders and dried parts of mythical beasts, the creatures so prevalent in all her father's beloved books. He had especially cheered up when she related her discovery of a bottle of powdered 'unicorn horn'. And he listened with rapt attention when she described the lurid procedures and odd medical devises that she witnessed in shop windows.

She paused and put her hand to her chest when she saw a man hurry by with a fully intact human spine in his hands. Delphia chastised herself. She had poured over secondhand anatomy books at the booksellers so that she could identify the organs and systems of the market's wax medical figures and explain them later to Father.

That spine was a medical model, she told herself, because real human vertebrae, had the spine been harvested right then, would have been loose pieces rather than rigidly connected, and hardly white. Though the model the man carried was probably of real vertebrae, she rationalized that it at least was not fresh.

Gruesome aspects such as those were why she avoided the row where the sawbones resided, with their loitering, grave-looting thugs. The equally gruesome, recent murders that had left London victims without their bones were also, she believed, causing the tension she currently sensed in the market proper.

On this day, progress through her usual market route was slow. Not only were medicine-buying customers standing about more than usual, as if indecisive or reluctant to part with money, but prostitutes—wearing cosmetics, bright dresses, and large bustles— loitered at the back exits to the obstetrician shops, blocking Delphia's passage. They fanned themselves and tensely chatted. The topic was of the Bone Stealer.

Delphia decided not to push her way through. Since her skirts were still short and therefore unrestrictive, she would attempt avoiding the crowd using an unconventional method. Unlike her aggressive brothers, Delphia liked to think she lent a feminine attitude to daredevilry.

An immense wooden statue of an elephant-headed deity sat before a fragrant stall selling Eastern cures. With a nimble skip, Delphia kicked up from the prominent belly of the statue and grabbed hold of the narrow ledge edging the second story of Medicines Row. She hoisted herself up. She quickly stepped along the ledge, high above the shop signs and women's hats below.

"Tssst! *Tssst!*" a skinny, curly-haired East Indian man tersely hissed at her, and waved his arms for her to come down. Delphia crossed to the opposite side of the alley via a wooden plank laid across opposing rooftops. She stepped down upon a sill ledge, and then to the ground, clear of the women and at a safe distance from the irate man.

"Such a monkey you are!" one of the women called out, and the others laughed as Delphia moved swiftly on her way.

Just ahead were the stalls of the blood-letters. In the section she had to pass through first, Delphia kept her gaze to herself. It was the area where the bodies harvested by the sawbones gave up their hair and teeth. Delphia ignored the shops with false teeth and wigs for sale.

A large man came crashing through the shop wall beside her, and Delphia leapt back. As he tumbled at Delphia's feet, a magnificently tall and unnaturally pale woman stepped over the torn partition. She glowed, and in one hand she held a skull wearing a top hat.

Delphia gasped, hands at her cheeks as she recognised the agent Artifice of the Secret Commission.

Upon seeing Delphia, Artifice tossed her the skull. Delphia caught it.

"My thanks, Friend," Art said. More men appeared behind her. She became immaterial and a fist whisked through her. Another man pounced and fell through her body. Delphia scurried backwards. Art solidified and with one sweeping backhand struck both men down.

"Turn me around! I need to see!" the skull cried in Delphia's hands. Shocked, she flipped him around.

Livus poked his head from the wreckage of his wall.

"She needn't be wholly alive! Take her!" he yelled.

One thug drew a knife and swung, aiming for Art's throat. She caught his arm and wrenched it aside. His blade cut into black cables hanging against the wall. Electricity crackled loudly, and Art and the man convulsed. As he fell away, his hand smoking, Art stiffly dropped to a knee.

She slumped over, her fist still clenching her walking stick.

"*Art!*" Jim cried from Delphia's hands.

Slowly, the men neared Art's prone form. One reached for the thug who lay unconscious, his blackened hand still smoking.

"Is he dead?" Livus called.

The unconscious man shuddered in the grip of the other thug.

A pool of blood formed beneath him.

"He is now," the other thug said flatly.

"I don't want him, get the woman for me!" Livus said. "Ten guineas for her body!"

"Art, get up!" Jim cried.

"Ten! She's mine, then," one man said. He drew a pistol.

Seeing him draw his firearm, the other thugs pulled their pistols out as well. They stepped warily towards Art.

"Damn it to hell!" Jim cried. "Not again!" He shook in Delphia's hands.

Delphia, realising that murder was imminent, ran forward and stood over Art. She thrust Jim out for all to see.

"*Shoot*, and he will *explode*, killing you all!" she cried.

Jim rattled noisily. When he began to glow, Delphia felt his heat in alarm but continued to hold him out. The men drew back.

"He'll kill you too!" a man cried.

"That's right!" Delphia said. "But the Secret Commission will bring me back! Can you say the same for all of you?" She threatened with Jim once more.

Art jerked. She slowly rose. Delphia turned quickly with Jim and dove into the nearest shop.

CHAPTER SIX

When the volts shot through Art, it felt as if a million needles seared into her every inch and locked every muscle. She thought her brain popped. Then, when she felt she could rise, she did so, heavily. Her vision was blurred, but she could still discern the pistols drawn and aimed at her.

She thought on how to disarm the men and heard the frightened voices of women behind her. One thug set his jaw and he cocked his revolver.

No bullet shall pass, Art resolved and imagined herself an impenetrable wall, thick as a mountain.

He fired at Art. Twice. The force of the shots sent her back. She heard screams behind her and the sound of people scrambling. She steadied herself. Two bullet holes in her chest bled pale blood. Her insides, made dense by her concentration, had stopped them from passing through.

She also felt as if the thrust of both projectiles had pulverized the interior of her chest.

"Put thy weapons down," Art said through gritted teeth.

The men fired. More bullets entered Art's chest and abdomen, driving her back further. None that hit her exited. The men advanced, and she swung, sending her fist into the face of the thug nearest her. Her stick came down with a wallop upon another, crumpling the man to the ground. She grabbed two more just as both men emptying their revolvers into her body. She smashed their heads together until their weapons fell clattering to the ground from their nerveless hands.

Art dropped the men and stepped forward for Livus.

"Thee," she said as he cowered behind his broken wall. Then she doubled over and vomited.

White, glowing matter and bullets poured from her mouth and splattered on the ground. The ectoplasm quivered like jelly and evaporated in a hissing mist.

"Art!" Jim cried from the cover of the shop. "So that's what your insides look like!"

"Ten guineas for her body!" Livus yelled. He pointed at Art as he cupped a hand to his mouth. "I will pay *ten guineas!*"

Two men fell upon Art, attempting to force her down. She focused on ghosting and nothing happen. With a great heave she threw the men off. Another man moved in with a knife. Art tried to dematerialise again as the blade broke against one of her corset plates.

I've lost the ability, she thought frantically, and punched the man in the face. Another man in a bowler hat whipped his walking stick at her, and she met it with her ironwood. He brought his cane down again and again, their woods loudly cracking. Art kicked him between the legs, and the man curled up in agony.

"*Ten guineas*, do you want it or not?!" Livus cried. More men in bloodied aprons, wielding bone saws and cleavers, ran at Art.

"We must retreat!" Jim bellowed. "Art! Let's go!"

∾

"The exit's this way!" Delphia said, emerging from the shop. "Can she follow?"

"She must!" Jim said as Delphia jumped on a stack of crates to avoid a man thrown by Art, his bone saw spinning away from him. Delphia rapidly climbed for the second- storey ledge.

"By the way!" Jim said as she sought her balance. "How did you know we're the Secret Commission? We're not wearing our badges!"

"A ghost woman carrying a skull?" Delphia said. "You've been in the papers, sir!"

"Then you know I'm Jim Dastard! And you?"

"Delphia Bloom! And if you don't mind—"

Delphia braced herself on the second- storey ledge and gave a mighty kick. She sent the stack of crates tumbling upon the men in aprons. Art briefly looked up.

"Well done, girl! *Art!* Follow us!" Jim yelled. Delphia walked quickly upon the ledge. Art smacked another man with her stick and staggered to keep up.

Livus continued to shout his bounty as prostitutes screamed and scurried out of Art's way. One lay wounded from a stray bullet as her companions tried to drag her to safety. Even as Art stepped over them, men ran forwards with their fists or with weapons in hand. She walloped them and flung the others away. Two nooses from either side of the alley flew down.

The nooses snagged Art neatly around the shoulders and slid up to tighten around her neck. Two East Indian men stood on opposing rooftops and pulled the lines taut, trapping and choking her. A third man ran out of a shop with a Royal Indian Army, breech-loading rifle. He aimed at Art's chest and fired. Art jerked as she absorbed the blast. He turned the rifle to empty the casing to the ground, reloaded, and aimed for her head.

"Damn it, those men with the nooses are above us and we need Art freed!" Jim yelled.

"My apologies, sir, but I must try something!" Delphia said. She took his top hat and put it on, stuffed Jim into her apron front, and unpinned her shawl. She flung it around the taut rope above her, gripped both ends of the fabric, and leapt.

As she fell, her weight on the rope brought the man on the roof down. The ground rapidly met her just as she lost hold of her shawl and saw Art heave on the other rope. It whipped free, bringing the other man down and Art sent it in a lashing arc at the man with the rifle. He ducked. His second shot went awry and shattered a window front.

When Delphia regained her feet and pulled Jim out of her apron front, Art was already thrashing the rifleman with her stick. Delphia ran up as Art threw him away.

"Art! This is Delphia Bloom!" Jim said.

Art bent over and vomited again. Bullets and buckshot fell amid the splatter of ectoplasm.

"Never mind! We're pleased to meet you!" Jim said to Delphia as she tried to help Art loosen the noose ropes and take them off. "Now, may I have my hat? And keep going, Bloom! Lead Art out!"

Art, freed once more, lumbered forwards. Delphia saw a woman emerge from the shadows, a long metal syringe in hand. She lunged and aimed her needle for Art's back.

Delphia thrust Jim in her path. The woman's hand met one of Jim's eye sockets and compressed the syringe.

"Arggh! Morphine!" he cried. "How *dare* you, madam, a needle to the eye socket!"

Delphia pulled Jim away, the syringe flying through the air. The woman backpedaled and fell. Delphia cringed as Art's fist flew over her head and hit a man who'd run up, ready to bring down his cudgel.

"Go before me, now!" Art said to her.

"Ptooey! It's affecting my sense of taste, *ha ha!*" Jim laughed. "Wee! We are floating! Oh this is terrible! Hee hee!"

Art punched another man. An old, wizened woman stepped up and blew snuff into Art's face. Art punched her as well. Blinded, she stumbled against Delphia, and Delphia fell, sending Jim rolling. As Delphia crawled to retrieve him, she saw the polished shoes and pinstriped, pressed pants of a gentleman. She stared at his walking stick.

The stick, from brass ferrule to the femur-head handle, was a long stack of human vertebrae. Delphia looked up and met the cold eyes of a pale-faced man. He was tall and gaunt, his small, elegant moustache grey. He had a distant icy gaze and stared down at Delphia as if she were a strange bug that had disturbed him. Two silent men stood with him.

"Yibble wibble!" Jim said on the ground. Delphia picked him

up and ran to join Art. Art shook the remainder of the powder away. She punched another woman who held a blue glass bottle. The bottle shattered, and smoke rose as acid ate the ground.

Delphia hopped about, realizing she could not make further progress through the throng that blocked their path. People were either crowding in to collect on the reward or gawking in morbid fascination.

Art advanced and swept her stick through the air in front of her, dispersing the onlookers. Delphia ran forwards. At the entrance of Medicines Row, shacks on either side had scaffolding erected for repairs. Delphia looked back and saw more men and women follow menacingly. Art took hold of a nearby scaffolding pole.

"No, not that one, he's a good doctor!" Jim cried. Art let go of the pole and lunged for the support beam of an apothecary.

"Yes, them!" Jim shouted. "They threatened to grind me into an aphrodisiac! Put this into your mortars, you fools! *Ha ha!*"

Art pulled hard, and the scaffolding and building façade came tumbling down. Debris and billowing dust lay between them and their potential attackers. Delphia ran ahead as Art staggered after her for the exit curtain of the Black Market.

～

Art followed Delphia behind the curtain and into the darkened room. She heard Jim chortle and gibber and wondered what was wrong with him. Then something smacked her on the top of her head like a hammer for a gong.

Art's ears rang and she saw stars.

"Good God! She went for the hat!" Jim cried when Delphia spun around.

Ellie whipped her stick up as Art's right fist shot out. Ellie neatly sidestepped and trapped Art's arm by locking it with her right. She whacked Art hard in the middle of her back. Art's corset dented over her kidneys. Ellie hit her again. She brought her blackthorn down in rapid succession on Art's tailbone, below her right calf muscle, and the bone of her right ankle. Art swung her stick and missed. Ellie whacked her in the anklebone again.

Art lifted her foot in agony and felt her right arm released. Ellie spun. She walloped Art in the abdomen and bent her in two.

"Oh, Ellie, for ten guineas?!" Jim cried.

Art rose and felt Ellie's blackthorn hit the back of her neck like a sledgehammer, rattling her teeth. Art arced her stick up and brought it down. Ellie sinuously moved, curving her body out of the stick's downwards trajectory.

Like a snake, Art thought. Then Ellie twisted and smacked her stick into Art's nose.

Art felt as if her head had been shoved into the next dimension. Her knees gave way. She could sense Ellie leap up to bring her stick down and Art drew back her fist.

When she straightened her arm, her knuckles connected with Ellie's chin.

Ellie's head snapped back, and she fell against the podium. She collapsed to the floor and remained still.

"*Good show*, Art!" Jim said. "You bluffed with a disability and thereby managed to tag her!"

"Friend, that was no bluff," Art gasped. Her nose was a giant pulsation of pain. "Let us—out—now—"

"Door! Door! Once outside we'll be all right, they can't attack you in the open and risk attention!" Jim said.

Delphia flung the door open and sunlight poured in. Art stumbled out and came to an abrupt halt. Her hand that gripped her stick's handle shook.

"Art! We'll run ahead and fetch you fresh fish! We'll be right back!" Jim cried.

"Fish, sir?" Delphia said.

"Yes, run, girl!"

Delphia did, moving quickly through the maze of seller's hampers for the Billingsgate arcade.

Art stood hunched in the sunlight and felt blood trickle in streams from her nose. She was certain that her corset was holding together what was left of her bullet-riddled midsection. Everything, from the top of her skull to her ankle, felt cracked. She had a keen desire to faint. Then she realised; Ellie Hench still lay unconscious within the Black Market.

With great effort, Art turned for the door. She flung it open and lurched back in. Inside, two men were lifting Ellie from the floor. Ellie still clutched her stick in one hand, though she seemed unconscious. Art stumbled towards them and swung. She hit the man holding Ellie's legs while the other dropped their burden and fled through the curtain. The man she hit scrambled away.

Art picked Ellie up by the scruff and dragged her out through the door.

CHAPTER SEVEN

Delphia held Jim up while he negotiated with a fishmonger to bid on a lot of haddock for them. She didn't understand why they were doing so, since there were basketfuls of dried fish outside. She could only conclude that fresh fish benefited Art better. As the auction progressed, Jim hopped about in her hands and giggled.

"I need to blow my nasal cavities, I do!" Jim said. "Confound this morphine!"

"Sir, I haven't a handkerchief, so . . . here," Delphia said. She bent to offer Jim her skirt. He blew into it mightily. When he was done, Delphia gingerly dropped her skirt.

"I think that's better, I think my head is clearing," Jim said. The auctioneer suddenly smacked his hands together. "Good, the lot is won! Hurry and load, man!" Jim said to the fishmonger. "We've a ghost to feed!"

When Jim and Delphia ran back, Art's eyes were shut. She was leaning precariously over her stick and seemed ready to topple over. She was shivering. The fishmonger quickly pulled his cart up.

"Art!" Jim cried. "We've brought you that most toothsome of fishes, the reliable hadd—"

The haddock flew out of the cart and over the fishmonger's head in a stream of glistening, scaly bodies. They sailed directly into Art, slapping loudly. As they entered she began to straighten, her arms opening. Her nose righted itself with a crack. The glow of her body grew bright.

"That's it!" Jim cried. "All your insides are mending!"

When Art absorbed the last fish, she stood at her full height. Though recovered and no longer leaning heavily, she looked weary. She slowly pulled out her kerchief from her cuff and wiped her nose. The fishmonger nervously touched his cap and pushed his empty cart around to head back to the arcade.

"Art!" Jim said. "Ellie's outside too!"

Ellie sat slumped like a rag doll next to the door of the Black Market, her blackthorn still in hand and her hat crooked. With her black spectacles perched on her nose, she appeared to be either drunk or sleeping.

"Aye," Art said tiredly. "I thought it best."

"You thought right. No! Don't touch!" Jim said to Delphia when she moved to help Ellie. "She might hit you upon awakening."

"Some water flung, then?" Delphia said as she stepped back to a safe distance, away from Ellie's long stick.

"Yes, but won't be by us, I'd rather she and Art not confront again. She's fine where she is. Ellie, if you can hear me, it was nice seeing you! Next time, I'd like to buy you a coffee! Let's go, Art. We need to get more food into you. I think we've outstayed our welcome."

"Aye," Art said. Though she felt her insides were whole, Ellie's many blows were still making their presence known. Her nose ached. "I made a mess of it, Friend."

"Fighting your way through all of the Black Market to get us out safely? And Ellie too? No my young friend, you did very well! Can you walk? To the arcade, then!"

"I can, but I feel oranges will aid at this time," Art said. She headed for the market courtyard's exit, leaning a little more on her stick than usual. Her sore ankle protested.

"To the street, then!" Jim said. "With this young colt here, acting as my legs!"

"Thy help is most appreciated, Delphia," Art said, as Delphia trotted by her side. Delphia was a girl nearly a woman; Art guessed her age at seventeen. Just as Jim described, she had the youth and long limbs of a colt. Though her clothes were working class, her well-mannered bearing was graceful. Her face was thoughtful and honest, and her grey eyes quietly earnest. Right then, Delphia's bright gaze held a light Art recognized: the exhilaration inspired by danger.

"Miss, it's an honour, really, helping His Highness' supernatural agents," Delphia said.

"Call me, 'Art', child, no title needed," Art said. They entered the muddy street with its congestion of vehicles. "I am sorry thy lip was injured. Thy fearlessness has impressed."

"Mi—Art, I don't believe it was fearlessness," Delphia said. "I only saw that you needed help and therefore gave mine. And as for my lip, well, that occurred before I entered the Black Market."

"Was it by the stern hand of a sweetheart?" Jim asked curiously. "Or of a father?"

"Not those at all," Delphia said. "If I must confess, I was caught unaware, standing where a girl's fist also decided to be."

Jim laughed.

"Thee was not napping when I called upon thy aid," Art said. "Thy swift cunning and action saved both our lives." She stopped before an orange seller.

After asking the seller for his fair price, Art bought an entire crate of oranges. She took one large fruit and bade Delphia accept it. Then she absorbed the lot. They tumbled into her body. Her soreness fled, and her nose stopped stinging. Her glow brightened.

"Huzzah!" Jim said. "Art, I will never tire of seeing my queenly Clydesdale returned to perfect form!"

"Thee likes thy horses," Art said, smiling.

"I do. I called Harold a thoroughbred. Like you, he was also a regenerationist," Jim said. "He could come back from anything. Once he'd eaten as you do. Meat—red meat. Cooked or otherwise, and potatoes, bread, barley, sweets, and pies. That man loved his sweets. Pails of fresh milk. You should have seen the dinners Catherine had ready for him."

Art looked at Jim when he abruptly paused. To her, it seemed a shadow fell across his bone features.

"An indestructible man," Delphia exclaimed.

"He's dead," Jim said.

He made throat-clearing noises.

"Is thee well, Friend?" Art asked.

"Art, I don't know if you were aware during the heat of battle, but a woman sought to poison you with morphine, which I received in the eye socket for you," Jim said self-importantly. "I admit it's still affecting my faculties."

"Sir, I'd only hoped you'd break the needle," Delphia said apologetically.

"No matter, Bloom, I was happy to do my part. But I see ice over there, and a few chips chewed might clear my head more. Then I can consider our matter at hand."

As Delphia approached the seller with the ice, Art noticed a woman in an azure coat, riding a treadle penny-farthing. It entered the bustling street as the woman toed the treadle. The rider was Helia.

Helia had a leg against her steering bars as she sat sidesaddle, one hand holding a match and the other holding a shiny match safe. At her smirking lips was an unlit cigarette. Her penny-farthing rolled along at a speed Art thought daring. She admired Helia's utter disregard for how smoking in public made her both disrespectful and disreputable. Where Helia was concerned, Art had no problem with either quality. Helia struck the match against the safe.

She turned her head. Upon seeing Art, her smirk faded.

Helia tossed the match and match safe into the air and put her hands to her face. Her wheel crashed into a lettuce cart, and Helia fell off.

Art hurried to her aid. Delphia followed. They helped to pick Helia and her wheel up as the seller bemoaned the state of her cart. While Jim and Delphia dealt with the seller, Art spied something shiny among the fallen lettuce.

She picked it up; it was Helia's match safe. The souvenir bore a colourful, celluloid panel. The illustration was of an airship with a crest. It flew above a glass, iron, and stone building.

"SKYCOURT AT THE ROYAL AQUARIUM EXPOSITION, 1876", the advertisement read.

When she offered the match safe to Helia, Helia was staring at her. Art put a hand to her chest. She would have liked to cover up. The beautiful bodice Charlotte had designed was riddled with holes, and she'd bled all over herself.

"You've been shot!" Helia said.

"Aye—"

"Many, many, *many* times!" Helia said. She grabbed both of Art's arms, staring up and down her ruined bodice. "Shot, but can't be harmed," she whispered. "Shot but can't be harmed." She smiled suddenly, the expression almost maniacal. Stepping back, she picked up her skirts and did a little dance. "Shot but can't be harmed! Shot but can't be harmed!"

"Believe me, I am celebrating with you, Miss Skycourt!" Jim said as Delphia joined them.

"Is this because I was once shot dead, Friend?" Art asked, remembering the bullet scar over her heart.

Helia stopped dancing. Art watched, alarmed, as Helia's wide eyes slowly grew haunted.

Art reached out. "I am alive," she said gently. "Suffer no more."

"Art," Helia said, her voice strained.

"Erhm-hrm!" Jim interrupted. "Miss Skycourt, I caution. Such knowledge as you possess—should you consider sharing it, please refrain. Even my stoic partner may fall to hysterics, or worse yet, some brain fever brought on by knowledge too crippling to bear. We agents come back to this world cleansed of our past for a reason."

"I . . . agree, Mr. Dastard," Helia said. "This is not the time. Perhaps there will never be a time. Yet, Art, if you wish me to share . . . I'll try."

"I understand, Helia," Art said.

"Oh, look at your lovely dress!" Helia then said. "Lottie will have a fit! She must make more for you. Do you know where she is? Here, I'll write it down." Helia reached in her dress pockets for her notebook and pen.

"Thee knows my dressmaker?" Art asked in surprise.

"She's ours. Well, Helene's. Lottie is a genius; she knows how to design things," Helia said. "For the active woman." She tore off the paper, folded it, and with a tremulous smile placed it in Art's dress pocket. "Don't go to any department store, milliner, bootmaker, or armourer," she said. "Ask for all that you need from Lottie."

"Armourer?" Art said. She thought of her corset with its plating that had looked like armour to Jane Finch, the seamstress.

Helia only smiled and patted Art's hand that held her walking stick.

"Helia," Art said. "I thank thee. Thee is here to visit the Black Market?"

"Oh, yes. It appears you have already visited. Did you find out anything? I hope you beat them all soundly for shooting you!"

"I did, Helia," Art said. Helia clasped her hands in delight.

"And we learned nothing, I'm afraid," Jim said. "Art's Quaker stoicism overwhelmed the good senses of the denizens and frightened them into lethal action. Miss Skycourt, may I take this moment to introduce this young lady who is graciously holding me? Lady Helia, I would like you to meet Miss Delphia Bloom."

"M'Lady, how do you do," Delphia said and curtsied with one hand.

"Oh, manners! I haven't any, for I grew up a heathen child. How do you do," Helia said and offered her hand.

Delphia took it, and because Jim was in her other, she merely bent her knee again.

"And Miss Skycourt, if I may be so bold again!" Jim said. "We must ask of you a favour. Since you're about to enter the market, perhaps you can find out what Art could not?"

"And what might that be?" Helia asked. "For if you've the context of the query, both our objectives may be served."

"And served well! Here is your context, madam. There's to be an exclusive demonstration," he said. "A sharing of secrets.

The Bone Stealer intends to show a select few the manner of his bone-transference. We must know when and where this will be."

"I will do my best, Mr. Dastard," Helia said.

"No," Art said. "'Tis dangerous."

"Art, she's a journalist," Jim said. "She knows how to be cunning. And charming. None of that coy silence you exude. And she might even have a ready crown or two?"

"I do," Helia said with a grin.

"No," Art said firmly. Helia looked up at her tolerantly.

"I'll be safe. I've been in there many times. I don't even need an invite, and today, I've a guard. Please don't worry, Artie."

Art said nothing, surprised at the familiar use of her name. Jim chuckled.

"I'll be a short while," Helia said, her eyes twinkling. "As today is not my treatment day. But you should leave. The outer market has its lookouts for those inside. Expect a note at the Vesta later whether I learn anything or no."

"Thank you, Miss Skycourt," Jim said.

"Thee has a guard?" Art stood in frustration. When she realised Helia intended to enter the Black Market, she had attempted to ghost, to no avail. She would accompany Helia while invisible if her ability would only return.

"Yes, a stick for hire," Helia said.

"Oh," Art said.

"She even bodyguards for the suffragettes. Ellie is very good."

"She lies insensible, at the moment," Art said.

"Oh," Helia said. "Did you two fight?"

"Aye, but her stick was superior," Art said.

"Really? Was her skill with her wood most impressive?" Helia asked, smiling up at Art.

"'Twas," Art said. "Hard and fast, did she drive her weapon. She hit my crucial marks many times. I was nearly insensate from it."

"Oh! Art," Helia said.

"And when she struck true, right on my most sensitive spot!" Art said, pointing at her nose.

"Gentlewomen," Jim said. "Such flirtations before my stalwart colt here! Who, need I remind, is of tender years."

"No need to worry, sir, I've read the Bard," Delphia said.

"And her stick's size rivaled mine," Art said to Helia.

"Art!" Jim yelled. "I've a thought. Let's hire Bloom to be my legs. It's most advantageous to have your fists and stick, which you are so fond of discussing, free during this case. And the girl knows how to squire you, in times of action."

Art turned her attention away from Helia.

"Our work is dangerous," Art said.

"Yet, Bloom has proven capable. And you said so yourself, we are indebted to her!"

"Well—" Art said.

"Fearless! Thee had said. Let's try her services at least," Jim said. "For this case. With pay of course. And if she wants to leave at the end of it, she may do so. What do you say, Bloom?"

"Art and sir, I am in need of immediate employment and I can think of no better position," Delphia quickly said. "Let me join you in your work and I shall do my very best."

"Jim, we must talk," Art said.

"Absolutely! But later! Miss Skycourt must be off, and we need to be scarce from this scene! Might we have that dressmaker's information that Miss Skycourt was kind enough to share with you? Delphia can walk me there, and we can order more garments for you!"

"I've a perfectly fine dress at the Vesta."

"Oh, for now," Jim said. "You can't borrow, remember? Due to all the women being of woman-size, next to you."

Art looked at him, and then sighed. She pulled out the paper Helia had given her and handed it to Delphia.

"You should go immediately to the Vesta and refresh, Art. You look a ghastly sight," Jim said. "And fix your hat, for the women will talk. Leave everything to Miss Skycourt. *Don't* return to the Black Market. Miss Skycourt! Good luck! We eagerly await your information!"

"Mr. Dastard," Helia said, smiling.

Delphia turned for the street with Jim. She hesitated and

looked back at Art.

"Delphia, he shall guide thee well, or else I shall scold him," Art said. "I will see thee soon."

Delphia smiled and proceeded down the street.

Then alone with Helia, Art found her earlier ease with conversation deserting her. Being tall, broad, and bloodied, she felt the oaf next to Helia's petite and trim figure. She admired Helia's bright eyes and the rosiness of her cheek again. Art realised she should say something, for Helia looked at her expectantly.

After a moment of awkward silence, Art decided that her lack of tongue was, unlike how Jim would have it, neither seductive nor coy.

"I . . . best get my wheel there," Helia finally said with a smile, turning away. She glanced back at Art and took hold of her penny-farthing. She hopped on the back step of her wheel. She was about to push off when Art suddenly caught Helia's free foot by the ankle. Helia dropped from the step to the ground and laughed in surprise.

"Oh Art, what is it?" she said, looking back. Art was staring down at the boot in her hand. Helia's heel had the silver cap tapped into it, just like Art's boots. Only Helia's was inscribed with the word "SKY".

"Won't you give it back?" Helia said, smiling.

Art realised what she'd done. She had only wanted to see what was on Helia's heel. In apology her thumb rubbed against the ankle; another impropriety.

"I am being forward," Art said in self-reproach, looking up at Helia.

"I don't mind," Helia said. Art let her foot go and rose.

"I've 'Art' inscribed upon my heels," Art said. "Yet 'tis odd, for I named myself before seeing them."

"Not so odd," Helia said. "We had those made for you. 'Art' is short for your own Christian name, which is no more Christian than mine."

Art stilled, her heart beating rapidly at the thought of learning her human name. Helia looked at her searchingly.

"I shall remain 'Art', for now," she finally said. "I thank thee for my boots."

Helia smiled and nodded.

"Thee be careful."

Helia gasped, the sound almost a laugh. She blinked several times.

"For you I will," Helia promised. She pushed off and rolled her wheel for Billingsgate's courtyard and the Black Market.

Once Helia disappeared into the courtyard, Art stood holding her stick, considering then discarding numerous options. In each scenario where she imagined re-entering the Black Market with the price of ten guineas still on her head, she also saw herself endangering Helia.

In deep self-chastisement, Art finally turned away.

She looked down at her hand; she still held Helia's match safe. Art put it safely in a pocket.

Still unable to ghost, and therefore fly, Art hefted her stick and began her run back to the Vesta.

CHAPTER EIGHT

"Bum bum, bah dee," Jim hummed as Delphia wound through pedestrians and carts for the thoroughfare free of Billingsgate congestion. A few things crossed his mind as Delphia crossed the street. One was the surprising bounty placed by Livus on Art's body; two was Helia Skycourt. Three was their mysterious black arts surgeon, and four was the girl presently carrying him in hand.

Jim sniffed mightily and felt, indeed, that he was still addled by the morphine. Until his thoughts settled and enlightened him regarding the previous three, he at least had the mental capacity to take care of issue four.

"You seem to know your way about these London streets," he said as Delphia hurried to reach another corner.

"I only know some, sir, and not beyond Bishopsgate. I hope to see a policeman who might tell me where this address is," Delphia said, looking at the piece of paper in her hand. "Unless you know, sir?"

"A driver would. But before I bid you catch a carriage, place me on that mail post there. Let's have a man-to-squire talk, you and I."

"That, sir, I can do," Delphia said, doing as Jim instructed. "Do you mind if I eat my orange?"

"Eat away! How's my hat?"

Delphia set it at a rakish angle for him.

"As my partner said, this is dangerous business," Jim said.

"But you've faced a significant bit of that business with us, bullets and all. I'm happy to employ you and I feel that sex and youth are not an issue when it comes to merit and mettle. However, the fact still remains, you are still just a girl."

"Yes sir," Delphia said. She had already peeled her orange and was eating it.

"Therefore, I must speak to your parents."

Delphia coughed suddenly, hard enough to bring tears to her eyes.

"You do have parents, don't you?"

"Yes sir, I do," Delphia said glumly. "And Mother has yet to know I've lost my position at the green nursery today."

"I see! In the doghouse before we've yet to *really* put you in there! What I want to know is how will they receive the announcement of your new situation?"

"Well, sir, we do need the money," Delphia said. "And I'm unlike the other girls, I'm hard to place. If we could afford more education, I would aspire for better positions, but it can't be done. I've even thought of leaving, for a different life, but my brothers are already gone, and I don't want to leave my parents alone."

"Older brothers?" Jim asked.

"Yes sir. One's at sea and the other is . . . gone out to the world."

"Ah. And this 'different life' you speak of?"

"In all seriousness, I was considering becoming a performer," Delphia said. With gravity she finished her last slice of orange.

"Let me guess, tightrope walker?"

Delphia smiled at Jim.

"Modest, are we?" he teased.

"I can only walk a little ways," she said. "Just for play."

"More than some can say. Up I go, then! It's time to meet pater and mater," he said. Delphia picked him up. "Hail us a hackney carriage. Then lend me your most intelligent ear, for there are particulars I must share. We've a dire case, and I fear there will be a fifth victim before we can get ahead in the game."

～

Once at the Vesta, Art entered through the iris portal. She hurried by the doorwomen who stared wide-eyed at her bullet-riddled bodice. Occupants of the library and Curiosities and Mechanical Room started in surprise upon glimpsing her spectral form. Milly Sedgewick stepped out of one of the drawings rooms and called to her.

"Oh my," she said, and inhaled from her cigarette. "Are you well, Art?"

"I am. My thanks for the concern," Art called. She did not look back but walked quickly for the stairs. Alice, stationed at the foot, followed her.

"Miss!" Alice said. "The bullets didn't exit your back! Should I get a surgeon?"

"No need, I . . . I ejected them," Art said. She reached the third floor and headed for her room. Alice nearly ran to keep up.

"Seeing that you are in a great hurry, I'll help you myself, miss, until the maids come."

"Alice, I thank thee. I must change and return immediately to the work," Art said. She needed to see if Helia was well. Art had intended to go back to the Black Market, but after Jim's admonishment, she thought then to find out where Helia might go next.

Her sister may know, she thought.

Art opened her door and she and Alice entered. "And Alice, between thee and myself, please, call me 'Art'."

"Oh, Art, I know you asked before, but consider my position. It's just not right," Alice said.

"Very well," Art said, smiling. While Alice took down Art's newest outfit and laid it on the bed, Art remembered Jim's parting words about her hat and removed it. There was a significant dent in the crown that Helia no doubt had seen, and the ostrich feather was bent.

Art sighed in dismay. It was no wonder that the costerwomen seated with their baskets had been pointing at her hat and then at their own, talking amongst themselves. Art knew that no matter how poor or hardworking the woman, her hat was a prized possession to be protected at all costs. Though Ellie was the one who lay defeated, Art was well aware that she had suffered the greater disgrace.

"Miss?" Alice said, looking up from her task of laying out Art's undergarments.

"'Tis nothing," Art said soberly as she fixed the hat. "Only an eldering, duly received."

Alice helped Art out of her outfit. The dried blood was like glue. Art's bodice stuck to her underclothing, and the corset to her body. The ragged bullet holes in the corset's plates cut Art anew as Alice pulled the sticky garment off. Art's fresh, white blood bloomed in spots on the chemise fabric and spread.

"Oh, miss!" Alice said, horrified.

"'Tis nothing, Alice, 'twill stop," Art said. Wanting to assuage Alice, Art concentrated to make that happen. To her surprise, the bleeding did.

"See, the wounds are no more," she said, pulling up the bloodied chemise for Alice to see. "Won't thee take these ruined things? And I'll wash. The basin will do."

"I will fetch the maids," Alice said, her demeanor unsettled.

"My thanks, Alice."

~×~

In a room on the third floor of the Vesta, Manon lay in bed with Arlette's dark head on her chest and ran fingers through Arlette's hair. She heard Oleg outside the door and then his quiet entry. He nodded, signaling that they were then truly alone. He looked at Arlette and smiled, his waxed moustache lifting. Manon felt Arlette's smirk against her breast.

The door closed behind him. They had a little while until their next client, Mrs. X. A widow of indeterminable age, Mrs. X always arrived with her face heavily veiled and dressed entirely in somber black. At first, she preferred to peep while Manon and Arlette performed. After a few visits, she decided to join them in the room, her black-gloved hands politely folded while she sat in a chair by the bed. Then, at her last visit, she paid for the privilege to touch.

Manon believed that this time she would not have to coax Mrs. X's timid hand to caress her.

Arlette pulled out the folded newspaper she'd hidden beneath the pillows. She shifted to her back, laid her head on Manon's belly, and began reading. In a few minutes, Manon expected Arlette to be fast asleep and drooling. This morning's breakfast with Art had been unlike their usual schedule. Manon settled herself and closed her eyes.

Voila, she thought. A presence she was becoming used to pricked at the edges of her awareness. Art's eldritch warmth signaled that she had just set foot in the Vesta.

Manon did not sense Jim with Art. His energy was more a dancing, white flame next to Art's powerful, roaring, and comforting hearth. Though Manon was skilled at hiding her own true nature, she never knew Jim to apply his abilities and attempt awareness of her. Instead, he had the consistent habit of sending pages to seek her out. And Art, being so new, was unabashedly oblivious. Even then, Manon could feel Art move for the third floor to her own room, not knowing that Manon was only a few doors away.

"Can it be a beast?" Arlette suddenly asked. Manon knew what Arlette was referring to without having to look at the paper. "People are being fed to it, perhaps?"

"*Non*," Manon said. "A bone-eater would not eat like that."

Arlette sighed. "I wish you had said there was no such thing. Then it is a man, or a woman. A very dangerous vivisectionist."

"*Oui.*"

"May Monsieur Dastard and Art bring swift justice!" Arlette said. She yawned widely. She turned the pages of her paper until she reached the section on politics and empire affairs.

"What is a 'vivisectionist'?" Manon asked.

"A man of science who studies anatomy, by cutting open living animals," Arlette said.

"*Atroce!*" Manon said. "It is a new name for an old thing, like your silly 'Fourth Dimension'. That is torture."

Arlette looked at Manon and reached down for Manon's left foot. She stroked it comfortingly. Manon felt her fingers explore the faint scars she had explained were from a time long before Arlette was born, and the Catholic Church more openly cruel.

"Please read," Manon said. "I am well."

When Arlette returned her attention to the paper, Manon idly played with Arlette's hair.

Manon did not sense the presence of humans as she could eldritch beings. It had taken her a great number of years just to learn how to do that, and despite her longtime experience living among humans, they still baffled her. She had Arlette and Oleg deal with their own kind, and by secluding herself and her partners at the Vesta she kept them safe from the more predatory, eldritch creatures that liked residing in cities.

Manon's otherworldliness had been one of the assets that persuaded Catherine Moore to transport her and her partners from France to England. However, when Catherine visited at the request of Manon's master, Lucius Blanc, he had a difficult time convincing his old friend to employ his strange, yet beautiful mistress.

"Lucius, she is pretty, and perhaps very well skilled, but she's hardly charming and for the most part, she merely stares!" Catherine said. "Can she really speak English or is she a mimic? I see nothing very special about her that I can't find in girls already in England."

"She has not worked her enchantments upon you? Ah, Manon, she hides her nature!" Lucius said. "I will tell her to show you. Catherine, she can make your Vesta richer. She can do that, and more. And I don't say this because I'm an old, dying man, so very fond of *ma petit fleur*. I want her well cared for when I'm gone, *oui*, but she is *worth* that care, my friend."

After Manon had overheard the conversation she fled back to her room, wondering what she could do to convince Catherine of her worth. Her master was, indeed, dying, and Manon felt that she'd been in one place long enough for her lack of aging to be noticed. Her master loved her eldritch nature, but that aspect did not always enchant humans. Sometimes the reaction to her beguilements was hostile, born of fear. Manon didn't think Catherine would be receptive to bewitchment.

Manon found Arlette in their room, chuckling as she read an English magazine.

"*An Englishwoman's Friend*," Manon read slowly. The cover had an illustration of two very pretty women, one with her head in the lap of the other. "Did you purchase this at the aeroport?"

"*Oui*, I asked for it especially. It is about the Englishwomen and their affections for other women," Arlette said. "So many letters and stories. So many sighs! If we are going to a deviant English brothel, I thought to know what it is the women like. This is romantic . . . sentimental! But some speak the language of desire!" She laughed and turned the page.

"The Vesta is not a brothel, it is a club," Manon said. "With women who like to be male. It may not include such women as in your magazine. What do they mean by 'friends' . . . do they mean 'sexual'?"

"Some boast of such, but many do not," Arlette said. "In these friendships are unrequited affections, obsessions, and passionate amity. Then there are the stories that I can only recognise as pornography. Very surprising!"

"How so? We are French women. By merely breathing, we are pornographic to the English."

"Birching," Arlette said.

"I find no passion in disciplining. *C'est stupide*," Manon said. "I dislike striking others, most of all, you."

Arlette grasped Manon's hand and returned her attention to her magazine.

"Was that a romantic English gesture?" Manon asked.

"It would have been more romantic had I taken your hand, pressed it to my breasts, and kissed you. In a flower-filled glade, under the approving face of the moon. But should these Englishwomen desire to know more than kissing, we can show them if they come to the Vesta, *oui*?" Arlette put the magazine down. "Now, are we going to England? Has Madame Moore accepted us?"

"She will, once I speak with her," Manon said. "She is a businesswoman. We will make her more money. Your magazine has given me the reason."

That night, with her master listening approvingly, Manon explained to Catherine how she and Arlette might entertain, educate, and satisfy the sapphic curiosity of English women. She made certain to mention *An Englishwoman's Friend*, and the sort of society—the British society—that encouraged romantic female friendships.

"Did Sarah Ellis not write in *Daughters of England*," Manon said, discreetly consulting the notes Arlette had written on her arm. "That the Englishwoman must understand her own femininity through other women before fully appreciating her place with her husband? Would it not be her rite of womanhood, then, for the sake of marriage and for her maturing identity, to learn about her own sexual nature and strengthen it . . . with another woman?"

Manon thought she could see the coins being stacked inside Catherine's head.

"But we can't have very vulgar acts," Catherine said. "I mean . . . well, the toms are as bad as the men when it comes to pornography, in which case whatever you do for Monsieur Blanc is probably appropriate. But we are discussing the possibility of having respectable Englishwomen enjoy the club."

"*Oui*," Manon said. "For them, we can be beautiful and romantic. We will be the proper Englishwoman's ideal of passionate"—Manon consulted her arm again—"amity, and bring pleasure to those dreams."

"'Amity', and not *l'amour*?" Lucius asked in curiosity.

"I will not assume for the Englishwoman where her heart lies," Manon said. "We are here only to explore her desires."

Lucius smiled broadly while Catherine pondered.

"Yes. You do make sense when you're not just staring at people," Catherine said. "And your English is satisfactory."

Lucius laughed. "Trees do not care for talk, Catherine! They can only show. *Bon!* I am glad this pleases you. And now you must know. Manon may also be of help when your son Harold is resurrected."

The revelation of Manon's true nature as an eldritch creature finally convinced Catherine of her worth. At Lucius' passing, Manon came to England with Arlette and Oleg and made her new home at the Vesta. The toms and their women loved engaging Manon and Arlette for lascivious acts, just as Catherine said. Then, anonymous letters appeared in *The Englishwoman's Friend*, extolling scenes of tasteful intimacy that could be witnessed at the Vesta. Manon worked with Arlette on sensual romantic display, and their discreet and discerning clientele began to build and return for more.

Once Harold was resurrected and an agent of the Secret Commission, Catherine expressed a keen interest in excluding possible otherworldlies from Vesta membership. Though Manon thought Catherine read too many Gothic novels, her employer's concern was legitimate. Some creatures had wealth as well as title and indulged in the privileges of class, which included exclusive club memberships. It was one reason why Manon had her peculiar rules and demanded to weigh clients beforehand. It became Catherine's habit to have Manon look at any Vesta visitor who seemed suspiciously queer.

"What do you think of Mrs. Grave Childs?" Catherine once cautiously asked Manon in the privacy of her office. "She's been here only two nights, and her sexual requests are practically scaring the staff."

"She is human," Manon said.

"You have seen the correct woman? Petite, young, pretty, dark-haired, but with eyes like ice. And Milith has a deliberately slow and disturbing way of speaking."

"*Oui*. She is human."

"Pity," Catherine sighed. "I was about to try looking at her with a mirror, wondering if she'd cast a reflection. I shan't have Harold expel her, then."

Despite Catherine's eagerness to discover creatures in the Vesta's midst, her greater problems were always human-related.

Humans who practiced dark arts were equally dangerous. Manon had yet to sense serious practitioners visiting the club. Catherine even frowned upon drawing-room pastimes like séances, "talking" boards, and the parlour favourite, the Willing Game, where a lucky participant was "willed" by collective mental focus to perform the mysterious—and this being the Vesta—sexual directive of the rest of the players. Manon never allowed herself to be hired for such frivolity, and Arlette had explained that the queer English pastime involved no mentalism, just clever prompting and the motivating excuse to kiss and do more with the partners and wives of others.

Whenever Manon found herself agreeing with Catherine, it surprised her, but she thought it wise to keep juvenile games— and their foolish repercussions—from disrupting the discreet and trouble-free environs of the Vesta.

For the first time in a very long while, Manon enjoyed predictability and peace. Art's sudden presence at the Vesta was like a towering signal fire to her awareness. Art's energy felt like purity, power, and resilience. Against all of Manon's precautions, she had needed to witness this extraordinarily fresh being and measure its newborn state herself.

Arlette snored against Manon's belly, finally fast asleep.

Manon wrinkled her nose.

Something distasteful was in the air, niggling at her. It was an old sensation—so old she had forgotten why it gave her dread. It made her want to flee, put rivers between herself and whatever it was, and swiftly enclose herself within a stout and long-lived tree to block out sound and feeling.

The memories returned to her in a jumble of violent images and sounds that were of men, iron, and fire. It was the scent of killing.

Manon leapt from the bed, upsetting Arlette. She swiftly donned her dressing gown and flung open the door. Oleg, seated by the door, turned to look at her in surprise. Alice was stooped over with an armload of clothing in the hall, attempting to pick up a soiled and mangled bodice decorated with mother-of-pearl buttons. She had accidentally dropped it. The scent of violence spiraled from the clothing.

"Is something wrong?" Alice asked Manon.

~

When Alice left with Art's damaged clothing, Art stood only in her stockings, boots, and ruined chemise. It seemed best to send Alice away before something upset her further. Art still bled in places from the stuck corset. Healing herself was not terribly easy, no more than her attempt at halting bullets with her own body. With great concentration, she closed the new wounds.

Since it appeared she had finer control of her flesh, she tried to dematerialize. Nothing happened. She tried again.

Art sagged in despair. Without the ability to ghost, she was a mere thug, as proven by her disastrous handling of the Black Market affair. That debacle, her failure to see to Helia's continued safety, and the state of her hat were enough to make Art feel very foolish and inadequate.

She moved for the washbasin closet and the door to her room burst open. Manon suddenly hurtled towards her.

Manon landed upon Art, legs wrapped around Art's waist. Art staggered back and fell upon the bed. Manon's dressing gown parted. Her green eyes were wide and pale. She franticly pulled Art's chemise up, revealing Art's torso. Art could feel the hair between Manon's legs brush her belly.

Manon touched where the damaged corset had previously cut Art and brought her fingers up, stained with Art's white blood. Her nostrils flared. She tasted her fingers.

She then kissed Art urgently.

Art heard Arlette exclaim, "Oleg!"

Art felt Manon pulled from her as their lips continued to meet. Oleg held Manon aloft. Arlette quickly touched Art's bared flesh.

"Forgive me, I do this only because she's such a creature," Arlette said to Art. She stained her own lips with Art's blood. "*Regarde!* Art is here," she said, pointing to her own mouth. "Come for me, come!"

Manon made a sound. Art felt the sensation of vines bursting forth, reaching. Manon sprang out of Oleg's arms and pursued Arlette, who ran quickly out the door. Oleg ran after them.

Art heard Arlette shriek. A door slammed.

Art's heart thundered. She ripped the ruined chemise off and hurried for the washbasin. She poured a pitcher of cold water down her face.

Several doors down, "Mrs. X", as Catherine discreetly referred to the heavily veiled client, was waiting patiently in a chair near the bed. Dressed from head to toe in mourning black, her gloved hands were neatly folded in her lap.

The door slammed open. Arlette rushed in with Manon in pursuit. Manon grabbed Arlette's dressing gown and pulled it roughly from her body. She pushed Arlette to fall back on the bed and fell atop her. She devoured Arlette's mouth. The newspaper crumpled noisily beneath them. Oleg reached in and quickly shut the door.

Manon grabbed the newspaper and flung her arm back. The pages ripped.

Mrs. X pressed both hands to her chest as the pieces fluttered down.

Manon pinned Arlette's wrists above her head. Her own dressing gown still hung from a shoulder. Arlette gave little cries as Manon caressed her. She parted Arlette's legs with her own.

Mrs. X cautiously rose.

She hesitated. Then she crept to the bed.

Very gently, she pulled the dressing gown away as Manon moved. She laid a trembling hand on Manon's back and caressed down.

In her room, Art vigorously washed. Her mouth still remembered the touch of Manon's. She shook her head and smacked her cheeks repeatedly. While drying her chest with a towel, she briefly marveled that her body appeared to have no other scars except the old bullet one over her heart. The maids arrived. Alice also returned, carrying Art's badge and other pocketed necessities. Among her things was Helia's match safe.

Once Art was laced, dressed, gloved, and her hat back on her head, she thought to try ghosting again.

The maids jumped when Art disappeared, and then reappeared. Art smiled in relief.

"Very good, miss," Alice said.

Art wrote a note for Jim, telling him where she had gone, and left her room with Alice. She saw Oleg standing outside a door.

Art stopped. She wondered how Manon was.

"Miss . . . Manon has a few clients to attend to," Alice said in a low voice.

Art nodded. Perhaps later she might find words, or understanding. She quickly left for the stairs.

~

Jim and Delphia's carriage stopped near her Bethnal Green home. When she disembarked with Jim, Delphia was both thoughtful and solemn.

"Well, Bloom, do you still want this position?" Jim asked.

"Sir, we must do all we can to save the next life," she said.

"Good to have you," Jim said. "We should return to the Vesta, where Art and I reside, and see what information Miss Skycourt has sent us. But first—"

"My parents," Delphia said. "They will both be home, sir." She walked them to the door of her modest home and called out to let her mother know she was there.

~

A mile over, between Shoreditch and Spitalfields, a middle-class woman, unusually tall and lean, disembarked from her omnibus and hurried down an alley. She was headed for the back entrance of Cambridge Music Hall. Miss Felly Pritt had short curly hair and a handsome face. Not yet in her mid-twenties, she had taken to playing bit roles of supporting males who stood in the background or engaged in swordfight melees. She was content to not have prominent roles but was gaining a little notoriety among the female theatre-goers who fawned over male impersonators. Felly didn't think she was quite as good as the more famous cross-dressers, but she was having great fun and enjoyed donning trousers. Her employer was also happy with the additional audience attendance thanks to Felly's androgyny.

Therefore, a stage boy happened to look out a second story window for her, due to her lateness for afternoon rehearsal. He gave an alarmed shout to Felly as men in gas masks descended from a waiting delivery wagon and grabbed for her.

Felly swung her parasol, cracking heads as she did so. One man came behind. She felt a rag soaked in chloroform pressed against her face and knew she was done for. She struggled for as long as she could. The masked men picked her up. Theatre hands shouted and ran to her aid. Amid the scuffle, Felly was dropped on the street. Her neck snapped.

Her assailants abandoned the abduction and escaped in their wagon.

~

At the Vesta, Mrs. X departed thirty minutes later. She was euphoric, and twenty guineas poorer. Oleg poked his head into the room, his eyes round. His moustache twitched. Arlette only rolled her eyes. He closed the door.

Arlette sat up and looked at Manon.

"What just happened with Art?" Arlette asked.

Manon's eyes darted. She considered a slew of thoughts.

"I will guess, then," Arlette said. "Art was wounded, her blood everywhere, and this impassioned you, yes?"

Manon gave no answer.

"When Monsieur Harold would return, covered in his own blood, it never bothered you before. Why is it so different with her?"

Meat, Manon thought. Monsieur Harold ate of hooved animals and smelled of red meat—like the humans around them.

The scent of his blood should have reminded her of war, of the desperate and frightened men who screamed and killed each other in her woods, but it never did.

"And then you tasted hers!" Arlette exclaimed. "Are you changing? Do you need more to savour, beyond dirt and trees?"

Manon suddenly gripped Arlette. *Art was like trees*, Manon thought. Her blood tasted of the sea, but mixed in the salt and water were rich and thick-leaved green things. Art's white blood had reminded her of the bleeding of trees, falling to their deaths before cannons and axes.

"Ah! *Ma fleur*, such a face! I am sorry, please forgive me," Arlette said, hugging Manon tightly. Manon clung to her. "You will tell me when you can. Forget now, everything is well. All is well."

Manon listened and allowed Arlette's voice and touch to soothe her. The effects of a long ago time will fade once more, she thought, and when she saw Art again, Manon would know better how to deal with her.

CHAPTER NINE

Art had flown nearly halfway to Helene's tenement before remembering that Helia was meant to send a note to the Vesta. Had Art waited for the note, she would then know that Helia was well.

Art chastised herself for not thinking clearly. But remaining at the Vesta with Manon in such a queer state also didn't seem prudent. She resumed her ghost flight. Her ability to fly was less effortless than usual; she felt heavy and fatigued. She landed and solidified.

She saw an odd mechanised buggy before Helene's building. It was small, red with black trim, and with a black leather-upholstered seat that could fit two. A long, sturdy wicker hamper was mounted on the buggy's front, a gas lamp on either side of the hamper. There was a steering tiller with a black rubber bulb horn attached.

A group of ragged boys loitered nearby, staring and jostling among themselves. Helene, in her long, austere black coat, stood by the vehicle and conversed with a young West African man sporting short sideburns. He wore a bright red tie, a finely patterned waistcoat, and a bowler hat. He glanced at Art, his brown eyes curious and bright. They widened as much as the big grin on his face. Art immediately felt at ease.

Helene noticed Art and motioned her to join them.

"Perseus, I'd like you to meet Art, an agent of His Royal Highness's Secret Commission and an artificial ghost," Helene said. "She was a former family friend, now risen from the dead and entirely without past memories."

"I am six days living," Art said to them.

"And Art, this is Perseus Cassius Kingdom," Helene said. "Inventor. His brother Taurus is a captain of our airships. Well, you don't remember. Taurus Midas Kingdom was the first man to captain an airship across the Atlantic. And we've his pilot and crew in our employ too."

"My admiration for thy family, Friend," Art said, smiling as she offered the young man her hand. He raised his hat, took her hand, and shook it firmly.

"Thank you. And it's a pleasure meeting you. My first supernatural acquaintance, if you don't mind my saying, Art," Perseus said. His accent sounded American, and Art was pleased that his informal manner precluded formal titles between them.

"Thee has fine names. Thee is American?"

"I am. My emancipated father took the name Kingdom," he said proudly.

"'Tis weighty," Art said. "As I'm newly living, I will choose a surname myself, when the time comes."

She thought Helene stiffened, and realised that like Helia, Helene would also know Art's original name.

Art gave the thought fleeting consideration. She let the moment pass.

"Perseus is also an exceptional mechanician," Helene then said, returning their attention to the small buggy. "For this electric vehicle—"

"The 'Picnic-hicle'!" Perseus said.

"A name which needs work, Perseus," Helene said. "Was designed by him, and as you can see by the prominence of the wicker basket, we hope might be a popular new means of transport for well-to-do women."

"The hamper locks so ladies can secure their purchases! Shopping, outings, visits with friends!" He walked around the vehicle as he spoke, demonstrating with his hands. "It runs on electrical power. The battery is fixed beneath. No legwork needed like the tricycle, no spokes or gears to catch the skirts on. No having to worry about noise, oil, smoke, fire, or having to touch a dirty engine. It needs only be hooked to a station for a recharging of the battery. It's clean, smooth, silent, swift, and safe for traveling! Perfect for ladies!"

"It sounds wonderful, Friend," Art said in admiration. She glanced at Helene. "Would Helia give up her wheel for such a fine buggy?"

"Well," Helene said, looking slightly taken aback by the question. "I suppose. Her penny-farthing can get her in tighter spots than this can. But she might use the basket top as an excuse to put her typewriter on it and type whilst driving. So I rather she not have one of these. But you didn't come here to discuss horseless carriages, did you?"

"I've come to discuss Helia," Art said. "I let her enter the Black Market alone and am worried."

"Ah," Helene said. She glanced at Perseus. "If you'll excuse us a moment, Perseus."

"My apologies, Friend," Art said to him.

"Please, ladies," he said, smiling as Helene and Art stepped away. The ragged boys approached and began peppering him with questions.

"Is this about the Bone Stealer?" Helene asked Art.

"Aye," Art said. "A . . . conversation in the market went awry. I was attacked, a price placed on my body, and therefore attacked more for harvesting. Thus, I was in no helpful condition to accompany Helia when she entered."

"You look in good health now," Helene said. "You must be a regenerationist, like Catherine Moore's son, Harold. Why didn't you ghost back in, or can you turn invisible?"

"I can, but I've discovered I've a weakness—"

"Wait," Helene said, raising a hand. "You're being foolish again. Never share a weakness. Not publically or with anyone. You don't even know me, Art."

Art held her stick. Though she disliked Helene's abrupt manner, she knew she was right.

"Good," Helene said. She lowered her hand. "We've an escort for Helia, for she goes to the Black Market regularly. Did she tell you?"

"She spoke of her visits."

"If you saw Helia enter, then her stick for hire was waiting."

"I trounced Ellie Hench."

"Oh," Helene said.

"Where would Helia be, if finished with the Black Market?" Art asked. "Her card tells me nothing."

"You let Ellie hit you on the head, didn't you?" Helene said.

"What?"

"Your feather's dented. No proper woman in a brawl would have allowed that."

"Thee does not wear a hat."

"Many a fighting woman would allow her garments torn, but never must her hat be harmed," Helene lectured.

"Will thee tell me where Helia lives?" Art said in exasperation.

She watched incredulously as Helene tamped down the smirk that threatened to appear on her mouth.

"She stays at the Royal Aquarium Exposition Palace and Pleasure Gardens," she finally said. "She's been living there since you . . . died."

Art recalled Helia's souvenir match safe. "'Tis in Westminster. Helia is at the Palace Hotel?" she asked patiently.

"No, she's in the aquarium exhibition itself," Helene said. "She keeps no apartment or hotel room. She sleeps in one of the airship replicas we've on display at Skycourt Pavilion, uses the Turkish bathhouse in the Palace, and eats at the cafes. She works from one of the tables, typing her stories."

"She lives in an exposition and retires in a balloon?" Art said. She had to see this for herself.

"Well, she obviously is not supposed to be there, but somehow she manages it," Helene muttered.

"More than an hour's passed since I left her at market.

Perhaps she's not yet returned."

"From Billingsgate? No, she'd be back at her table by now. It would only take her twenty minutes by wheel. Thirty if she crashes."

Art recalled Helia's last crash and her own alarmed reaction.

"I'll leave thee, then," Art said, "and go to Westminster."

"We'll take you," Helene said. "I have to bring this 'picnic' thing—"

"Picnic-hicle!" Perseus said, turning from his conversation with the ragged boys. "And sorry, didn't mean to eavesdrop, ladies."

"To show my uncle," Helene continued, giving Perseus a look. "And his offices are near the aquarium. I'll see first if she's there. Come up." Helene walked to the entrance of her building, and Art fell in step behind her, curious to see Helene's living quarters.

Jim had been in many an abode and knew the difference between rich, poor, working class, and the growing middle class. Delphia's street in Bethnal Green was one of the working class amid other streets where abject poverty prevailed. Sturdy women with beefy arms hung laundry or stared with arms crossed when Jim and Delphia disembarked from the carriage. A fancy-wares dealer at the corner stood patiently by his barrow. Women with babies gazed at his trinkets. A dog and eager children ran past to surround a man and a boy setting up a street puppet show.

When Delphia stepped into her home, a ground floor of a larger, dilapidated house, Jim saw that it was worn, simple, and lacking certain amenities but it had the warm touch of a woman's hand with patterned drapes, tablecloth, and a quilt thrown over a chair. It was comfortable, at least. But scattered about the modest home was evidence of better times; a worn Persian rug with a once bright pattern lay on the floor. Tiny portrait paintings in round silver frames stood on a cabinet, and books—many, many books—with tooled leather bindings, gold lettering, and ribbons between the pages, were stacked in a cracked cupboard that no longer held china or silverware.

Volumes were piled around one chair in particular in the room Jim assumed acted as living room, dining room, and sitting room. In that chair sat a bearded, sad-faced man. He did not seem to stare at anything in particular. Very thick spectacles were in his one hand and a round magnifying glass with a horn handle in the other. In his shawl-covered lap was an open, illustrated book. The man looked weary.

At the table, a woman with a lined face and firm mouth pulled upon a large curved needle. She was mending saddlery. Pieces were laid on the floor.

"Delphia, you are home far too early," the woman said without looking up. Her hands worked quickly. "I'm afraid of what you'll tell me."

"I'm afraid you're right, Mummy," Delphia said. "I've lost another situation today."

Mrs. Bloom sighed heavily and put her work down. When she looked at Delphia, she saw Jim in her daughter's hand.

"What is that?" Mrs. Bloom exclaimed.

"Mrs. Bloom, I presume?" Jim said.

Mrs. Bloom's strangled shriek in answer revealed several things to Jim. One were the two children who had been playing in the bedroom, a small girl with pale hair like Delphia's and one bigger boy, who immediately responded to their mother's reaction by coming to the door to gape. Two was Delphia's poise and deliberate calm. Three was Mr. Bloom's reaction.

Mr. Bloom quickly donned his thick glasses and swiveled his head this way and that.

"What is it? What's happening?" he said fearfully. He stared, unable to discern anything with his magnified eyes.

"Mr. and Mrs. Bloom, if you please," Jim said. "I'm Jim Dastard, agent of the Secret Commission. Forgive me for not having my card, as I've misplaced my pockets. I am here because I would like to offer your daughter a position."

❧

Once up the stairs of the tenement, Art saw the thick construction of Helene's door and its metal security plate. Helene slid the plate back, pressed a combination of lettered brass keys within, and turned the handle to open the door. Art heard the gears shift and watched as the heavy door opened outward. Helene entered and Art followed.

She noted the sparse, small space. There was a narrow bed, two chairs, a desk, a stove, a case with books, and little else. It was very much an ascetic's cell. There was nothing present that might comfort—of color, object, or beauty—though Art did spy a tintype and two daguerreotypes in framed casings at Helene's desk, lined with deep red velvet.

Helene went to her desk and laid the tintype facedown before Art could see what it was of. The other photographs, a dual case sat open like a tiny book, held the portraits of an upper-class woman and man. Art thought they might be married. The woman looked very much like Helene.

Helene opened a shelf cabinet at her desk. Within was a telegraph and teleprinter. Art marveled at the sophistication of the shiny devices.

"Thee has a wire from here to Westminster?" Art said.

"No. This is wireless. Much like your badge except without the black arts element," Helene said. She switched on her telegraph and tapped a brief message. "We'd have voice-to-voice communications by now if the patent wasn't tied up in litigation these past ten years."

"Speech, at long distance?" Art said. She and Jim had practiced "far-speaking" thanks to inventions by the Secret Commission, but she still found the idea amazing.

"Yes, it's called the 'telephone'. Though we'll still make do with pigeons for our airships," Helene said. "So. This 'Bone Stealer' Helia has been writing about. Since you were at the Black Market, I assume you're close to capturing him?"

"With Helia's help, perhaps."

"I see. Well, here's your answer." The teleprinter slowly printed a strip of paper, one character at a time. When it was done, Helene tore the strip off and handed it to Art.

AM HERE, the strip read.

Art smiled.

"Let us go to her," Art said.

Helene retrieved a black hat from her closet. Its brim was upturned on three sides: a tricorne. The form of it was not so much like the old tricornes of years ago, Art thought. The folded brim was snug to the crown instead of curled and spread. The triangular top was higher, like a riding hat. To Art, it was very fetching once it was on Helene's head. Helene fastened the hat with a long and deadly looking jet hatpin. Art spied the clothing hung within the closet. All were simple, black outfits.

Dress of mourning, Art thought.

Helene seemed satisfied with the fit of her hat and gave the top a rap. It sounded as though she were knocking on wood.

"Thy hat is hard?" Art said. "Yet thee has an untouchable head?"

When Helene looked at her, her mouth was suppressing a laugh.

"Oh yes. I needn't worry about others disgracing my crown, but when thrown from a horse or buggy, well, a hard hat is prudent."

"Ellie Hench had the elder hand, 'twas no disgrace. Can Charlotte Thackery provide me such a hat too?"

Helene looked at her in surprise.

"Helia said we've the same dressmaker."

Helene sighed.

"Do you want one just to allow others to hit you on the head?" she said.

"Thee was not there to see the fight."

Helene stepped forward, her eyes bright like Helia's.

"Show me," Helene said. "Pretend I'm you and you're Ellie."

Art was hesitant but at Helene's insistence, did as asked. Slowly and carefully she explained what happened with re-enactment. Helene was smaller and slim like her sister, but when Art locked Helene's arm as Ellie had done to her, she felt the strength tightly coiled in Helene's body. Art imagined a small, powerful engine, waiting for the press of an accelerator, or as Jim might describe, a fresh young Arabian, ready to start at the gate.

"Right for your kidneys!" Helene exclaimed when Art demonstrated the blows Ellie gave to her back. "Did the plates of your corset help?"

"Aye," Art said. "But her blackthorn dented them."

As Art replayed each hit, Helene easily submitted to Art's role as antagonist. Helene moved with such ease, seeming to anticipate what Art would do, that Art suspected Helene could exhibit more had she wanted—whether movements in defense or to subdue. Art gently took up Helene's right wrist. Helene made a fist as Art directed it for her own chin.

"I hit her thus," Art said. "And the fight was ended."

"Knowing your previous skill, one well-placed blow would have done it. But you've superior strength now, haven't you? All you creatures of the Secret Commission do."

Art didn't answer.

"You're still a very good teacher, Art," Helene said.

Art let go of Helene's wrist. "I . . . taught thee how to fight?"

Helene laughed.

"No," she said. "But you did teach others."

Art did not know what to think of that revelation.

"I would still like a hat like thine," she finally said.

"You never forget, do you? Very well, you may have a hard hat too," Helene said begrudgingly. "But don't tell everyone of Charlotte's designs. We must be selfish and keep her to ourselves, agreed?" She winked at Art.

Art stilled. When Helene winked it was not like Helia's, yet it equally enchanted her.

"Yes, Helene," Art said slowly as Helene moved for the door.

∽

"Now then, Perseus, let's go see that uncle of mine," Helene said once she and Art were on the street again. Perseus hopped out of the front seat where he had been lounging and rubbed his hands in glee. He bade the street boys to step back, reached behind the vehicle, and pulled out a high seat. He locked it in place and climbed into it.

"Art, please take the front seat and enjoy," he invited with a grin. He put on the goggles he had perched atop his bowler's brim.

The front seemed small. Sitting next to Helene would be intimate, Art thought. She didn't mind it though she did have one personal concern. She focused on the density of her body.

Helene mounted the driver's side, snapped a pair of dark blue lens to her spectacles, arranged her skirts, and then looked at Art. She laughed.

"You've gone translucent! But only by so much; you're still solid, aren't you? Are you making yourself lighter?"

"Aye, I may be as much as thirteen stone; I may tip this buggy," Art said. She carefully boarded and sat next to Helene. As she thought, it was a snug fit.

"Tut, we'll be fine," Helene said. "It's all that muscle of yours. I'm heavier than Helia by half a stone."

"Thee is also unsexed?" Art said.

Helene looked askance at Art. She also glanced behind her. Perseus sat above in the rumble, grinning and already holding the seat's sides. Art's arm was draped on the upholstery of Helene's seat back. Were she to lean back while driving, Art would have an arm around her. Helene looked at Art.

Art chose not to acknowledge her impropriety and set her stick to the vehicle's floor.

"Still incorrigible," Helene muttered. She released the brake lever and honked the horn. "Hold on to your hats!"

With one hand on the throttle stick and the other on the steering tiller, Helene stepped on the accelerator pedal.

The vehicle jumped from stillness to swift motion so rapidly, Art had to raise her arm for her hat.

CHAPTER TEN

Jim had laid out all that he could offer in way of a position for Delphia and awaited the resulting family argument. With a little more query, he learned the mother's name—Gaiety—and the father's, which was Peter. When Gaiety was younger she had been a fresh beauty, but Jim could see that the family's economic fall, accompanied by a disabled, dreaming husband, had taken its toll on her countenance, if not her spirit. Peter, with his precious piles of books, was blind in more ways than physically.

The proper thing was to give the Blooms their time to discuss and have Jim come back on the morrow, but time was of the utmost importance in this case, and Jim was eager to use his new "legs". Motherly concern took the conversation from wary to passionate. Jim felt a surprisingly harsh headache begin, and a deep nausea in his phantom organs, though he very well knew he had no stomach with which to feel ill. He tried to stay focused on the discussion.

"She is still just a girl!" Gaiety said to Peter.

"Mother," Delphia said. "You know I can do this."

"Hush! This is more than about position and pay!" Gaiety said.

"Oh dear! Forgive me!" Jim said, and he suddenly vomited coins, cigarettes, his badge, a bag of tobacco, several wrapped sweets, a tobacco card of Queen Victoria, and a marble.

"Mr. Dastard!" Gaiety said, standing.

"Sir! Are you unwell?" Delphia said.

"Ohhh. I never did get to chew that ice. Tell your parents of the morphine attack," Jim said piteously. "I believe it's made me terribly ill."

He vomited three more marbles and a carte de visite of a burlesque performer.

Thus, Jim found himself with his hat off, laid on a comforting blanket, and a cold compress on his forehead. He tried to explain that he needed to smoke to feel better, or at least eat a match, but Delphia was busy sharing with her family a very simplified version of their adventure in the Black Market, as well as what she'd read in secondhand medical journals of morphine withdrawal and its aspects. Hearing their adventure retold, Jim finally learned why a girl like Delphia happened to be in the Black Market in the first place. Peter was terribly curious and entertained while Gaiety listened, tight-lipped but reluctantly impressed. The Bloom children stared at Jim and took turns giving him sly pokes. He told the children to help themselves to the sweets and marbles.

Finally, Gaiety relented. Delphia would be allowed to work for Jim and Art. Gaiety put on a brave front as Delphia hugged her, but Jim saw the desperate desire in Gaiety's eyes to protect her child. A small voice in Jim's mind chided him for causing this maternal pain, but he chased it away.

For, he thought, everyone was someone's child. One only had to look at his deceased partner, Harold.

"And what happened to your mouth, Delphia?" Gaiety then said. "Was it Hettie O'Taggart again?"

When Delphia stepped out of her home, she was wearing her coat and had discarded the grey apron. Jim had his hat on, his possessions back inside him, and was smoking a comforting pipe. He still had a headache but at least his nausea had receded. His eye sockets suddenly glowed.

"Ah! Buzz buzz! It's a message via my badge! I'll take it!" Jim said as Delphia looked in confusion at his glowing eyes.

After a while, Jim spoke.

"She's at the Metropolitan Free Hospital in Spitalfields."

"Art?" Delphia said apprehensively.

"No, our near-fifth victim," Jim said. "Or we will know that for certain, once we get there. To a hansom cab!"

Delphia ran for a street where she could wave for one. The driver of the two-wheeled carriage, its roof smartly folded back to reveal the clean, leather seat, trotted his horse up to where she stood.

"Being that you are a fledging adventuress, young Bloom, do you mind our taking a hansom cab?" Jim said.

"Should I, sir?" Delphia said. "It would be my first ride in one!"

"Then by all means, enjoy!" Jim said jovially.

"I'm still keeping in mind that we were meant to go to Art's dressmaker," Delphia said when they had boarded the hansom cab.

"Ah, yes! And I meant it, for Art goes through clothes like a boy through penny bloods. And I've another task for her dressmaker too, once we visit her. But first, we must meet the police!"

Delphia stiffened.

"The police, sir, of course, sir," she said.

"Is something wrong?" Jim asked. He puffed contentedly on his pipe.

"I think not. It will be a short ride," Delphia said.

"Allow me to spit the fare into your hand," Jim said, and when Delphia obliged by removing his pipe and offering her palm, he spat out a few coins.

The ride from Bethnal Green, through Shoreditch, and down Commercial Street to Spitalfields was short indeed. Delphia paid the driver through the trapdoor in the roof, hopped out of the cab before the gates of Metropolitan Free Hospital, and walked to the entrance. Inspector Risk waited.

"Quite the affray you and Art had at the Black Market earlier today," Risk said drily when Delphia and Jim neared. "You even incurred a bounty."

"Well, Art certainly did," Jim said. "Since it reached your ears, we must have left the place in suitable disrepair and with a sizeable impression! Inspector Risk, this is my new assistant, Miss Delphia Bloom."

"Sir," Delphia greeted.

"'Bloom', eh?" Risk said. He looked at Delphia closely. "I know a 'Bloom'. . . know him well. And I must say that's quite the family resemblance. He liked to be called the 'Acrobatic Thief'."

"It was the papers that liked to call him that, and he has a name. It's Philosophy," Delphia said.

"True, 'Phil Bloom' was his name," Risk said. "He certainly made a reputation for himself, with his wild antics evading the police. We caught him finally because the last robbery he tried to flee from, he tripped over his sister."

"Were you that sister, Delphia?" Jim asked curiously.

"I was," she said.

"Court didn't find you an accomplice, even though you were present at the crime, else you'd been transported like him," Risk said.

"And Philo is getting on well in Australia; he may return in two years," Delphia said.

"Return, so you two can resume your former habits?" Risk said.

"Return, knowing he'd paid his price and we may resume being a family again," Delphia retorted. "And since you say you know him well, sir, then you should intimately know the case, and therefore recall what I said in court, and that is all I have to say."

"Very well," Risk said. His thick moustache seemed to hide an amused turn to his mouth.

"Delphia, let me add to my earlier statement about sex and youth. I shall also add 'history'," Jim said. "You are still my assistant."

"Thank you, sir," Delphia said quietly.

"Come along, then," Risk said. "Let's see if our victim's still living."

Risk stood aside so that Delphia entered the hospital first.

~

"We've a Miss Felly Pritt," Risk said as they walked into the crowded waiting room full of ailing women, men, and children. They found a spot to wait for a nurse to become available. Risk explained the entire circumstance of the attempted kidnap and subsequent accident.

"And what leads you to believe this is related to our Bone Stealer?" Jim asked.

"Her fellow actors who foiled the kidnap said the fleeing men spoke German," Risk said. "Cursed in German, to be exact. When Miss Pritt was seen breaking her neck."

"That's quite an assumption," Jim said. "The connection is thin."

"True, but I don't think this will waste our time," Risk said.

A nurse came who led them to the ground-floor orthopaedics ward where a doctor was present. Within the quiet ward, patients lay in the beds, their limbs or body parts in splints or plaster casts. Many were attached to pulleys and ropes that kept them in traction. After introductions, Risk looked about curiously for their victim.

"Miss Pritt was given a private room," the young doctor said. "Payment was provided by the Music Hall Benevolence Fund, and they insisted. And since she has such an odd visitor present at her bedside, I have to agree that it's best she rest in private."

"Odd?" Jim said.

The doctor started when Jim spoke and stared at him, flustered.

"I-I didn't know—I mean." The doctor cleared his throat. "Well! Her odd visitor. Miss Pritt had a note pinned in her purse. It said that if anything should happen to her, this man should be summoned. And so he's here. He's supposed to be her doctor."

"A pinned note. That's a good idea," Risk said. "I'd want the doctor I favour to come to me when something happens. Even if he were a magic toad."

"Well, yes," the doctor said.

"Let's see them, then. Doctor, thank you." Risk walked with Jim and Delphia towards the private room.

Delphia would have been nervous about participating in her first investigation were she not still feeling indignation from her conversation with Inspector Risk. Therefore, she walked down the orthopaedics ward with her chin held higher than she usually would, and with a variation of the swagger she learned from the chocolate factory girls. Her airs ended once Risk motioned her into the private sickroom. There, Miss Pritt lay, supine and fragile in her bed.

Miss Felly Pritt had a sheet drawn up to her chest. Her black-stocking feet poked from the bottom and hung a little over the end of the bed. Her neck was encased up to her chin in a steel-and-leather corseted brace that rested around her shoulders like a collar. The bottom of the brace was strapped criss-crossed to her chest. Miss Pritt's mouth was a tight line and her face grey.

A white-whiskered Chinese man, his high cheekbones prominent in his lined face, sat near the bed. He was dressed in a short black jacket with spacious sleeves cuffed neatly at his bony wrists, over a long green shirt. He wore black trousers tied off with ribbon at the ankles of his thick, white socks. Hard, shaped slippers were on his feet. A round black cap was on his head. He held a long, thin-stemmed pipe, the small bowl carved in the shape of a crane's head. He puffed quietly upon it. The air smelled sweetly of jasmine and tobacco.

The old man's gaze came to rest on Delphia, and she thought that despite his thinness and age, his solidity and calm presence seemed to speak of firm health and strength. He sat with a straightness and balance that she admired and she briefly wished that her father, bowed with melancholy, might benefit from half the body-awareness this man had.

The man rose suddenly and walked purposefully for the door in a direct manner that made Delphia step back. The man exited and promptly took a seat in the chair placed beside the door. Delphia followed and stood before him. He sat with legs splayed and feet planted, the pipestem back at his lips, just as he had sat within the room.

"Hello, sir. I am Jim Dastard, and this is my assistant, Delphia Bloom," Jim said.

The man merely stared at Jim, his gaze contemplative.

"You are Miss Felly Pritt's doctor?" Jim said.

"Yes," the man answered calmly.

"I think I know you, sir. Don't you have a shingle hanging in the Black Market?" Jim said.

The man slowly exhaled smoke.

"Yes," he simply said.

"Interesting cartoon on your sign," Jim said. "It's of the whole body but with great, red circles drawn on it. What can they mean?"

The man did not answer and merely smoked pensively.

"I've seen your shop too, sir. When I go to the blood-letter's," Delphia said. "There are many men and women who like to visit you. I've always been curious as to what manner of healing you practiced."

"I am Dr. Lau," the man said. "A nerves-setter."

"Nerves!" Jim exclaimed. "Instead of bones, intriguing, sir! And what did Miss Pritt visit you for, Dr. Lau?"

"Balance," Lau said.

"A correction of her—?"

"Pelvis."

"Ah. She's an unusually tall woman, Miss Pritt. She looks practically Art's size, don't you think, Delphia?"

"Such a rare height, but seems right," Delphia said. "How tall is Art, sir?"

"She's six foot two inches. Would you say that's close to Miss Pritt's height, Doctor?"

"Felicity is so," Lau said.

"Dr. Lau," Jim said, "I believe that someone in the Black Market has a special interest in unusually tall females. Someone with a measuring eye and an intention of harvesting."

Dr. Lau stilled. He removed the pipestem from his lips.

"A chop man?" he said, his tone cold.

"A sawbones? Yes sir, I do believe so. Would you happen to know about the surgeon stealing people's living bones? Miss Pritt might have been his fifth victim had she not had the misfortune of breaking her neck."

Dr. Lau returned the pipe to his lips. He thought a while, his face solemn.

"I do not," he eventually said.

Jim thanked him. Their conversation ended, Dr. Lau rose and bowed low.

"Doctor," Delphia said before Dr. Lau could return to his patient's bedside. "Will Miss Pritt recover?"

"Tomorrow we will know," Dr. Lau said. He re-entered the room.

Delphia and Jim retired down the ward with Inspector Risk.

"Miss Pritt's relations live outside of London, but her sweetheart is here," Risk said quietly. "Roger Flannagan. He works at the same music hall. I spoke to him earlier and sent him on an errand to calm him down. But he did say that Miss Pritt's been injured before. 'Crushed' would be a better word. Was her pelvis, in an omnibus crash. She was told she'd never walk again."

"No mystery that she has this doctor, then. Let's hope Lau can repeat his miracle. Her neck may be broken, Risk, but she may still be a target," Jim said. "Whoever needs her bones may want them that much."

"I'll have men on guard here, and Flannagan intends to keep both eyes on her as well," Risk said. "I doubt Dr. Lau will be leaving soon, either. So, tall girls, is it? That price placed on Art. Hardly coincidence."

"Yes," Jim said darkly. "Risk, the man you must take from the Black Market is Livus. He's the one who's been measuring unfortunates for the Bone Stealer. After this failed kidnap, a wiser murderer would retire for the time being, but there are other players in this game."

"The buyer," Risk said.

"Indeed," Jim said. "I'd like to know which rich, and unusually tall, young woman thinks she can pay enough to steal the bones from the likes of Art and Miss Pritt."

~

Art had a firm hold of her hat as Helene sped them down the

streets of London. The "Picnic-hicle" rattled on stones as a horse carriage did and was driven by Helene with as much recklessness as a racing coach-driver. But the ride was smooth, swift, and unlike anything Art had ever experienced before. The little buggy was so instantly responsive as it weaved and accelerated ahead of cabs and carts that if Art hadn't seen Helene's firm hand upon the steering tiller, she would have thought the vehicle behaved of its own accord, and in a manner most artificial and unnatural. She could not imagine a horse behaving thus—changing, slowing, and then speeding at every unpredictable whim of Helene's. It even rolled backwards, a movement Art found alarming.

'Tis a toy, Art realised. Passersby and drivers gawked, and more than a few boys pursued them. Perseus waved, shouted, and pointed. By the time they swerved into the broad streets of Westminster and sped by the Abbey, Art felt oddly nauseous. She didn't notice when her badge suddenly glowed, the signal stopping as suddenly as it had started.

Helene slowed the buggy and entered the oval courtyard before the Royal Aquarium Exposition Palace and Pleasure Gardens. Though the ride had been adventurous, Art realised that it had saved her from the exertion of ghosting and flying to Westminster. The short flight to Helene's tenement had been surprisingly trying on her body. Helene circled them before the ornamental stone-and-iron façade of the aquarium's great hall. Art saw the poles above bearing the waving flags of various nations besides those of the British Empire.

"Out you go!" Helene said when she brought the buggy to full stop. She pulled upon the hand brake. "Helia is within the exhibitions, past the sea tanks and across from Skycourt Pavilion. Her café is the Blue Vanda."

"I've no knowledge of this place," Art said. As she rose, Perseus hopped out of his rumble seat to help her disembark.

"You've been here at least once when alive, that I know of," Helene said.

"'Tis multinational?"

"It is British-owned, but what has saved it and the pleasure gardens and Palace Hotel from languishing is foreign tourism," Helene said. "The many embassies are in this area, after all. Thus, there are businesses within catering to the various cultures, as well as those of the Empire. The food served at the Blue Vanda, I can attest, is native. It's no wonder we like to tarry here, as we were not born in England."

Art looked at her in surprise. "Thee and I?"

"Oh no, Art," Helene said, appearing deeply amused. "You were born on English soil. Helia and I were born in Nepal."

"A marvelous kingdom I'd like to see someday, since Skycourt has the air route to there, perilous as it is," Perseus said. "The nearest experience I can savour is from its neighbor, India, found in the form of the Blue Vanda." Perseus rubbed his hands in delight. "Delicious curry. Would you like me to escort you to your destination, Art?"

"Friend, I mustn't keep thee from thy task any longer," Art said. "But I am very grateful for the transport. Thee has created a magnificent vehicle." She looked at Helene. "Shall I tell thy sister hello?"

"Certainly. Why not?" Helene said.

Art bade them both farewell and strolled towards the great doors of the Royal Aquarium.

❧

When Art disappeared within, Perseus hopped into the passenger side of the buggy.

"Take the driver's seat," Helene said. She disembarked on her side. "I won't be accompanying you to my uncle's."

Perseus looked at her in surprise. "Wha—?"

"Don't worry, you'll do well," Helene said. She removed the dark lens from her spectacles and moved around the vehicle. "Uncle Cadmus likes you. Good luck!"

She walked purposefully for the entrance farthest to the left.

❧

As she had at Billingsgate, Art faced a massive space inside the Royal Aquarium, stretched high and wide and topped by arching glass and iron. The sounds of milling people echoed upon the columns and walls, and Art perceived an underlining hum of excitement. Above, palm trees stretched three stories to the iron arches. Art saw dust-speckled sunbeams shine down from a great glass dome in the distance. Dirigibles hung in the serene illumination.

She stepped farther into the arcade proper and strolled to where the great, blue tanks stood. As she did so, people who noticed her hurried out of her way.

The thick glass of the tanks stretched sixteen feet high. At their bases were brass railings against which visitors leaned. A large plaque explained the water replenishing and circulation system. To the arcade's left, the great tanks had floating balls, hoops, and swings suspended above the water. Here, performers took turns diving and executing aquatic tricks. Spectators crowded the glass and watched every twist and turn of the scantily clad swimmers. The sole female diver swam close to the glass, her dark hair waving, and smiled for the crowd.

"Once more! Once more!" a group of women cried, waving their handkerchiefs to a tall, well-muscled male diver standing upon a swing. He jumped and smoothly dived in, to their vocal appreciation. To Art, the women's accents sounded American, and she smiled at their brazen manner as they tittered to each other.

Provocative performers did not hold Art's interest long. She turned to look at the tanks to the right, where fronds of sea fauna waved as colourful fish swam and darted. Many were very small, but Art saw giant sturgeon glide slowly by, longer than the length of her arms. Their tiny eyes stared from the sides of their heads, and she looked back with longing.

Art nearly bumped into young sailors who were consulting their small guidebooks while studying a tank. The aquarium glass had a notice fixed to it, declaring that the huge tank held a giant clam, lobster, and crab, though Art could not perceive of any such animals hiding within the sand and sea grass. Girls in straw hats quickly passed her carrying a pictorial foldout map. She had the sudden desire to purchase a souvenir guide herself, for she felt there was far more that she could learn and discover than by merely viewing exhibits and reading plaques.

Such visitors were so absorbed in where they wanted to go and what they wanted to see, that Art as a supernatural presence hardly registered to their awarenesses. But any who might turn after watching the acrobatic divers or the darting fish stared in either surprise or terror at her. Some hurried away, urging their spouses, friends, or children to follow. Their viewing spaces before the glass filled again with spectators who paid no heed. She saw schoolchildren approach and moved to walk to the left side, causing more people to notice her and press back in alarm.

Charity school girls, aged six to ten, in their blue dresses, pinafores, and bonnets, walked hand in hand in two rows. Their teacher came to an abrupt stop and paled at the sight of Art.

"Children, hold your buttons!" the teacher said. "Do so, now!"

When the girls saw their teacher clutch one of the buttons of her dress's chest front, they did the same, reaching inside their pinafores. Art looked at their large eyes as they stared up at her and her heart ached. To hold a button meant they were protecting themselves from an omen of death.

"Be not afraid," she said to them gently. "Thee will grow." She said this to each child she passed. She did not look back so as not to alarm them further.

As she approached the end of the row of tanks, she saw country folk in their best, holiday dress. They had brought their picnic baskets, and finding ledges and benches to rest upon, sat with their paper-wrapped meat-and-mustard sandwiches and watched the crowd. When spying Art, they chose not to flee, but stared wide-eyed with food in their mouths. Retreating at the sight of her would mean having to repack all their utensils and provisions. Therefore, they sat still and in amazement, even as she drew near and strolled on.

She entered sunlight and the great dome proper. Replica airships, balloons, and other flying contraptions from various British, German, and American manufacturers hung suspended high above her head. Art looked up at the impressively large dirigibles and smiled in wonder.

In the area of the pavilions, amid presenters and salesmen ready to discuss air flight, she saw the other exotic characters English folk gaped at. Tall Africans in ornate kaftans strolled, pointing and loudly discussing the various models above. Bearded Indian men in turbans and silk walked solemnly with hands clasped behind their backs. Art saw Asian men in dusty coats, their unruly hair long and tied back, seated at a café patio table. One dozed against his folded arms.

Building façades lined the sides of the exhibition space and housed cafés for coffee and tea. Other storefronts held souvenirs, imported sundries, and newsagents who carried papers in different languages. Art saw that some façades were fanciful representations of the great Empires, including those of Germany, Russia, and Japan. Beside the cafés, leisure areas were hidden behind planters and small palms. There, loungers sat in wicker chairs around gently cascading fountains and smoked, read, or played chess.

She walked farther. She came upon a French restaurant with an ironworks entrance of twisting vines, berries, and female figures. The patio held mosaic-topped tables, delicate, wrought-iron chairs, and an oxygenated glass tank, bubbling and filled with living crawfish. A server fished out a few on to a plate and hurried inside. Art admired the allegorical females painted on the restaurant's colourful signboard. Amid the aromas of cream-rich haute cuisine and poured wine, diners amicably chatted.

But it was a spicier scent, enticingly aromatic and heavy with fresh herbs that caught her attention. Somehow she knew what the fragrance was, mixed with the scents of steamed rice, mango, coconut milk, and chicken; it was Indian curry. Art looked towards the crowded patio of a café at the other end of the pavilions area. The long café façade was ivory-white with gracefully ornate Indo-Saracenic arches and slim columns. Airship models with the crest of 'Skycourt' floated high above them. Art strolled towards the Blue Vanda.

～

Helia sat at a Blue Vanda patio table with her portable Baby Fox typewriter, a scattering of written-on paper, three pencils (one lost beneath the table with a few balled-up pieces of paper), a dish of half-eaten tikki masala, and several used cups of tea. Whenever the café staff—all Indian men in long embroidered kurtas and trousers, their waists wrapped in long white aprons—approached to clear the table, she shooed them away. She didn't like to be disturbed while working.

Right then, she was wording a telegram to be sent to Germany and a discreet contact there.

Bitte informieren Sie Vivisektion von Verbrechen und ihre Standorte.

Please inform of vivisection crimes and their locations.

She released the paper from her typewriter and pulled it out. A waiter accepted it from her. Though there was a perfectly well-run telegraph office nearby, behind the aquarium ice cream stand, the waiter would take Helia's note into the Blue Vanda's office. There, the head of staff would privately send her message.

Helia fed a fresh sheet of paper into her Baby Fox and tapped her pencil fretfully. A telegram like hers was something Inspector Risk would have already thought to do, if not already, then soon. Helia felt in this respect she was only carrying out the procedure of investigation, and not enquiring for clues that might answer the question currently nagging her.

She had learned what manner of person the Bone Stealer was. She just hadn't discovered his name.

Yet, though there were more direct queries she would rather pursue, she refrained. This was one of those rare times where she chose to be cautious, for this man they all wanted was not one to be trifled with.

Helia ate another spoonful of her meal and began typing. She glanced up and noted that her favourite string quintet had slowly trooped single file into the pavilions proper, each musician with a hand on the next person's shoulder. Made up of a female conductor, two male violinists, a viola player, a cellist, and a flutist (the last three being female), the entire group was blind except for the flutist, who was mute and presently leading them. They found their customary seats beneath the raised patio of the Blue Vanda and unpacked their instruments. As they seated themselves, they laid their Braille music sheets on the floor and took off their shoes and socks, the women demurely so. The women obscured the sheets with their skirts, but the men could clearly be seen tracing their Braille sheets with a bare toe.

The conductor knocked about until she found her music stand and placed her sheets upon it.

Helia leaned over the rail and waved happily, though only the flutist could see her. The flutist, nicknamed "Eyes", waved back. Feeling cheered, Helia adjusted her chair and returned to typing.

She'd learned a little bit about the Bone Stealer once she'd left Art and entered the Black Market. Art had left the market in impressive disarray, and when Helia saw the extent of Art's Amazonian damage, she thought it fortuitous. With the denizens of the Black Market distracted, Helia would be free to enquire discreetly and leave quickly. Ellie, roused by water thrown at her face, walked by her side and looked appropriately threatening, though uncharacteristically stiff and stoic. Helia didn't doubt that Ellie suffered silently from some mild concussion, but it was an ailment that had to wait until Helia had obtained her information.

She went directly to a second-storey shack that had no shingle hung or marks on the door, hidden in Surgeons Row. Its windows were papered over. The office belonged to her eminent scientist friend and Black Market resident, Arthur Fellows.

Once she identified herself, Arthur let her and Ellie in. He was a handsome man, with a mane of thick dark hair that rose from his high white forehead, but his blue eyes were faraway and solemn, and his pale face grave, as if he were preoccupied with secret knowledge that haunted him.

"How goes it, Arthur?" Helia asked gently.

"Not well," he said. "I've failed again."

His dimly lit office had a lingering stench, slightly sulfurous.

Diagrams and drawings were pinned up on the walls, all of dissections and of internal organs. Texts and books lay piled, some filled with Egyptian hieroglyphics. A cloth was thrown over his desk, but from beneath peeped the end of a silver-tipped stick of black wood. On his lab table were two rabbits, both dead.

"It was a successful organ transfer," he said. "I tried it with their livers, a phantom transference, no incisions. Each rabbit had the liver of the other. I thought I'd found the right ritual at last. And perhaps I did. I measured everything precisely. They were perfectly matched. But their bodies could no longer tolerate their new organs."

Helia looked at the rabbits. "Are you saying they were healthy and living, for at least a while?"

"For a week," Arthur said. "One beautiful week." He sat down, seemingly devastated.

"I'm sorry Arthur," she said and joined him.

"I miss Emily." He touched a jet mourning pin he wore on his chest. The crystal centerpiece contained woven hair. "I miss her terribly. I couldn't save her from her weak heart, but this work I'm doing . . . if it could save others. It's all I have to keep me from going mad."

"You are doing good work, Arthur, despite what family and friends think."

"Taking an office in the Black Market so that I may study in secret and in peace has hidden me from their scrutiny, surely. I'm still a respectable man. But I'm certain that everyone now believes I'm supporting several Convenients." He laughed bitterly.

"Arthur, I must ask," Helia said quietly. "A secret event is about to occur, demonstrating surgery very similar to yours. Have you been invited?"

He looked at her. "I have," he slowly answered.

"Do you know where?"

"I do not."

Helia had found that when a person looked unblinkingly into her eyes when answering, as Arthur was then doing, it was a good possibility that they were lying. But such a person was often a practiced criminal, and Arthur was that sort of sheltered, earnest gentleman who would not be good at deceit, or willful criminality.

"A time and place was not offered, then?" she said.

"Due to the nature of this . . . most dark enterprise of the event's host, I believe such specifics will be passed to me, eventually. Perhaps right before it is to happen. You must understand, Helia. These invitations are sold, and the price is high. They are not just offered to surgeons like myself, but to the wealthy."

"Perhaps to convince future clients of his skill," Helia said.

"I did not buy my invitation," Arthur said.

"It was merely given you? He must think you a worthy colleague, Arthur. Have you met him?"

"I'm glad to not have," Arthur said, looking at her with his haunted eyes. "For by chance I heard a little about him, and it really is best not to know."

"I must know, Arthur," she said.

"Of course you must, Helia. I can only give you this much. He's titled, and he is not from here, he's a foreigner. And his sorcery, and heartlessness, is of a depth and scope where any connection with him can incur death. And frankly, I miss Emily so much I might consider it an opportunity. I'm still young, and in good health. It will be too long 'til I see her beautiful face again."

"Arthur," Helia said, "but your work."

"So many I would like to help." He turned away. "I am being morose. I should persevere."

"Yes, Arthur, you must," Helia said.

Arthur grew silent, and she waited patiently. "Please let me know where and when," she finally bade. "For that knowledge, too, will save more lives."

"I will try," he said, staring elsewhere.

As Helia moved to leave, he caught her arm and rose. He whispered urgently in her ear.

"He's a *Durchlauchtig*," he said. "A Serene Highness."

When Helia left Arthur's office by the back entrance, she did so quickly, hoping she and Ellie were not noticed.

"Wanted the rabbits. Could've et 'em," Ellie murmured to her.

"Best not with his rabbits," Helia said as they walked for the market exit. "With those queer senses of yours, didn't you feel the taint of black arts on them?"

"Yer tainted, and yer perfectly well," Ellie said with a grin. "And when such taint are eaten, some 'earty luvin' can easily cure."

"Oh! Ellie," Helia said.

"It's the good feelings that chase away the bad. With those rabbits, has to be lots o' luvin'," Ellie said.

"Your head will be getting a proper look," Helia said. "Please try not to cure your concussion with men."

"No promises," Ellie said, smiling, and she stepped through the curtained exit first, using her stick.

❧

Helia stifled the great yawn that came upon her and shook off her fatigue. She worked on the wording of her next telegram, this time to the Vesta. The blind quintet was in the midst of a surprisingly well-performed Boccherini (No. 4, in D major, Op. 19, G. 428), when Helia heard a murmur rise around the patio. She looked up.

Art was walking into the pavilions proper, her spectral presence parting the crowds as if she were a slow-moving yet dangerous bull, let loose among them. Apparently oblivious to the disturbance she was causing, Art was gazing in gentle amazement at the dirigibles above.

Helia jumped up, ecstatic, and danced a brief jig. She hastily picked up her used cups and balls of paper. A waiter ran up to help her. Soon her table was clear of everything but her Baby Fox and papers. She saw Art notice the Blue Vanda and approach.

Helia gestured frantically to the quintet below.

"Eyes, Eyes, Eyes!" Helia said.

Eyes suddenly stood, nodded vigorously to Helia, and tooted her flute at the conductor. The music sagged as instruments slowed and petered out.

"A processional! Tell her I want a processional!" Helia hissed.

Eyes made shrill sounds with her flute at the conductor, who raised her head in Helia's direction.

"We can *hear* you," the conductor said. "We're blind, not deaf. Eyes, sit back down and cease that racket." She rapped her stand with her baton.

"The Mendelssohn march," she called out. She stomped a hard, deliberate beat with her foot. The music began.

"No, no, nonono!" Helia said, jumping up and down as the musicians warmed up to the new score. "Oh, horrors!"

The conductor gave an exasperated sigh.

"Stop!" she ordered. She flipped through her pages of Braille notes.

"*Queen of Sheba*," the conductor called out. The players rapidly toed through their Braille music sheets. As the conductor stomped out the count, the slow and nearly discordant notes rang out in the great exhibition proper.

With a wide smile, Helia looked towards Art. The celebratory sounds lagged in almost a lazy manner as the blind musicians played, but the composition's flowing beauty still remained, traveling down the great dome space and arcade. Art returned Helia's smile, her walking stick tapping, and Helia thought of sweet-smelling flowers that floated like Handel's notes, down a sparkling river.

Art mounted the Blue Vanda patio steps and walked up to Helia.

CHAPTER ELEVEN

Art hadn't the opportunity to hear much music in her brief second life, but she was certain the odd quintet below the Blue Vanda was playing a bit poorly. It didn't matter to her. The composition itself was still beautiful, and perhaps the lagging music was less painful because Helia was there, beaming and her eyes bright.

Art stopped before Helia's table and smiled. She prepared to speak.

Then Helia turned, balled up a piece of paper, and threw it at the head of the conductor. It bounced off the woman's hat.

"Gracious!" the conductor said loudly. The musicians responded with an abrupt squeak of bows. She stared up into the air. "You only have to tell us to stop, and we'll stop!"

Helia returned her attention to Art and smiled happily.

"Ha," Art said. She raised a hand to her mouth in surprise.

"'Twas my first laugh," she said.

"Hahaha!" Helia said in delight.

"Why did thee throw the ball of paper?"

"Why, because they're blind," Helia said.

"And a wee deaf?" Art said, glancing down at the quintet. The musicians were busy toeing through their music sheets to begin a new selection.

"Oh no, they've working ears. I just like to throw things. I'm so glad you're here," Helia said.

"And thee is safe and well," Art said warmly. "Thy sister and Perseus Kingdom send greetings."

Art handed Helia her souvenir match safe.

"Oh! Thank you, Art. I would have missed this. When Helene sent that message, I knew you and she would come. Please, sit."

A server came and helped seat Art and Helia.

"After viewing the contents of the aquarium, you must be

hungry," Helia said. "And today, I remember my manners. For it is time for tea."

Art realised that she did have an appetite. Perhaps she was still mending from her Black Market adventure, she thought. Helia gave a detailed order in Hindi to the waiter.

"Fruit, I can have," Art said when Helia ceased speaking and the waiter bowed. "As well as greens. But edibles made of flour I cannot," she added in a tone of regret.

"A tea will be fashioned that you will enjoy," Helia said. The waiter smiled at Art and bowed once more to take his leave. "And I will have something equally enjoyable."

"Thee and thy sister paid for my clothes upon resurrection," Art said. "And perhaps thee pays still, for I've received no bill from Charlotte Thackery. I will pay for my tea."

"Nonsense, I can't allow it. You mustn't worry, Art, I've an account," Helia said. She leaned in to whisper. "It's Helene's."

A memory of what Helene had said spoke in Art's mind: *I only pay the bills.*

"Has thee no money of thy own?" Art asked.

"I've none," Helia said. "And what the *Times* pays me goes to my everyday expenses."

Art wondered. Both sisters lived in poverty; in Helene's case, by choice, yet Helene had the responsibility of her family's money. Art did not believe that in her former life she had been rich. How did she come to know such women? she thought. So many questions she could ask, but Art felt an odd reluctance, once again, to learn more about her old life, and her old self.

The quintet below had begun a lulling composition, pleasant and introspective. The musicians leaned in unison. Their bows drew a sound from their instruments that surged. Art absorbed the sensation, and it welled within her.

"Thee and Helene are many things," she said. "And my questions are equally many. Yet I may understand nothing."

"Do we overwhelm you?" Helia asked gently. "Helene and I are strange, I know. Sometimes England doesn't know what to think of us."

"That I can understand," Art said, smiling.

"Ask what you like. I'll try to answer," Helia said.

"Thee was my good Friend?" Art asked.

"I still am," Helia said.

"Thee was my . . . heart-Friend?" Art asked hesitantly. "In the manner of the Vesta?" Art felt her heart pound.

Helia turned to her typewriter. She typed enthusiastically.

"Words, words, happy words!" she cried. She turned back to Art.

"Art . . . you were mine," she said.

Helia's eyes shone. In that bright gaze, Art felt immense, like a balloon swelled with feeling that she could barely contain.

Helia is so beautiful, she thought.

"I am only six days living," Art said. "I must know thee, again."

"Yes, Art," Helia said.

"And I must make confession," Art said. "And if 'tis wrong for me to burden thee with the sharing, thee must tell me so. I'll say no more." She took a breath. "Just as I caught thee by the ankle, I placed my arm around Helene."

Helia burst out laughing and covered her mouth. Her eyes were merry.

"And she did not throw you?" she said. "She's learned in jujitsu!"

"Jujitsu," Art said thoughtfully. "'Tis good to know. No, she did not. I've no understanding why I did it, for 'twas rude like the actions of a coarse man. Yet perhaps I was always thus."

"No, Art," Helia said, smiling. "You've fondness for her as well."

Art did not know what to make of that. Especially when Helia did not seem to mind.

"And perhaps thee will not find humour when I say. . ." Art rallied her courage. "That I have enjoyed the company of a woman at the Vesta. We have kissed."

"Was it Manon?" Helia asked.

"Aye," Art said in surprise. "I desire her friendship, for she is . . . she has understanding. Like thee. Of otherworldly things. But in deference to thee, I will cease affections."

Helia shook her head, smiling. "Please don't. Yes, you're

a creature now, Art. How can I know better what that's like? Companionship with someone like yourself will help."

Helia knows about Manon's true nature? Art thought.

Before Art could ask, tea arrived, and the servers brought an extra table to place Helia's typewriter on. Art watched as fragrant Darjeeling white tea was poured. Three pieces of fried pastry was laid before Helia. They smelled of potatoes and curry. Before Art, four small plates were placed containing glistening raw salmon, turbot, tuna, and trout, cut into square cakes. They were garnished with tiny slices of green onion and chopped parsley. A curl of orange slice lay atop each salmon cake.

"Oh," Art said in awe. "'Tis wonderful. Thee will not have more than thy little curry pastries?"

"These are samosas, and are my favorite, but I'm too nervous to eat more," Helia said. She was adding milk and sugar to her tea and mixing it. Her spoon made no sound. Art thought that for someone who professed to have no manners and had a brazen attitude in public, Helia's table etiquette exhibited a clear ease that spoke of breeding.

"'Tis my first experience with each fish laid here," Art said in gratitude. "I thank thee for sharing tea with me."

"The things I want to say to you," Helia murmured.

Art opened her hand. Each small stack of fish cakes flew into her body. She took her time so as to savour their distinct flavours. Art glowed.

A murmur of astonishment rose from the tables surrounding them, but Helia only clapped happily and turned to her typewriter again.

"Eating, eating, delightful eating!" she said, typing.

When Helia turned back to her tea, she did just that, her body and motions falling into the graceful deportment expected of a lady. Art attempted to drink her cup but found herself distracted with watching Helia. She merely touched the brim to her lips, and the scent of white Darjeeling wafted before her nostrils. She watched Helia sip her tea and lay her cup down on her saucer,   the china making no sound. Art endeavored to do the same with her cup, and her saucer clinked lightly. Helia ate her samosas, drank her tea, and appeared to have no further thoughts on Manon.

Helia paused to demurely cover a yawn with her napkin. She gave no excuse for her minor indecorum and only resumed her tea. Their companionable silence seemed to Art a familiarity grown from longtime understanding. It was one Art had no context and history for, but Helia's acceptance lessened Art's own otherworldliness and for that, Art was deeply gladdened.

She gave private thanks and decided that what little she recalled of social morality and propriety she would discard right then, for with Helia and Helene, everything was new.

"Thee once was a Vesta member. Thee has been with Manon?" she asked in curiosity.

"Oh no, Art," Helia said. "I wasn't at the Vesta for that. Nor Helene. But now Helene will be known for such!" Helia burst out in laughter again behind her napkin.

Art smiled. She did not understand that last remark, but Helia's mirth made her happy.

"Manon is gifted to me," Art said. "I know not by who."

"Yes, she is. And please don't think badly of us, Art." Helia put down her cup and smiled hopefully. "For right over there is the one who is paying for Manon."

Helia pointed out into the pavilions proper and indicated Helene, who stood, a figure in black among the other visitors of Skycourt's exhibit. Like a tiger discovered, Helene became motionless. Art stared at Helene in surprise and came to a sudden realisation.

"Thee both enquired about my breakfast this morning," she said.

"At my request she pays for the arrangement," Helia said, looking out at her sister. "And to preserve your respectability, we decided that Manon's services should look like Helene's indulgence. Or as it's said, she shall be seen as Helene's Convenient." Helia glanced back at Art and smiled. "Her reputation can stand it." She then waved enthusiastically to her sister.

"Come! Come join us! Oh, do come!" Helia said, waving and

gesturing. Art thought Helene looked flustered. Perhaps to cease Helia's antics, she finally stepped forwards. But before she could cross the exhibit, two small Japanese men in top hats and carrying umbrellas approached her. They bowed low, and Helene had to stop and bow as well.

"Well! Despite her efforts, she is always recognised! Serves her right for running off to Japan while I was in China!" Helia said. "Oh look, I believe a dispute is about to happen."

Art watched, concerned, and saw the dusty, disheveled Asian men she'd seen earlier approach. With them was a very large Japanese man, tall and broad, with a thick neck, shaved pate, and topknot. On his feet were sandals, and beneath his coat he wore a patterned robe.

Wrestler, Art thought. She wasn't certain how she knew, but as with the muscular Russian, Oleg, somehow she recognised the body traits of such athletes. The large man bowed to Helene and spoke, indicating himself and the men with him.

"She'll be a time," Helia said, watching the group. "Might be about ship purchasing, or airfield locations, or labour conditions. Such tedious affairs. Helene hates such stuff but she is very good with business." Helia turned back to her tea.

Art continued to observe. The dusty men had begun to bluster and express what looked liked accusations at the men in top hats. Helene stood between them, completely still and with an expression Art thought quite irate.

Art returned her attention to Helia.

"I don't know what to say about thy gift of Manon," Art said. "Were she independent and agreeable to the hiring, t'would still feel like she were chattel." She picked up the teapot and carefully refilled Helia's teacup. Steam rose as the liquid swirled.

"Art, you would never treat her so. I'm sorry this has the taint of transaction."

"'Tis no worry. 'Tis her work, and I've no wish to insult it." Art set the teapot down. "Thus, I gave her choice. However the nature of our relationship may progress, I leave it to her."

"You are wonderful. Do you like her?" Helia said with a soft smile.

"Aye. She is unique of Light. And she is of God's first temple, the grove, known without words and immutable. 'Tis an aspect that can terrify me."

Helia reached and grasped Art's hand. Her hand was bare. Art took hold of Helia's ring finger and rubbed it with her thumb.

"I've gratitude for thy generosity and strange understanding. Thine and Helene's," Art said. "And I've unkind thoughts towards myself. Were my appetites so uncontained in former life? 'Tis appalling. E'en now, had I opportunity, I'd catch thy ankle again."

"And as I've said, I don't mind." Helia's cheek grew rosy.

Art smiled.

"But may I have my hand back?" Helia gently asked. "I must give you something."

Art let go and Helia fished in her pocket.

"Here," Helia said. She offered her palm to Art. In it was a small key. It was stamped with a tiny letter: V. A little red-paste stone was set in it.

The key, though tinier, matched Art's room key at the Vesta.

"'Tis the key to my room's peepholes. Thee is my peeper," Art said in surprise. "Thee slept in the passageway," she added in mild accusation.

Helia blushed more.

"It's because I'm banned from there, Art. I must sneak if I wish to see how you are," she murmured. She dropped her gaze.

Art looked at how Helia's eyelashes rested on her cheek. She took Helia's hand and gently closed Helia's fingers around the key.

Helia raised her gaze in surprise. Art held Helia's fist firmly closed. She watched the breath that came from Helia's lips, flustered and giddy. Helia finally drew back her hand.

With a shy, excited smile, she pocketed the key.

"Dost Helene have a key?" Art said.

"Oh no, Helene would never," Helia said. "She's not at all like that."

Helia looked as though she might type again, her fingers wiggling. She turned to put more milk and sugar in her tea instead.

Art glanced to where Helene had been. She had retreated to an area of the Skycourt exhibit that was less in public view. She stood between the men in top hats and the men in dusty coats, her pose authoritative and her hands firmly gesturing as she discussed matters. Art wondered if Helene was speaking to the men in their native tongue.

"Thee was born in Nepal," Art then said to Helia. "And thee lives in a balloon, here."

"Yes! I'm so glad Helene is conversing with you, she's much friendlier to you, now."

Such manner is 'friendly'? Art thought.

"Oh, Art. We both love you, you must know."

"How did I gain thy love?" Art said in wonder.

"How do you imagine it?" Helia asked.

Art thought of how she would like to be close to Helia, right then, and have her arms around her.

"I seduced thee," Art said.

"With your beautiful heart, and your beautiful soul," Helia said. "Yes, you did seduce me. With your big bonnets and queer sayings, ugly shoes and porridge-eating! Even when you didn't understand, you always forgave me." Her fists came up, shaking. "Always! How could I not love you?"

Art reached to soothe Helia's sudden anguish. But something—a shadow—in the masked side of Helia's face gave her pause. It was not on the leather's surface but somehow beneath, within Helia's flesh.

It moved.

Art stared harder. She only saw the leather, and Helia's unhappy eyes looking elsewhere.

"I was not a good person, before," Helia said. "I hurt everyone. I thought I cared for nothing. And I hurt you."

"I am unhurt, now. Thee was a libertine?" Art softly asked.

"That soubriquet suggests that I'd great sport," Helia said. "And for all appearances, perhaps I did. I was a black soul, Art. A rakehell. It's my fault you died."

"'Tis no matter, Helia," Art said.

"It does matter. It does!" Helia said in a hushed voice. "It will matter when you know how it happened."

"Not now. Worry not. As way opens, when 'tis time."

"Art," Helia whispered.

"Won't thee finish thy tea?" Art gently asked. "Thee is far thinner than thy sister."

"I'll try." Helia picked up her remaining samosa. "We couldn't eat, even . . . even before. But Helene eats porridge, so she remains quite fit."

"Porridge, 'tis satisfying fare, and good for thy vitals. Helene could throw the big man with her," Art said.

Helia gave a brief chuckle. "Yes, she can."

Art replenished their teacups. Once Helia had resumed her tea and eaten her last pastry under Art's watchful eye, Art looked in Helene's direction. The Japanese men were gone. Helene was walking determinedly towards the Blue Vanda when a salesman approached, escorting the two tall African men Art had seen before. They greeted Helene and she stopped for them.

"Oh, that will be a difficult situation, poor Helene," Helia softly said. Her eyes shut as she sipped from her teacup.

Art studied Helia. She looked at the three, delicate forget-me-nots painted beneath her masked eye and the studs and wear upon the polished leather. Helia seemed recovered from her moment of confession. To Art, Helia's half-mask appeared to be what it was; she could detect nothing more on the surface of the leather, or beneath. But as with the "blanket" over the Black Market, she knew something more was there. She sensed a veil, somnolent in effect, keeping something still.

"Thee refers to the African men?" Art asked.

"It's a political matter. Depending on what part of Africa those men are from, England may not want them to have airships, if at all."

"No African ships, because of colonisation," Art said. She was surprised she'd recall of such politics, for to her, Africa seemed very obscure.

"Yes, dear," Helia said, smiling. "They've no ships of their own.

But if not for our airship routes, Africa would be as distant to us as the moon. Then, the unseemly efforts of colonisation would not be commonly known. Africa is beset with the French, Danish, Portuguese, and yes, we British. That continent has no unifying ruler or empire, and the Ottoman Empire is crumbled. It's each small nation for itself, and they haven't much chance against all of Europe and its influences."

"But if Africans have ships, they'll have strength," Art said.

"Perhaps. However, if they buy ours, the ships mustn't be used in civil wars or the trafficking of slaves. Enslaved Africans are still exported to certain parts of the Americas. And all over Africa, tribal warfare is constant. They are being fed guns, you see."

Helia nodded towards the pavilions area, and Art realised Helia was indicating the façades around them, representing the various European countries and empires.

"It's just too complicated, and not worth good intentions or profit. But that is my opinion. It is Helene's decision. She knows more, and I'm certain has already formed thoughts for a solution."

"Thee does not seem so insane when speaking of world affairs and business," Art said.

"Oh, but I am! That's why I'm not given money. And now you've reminded me of my work. I was meant to send a telegram to the Vesta, to your partner." Helia set down her cup and turned to her typewriter. She pulled out the sheet she'd randomly typed on and fed a new one into the roller.

"Thy visit to the Black Market." Art chastised herself for having forgotten. "Ellie escorted you?"

"She did." Helia finished typing and pulled out the paper. "You may read it first before I send it." She handed the sheet to Art.

Art read:

"*Helia-Vanda. Your quarry, name and location, the expected event, time and place, all unknown. Dastard-Vesta.*"

Art returned the paper to Helia.

"'Tis disappointing," she said.

"I'm erring on the side of caution. I will tell you what I know, and then you may tell Mr. Dastard. It isn't much, but it is everything.

The Bone Stealer is of title."

Art waited patiently.

"And that is all I can tell you," Helia said.

"Thee knows more," Art said.

"I know the title itself," Helia said slowly. "But better that you and Mr. Dastard, and the police, not know."

Art looked at her, perplexed.

"Will thee pursue knowledge of his identity?" she asked.

"Perhaps," Helia said. She sipped her tea.

"Thee is afraid," Art said in concern.

"I'm usually not. It's quite a surprise," Helia said lightly. "I must want to live, so that we may know each other again!"

Helia laughed, but Art saw the brief bleakness in her eyes. Art unfastened her glove and removed it. She reached over and laid her fingers on the inside of Helia's bare wrist. Helia leaned into the touch.

"The same, the same again, oh, how you are," Helia whispered.

"Hush," Art soothed. "I know not why I do this, but it pleases me to feel the beat of thy heart. There, such a strong vein. Thee is healthy and whole."

"It's beating fit to break my chest," Helia said.

"Worry not about the Bone Stealer," Art said. "We will stop him."

"How to explain!" Helia said. "Without knowledge of his name, then you and Mr. Dastard may act as agents do, and all that is about identity may be known after."

"After . . . that we should have him?" Art said.

"If that is the result," Helia said.

What other result could there be? Art thought.

"I must hand away the telegram message," Helia said with a smile.

Art let go of Helia's wrist. She watched her give the paper to a server.

The quintet ended their music selection with the flutist rendering a final, pure note. Spectators applauded.

Slowly, Art put her glove back on.

"I thank thee and Helene for my tea," she said. "Thy company is precious to me. But when I see that telegram being sent to my partner, I feel I mayn't tarry any longer. I must return to the work."

Reluctantly, she rose. Helia stood as well. Art felt there was too much to ask and to know. But most of all, she wished to stay with Helia more.

"I will see thee, again," she said.

"Yes, Art," Helia said, looking into her eyes. She picked up the sheet of paper she'd randomly typed on, folded it, and gave it to her.

"How shall you leave, Art?" Helia asked curiously.

Art then realised that though Helia had seen her eat in her eldritch manner, she'd not seen her fly. She smiled.

She became transparent and watched Helia's delighted eyes grow wide. Slowly, Art rose in the air. She continued to rise, floating higher and higher, the people of the Blue Vanda and of the pavilions proper staring up in astonishment. Chairs fell over as people scrambled to look. The blind quintet had picked another selection and begun to play. She passed the three-storey façades with the people gaping from the windows. She reached the space belonging to the model balloons and airships. She kept her gaze upon Helia for as long as she could. She entered the dome area, girders, and the iron arches. She passed through the glass and felt the air of London hit her.

A strong breeze blew from the Thames and sent the many flags atop the building flapping. Art came to rest upon the glass dome and solidified. Helia's paper had passed successfully with her.

She unfolded it and read:

Art is here! OH my heart, how I love you. Your gaze is a joy to me. Your smile uplifts me. Your voice is a gift to me!

The life you now have is the Victory that overcomes the World!

May you never hurt as you once did. May you never die before we do.

Art pressed the paper to her chest. The wind blew, and she felt drops of moisture strike her face.

She saw the sky cloud and become dark and grey. Art turned

from the wind and carefully folded Helia's note into a small parcel. She put her walking stick beneath her arm and unhooked her bodice. After some effort, she had the note safely tucked away inside her corset, beneath her breasts. She refastened her outfit. She turned towards East London and became a ghost. She took to the air and flew away.

The pavilions area was in a state of confusion and awe, the great space echoing with astonished voices. More people joined the crowds, enquiring and hearing of Art's spectral departure. They also peered above. A few women had swooned, and others were reviving them.

Helia ignored the commotion. She gazed far above to where Art had disappeared.

"Was that your first time seeing her ghost?" she heard Helene say. "I've witnessed her flying about, twice. And for a woman of her size, rather willy-nilly. She even sat by me, translucent."

Helia dropped her gaze and looked at Helene. Her sister stood by her side.

"Was that when she put her arm around you?" Helia said. "Apparently, you gave no fuss."

She watched Helene blush.

"She's still incorrigible," Helene muttered.

"Pot calling the kettle black," Helia said. "You lurked and didn't bother to come sit with us. Have you an explanation?"

"Come, we must talk," Helene said, and walked away to descend the patio steps. Helia took a breath. For Helene, 'talking' meant going somewhere inaccessible and therefore very private. The staff of the Blue Vanda knew to watch over her typewriter. Helia buttoned her coat, found her gloves, and followed her.

A few minutes later they were both climbing a metal ladder for a roof hatch high above in the aquarium dome. Helia thought they would walk the iron girders that arched above her replica airship and take refuge inside the model, despite being within sight of the still gaping crowds below. But Helene needed more privacy.

Helene opened the hatch and the winds blew above them. She helped Helia to stand on the glass roof and shut the hatch.

"It's Art!" Helia cried, pointing.

In the far distance was a woman's ghostly figure, distinctly Art's shape, flying swiftly past Parliament and Big Ben.

"I can't imagine the wind affecting her when she's immaterial, but look, see how her skirts flap," Helene said, also pointing.

"That is odd, and yet she has no need to hold her hat," Helia said. "My, how fast she goes."

"This whole 'artificial ghost' business," Helene said. "Can't help but wonder. Perhaps in that state, she forms her own reality."

Art soon disappeared from their view. Helene turned and sat down against a girder, helping Helia do the same. She and Helia arranged their skirts.

"Well. I'm now of the proper inclination to rid the world of evil," Helene announced. "And in permanent fashion. Please tell me that this Bone Stealer is as irredeemable and completely corrupted as the worst I've faced."

"The blackest, and to the core. Arthur affirms," Helia said. "But you will not be the one to rid the world of him."

"Why not?" Helene said in surprise. "All this time you've nagged me to come out of mourning and do something. I've gone and sharpened my blades, among many such preparations!"

"You had felt the need to hang up your pistols and no longer ride out into the night, and for this situation, now I agree," Helia said.

"You *never* agree with—very well, what is it?" Helene said. "Why are you declining my help?"

"Because you will be Countess Skycourt," Helia said simply.

Helene looked at her sharply.

"Do we know this Bone Stealer?" she demanded.

"I highly doubt it," Helia said. "But I believe the royal family might."

"German," Helene said in realisation. "Are you saying there might be a connection through His Royal Highness? Is the Bone Stealer of their blood?"

"That, I don't know, but he is a prince," Helia said. She looked out in the direction of Big Ben, where Art had disappeared.

"A prince?" Helene said. "Not a crown prince but a minor prince, you mean?"

"Yes," Helia said. "A Serene Highness."

Helene snorted. "A Serene Highness! Not all houses survived the new German Confederation, there are . . . less than two dozen such families left! He's been committing his crimes for money, hasn't he? No noble would dare work for money. Well, except for you. Therefore, his is a diminished or deprived house. His family may have already lost sovereigntry."

"Lost sovereigntry is a very good possibility. But a Serene Highness is thus, and ever so while he's still living, whether his house still exists or no," Helia said. She turned to look at Helene. "We are talking about Germany and our own royal family. When Uncle Cadmus is gone, you will be countess. As heir to the earldom, you mustn't get involved because you cannot *risk* it."

"To hear you talk about titles and blood ties!" Helene said. "You never cared!"

"I still don't, but I care about you and Art," Helia said. She looked earnestly at Helene. "You will have Skycourt, Helene. And you've more respect, influence, voice, and authority than any of our sex who are of privilege. Men listen to you. Uncle Cadmus knows this. You've been given the airship business, and there's only myself to challenge you for it. You are our future. And I want Art to have a future as well, one that is with us."

She laid a hand on Helene's arm. "Can't you see? She's an eldritch being now. I paid Dr. Fall everything I had to make it so. Art may be on this Earth a long time. How can I guarantee her well-being, her happiness, except through you? *You* are Skycourt. You can ensure it. You will create a lasting company, therefore lasting security, for Art, for generations to come."

"You have truly become queer," Helene said, staring in wonder into her sister's eyes. "I've never heard the like come from your mouth, ever. Art is very good for you, just as you've said."

"Don't pursue this man," Helia warned.

"So, we're to leave it to His Royal Highness' special hounds?" Helene said. "You talk of a future with Art, and yet would send her into the bear-ridden forest! She and her skull friend did well with the re-animationist, but what can they really do once they've apprehended this prince? Through the Secret Commission, he may be given his chance to gracefully disappear."

"I disagree, Helene. You've seen how Art is now. She's magnificent," Helia said. "She's the equal of all those bears in your fictitious forest, and Prince Albert's creature-hounds run at will as those without a master do. It's his Secret Commission, but he does not give direct orders, and he does not oversee. Art and Jim Dastard don't know who the Bone Stealer is, but when they have him, they may see this to its rightful end."

"Really? Art, who is Quaker?"

"Yes, Art, who is Quaker, and for whom class, and therefore princes, mean nothing."

Helene turned away. Helia waited patiently as the wind blew and Helene scowled.

"That was my task for five years," Helene finally said.

"Of course you'd miss it," Helia said. "I was surprised you stayed in mourning for as long as you did."

"I know that this Art is capable," Helene said. "And she's mettle to prove. Make certain that she has the proper scent, then. And as for myself—"

"You've Skycourt," Helia said adamantly.

"Sanity is unbecoming in you," Helene said.

Helia sat closer and took Helene's arm. She put her head on Helene's shoulder. Helene tutted but didn't shrug Helia away. They sat together and watched the airships in the grey skies above the Thames.

CHAPTER TWELVE

Delphia counted as her blessing that her new employer was a mere skull and therefore made decisions with his mind more so than, say, with his non-existent genitals. For this reason, he could see past her sex and consider her capable of the tasks at hand. But one downside of such *laissez-faire* was the fact that a young girl's place in society was still that—a position burdened with societal concerns. Delphia stood before the gleaming iris portal to what was undoubtedly a gentlemen's club—in the unsavory part of East London—and held Jim's entry key in hand.

"If I may ask, sir, what manner of club is this?" she said. "It looks quite a well-to-do place. Is it dedicated, perhaps, to the passion of ponies or politics?"

"Ah, no, it is dedicated to deviant behavior," Jim said. "Though one may find conversations entertained within pertaining to ponies and politics! Don't worry, Bloom, I am your chaperone, and this is a most respectable club. Why, unlike any club in London, the Vesta's services are solely provided by women!"

"I . . . see, sir."

"And Bloom. Should any so much as look askance at you, their class or position is of little concern to a Quaker like Art. She'll thrash them for you! Now, are you assured?"

"By a very small degree."

"In we go!" Jim said.

She put the key in the lock and turned it. The metal blades of the iris door spun open, and Delphia stepped inside.

The club was, as she expected, quite grand. Wood paneling with green-and-gold detailing stretched to a vaulted ceiling. Gaslights hummed behind glass filigreed with fine ironwork, and inside small wall niches, nude Greek marbles stood. Thick red glass was set in the foyer partition leading into a great hall beyond.

But despite the size of the place, its dark colours, red glass, and polished wood gave it an intimate atmosphere and warmth. There was the lingering, earthy scent of pipe tobacco and mixed in, of fresh flowers. Delphia was reminded of taverns. Two tall uniformed footmen stood in the foyer, and when Delphia glanced at their faces, she realised they were women.

Delphia calmly stepped forwards, her head ringing with the strange revelation. Her shoes made no sound on the thick carpeting. Jim jovially greeted the footwomen, one of whom he called Doris. Delphia thought they might take Jim's hat but when they didn't, she moved on, entering the great hall. An older woman approached, completely outfitted in gentlemen's attire and an overcoat. She had a walking stick and top hat in hand.

"Milly!" Jim said. Delphia stopped and held him up so that he could converse more easily. "Going out, I see?"

"I am, Mr. Dastard. And I must say, I can only suspect what a day you're having. I had seen Art not too long ago, in a most surprising condition," Milly said. She looked at Delphia, her eyes taking in all of her appearance. Milly returned her attention back to Jim. The assessing gaze had barely taken a second.

But Delphia had been surprised by the glance, and just a little perturbed. In her experience, the rich merely regarded people like herself as invisible.

"Milly, it *has* been quite a day, and more to come! But allow me this opportunity to introduce my new assistant. Baroness Millicent Sedgewick, I would like you to meet the very capable Miss Delphia Bloom."

"Your Ladyship," Delphia said and curtsied.

"How do you do," Milly said, smiling, and offered her gloved hand. A jewel gleamed in her starched cufflink. For a moment, Delphia was nearly confused, because though Milly was obviously a woman, she was in gentlemen's dress, and to be offered "his" hand played brief havoc with Delphia's decorum.

Delphia took Milly's hand and curtseyed again.

"Jim, I was leaving for tea at the Empress, but there's still time for me to meet my party there. I *must* hear what has happened with regards to this Bone Stealer," Milly said. "Come, I will walk a little ways with you, and then you must share."

"Since you insist!" Jim said.

Delphia walked by Milly's side as Jim talked, and found herself moving at that pace that was distinctly upper class: with leisure. During such slow progress down the hall, Delphia gave discreet attention to the various rooms. She tried her best not to stare openly at the library, but the artifacts within the Curiosities and Mechanical Room could not help but arrest her eye. More women in men's hats and dapper dress were concentrating on a solemn game in the card room, their cigarettes dangling from their lips and their drink glasses at hand. The smack and roll of billiard balls could be heard, played on a table out of view. She saw a woman's skirt swing within sight of the door and a cue stick briefly dip.

Delphia pensively turned her attention away to focus more on the Vesta's overall surroundings. She could ponder more on the odd denizens of this club but she'd a mental task to see to first. As Philo always advised, one should familiarize oneself with every possible exit should one need to jump out a window.

It was good practice, the study of one's surroundings. Philo had been adamant that Delphia always apply such mental exercise in case fire or other forms of disaster befell any of her factory situations.

"And not only that," her brother Gavin would add. "You'll learn how to more easily flee or hide from Hettie O'Taggart and her fists!" Then both her brothers would laugh.

Milly stopped before a drawing room where two upper-class women in proper, feminine dress sat upon a settee, both reading books. Jim was extolling highlights of the Black Market adventure, and Delphia noted that he kept his narrative entertaining, but devoid of details pertinent to the case. While they dallied by the drawing room, she glanced to the one across. The question of why there were two drawing rooms was answered for her. From what she could discern, the one she stood by was for women, and the one opposite was for men. And it was for men who very much preferred the company of their own sex.

The group of well-dressed men was of bachelor or university age, with the youthful, fresh faces yet to have the gravitas of responsibilities. Two men sat in the laps of two other men as they all laughed and discussed something in earnest, while another two stood propped against the fireplace, smoking and with an arm around each other. But the embrace did not seem so fraternal to Delphia, for one man's hand seemed to idly caress the other's thigh.

Delphia brought her attention back to Milly and Jim, not wishing to intrude more on the men with her staring. She was beginning to have an understanding of what the Vesta was, but she thought to reserve opinion until she learned more. The cross-dressers like Milly and the card players, Delphia understood; if they weren't music hall performers, then they were indulging in an aberrant passion for male dress. She just wasn't completely certain that something especially deviant was happening at the Vesta.

Because for all she knew, with regards to the affectionate boys in the drawing room across, perhaps that was how boys were, like beautiful Tom Frye. Delphia understood the affectionate relationships of women, but men were another matter. Since men saw fit to make certain they were the only ones who could populate clubs, academies, places of government, institutes, and places of higher education—as well as any venue of entertainment where proper women could not go unescorted—it was very possible this was how they generally behaved with each other, out of sight of women. Delphia corrected herself; at least out of sight of properly dressed women.

She and her brothers were close, but Philo and Gavin more preferred the community of their own sex. She wished they were not so far away so she could ask them if the real society of men was thus.

"Milly, I mustn't keep you any longer," she heard Jim say.

"It was worth every minute," Milly said. "And gives me the opportunity to introduce our latest guests. They've come from Canada and they've just declined joining me for tea. They insist instead on remaining and enjoying the quiet comforts that is the Vesta."

Delphia followed Milly into the drawing room. She saw another woman in male dress—trousers and tweed coat—sunk in an armchair facing the fireplace. In contemplation, she smoked a small pipe. The smoking woman ignored their entry. Delphia turned to the ladies seated in the settee.

The women were holding hands as they read their books. They looked up, and Delphia saw that they appeared of spinster age, quite handsome and with friendly, receptive faces.

"Miss Eustania Dillwick, Miss Lizzy Fesque," Milly said. "May I introduce Mr. Jim Dastard, agent of His Royal Highness' Secret Commission, and his capable assistant, Miss Delphia Bloom."

If Miss Dillwick and Miss Fesque had any great, emotional reaction to Jim being an animated skull, the two women hid it well. They were wide-eyed once Jim spoke, but genial in manner and in conversation. Delphia thought them enthused at having the opportunity to converse with a skull. They answered Jim's queries while completing each other's sentences. Delphia learned that the two had grown up as schoolgirls together. To her, their mutual fondness was clear.

She also wondered if they might be spiritualists, for she'd a notion, from reading papers, that those of the American continent were fervent enthusiasts of the supernatural. She didn't know what clues to spy that would reveal such a sensibility. The one remarkable thing the women did was to remain clasped in hand. During introductions, they had preferred to put down their books in order to offer Delphia a hand to take.

That was when she noticed that they wore matching gold ring bands.

After more small talk in which the ladies expressed their appreciation of London and the Vesta, Jim and Milly took their leave, and Delphia curtsied. Then, outside the drawing room, Jim and Milly formally parted, and Delphia curtsied again.

She did her best to avoid another glance into the men's drawing room, even as male laughter suddenly ensued. She walked towards the grand staircase and saw a young woman—not much older than herself—with short hair and wearing the male clothing of a page, standing by the landing.

"Alice! My new assistant, Miss Delphia Bloom," Jim said. "It's come to my attention that it's time for tea! Have some sent up to us, won't you? Is Art upstairs?"

"No, sir, she departed, and very quickly. I'd say more than an hour ago," Alice replied. Delphia followed her up the stairs to the third floor.

"No matter, she'll return in due course. Alice, let's place Delphia in Art's room, and then you must walk me to Catherine's."

"Yes, sir, I'll do that. And Art left a note for you, sir," Alice said. She led Delphia to a pair of doors near the end of the third floor hall.

"Note, yes! And might there be another, from a Miss Skycourt?" Jim asked.

"Why, yes, a telegram," Alice answered. "You'll find both in Art's room." Alice opened the door.

Delphia stepped through and into a deeply red bedchamber wallpapered in red and gold. The room was furnished with plush, carved-wood furniture, heavy red drapes swirling with a gold, Persian paisley pattern, and thick oval rugs laid over the polished floors. There was a large black hearth stove, fat, squat, and inviting. Delphia resisted the urge to coo.

Alice took Jim from Delphia's hand.

"My notes! My notes!" Jim said.

"Yes, sir, over here," Alice said. She carried Jim to a table by the windows. He murmured to himself as he read each piece of paper Alice showed him.

"Bloom, read these as well and then set them aside on Art's dresser. We'll be right back, Delphia!" He said as Alice walked him out the door. "Make yourself comfortable and tea will arrive shortly!"

The door closed behind them. Delphia retrieved the pieces of paper, read Art's note to Jim, and then Helia's telegram. After placing them on the dresser top, Delphia caught sight of herself in Art's full-length mirror. She saw her shabby coat and shoes, and her thick black stockings. She had a healing scab on her lip.

"Well," she said dolefully. "At least my hair looks acceptable." She took off her coat. There was a knock at the door, and a young woman entered, also dressed as a page. She rolled a teacart in and began setting the table by the windows with china and two place settings. Plates of sandwiches, tarts, biscuits, delicate little pastries, and small cakes were laid out.

Delphia clenched her fists. It was a proper tea, she thought, and her stomach responded. Despite her hunger, she was not going to cause a spectacle by flinging herself at such bounty. She deliberately walked about the room, studied the windows and furnishings, and thus found the door standing ajar that led to a tiny study. Delphia entered. She stared at the book titles on the shelves and tried to read them. She could hear the page fuss with the plates.

"Intestinal valour!" Philo would say. He would repeat it like a song. Then Gavin would take up the chant and Delphia would join in. In this way, those hungry times in the Bloom household as they became poorer and poorer were staved. Father encouraged them to run wild; "burn your needs like a steam engine", he would say, so that they might not remember the wants of the body. But whenever food was on the table, it was every Bloom child for his or her own self.

Delphia resolved to eat only enough so that she could take the rest home. She re-entered Art's room just as the page finished with setting the tea and left. Delphia looked at the table and saw that the second place setting was meant for Art. It seemed to explain why fresh, bright watercress was spread in a pile on one plate, black and red raspberries on another, and a small stack of raw herring on a third.

Delphia seated herself, looked at everything, and brought her hands together briefly to give thanks.

Jim returned just as Delphia had separated out a portion of the tea for herself. Alice brought him to the table and took her leave. He hopped to look at Delphia.

"Art and I, being spectres, don't always remember about things like tea!" he said. "We eat when we feel like it, and we can go quite long without. When you're hungry, Bloom, just say so. This tea looks a treat! It's good, yes?"

Delphia was attempting to eat and drink as slowly as possible.

"Yes sir, I'm very grateful for the thoughtfulness," she said after she'd swallowed.

"Just make sure I stay thoughtful. So! Now you've seen the Vesta. What do you think of it?"

"I don't know, sir," Delphia said, putting down her teacup. "It seems very comfortable, and yet . . . is this what some might call a 'lair of deviancy'?"

"Lair? Ha ha! I know what word you want to use," Jim said.

"I don't want to offend," Delphia said demurely.

"'Brothel'. There, I said it for you. No, it's a proper club. A very exclusive club. For wealthy mandrakes and toms."

"'My," Delphia said thoughtfully. "When I had my chocolate factory position, I earned enough to afford membership with the Working Girls Club in Bethnal Green. I liked it. It had a library, classes, dances, and even debates."

"Very proper!" Jim said. "The members of the Vesta require somewhat the same, though with consideration to their particular interests."

"Since you've mentioned 'particular interests', I shall be forthright and say that I am confused," Delphia said. She thought again on the intimate touch she had witnessed in the men's drawing room. "For, on the one hand, there is deviancy, and on the other, there's 'noble affection'."

She'd read of such ideal male relationships in her father's books on ancient Athens, but reading about such an explanation for "male love" was one thing. Seeing men in the drawing room, commingling in affectionate familiarity, was quite another.

"Noble—now where did you get such a term?" Jim said with surprise. "In your father's book piles? Ha! Well, it's a concept gaining renewed attention by those Oxford fellows. Don't feel you lack understanding. You are a youth, still learning your body and heart."

"But can you clarify, sir?" Delphia said. "For the youthful mind."

"I am a skull; I am no more a mandrake than Art is. Such aspirations for male 'spiritual love' are bandied about the drawing rooms, but I am not much for sentimental talk of the glory days of Hellenism! One may develop one's emotional maturity—especially in anticipation of marriage—with love and understanding experienced with one's own sex, yes? But really, sex is *sex*. I hope I don't have to explain what I mean by the use of the word. *Is* it 'deviancy', really? Such matters of the heart and body seem to only offend certain established opinions. We call it deviancy, but you must decide what it is to you."

Delphia chose not to be offended by Jim's frankness. She'd heard "sex" used to describe carnality, among other cruder words, from the girls of her street. She knew of girls who made a better wage doing such. She thought of the two women in the drawing room, sitting close and reading books while holding the hand of the other.

For, she realised, the sight of the two women reading had reminded her of happier times, when the Bloom family had been well-to-do. When she had been very little, her parents had sat together in much the same way, and such affection was neither lofty concept nor sinful indulgence.

"I know someone," Delphia said. "Who's a man and he loves men very much. So he chose a vocation where there were men like himself."

"The navy?" Jim said.

"Sir?" Delphia said. She put a hand to her chest. Had she so easily given her brother Gavin away?

"Forget I said," Jim said with humour. "Very well, the mandrakes don't bother you. What of the toms?"

"The Baroness Sedgewick, she may be of class, but I rather disliked a bold look she gave me," Delphia said primly. "And looking is almost acceptable, but not so much one, however brief, that might make me question my own virtue. Were I of age,

I would have liked to have expressed my indignation."

"And well you should. Honour is what you must preserve. Let no one trod on it. But while here, have Art and I speak for you. Now, Milly, you must know, she's a toff who slums. Other classes are of great entertainment for her. I won't excuse her boldness, but at the same time, such treatment is to be expected. As a whole, I believe the women who frequent the Vesta are quite all right. The stranger ones keep to themselves. Why, I've even seen a sapphic couple from the country come stay," Jim said in hushed astonishment. "Wearing *big* bonnets."

"Not so very 'tom', sir?" Delphia said, smiling.

"Oh, putting forth the thought they might try trousers for the novelty of it made them giggle! For days!" Jim said. "Two widows in romantic friendship. They'd combined their properties and fulfilled the legalities for contractual female marriage. Shrewd, eh? Pleasure to talk to, but it was like conversing with lovely, brown-eyed cows, come for a grand time at the world fair."

Delphia laughed. "Such folk are as you like to say sir, 'all right'; I nearly prefer the boys that are so. As long as they've a good heart, and kind eyes."

"Oh? Didn't notice the well-bred bucks, below, then?" Jim teased. "They were a surprisingly handsome lot."

"I did, but as you've said, gentry can be of a certain nature to one such as myself, and I've no need for such frivolity."

"My, you do like them simple."

"I've yet to have a sweetheart, but I would like a good and honest fellow."

"Ha! Were Art a man, I'd see myself matchmaker," Jim said.

"What an interesting thought," Delphia said. "She is quite wonderful."

"Ah," Jim said. "I knew it. You've a girl's adoration. We may disappoint you yet."

"The same may be said of myself. Let us agree to do our very best by each other," she said.

"Agreed," he said.

Delphia resumed her tea with enthusiasm. She felt an odd

displacement of air in the room. Though the windows were not opened, the curtains moved as if blown by a breeze. Delphia turned in curiosity. Art materialised through the window, landed on her feet, and solidified.

～

When Art flew into her room and saw Delphia, she was both warmed and concerned. Art felt the Vesta wasn't a very proper place for a young girl, though many girls Delphia's age were undoubtedly working, right then, in places far worse than the Vesta.

"Delphia," she said warmly. "Thee is well?"

"I am. Thank you, Art," Delphia said, smiling.

"Is thee comfortable here, at the Vesta?" Art said as she removed her gloves. "'Tisn't a typical place."

"So I've learned. Mr. Dastard has assured me it's not a lair of deviancy."

"But, 'tis," Art said with a perplexed expression.

"Art!" Jim hopped. "Were you successful in finding Miss Skycourt?"

"I was; she is well," Art said. Smiling, she set her stick aside and took off her hat. She bade Delphia to resume finishing her tea.

"Tea is the body's tendering," Art said.

"Your latest outfit becomes you," Jim said in admiration. "I was right about those lapels. Come sit down. I must tell you what Bloom and I have been up to. Developments have occurred."

"Friend, I shall, but allow me a private moment with thee," Art said.

"Oh? Have you news as well?" Jim said.

"Aye, but first, a discussion needs finishing," she said and picked Jim up.

"Ah—Delphia! Please continue with your tea! We'll just be over here!" Jim said as Art carried him into his study. She shut the door behind them.

"Ahem! Now Art," Jim said as she laid him down on his table.

"Thee brought the child here," Art said.

"Well, she's not that much of a child, she's seventeen years old!" Jim said. "And this is no place of ill-repute—"

"Thee knows pests may be of any class or sex," she said. "I will not let her be harassed."

"And I've thought of that! She's our squire, and I plan that she be clothed properly. It'll send a clear message, Art," he said.

"Jim, heed me," Art said with severity. "One does not subject a girl to such sights and sensibilities as are indulged at the Vesta."

"Arr!" he said.

"Thee also did not think on her reputation, and gave disregard to her future respectability and safety. Was not thee aware that there are peepholes in my chamber?"

"Oh, Art," Jim said. "I mean—er. Hm."

"Now thee thinks," Art said.

~

Delphia dropped a tart into her lap upon overhearing 'peephole'. As Art's and Jim's conversation lowered in sound and intensity, she looked about the room in alarm. She found herself with one foot poised from the chair, ready to flee this assistant position that had seemed so perfect just moments before.

Then she reminded herself, as Philo would have done, to weigh the situation honestly.

"Think quickly," he often said, "and decide. We see how animals do it, don't we? But creature instinct also needs knowledge— information. Yes, trust our natural senses, but if we act solely in fear, it'll just get us into trouble, Delphia. When you have your information, then do the best thing."

Such an approach had made Philo a very good thief, able to outwit his pursuers or escape any situation. Delphia knew her poised foot was about fear. Knowledge, however, brought understanding. Art was right then scolding Jim, just as she'd promised, because she had Delphia's best interest at heart. And Jim had said earlier to let no one trod on her honour, which Delphia was certain was a behest that included himself.

The conclusion, she mused, was to see further how things

would develop. For this was only the beginning, and she would like, after all the situations she'd been dismissed from, to see a position through.

She settled back in the chair and resumed her tea.

            ❮

Once Art was certain that Jim was suitably chastised, she opened the connecting door and brought him back to the table. She smiled reassuringly at Delphia, who did not seem upset, and set him down.

"My ears are burning," Jim said sourly.

Art said nothing and merely took her seat. She poured herself some tea.

"Delphia, I regret any discomfort suffered by placing you in this provocative environment," Jim said. "No doubt it has caused hardship to your youthful sensibilities. You're a most resilient squire. Perhaps it would be wiser to have you face bullets and the horrifying dens of murderous creatures than circumstances that challenge your fledgling sexuality. I have shown great lack of consideration, and hope you'll forgive me."

"'Tis also about respectability, Jim," Art said.

"Yes, yes, of course. It's just hard to remember that when I'm living with you," he said.

Art cocked an eyebrow and raised her teacup. When she looked at Delphia, the young woman seemed lost in thought.

            ❮

Delphia was pondering the odd observation Jim had just shared.

Would she rather, she reflected, fling herself into dangerous situations than endure some naughty person spying while she drank tea? Would she prefer being shot at than risk walking in on the young men below, kissing?

Delphia could imagine what Philo and Gavin would say.

"My," she murmured to herself, "That's a very sad thought."

"Delphia?" Art said.

"Art and sir," she said. "After my own serious considerations,

I feel you both have the best intentions, and as it is a unique situation, doubtless there is much I'll learn and become aware of, and it would seem you, sir, you will learn too. I see it only benefiting myself, as much as I hope my service will benefit you."

"Well said!" Jim said. "Huzzah!"

Art looked at Delphia, measuring.

"As thee wishes," she said gently.

"Art, can we discuss the case, now?" Jim said.

When Art consented, Jim told her of Miss Pritt and the near-kidnap. She listened gravely, and to keep Delphia at ease and eating, she continued with the tea by absorbing her watercress, berries, and herring. She noticed that Delphia deliberately kept a great portion of the tea untouched.

"Such a handsome girl, I hope she rallies," Jim then said. "Didn't feel the need to mention it to Risk, but I am aware of Felly Pritt's work. She plays male roles, and as you know, Art, I've such a fondness for the male impersonators."

"Olivia Hill's masculine airs did impress me," Art said.

"None can rival you in how unsexed you are, but you could never be a male impersonator," Jim said regretfully. "That chest of yours defeats the purpose."

"I am fond of my bosom," Art said.

"Aren't we all? Ah, and I must let you know of an additional turn in events," Jim said. "Someone is also fond of your sturdy bones."

"My bones?" Art said in surprise. She set her cup down.

"Livus put a bounty on you," Jim said. "And it was no ploy on his part in order to drive us out of the Black Market. You and Miss Pritt share the same impressive stature to the inch! With her neck broken, we must assume you are next in danger."

"'Tis melodramatic, Friend," Art said. "How might they take myself?"

"Tut! 'Be not above thy gas lamp', as you Quakers say," he said.

"'Tis, 'be not above thy Light', but I hear thee, Friend," Art said grudgingly.

"Good! With Miss Pritt injured and you such a large and hard-to-ignore target, I must ask that you confine yourself to the Vesta," Jim said. "Until we learn more—ghost about! Play phantom cards, or treat yourself to some of Manon's company. Now would be a good time to find *Black Beauty* in the Vesta library."

"But, the Vesta library, 'tis mostly erotica," Art said.

"You've already looked?" Jim said. "Anything new?"

"Oh dear," Delphia said. "This place really is a lair of deviancy."

"Delphia," Art said. "'Tis a sex club."

"It's not a—the *things* you tell our squire!" Jim said. "Make this very clear to your parents, Bloom, that this is a most respectable club! Why, I would tell you what esteemed women of society and nobility are members, except that's secret. Pastimes of a certain nature do go on, but, as was explained most sternly to me, well—now you know! Just as you've said, consider such enlightenments a learning of human nature."

"She needn't know all truths," Art said.

"Then why do you keep telling them to her?" Jim said. "Well, whenever you've questions, Bloom, ask Art. As you no doubt already know and admire, Art is of upstanding character. And stern. And a sapphist," Jim added in a loud whisper to Delphia.

"Sir," Delphia loudly whispered back. "I'm just very relieved that your particular interests won't have me dressing as a boy."

A sound of mirth suddenly emitted from Art. Jim hopped in place.

"Art! Actual laughter? We may make a real woman of you yet!" Art touched her mouth.

"'Twas my second laugh," she said. "I laughed today, at Helia . . . though that sound was more queer."

"Six days is a good record! You sprang smiling out of Zeus's split pate, and I am very glad of it. Don't you agree, Bloom? It's that funny quirk to the corner of Art's mouth that helps."

"Art has beautiful features," Delphia said.

"Thee are both kind," Art said. "Delphia, thee has only your parents?"

"She's two smaller siblings," Jim said. "Healthy little rascals. And two older brothers gone to find their fortunes."

Jim went on to describe his visit to the Bloom home. Delphia had finished her tea, her napkin on the table and her hands in her lap. Art opened her clean napkin and placed all the uneaten tea in it, including an uncut loaf. After wrapping the food, she tied the napkin securely and gave it to Delphia.

"Now! I want to hear about Miss Skycourt," Jim said. "We've her telegram here, and it is rather disappointing. Therefore, give us a little cheer. You visited their lovely pavilion at the Royal Aquarium? Saw the mighty replicas of what sails in England's skies? What did you think of Lady Helia?"

She looked at him in surprise. "I told thee in my note that I went to see Helia's sister. I had not yet planned to travel to the aquarium."

"Art. It's common knowledge that the mad and lovely Miss Skycourt larks about the aquarium exhibition, typing her lurid stories. Since Helia was your prime concern, no doubt you'd end up there, and did. And in case trips to the aquarium become a habit of yours, I'm particularly fond of the Turkish cigarettes, flavoured with apple, at the Palace Hotel's tobacconist."

"I shall note it. The exhibition is most pleasing, with a variety of cultures and peoples. I am . . . fond of Helia."

"And clearly, she's fond of you. Very fortunate—that she's not your former rival, bears a grudge, was your killer, that sort of thing."

"I've yet to learn if those may be true or whether I've harmed them in return," Art said.

"Them? Who?"

"Helene, her twin, who clearly, at least in the beginning, disliked me."

"Ah. There's too much you don't know, Art, and that is the nature of it," Jim said. "For even if a year of your former life was revealed to you, it's more than you can ever fully comprehend, in mere words told. In truth, it will always be another person's life."

"Yet, the history is mine, whether I am able to recognise it or no. A most emotional and challenging exegesis shall be in my future," Art said. "And still, all things may not be understood or easily accepted. I am not ready."

"It's good you know that," he said.

"Helia chose to be obscure in her telegram to thee," Art said. "Let me share what I've learned from her."

The information Art shared was brief, but it prompted Jim to request a cigarette lit while he pondered.

"If a woman such as herself chooses caution, then it's an eggshell matter, indeed," he said, almost to himself, as he smoked. "The title outranks her family's, no doubt. And one that's above an earldom? My. She was correct not to share what that might be. Catherine is discreet, but well, eggshells."

Before Art could ask him to explain, Jim twisted to regard Delphia.

"Bloom!" he said. "Pencil and paper! Art has some on her dresser. We must compose a telegram to Inspector Risk regarding this new information."

"Without mention of Helia," Art said.

"Correct. The higher the toff, the harder to fell him," Jim said. "But fell him we shall." After Delphia retrieved the pencil and paper and wrote out Jim's dictation, she pulled the cord by Art's bed to summon a page.

"Friend, I must also share something else," Art said. "And Delphia, what I share must not be told to anyone."

At Delphia's solemn acknowledgement, Art related how she lost her ghosting ability once the altercation escalated at the Black Market, and of the odd fatigue she experienced after flying.

"My, my," Jim said. He puffed. "Are you tired now?"

"I am not as I should be, 'tis true," Art said. "And I've ingested of a great many things since our departure from the Black Market, including this tea. As this is a matter of health, should I consult Dr. Fall?"

A polite knock sounded at the door, and a page entered. She accepted the note for telegraphing from Delphia and cleared the table of tea, leaving Delphia's napkin parcel behind.

"I am not the one to ask, for I don't trust him to be my doctor," Jim said. He ate the last of his cigarette as the page left the room with the teacart. Delphia shut the door.

"His interest in our functions is not medical, but scientific," he said. "One can easily return from a simple examination from him . . . changed."

"Then who may I have as a doctor?" Art said.

"Oh, someone reputable and knowledgeable from the Black Market," Jim said.

"Oh."

"But to the problem you mentioned. Perhaps a great shock to your systems—such as being shot numerous times—could result in your loss of the ability to ghost. Thankfully, temporarily," Jim said.

"If such were the case, Ellie smashing my nose would have done same," Art said. "Or my being pole-axed, as what happened with the re-animationist."

"That's quite an Achilles heel," Jim said. "If it were thus. And would occur far too frequently for my liking. In that respect, Fall would have left a great fallacy in his design of you, and he is not the sort to make such a mistake."

"Design!" Delphia said in wonder. "If I may ask, for I've been very curious about this, but is it true that the agents of the Secret Commission are created in supernatural storms? Even from Bethnal Green, we have seen the strange flashing in the night sky in St. Paul's direction, and it's the only time, we believe, that beings such as yourselves are being born."

"Reborn, you mean, and it's true," Jim said. "We come to be in electricity and eldritch fire."

"I saw such fire and lightning six days before. Then it was Art, being reborn," Delphia said.

Art thought of her rebirth and how she felt when electrocuted at the Black Market.

"'Twas the electrical shock," Art said. "That made me lose my ghosting ability. When the man's knife cut the cable. I had not felt such since my awakening."

"That very well may be your answer, Art," Jim said.

"I must stay away from lightning and electric cables, then," Art said.

"Done! And with that settled, it's time, my young friend, that you should sleep."

"Friend," Art protested. "'Tis barely evening."

"Art, did you not just confess to fatigue when flying off to seek Lady Helene? You've been riddled with bullets and you ate them rather than let them pass through you—commendable, though we all saw what that did to your insides. And you briefly lost the ability to ghost. As a physical culturalist, do you not agree that the body needs its time to recover, replenish, and renew? What did you just call it, 'tendering'? That rest is no doubt essential to the flesh's well-being, just as much as frigid dips, the beating of oneself with leafy oak branches, and the running of thy naked self, flippity-flappity through the snow—?"

"Very well, Friend! I will lie down and rest!" Art said, and she did just that, rising from the table and falling upon her bed.

"Good! Though please take off your boots. And other restrictive garments, I can't see how some of your women's wear can be comfortable whilst taking rest, attractive though it makes the lovely figures of your sex. Are you planning to sneak away?"

"Ah," Art said. "I am merely keeping clothed and ready for any occurrence."

"Tut! The only thing that will occur is your snoring! Bloom, you must know, Art has not taken proper rest since her rebirth. She must sleep, or else be jelly."

"Like the quivering matter she ejected with the bullets?" Delphia said.

"Ectoplasm! Amazing stuff! Not really like that, I merely make a figure of speech. Now, Art, shall I speak to you a lullaby?" Jim said.

"Well," Art said, as she contemplated the ceiling. The door suddenly opened. Manon entered and closed the door.

"Ah! No need, Manon will do it," Jim said. "Dear sweet! Art must sleep, and sleep deeply. Please help her, won't you? Bloom, let's go. We've a dressmaker to see. Art, stay here! Don't move! *Sleep!"*

~

Delphia rose, retrieved her coat, and picked up Jim and her parcel. She would have bid Art farewell, but Art had sat up and was entirely focused on her new visitor.

Manon stood before the closed door. Delphia approached. She was half a head taller than Manon, and in comparison, lankier of limb and legs. Manon was well proportioned, like a dancer, and her face had the pretty lips, well-shaped nose, and large eyes that rivaled the illustrated beauties in the magazines. Manon's blonde hair was down, her bodice loosely buttoned, and Delphia could spy bare toes peeping beneath her skirts.

But Delphia wondered why Manon was staring at Art with such deep and silent intensity. Delphia felt she had walked into the middle of a dramatic moment, infused with the dark sensuality seen in actresses from Philo's cabinet cards collection.

"Glades! Green shoots and dragonflies!" Jim said happily in Delphia's hand.

Manon broke her gaze with Art to look at Delphia.

Delphia found herself recipient of nearly the same focused attention, lessened in sensuality but just as silently assertive and purposeful. It seemed Manon was communicating something that Delphia, somehow, had no ability to hear.

Delphia stared back quizzically. Manon's gaze turned to surprise.

"Bloom!" Jim said. "We must depart!"

Delphia did so, managing the doorknob while holding Jim and her tea parcel. Manon returned her attention to Art. Delphia gave Manon one last curious glance and exited.

~

Art sat up. She hardly noticed Jim and Delphia's departure. Manon was dressed, but barefoot. Art saw green and blooming things given her in Manon's look. She saw dragonflies. But this time, she did not become lost in the gaze. Manon had a different purpose in her stare. Her eyes were direct and searching.

Art looked around, hoping Arlette might materialise.

Manon approached.

"How is thee?" Art said. She felt she should get off the bed, especially as she still had her boots on, but she wasn't sure if standing would make a difference.

"I am better," Manon whispered. She climbed onto the bed and sat astride Art's lap. She gently pushed Art to lie back down.

"I'm glad. I'm sorry I upset thee," Art said.

"I will not attack you again," Manon said. She pulled the pins from Art's hair. Her fingers ran through Art's locks.

"Oh," Art said.

Manon unfastened Art's bodice.

"*C'est belle*," she said, caressing the seam along Art's breast.

"I will try not to ruin it," Art said. Manon took hold of Art's face and looked into her eyes.

Art saw more green things, lush, full-leaved, and bountiful, in the places cooled by shade and light breeze, smelling of earth and pungent flowers. She smelled gardenias. Butterflies fluttered. She saw grass wave to and fro.

To, and fro.

To, and. . .

Manon loosened Art's corset. She was fast asleep by the time Manon unbuttoned both of her boots and laid Helia's folded note upon the dresser.

～

When Delphia left Art's room, she saw the two women from Canada in the hallway. They smiled, nodded to her and Jim, and entered a room across that Delphia spied was entirely decorated in green. But what surprised her was the sight of two desks—one with a typewriter and stacks of books while the other was covered in a systematic spreading of letters and research notes.

For women on holiday, Delphia thought, they'd attended right away to their respective projects, whatever those might be.

The door closed behind them. Such women of intellect were an interesting contrast to Manon, who Delphia surmised was a "knee-trembler", as evidenced by her unkempt appearance.

"Such a queer place!" Delphia said, more to herself.

"What's that, Bloom?" Jim said. "Is something happening to your youthful sensibilities, again? Ho! Another signal!" His eye sockets glowed. "I'll take it, must be Risk. Hopefully Art's fast asleep and won't notice."

Delphia halted in her descent on the stairs. She set Jim and her parcel on the banister while she buttoned her coat.

"Risk is at a police station near Bishopsgate," Jim finally said. "We'll meet him there and hear more. To the street, Bloom!"

"I am newly in your employ, and will serve as best I can," Delphia said as she hurried down to the first floor and for the Vesta's entrance. "But I must admit, I wish Art were with us."

"It does help to have muscles, doesn't it?" Jim said. "And Art would have accompanied us, for threats don't matter. Endangerment is a part of the work."

"Then why have her remain?" Delphia asked as she hurried down the first floor hall. She stepped out the Vesta's portal entrance that Doris opened for her. She held her napkin parcel up for a hansom cab. "Unless you believe she needs the rest."

"That, I would have foregone for her as well, had you not been here. But here you are, and what a good opportunity for you to prove your mettle!" Jim said. "To make up for your lack of muscles, I will see to it that you are armed."

"I—what?" Delphia said as Jim shouted an address to the driver who had driven his cab up. The driver pulled the lever, swinging the cab door open. Delphia stepped up.

"You mean . . . a stick, is that what you mean, sir?" she said when seated. "I wouldn't mind a shillelagh."

"Oh no, I mean *guns*," Jim said in glee, and with the sudden start of the cab, Delphia fell back.

CHAPTER THIRTEEN

Delphia, thanks to her unfortunate arrest when she followed Philo to his last, planned theft and tripped him, was familiar with the interior of a police station. She took Jim inside the small, busy station on Bishopsgate, avoided two squabbling women in torn clothes and the policemen who held them, and approached the front desk. The sergeant stood after they'd introduced themselves and led Delphia and Jim to Inspector Risk's temporary office. The sergeant closed the door as Risk rose and bade Delphia and Jim take a seat before his desk.

"Now then, where is Art?" Risk asked curiously when he'd sat down again. "That's twice I've not seen your partner. You've decided to hide her due to that bounty?"

Risk didn't sound impressed. Delphia hoped Jim's decision to keep Art at the Vesta wouldn't reflect badly on her.

"Truth be told, I'm giving our new squire the opportunity to quickly familiarize herself with our business," Jim said.

"Indeed," Risk said. "Enjoying your newfound autonomy, eh? Just make sure the one who can fight dragons is back on duty when we need her."

"It shall be so! What do we have, Risk?"

"That Livus fellow, for one," Risk said. "But we didn't have to catch him. He came to us."

"He's a snake," Jim said. "He came to you with information, then."

"He did. And with an 'ysterical plea for protection from the Bone Stealer himself. Considering what happened to our last man, we've this one completely locked up and hidden. I'm afraid I can't even let you see him."

"He's a true snake, Risk," Jim said.

"I agree. And he's now a snake with one eye. The other apparently resides among the Bone Stealer's curiosities."

Delphia and Jim sat in silence.

"Livus was bloodied and babbling from morphine when he stumbled into the station at Billingsgate," Risk said. "His fear was clear. I had him transported as swiftly as possible to another location, and so on from there."

"And what of his information, in exchange for such fine hospitality?" Jim said.

"I've a place and I've a time, for the Bone Stealer's little demonstration," Risk said. "We've until tomorrow night. Make sure Art is ready."

"She will be. But Risk. No name or clue as to this man's possible title?"

"I received your telegram, but hadn't opportunity to question Livus himself about the title aspect," Risk said flatly. "And no, he had no name for the man."

"Very well. But let me return attention to the secret soiree," Jim said. "It's been planned for quite some time now. An unusually tall and rich girl is waiting, and not only that, the seats have been selling. The only thing missing is the unusually tall, female victim. Miss Pritt is safely injured, and Art is ensconced at the Vesta. The owner there will not let so much as a supernatural flea squeeze through its iris portal. Therefore, where is our next victim? And is she already taken?"

"I'm working on the assumption that they haven't taken their woman yet," Risk said. "We've a warning gone to print in all the evening newspapers. Won't matter if the girl's even close to six foot two inches. Every young lady over five feet will be hiding by the time the news spreads, and if one is missing already, any who know her will soon let us know."

"That takes care of random opportunity, yes," Jim said. "But I was thinking more of a specific target. Namely, our local sideshows."

"*Barkley*," Risk barked. The sergeant opened the door and hurried into the office. "I need every sideshow in London and within thirty miles of London notified. They've their giantesses to lock up, understand? Any girl that stands over six feet, we are to send men for them!"

"Yes, sir!" Barkley said and quickly left.

"But in case the Bone Stealer's ahead of us in this game," Risk said, returning his attention to Jim and Delphia. "And has his victim already."

"Tomorrow night, we'll be there," Jim said.

With the Bone Stealer business more or less settled, Risk invited Jim to join his family for dinner. Delphia wrote a letter per Jim's dictation to Charlotte Thackery, Art's dressmaker, with paper borrowed from Risk's notepad. She made a mental note to procure her own such notebook and pencil. For her final duty of the night, she would take a cab to Charlotte's shop and from there return home.

"Bloom, here's fare for Bethnal Green as well," Jim said after he'd spat out the coins. "And make certain you take that hansom cab, understand? Or else Art will box my ears for letting you wander about at night, without a chaperone. Your parents will have to accept that your duties will last beyond nightfall, for that's when evil likes to do its business."

"I understand, sir," Delphia said.

"Oh, and write down that pistols are to be ordered for you too," Jim said.

"Wot?!" Risk said, turning from the small mirror he held up. He had been combing his thick moustache in preparation for greeting his wife.

"Pistols, Risk! She *is* wandering about the night, without chaperone," Jim said.

"I'd much prefer a shillelagh," Delphia said.

"You may have that, and a knife if it suits you, but pistols I will not approve of!" Risk said.

"But Risk!" Jim said.

Delphia gave her farewells and took her leave as Jim and Risk argued. She realised once she'd stepped out of the station that she didn't know when she was to come to the Vesta in the morning, but like any position she'd worked, eight sounded right and if too early, she could dawdle in the Vesta library. Despite the erotica, such a vast library would surely have many other interesting books.

Delphia stood on the walk amid the people hurrying for home and heard newsboys cry out the latest headlines. The sun was setting. Gas lamp-lighters were busy lighting the street.

"Bone Stealer after tall women!" the newsboys shouted. "See if that's you!"

Delphia hailed a hansom cab as people crowded the newsboys. She boarded it for Charlotte Thackery's dressmaker's shop.

The Royal Aquarium's glass dome reflected fiery red and orange, mirroring the sky over the Thames. Helia slept on Helene's shoulder while Helene sat in contemplation. As the sunset's colours faded and the sky darkened, Helia woke up.

"Oh, you shouldn't have let me nap, I've work, I've people to pester," Helia said sleepily, rubbing her eyes. "I want to eat peppers. My nose is cold!"

"A brisk wind brings appetite," Helene said. She helped Helia up and stepped for the hatch. "Down we go!"

Ten minutes later, the two were back at Helia's table at the Blue Vanda. Helene didn't bother to remove her coat. The blind quintet had long packed their instruments for the evening and gone back to their lodgings at the Blind Institute. Music could be heard drifting down an adjacent hall leading to the Palace Hotel, where another string quartet played in their lounging area. A wandering, Italian violinist was serenading the patrons seated at the French café.

"Progress, no progress, so very little progress!" Helia muttered to herself. She was staring at the blank sheet of paper in her typewriter. The telegram reply from Germany had arrived while she'd been on the dome with Helene. The information, a list of murdered people found in the same condition as the boneless victims of London, gave a disparity of crime locations. None pointed to a common territory, and therefore to a sovereigntry, for their vivisecting German prince.

"Experiments, mistakes, caprice, mere notions!" Helia said,

staring at her typewriter. "So many! And he likes what he will do."

"Well. I did say I would help," Helene said. She tossed the telegram on the table after reading it.

"And we've discussed that," Helia said. She glanced up and saw Perseus mount the steps of the Blue Vanda patio. He smiled, raised his hat, and approached. He had a newspaper beneath an arm.

"Ladies," he greeted. "So good to see you." He took the seat Helene indicated for him.

"Perseus, did things go well with our uncle?" Helene said.

"I believe it did, though another visit may tell better," he said. "I am optimistic! But I must bring up another concern. Is Art still here, at the aquarium?"

"Art departed quite a while ago," Helia said. Perseus opened his paper.

"That Bone Stealer business," he said. "I believe you ladies should see this. It's more information from the police."

Helia snatched the paper from Perseus before Helene could. She quickly scanned the front page.

"It says that now the Bone Stealer's after women specifically of the height six foot two inches," Perseus told Helene. "I've no knowledge about bone transference, but I believe the measure needs to be exact in order to work. Desperate men might not think on that, especially snatchers. My brother Taurus is six foot five inches. I thought Art was nearly the same."

"Art is six foot two and seems more when wearing shoes," Helia said. She flung the newspaper on the table and turned to her typewriter. She typed rapidly. "Oh! I hope she's at the Vesta!" She pulled out the typed paper and gave it to a waiter.

"As I'd said, into the bear-ridden forest," Helene muttered. She picked up the newspaper to look at it. "I expect you'll want my help again."

"Yes!" Helia said. "I'd no knowledge of the other tall woman nearly kidnapped, who is mentioned. I will go to her hospital tonight. But you, you must go to your Convenient!"

The people seated around them started at the words. A woman

lost hold of her fork.

"My. . ." Helene said, staring at Helia blankly.

"Tonight! As soon as you can, attend to your Convenient and then see if Art is well," Helia said.

Helene stared.

"Do I need to remind you," Helia said in a chastising tone. "Of how negligent you've been with your wo—"

"Very well!" Helene said. "Thank you, Helia. I *will* visit my Convenient, tonight."

A woman gave a strangled cry and fainted at her table. Men quickly rose to revive her.

Perseus cleared his throat and stared with great interest at the replica airships above.

"Mr. H. E. Dublow of Dublow American Aeronautics is seated over there, with his very fetching and provocatively dressed 'niece'," Helia then confided in a low voice. "He's in London on business, and traveling without his wife. No doubt now that he's heard you keep a lover, he'll consider Skycourt of estimable interest. I expect him to stop by and introduce himself."

"Does this mean I'm allowed to eat my curry?" Helene said. "Before rushing off to sate other appetites."

"Yes, Helene, you may eat your curry." A server came and handed Helia a telegram. She read it. "For Catherine writes that Art is at the Vesta and in her room. But you are to go there right away, after you finish your meal!"

"Yes, Helia. After such a meal, I'll need to indulge in the form of exertion you've suggested," Helene said.

Helia did not answer. She was busy typing again.

"No doubt those are specific instructions for how to conduct myself," Helene said, "as apparently, I've forgotten my abilities in such situations."

"Hush, you are causing Perseus all sorts of discomfort," Helia said. "And these instructions are for Catherine to make certain your Convenient is ready for you."

"Perseus," Helene said, her tone defeated. "As apology, please dine with us."

"I am happy to join you, ladies!" he said.

"And if you've no further plans for the night, I hope you'll take Helia in your buggy to her hospital destination," Helene said. "It would be faster than her wheel and would put me at ease."

"I am at Helia's service," Perseus said.

"Just don't agree to everything she wants you to do," Helene said. "You may find yourself wedded to a strange girl in the morning. Ah, food!"

Plates of chicken masala, bread, chutney, and rice were laid before them, steaming and fragrant. Helia finished typing her second telegram to the Vesta as Perseus gave his own dinner order to the server.

Later, when they were nearly done with dinner, Helene received a card from Dublow. His second dinner companion, the son of a Lord of Parliament and friends with Helia and Helene, made introductions for him. Helene and Dublow exchanged pleasantries and promised further meetings. The trio bade Dublow farewell and took their leave of the Blue Vanda. While walking to the aquarium exit, Helia laid a hand on Helene to allow Perseus to move ahead.

"I've seen Manon, and she, me," Helia whispered to her. She tapped her sister's spectacles and then her own face—the masked side.

Helene adjusted her bewitched spectacles and stared at Helia's face. Not once that day had she spotted even a shadow of the eldritch presence that lay hidden behind Helia's mask.

"Oh, it's sleeping," Helia said. "But it saw her and she saw it."

"When?" Helene said.

"When I sneaked into the Vesta to make arrangements with Catherine," Helia said.

"This Manon is a creature?" Helene whispered.

"A good one," Helia said. "I told you, not all that's different wishes us harm. Be civil, Helene."

"Of course I will be," Helene assured as they resumed their walk to catch up with Perseus. "I'll need to stop by my room first."

Delphia's hansom cab made its way from Bishopsgate Street and through the evening traffic for the equally congested Cheapside. The air was filled with stirred dust and the deafening clatter of wheels and hooves. Delphia stared at the thoroughfare known as the busiest in the world. When she craned her neck above the horse's head, she caught a glimpse of St. Paul's in the west. She thought of John Milton, who was born in Cheapside, and of the goldsmiths and markets that made the street legend. She spotted Bread St. and wondered where Honey Lane might be. All the other cabs crowding the street were filled with male passengers, reading, smoking, and sometimes they regarded her quizzically.

She remembered Jim's question from their first cab ride. Being that she was a girl and a poor one at that, she treated her singular female presence as just another freedom she might indulge in, just like the freedom of shortened skirts. Her cab turned down a side street off Cheapside and then turned again, into a small street lined with shop fronts. It stopped before *Thackery Fine Dressmaker, Tailor, & Outfitter.*

"Robin Hood's Row!" the driver called out. The roof's trapdoor opened, and Delphia handed up the fare. The driver turned the lever to swing the small door open. She jumped out with her napkin parcel.

"Shops are now closed, miss. As local laws must have it," driver said. She looked at the darkened windows of Thackery's dressmaker's shop and its three fully clothed forms on display. One was dressed in a white, lacy summer dress complete with open fan, the second in a woman's sharply cut riding habit with top hat, and the third in evening gentlemen's attire. But as the driver had noted, all the shops on the street had shut for the night, their lights out.

"Would there be a way around back, sir, an alley, perhaps?" Delphia asked. "I've a letter, and business can still be conducted, even through the dressmaker's workroom."

"I was 'bout to mention," the driver said. "For in the lane behind this row, that's where the better business is done. Hop back in, and

I'll not charge you more. I intended to go there as that's where I'll find my next fare."

Delphia did, and the cab moved forwards for the end of the row and turned left. In the side street were cabs, hackney carriages, a brougham, and one private carriage, the coat of arms on its side obscured by black cloth. A scattering of food stalls lined the walk, doing brisk business in meat pies, oysters, pickled eel, and fried fish. The driver let Delphia out before an alley lit by gas lamps. Shoppers, mostly men, walked about, peering into brightly lit back entrances. Haggling could be heard amid the cries of "pies, tasty pies!" Delphia looked up and saw the alley's street sign: Robin Hood's Lane.

She walked down the lane, passing the smithy of a burly armourer, his hammer hitting the anvil as men in top hats looked on. Swords and other metal weapons hung on his walls. Behind him, the forge glowed white. An apprentice heated a roughly shaped blade between his tongs. She passed the lit back entrance of a leather goods and saddlery shop. A leatherworker with tools, hammer, and needles stored in his work apron held an ornate halter replete with bronze medallions for a buyer to examine. At a milliner's, women in gaudy gowns tried on hats before mirrors and looked at purses, gloves, and parasols laid out on a table. A bootmaker watched from his workroom as a man and his servant departed with four long boxes that Delphia suspected held riding boots. She found a back door where two women emerged with even larger, flat boxes. From within, Delphia heard the whir of machinery. Such large boxes, she knew, were for clothing. She entered the building.

Inside the bright workroom, Delphia saw six treadle tables. Women sat, running the needles rapidly in their black sewing machines. Their feet stepped up and down. One woman worked the wheel of her machine with a hand as she slowly moved a hoop of cloth this way and that. Delphia realised she was embroidering with her machine needle. More women sat at two worktables, sewing by hand. Cut cloth lay on a third table. All manner of clothing hung from pegs. Scraps of fabric and lace were piled in baskets beneath the tables. One table held more baskets filled with spools, pincushions, and bobbins. Delphia picked up one fallen spool on the floor and laid it on the table. None of the women looked at her as they worked. She took that as a sign to continue on and find Charlotte Thackery's office.

She followed the sound of a woman's voice to a small lit room. Inside stood two women before a desk, both with shears hanging from their chatelaines and measuring tapes hung around their necks. They watched a small, thin red-haired woman, her brow furrowed. She showed them fashion plates from a Parisian dress catalogue. Beside Charlotte's Thackery's desk was a form wearing the dress Art had worn at the Black Market. It was cleansed but punctured with bullet holes.

"I believe these designs will be popular. Knowing Madame Duchamp's salon, they will pick these as well as the more ornate designs for the season. Whatever Duchamp will soon display in their showroom, our clients are certain to ask for a copy. But have this dress, which I've marked, cut and made tonight. It will be displayed tomorrow in the front window."

The fabric cutters accepted the catalogue and left the room. Delphia stood at the doorway and Charlotte noticed her.

"Good evening, what may I do for you?" she said.

"Good evening, Miss Thackery, my name is Delphia Bloom. I've a letter from my employer, Mr. Jim Dastard, partner to Art, whose dress from today I see hanging on your form," Delphia said. She approached and handed over the letter.

"Ah yes," Charlotte sighed. "I have three dresses worked on for her, and three corsets. I don't mind the business, but how distressing to see the dreadful condition she puts my clothes through." She opened the letter and began reading it, frowning. Delphia had noticed narrow stairs outside the office, leading up as well as down to a basement. The stairwell below was brightly lit. She wondered where the corsets Charlotte mentioned were being worked on. A boy suddenly ran past the office and down the steps, carrying an armful of stays and a huge wooden spool of lacing. He also carried thin metal plates.

"Nicholas, please don't run," Charlotte called out distractedly. She continued to stare at the letter and frown. Then she raised her gaze and stared at Delphia.

Delphia stood patiently and after a while, wondered if something was stuck on her face or her coat.

"He is requesting a style of uniform," Charlotte finally said. "Bright red, with gold buttons, epaulets, braiding, belt, a badge, fitted to your figure and with military hat and boots. Are you in any way a burlesque performer?"

"No, miss. He requests a uniform because I will be present at the private club known as the Vesta, which both Mr. Dastard and Art reside in."

"The Vesta! At your age! Dear God, what is Art thinking?" Charlotte said.

"Miss, Art thought the same as yourself, it was Mr. Dastard that had me come to the Vesta," Delphia said. "And now it's done, and I need to be seen as a proper assistant whilst in such an environment."

"This outfit he is ordering will only see you as a possible participant, like a flag raised before a bull. When I visited that club, I had not one, but three of those toms raise a hat to me as I made my way to Art's room. Their attentions were more polite than what one might receive from typical male pests, but one does not want such attention to overstep."

"Yes, miss," Delphia said.

"Come. I know what I'll have you wear tonight," Charlotte said as she folded the letter, placed it in a pocket, and came around her desk. "When Mr. Dastard sees it, he will understand why it will be appropriate for the Vesta and for your work. But for what he specifically requests, if he still desires it, I prefer he visits the shop and look at designs I'll prepare for him."

"Yes, miss," Delphia said. She followed Charlotte out, who went directly to a small room across from her office. She searched through clothes on hooks and drew out a young man's black coat.

"The boy this was made for unexpectedly died," she said. "His family moved away and abandoned the things ordered for him. He was slim and narrow of shoulders. Let's see if the fit works on you."

Delphia put down her parcel, removed her coat, and put on the black coat. It fell to the middle of her thigh, and Delphia found the sleeves and shoulders fit well. Charlotte turned her around, nodding her approval.

"Yes. I'll not have you fitted to it. The idea is not to show your figure, but give you some aspect of maleness. It looks as if you'd borrowed your brother's coat on a rash whim, or your sweetheart's."

"Such a bold idea, miss, but I very much like it," Delphia said. She admired the black, buttoned cuffs. It was a very fine coat.

Charlotte then led Delphia out her shop and to the alley. They went to the milliner's, where Delphia tried on gloves until Charlotte approved of a grey pair fastened with three black buttons. She handed Delphia top hats, sized for boys, to put on before the mirrors.

"No, that won't do, Lottie," the milliner said. Franny was shorter than Charlotte, plumper and with a pleasantly round face. One of her children slept in a basket beneath the table, sucking his thumb. "It should be a lady's riding hat, black, with no veil. And by the by, I sent another client to your shop, in need of riding habits."

"Thank you, Franny," Charlotte said. "And did two women come, in search of straw boaters?"

"Oh, they did, and were happy to order four! Now here, miss, try this," Franny said, giving Delphia a black riding hat, bowler-style, that Delphia thought very attractive.

"But Delphia must fraternize with toms, Franny," Charlotte said. "That's why she's trying stove-pipes, bowlers would seem too common. She assists Secret Commission agents who reside at the Vesta."

"The Vesta!" Franny exclaimed. After she and Charlotte tutted over Delphia's situation, Franny chose a lady's riding hat in the style of a top hat, but one short of crown. It had an elastic band. Delphia looked inside of it, wondering if she might be able to store things, as Jim did with his hat.

"And its size will not rival your employer's?" Franny asked.

"No, missus, his top hat is much taller," Delphia said. She put the hat on, and Charlotte nodded her approval.

Thus satisfied, Charlotte and Delphia left Franny's, and Charlotte consulted Jim's letter.

"I can have the badge he describes, designed and then cast, which I'll have delivered to the Vesta. You last need a weapon." She stopped in the middle of the alley and looked at Delphia. "Do I understand correctly, Mr. Dastard wishes for you to carry pistols?"

"Miss, a police inspector has expressed his disapproval of the idea. But I'm allowed a shillelagh," Delphia said.

"That, I'm willing to acquire for you."

Across from the armourer's smithy was the workroom of a walking-stick-and-canes shop. Inside, sticks, canes, and umbrellas dangled from the ceiling. Woodworking tools lay on a table with a cane of wood held in vises. A boy in a cap sat eating a meat pie.

"Hello, Aedan, is O'Nackey at the pub, again?" Charlotte said. The boy nodded vigorously, his mouth full of pie.

"Pick us a cudgel, won't you? For Delphia, here," Charlotte said, indicating Delphia. "Have you any skills with the stick, Delphia?"

"No, miss," Delphia said. "I assume Mr. Dastard shall provide for lessons."

Aedan studied Delphia while he chewed his food. He trooped over to a cluster of twisted blackthorns of various lengths, hanging on a wall. He brought down one that was eighteen inches long, with a large, gnarled head. A hole was drilled at the base of the long end, from which a leather strap dangled.

Aedan showed it to Delphia, but before she could take it, he walked back to a worktable. He retrieved an empty treacle can beneath the table and placed it on the tabletop.

He stood back and showed Delphia the position of his grip upon the stick. He set the stick back behind his shoulder, like a hammer. Then with a simple swing, he brought the head of the stick down on the can. He crushed it flat. To Delphia, Aedan had swung down so precisely and with so little effort, he could have just hammered a nail with one blow.

"'Tisn't 'bout strength, miss, it's how you do it," he said. He handed the cudgel to Delphia. "That's all you need to know, for now."

"Thank you, Aedan," she said.

They left the walking-stick workroom, and Charlotte invited Delphia to have evening meal at her shop. Delphia, who'd left her tea parcel and old coat in Charlotte's office, declined. She felt her mother might already be worried since night had long fallen.

"Delphia, I can't help notice, but isn't it time your skirts were lengthened?" Charlotte said in curiosity. "Oh, never mind my silly question. Your mother's not ready, is she?"

Delphia didn't know what to say. This was something the women of her street had noted as well, though not within her mother's hearing.

Charlotte sighed. "Thank goodness I've a few years yet for my Laura. You all grow so fast."

"Oh," Delphia said, abashed. "*Mrs.* Tha—"

"No," Charlotte interrupted. "You were right the first time in how you addressed me. I've two children, and I never married. It's one reason I don't have my shop in the West End. I chose here, Cheapside, between the poorer London and the richer West End. Were I among the other salons, my reputation would not survive the disdain of the upper class and the court dressmakers. My clients are the middle class, who can't afford the latest Parisian fashions but are willing to pay me to copy such designs for them. And I design my own devises as well, and patent them. I must work very hard to keep up my business. I am the owner."

"Oh," Delphia said. "I like that, Miss Thackery."

"Do you? Well, you know you shouldn't," Charlotte admonished, but her tone was light.

When they reentered Charlotte's workroom, the women were on evening meal break. They sat at the counter table against the window facing the alley, eating foodstuff from the stalls. One woman had a paper and they were in avid discussion of the latest news about the Bone Stealer. In the back, behind a folded screen, one of the fabric cutters could be heard talking while she measured a female client. Delphia, who had once attempted work in a sweatshop—and failed, for she sewed too slowly—thought it very rare to see so relaxed a workroom.

Delphia retrieved her napkin parcel and old coat. Charlotte walked with her to the back entrance. Upon leaving, Delphia curtsied to her.

"Wait, Delphia," Charlotte suddenly said.

Delphia, surprised, did as asked. Charlotte once again mused upon Delphia's appearance.

"It may just be a hat and coat, but when you wear clothes like these, you must act appropriately," she finally said. "Rather than explain, let's see if it can be shown."

Charlotte called to one of her employees, a young woman named Belle. Belle was an African, full-lipped, full-figured, and with a sway to her walk. She smiled at Delphia, and she and Charlotte stepped outside into the alley.

"This will be an exercise in fitting your manner to your new appearance," Charlotte said. "You mayn't speak to a woman you've not been introduced to. Therefore, let's imagine that Belle happens to approach a puddle. She stops, and as you are there, you shall, in a moment of sympathy and desire to give aid, make yourself known to her. Let's begin."

Belle walked towards the imaginary puddle, smiling and her hips swaying. She came to a stop and pretended dismay at the phantom puddle. Her hands touched her cheeks.

Delphia, standing to the side with her parcel, coat, and cudgel in hand, bent a knee in curtsey.

"No. Let us stop," Charlotte said. "You are not a gentleman by any stretch, but the attempt here is that you should affect their position of sex. Now, you've a hat. You're not the 'girl', you're an androgynous figure. Remember such manners. Let's try again."

Delphia nodded and hurriedly put all her items on the ground.

Belle walked back, and then approached once more. After she feint her dismay, Delphia bowed and raised her hat.

"How do you do, sir," Belle said, smiling.

"How do you do, miss," Delphia said. She nodded and tipped her hat again. "Would you like assistance across this puddle?"

"Please, sir, if it doesn't trouble you," Belle said. She offered her hand.

Delphia accepted Belle's hand and helped her to step across the offending puddle.

"Good! Very well done!" Charlotte said. "Now, Delphia, do you understand?"

"Yes, miss. It's really quite a difference," Delphia said.

"Affect this manner while working with the agents," Charlotte said. "And you may find yourself discovering benefits unknown to our sex."

Delphia bowed and tipped her hat to Charlotte. Then she did the same to Belle.

When Delphia walked back down Robin Hood Lane for the outer street, she held her cudgel, old coat, and parcel and felt, indeed, that she was different. Men looked at her, but either quickly dismissed her or respectfully gave her way. It was a pleasant change from the stares—open or covert—elicited for being a young girl out and about, and alone. Delphia hailed a hansom cab by raising her stick. Once inside, she practiced adjusting her coat to accommodate the act of sitting down.

By the time her cab reached Bethnal Green, her home's darkened street was devoid of people. All residents were safely inside, either already gone to rest, or if lucky, partaking of dinner. No one saw her disembark in her new outfit, but Delphia was glad of it, for she needed to see her family right away.

The reception once she was home and inside was warm and excited. Delphia handed over the leftover tea, and instead of taking off her new hat and coat, decided to go directly to the broom laid against the table and finish her mother's sweeping. Her siblings played with her cudgel as she shared the later day's activities with her father and mother.

"Helping those unnaturals . . . well, I don't know," Gaiety finally said as she portioned out the tea for the children and for her husband. "It's awful danger they face . . . fighting all the time, and seems for all their strange gifts they fare no better than the Nick Blackhearts. And we've not heard of the last Nick for months. She must be dead."

"Mummy, you've yet to meet Art," Delphia said. "She's a very queer Quaker, for she dresses prettily and fights! But my, she seems more than an Amazon. I feel safe with her."

"She sounds like Pallas Athene," Peter remarked, thoughtfully chewing on a biscuit. "A great warrior goddess."

"Yet a Quaker," Gaiety said. "I'd rather she were Nick Blackheart."

Later, as her family finished their meal, Delphia took the waste bucket out to the street's center gutter and emptied it. She took that moment to look up at the night sky and reflect on her good fortune. Then she felt a hand touch her arm.

"Oh! Elsepeth!" Delphia said, her heart in her throat. She nearly jumped out of her new coat. Elsepeth stood so closely, Delphia couldn't fathom how she missed knowing it. Elsepeth laid a white hand again on Delphia's arm.

"Delphia! Your lip is hurt!" she said. "I heard something terrible happened at the Black Market. And . . . my, what interesting dress you're in tonight!"

Delphia raised her hat to her, and Elsepeth smiled in surprise.

"Thank you for your concern, Elsepeth. I'm well, but why are you still out? You know these streets aren't safe at night, and you're always walking alone." She picked up the bucket and moved them closer to her home.

"You walk with disregard as well, Delphia, I could say the same to you!" she said. "But don't worry about me. After I heard what happened at the market, I had to see you."

"How did you know I was there today?" Delphia said curiously. "I never arrived at Von Fitz's shop."

"Oh. I guessed. I'd also heard you lost your position again! So I thought to bring you more invites."

Elsepeth held out the wooden cards in her hand. In the darkness, the illustrations of the leeches gave a subtle, eldritch glow.

"Thank you, Elsepeth, but I won't be needing them," Delphia said. "I've accepted a very good situation today. I'll be assisting agents of the Secret Commission! It's very interesting work. And I confess, I was part of the trouble that happened at the Black Market. So much so, that I don't think it would be wise for me to return."

"Agents? And you were part of the trouble? My, so much has happened to you! But Delphia, you must be exaggerating. Are you certain you can't continue to give your blood?" She offered the cards again.

"I believe so; the Black Market will not receive me kindly. Please save these for a girl who can help."

Elsepeth slowly withdrew her hand, her eyes wide.

"Elsepeth, are you angry?"

"Such a thing to ask!" Elsepeth said, but Delphia thought her friend's lip trembled.

"Elsepeth, forgive me again, but are you ill?" Delphia asked.

"What?" Elsepeth laughed. "Am I so very pale today? I thought that was the appearance the magazines advised was the most attractive to our present society." She smiled, her teeth white against her red lips. Delphia was always impressed by how beautiful Elsepeth's teeth were.

"I would expect just a little pink in your complexion, and not what's brought on by consumption," Delphia said. "Tell me the truth, are you the one who needs the transfusions?"

Elsepeth withdrew slightly, her eyes large with surprise. Delphia thought she folded a little upon herself, like a bird steeling its small body against some harsh wind. She stared searchingly at Delphia, a gaze clear in its desire for assurance, or deeper knowledge.

Elsepeth gave a slight smile.

"I need your blood, yes," she said finally.

"I thought so," Delphia said. "When you spoke of deaths from bleeding, I suspected you might be predisposed to a hemorrhagic condition."

"Goodness, you sound just like a doctor," she said, her smile widening.

"Well, I do like the words. 'Haemorrhaphilia'. I believe that's the term."

A silence fell between them, in which Elsepeth only smiled at her. Delphia blushed.

"I've met such interesting women today, so strong-willed and independent," Delphia said. "But I must count you among them, for you ought to be hidden away in a room somewhere, never to go out and possibly just lay about, in case you should bleed all over something. But you travel where you like and you solicit help for your own cures. I very much admire it."

"I'm not deserving of such admiration," Elsepeth said, looking down. "I only do what I must. And you're right, I can find other girls to help me."

Delphia took one of the invitations Elsepeth held.

"I still think I'll not be welcomed at the Black Market," Delphia said. "But perhaps later. When things are calm again." She laid a hand on Elsepeth's cool hand. "Please be well, until then."

"Oh! Thank you, Delphia," Elsepeth said, taking Delphia's hand. She held it between both her own. "I so look forward to it," she whispered.

Delphia went in to tell her mother that she would be escorting Elsepeth to where she could catch a carriage or hansom cab. At Elsepeth's insistence, Delphia would ride the same vehicle the short distance back to her home. Delphia retrieved her cudgel from her younger siblings and walked out into the night with her friend.

As she and Elsepeth made their way down the dark street, arm in arm, Elsepeth chuckled.

"Since you're in skirts, Delphia, I doubt a bobby will try to stop me this time and enquire as to my business. Unless he suspects us both of illicit intentions."

"Oh, Else'," Delphia simply said. Having been rude twice to Elsepeth, Delphia refrained from expressing another curiosity. Her friend had been dressing in finer clothes since their time at the boot-making factory. She no longer wore shawls, but fitted jackets. Her boots looked smart and new. But she did not dress overly prettily, with ribbons, bows, or bright colours, nor did she wear gloves, hat, or carry purse or parasol. Like Delphia, she still wore her hair down and her skirts short, though Delphia suspected Elsepeth could easily dress of age and be convincing as such.

Overall, it seemed an appearance not concerned with attracting attention. Elsepeth hadn't a face that was strikingly pretty—not like the magazine-worthy face that was Manon's. Elsepeth's brows were dark and arched, and her hazel eyes alert and clear, as if they missed nothing. Her nose was long. She wore no cosmetics though her lips were red, and Delphia thought them naturally so. But despite Elsepeth's unobtrusive appearance, the quality of her clothing was still apparent and could demand better respect, in Delphia's estimation, than usual working-class attire.

Delphia hoped Elsepeth wasn't really prostituting, though that was always an unfortunate option for girls of their class.

"Why are you dressed so, Delphia?" Elsepeth asked. "It is fetching but not quite the uniform I would envision for your new position."

"Well, Elsepeth, it's a matter of adaption," Delphia said. "My employers reside in a rather interesting private club, which caters to those who cross-dress."

"Really, Delphia," Elsepeth said, smiling once more in surprise. "Don't tell me it's the notorious Vesta?"

Delphia was beginning to feel as if everyone knew about the nature of the Vesta except for her.

Carriages and cabs were scarce in impoverished warrens like Bethnal Green. But Elsepeth said she knew where one would soon appear, and as they waited at a lit corner, she discussed the Vesta with Delphia. Not specifically the nature of the club, but more on how Delphia's position should be handled. Elsepeth seemed to have an understanding of how places of class worked, which brought another question to mind that Delphia also declined to pursue. Elsepeth was mannered and spoke well. Either it was because she had once been privileged, like Delphia, or was very thoroughly tutored as per the requirements of a well-kept Convenient for a rich man.

"In the morning, enter the club through the back entrance," Elsepeth advised. "That would be the kitchen. You *must* befriend the staff, and the cook, not the housekeeper, is whose favour you must win. I say this because housekeepers are head of staff and therefore loyal to no one but themselves and their mistress. Yes, you're of lesser class, but you don't work for her. Ally yourself with the downstairs, and that includes any prostitutes in residence, just so you'll get a share of the banquet leftovers that the servants enjoy, at end of day."

"And then I might see how the other areas of the Vesta are laid," Delphia said thoughtfully. "Elsepeth, today I was introduced to a lady, and I felt I acquitted myself well, but then I learned later that she was of an earldom! Then I was introduced to a baroness, and I called her 'Your Ladyship'. That sounds right, doesn't it, Elspeth? I'm certain to make a mistake at some point."

Elsepeth patted her arm. "You were correct, Delphia! And you needn't worry. The reason is that such secret clubs are a mix of classes. It isn't about gentry, it's about who has money. Mistakes will happen, and recognition of title is not the first concerns of such patrons, who would prefer to be incognito and therefore, free of convention."

Armed with such advice, Delphia hailed the hansom cab that finally appeared. Elsepeth laughed.

"A cab? Very well, Delphia," she said.

"Well, there isn't anyone who will see us, Elsepeth," Delphia said, grinning.

They rode it the short distance back to Delphia's home, where she disembarked. Delphia bid Elsepeth farewell and tipped her hat.

～

At the Vesta, Art woke up.

The light from her windows was fading. Evening had come. She rose awkwardly, finding her garments in disarray. Knowing that nothing untoward had happened between herself and Manon, it seemed odd to find herself in such a state. She stood, took off her bodice, buttoned her boots back on, and set about lacing herself back into her loosened corset.

Glancing around as she worked, she realised that Jim had scampered off with Delphia and left no note. Without an address to refer to, Art did not know where Charlotte Thackery's shop might be. The Vesta had fetched Charlotte once. Art could find out the information from Alice, but she suspected that Jim and Delphia were long gone from that location.

Art felt irked, and she knew why. Jim was working the case without her, and perhaps she was at fault for the rapidly growing gap between them. She did, after all, go in pursuit of Helia almost single-mindedly, and somehow Jim knew she would do that. He had been very tolerant and even jovial in his queries of her aquarium visit. And while there with Helia, she had all but forgotten about the case.

"I've a weakness," Art said to herself as she finished fastening her bodice. "'Tis 'skirts-chasing'. I must focus on the work."

She and Jim would need another discussion. She did not like this separation. True, he had found new independence by hiring "legs", but Art was also concerned that Delphia not be overworked. Unlike the agents, who could remain ceaselessly active and eschew proper meals, Delphia was human.

Art coughed. Suddenly, she felt terribly ill.

She rushed to her wash cabinet and vomited into the ceramic basin. Two smashed and shiny bullets clattered inside the bowl. None of her insides had come up, this time. After ejecting the bullets she felt immensely better.

"What manner of bullets are these?" she said in wonder. They looked very shiny. She took them to study under a gaslight and determined they were silver. If there was anything more to them, they might have been the cause of her fatigue. She had the absurd notion to give one to Helia.

Art then touched beneath her breasts. She wondered where Helia's note was.

Manon had laid Helia's folded, typewritten note on the dresser. Art picked up Helia's silver-engraved card and placed it and the prettier of the smashed bullets on the dresser along with her other objects. She realised that she had no proper box to store items precious to her. Or items that she might safely keep as reminder of life-events, like the tooth of one of the reanimated children. She laid the second silver bullet next to the tiny tooth.

Taking pencil and paper laid on her dresser top, she wrote a list of necessities:

Journal
Pocket Watch
Keepsake box
Dumbbells

She thought a moment, then added to "dumbbells": *4 stone each*.

She set the list aside and wrote Jim a note. He had cautioned her to not leave, but she was still skeptical that the threat of kidnap could be executed on her ghostly self. If she did not find him below, Art knew where she would go next. She would fly to Whitechapel Market and visit Fiona Bell, the widow of the slaughter man she'd accidentally killed.

While invisible, Art ghosted about the drawing rooms for Jim. She tamped down her mild irritation at not finding him, and then flew away for Whitechapel and its market. She solidified in front of the tenement Fiona Bell lived in. Those loitering outside started at her sudden appearance. She climbed the steps until she found the room. Fiona's mother, Cairenn, a greying woman missing teeth in her smile, let her in. Art saw the little ones, a young boy and a very little girl, nearly three years old, playing on the floor.

They ran to her immediately. Art didn't know why the boy had taken to her; he was four and missed his father dearly, yet somehow he understood that she hadn't murdered Dennis Bell, and that it had been an accident. Art hoped that his trust was not from lack of understanding. She didn't want him to grow to anger later.

He and his sister pulled her skirts, and she lifted them at the same time. Art saw a small pile of male clothing on one of the narrow beds. Dresses—bright and fringed—were among them too. She assumed they were Fiona's best outfits.

Art had given the family the Secret Commission's recompense for Dennis's death, but the loss of a second wage, and one made by a man, was still a blow to such a household. She didn't know how much a proper burial cost, but right then she assumed it had affected the recompense significantly.

Cairenn was pleased to see Art, almost to the point of giddiness. After the tongue-lashing Art had received on her last visit, she was surprised. Cairenn pinned on a shawl and a put on a hat decorated with artificial flowers while Art gave the children lifts into the air, much to their delight.

"I'm glad you've come!" Cairenn said. "Take us to market, then? Fiona won't come home 'til later 'n I've been inside all day!"

"Aye. I will buy thee supper and foodstuffs," Art said. She helped the children put on their shawls and coats.

At Whitechapel Market, stoic butchers had unidentifiable scraps of dark meat out, which poor women touched, tried to haggle over, and finally left on the table, unable to afford the ragged bits. Cairenn ignored such stalls and walked with a spring in her step. She heartily greeted women she knew and introduced Art, who held the children in both arms. Cairenn's friends were wide-eyed and wary of Art's presence, but tolerated her while gossiping. Art felt that were she on a leash, she might be Cairenn's spectral Russian dancing bear.

Art chased the boy when he wiggled out of her grasp. She gave Cairenn coins when asked. Cairenn treated herself to a few oysters from a stall, ate them on the spot, then bought milk, onions, day-old bread, potatoes, salt, tea, matches, two eel pies, and one dried fish.

Art had seen the small stove in Fiona's room. A precious possession, since it could warm the family in winter. But she knew that the poor could not afford to cook on their stoves, as wood, coal, and even paper stuff could be precious to obtain, so they ate from day to day. She suggested a bag of coal to Cairenn who looked skeptical and shook her head. Cairenn would know better what her family needed and how the coin should be spent, so Art relented.

"The children need clothes," Cairenn said. "They grow and grow. And I'll be sellin' 'er husband's."

"My next visit, I'll take thee to the secondhand sellers," Art said.

"We must sell 'is pole ax too," Cairenn said, her tone matter-of-fact.

On the walk home, Cairenn told Art of her day, complained about her neighbors, her aches and pains, and gossiped about Mrs. So-and-So. It was while chasing the boy again that Art heard Cairenn casually mention a friend of Dennis Bell's, a fellow slaughter man whom Art had also injured, and how that friend had a desire to marry Fiona.

Art thought that proposal was too sudden, though Cairenn didn't seem to mind the situation. Fiona was a beauty, red-haired, green-eyed, freckled, pale of complexion, and generous of hip and bosom. Art could understand someone wanting to marry her right away, but Fiona was also deeply grieved by the loss of Dennis. This, Art knew too well.

Fiona came home from the match manufactory just as Cairenn had finished storing foodstuffs away. She and her mother laid a meal for the table. It was portions of pie, some onions, and milk. Fiona was still angry with Art. Art hoped she might not ever see another woman's eyes flash so. But she felt that she should be present for Fiona to put that anger upon, that inconsolable grief, so that it mayn't stay inside of Fiona, grown bigger and long-lasting with remembrance and bitterness. At least Art hoped her presence helped as such. Fiona glowered but sat down to dine with her mother and children. She did not ask Art to leave. After the family had their meal, Art played with the children more. She finally bid them farewell.

Fiona accompanied her downstairs and out the door. She stood before Art in the dark street and folded her arms.

"I feel everyone's sitting on me chest, speaking fer me mind or wantin' something of meself, and for Dennis I can't properly mourn," she said.

"Would thee like it if I not return?" Art softly asked.

"No. Come back. I don't know why." Fiona's eyes became

bright with tears but she scowled the fragility away. "Except for my li'l ones, yer all that's left of him. Even 'is friends won't let me remember, but you let me. And perhaps that's wot ghosts are for. I'll need you a li'l while longer. Now, give us a kiss, then be gone."

Art understood. They were not friends. But a touch of the lips on each other's cheek was a peace offering. After she kissed Fiona, Art stepped back and flew away.

It was night; Art saw people hurry in the dark below, but already many streets were empty and windows were lit and doors closed. Smoke from the factory stacks and home chimneys billowed and descended, rolling down the roads. It seemed the perfect time, she thought, for those of ill intent to emerge. She rose higher and flew in the direction of Spitalfields and its Metropolitan Free Hospital.

～

On the second floor of the Vesta, a sumptuous buffet was laid, laden with meat dishes. The two women from Canada chose tiny, stuffed pigeons wrapped in bacon from the silver serving platters and listened to Milly Sedgewick and the rich widow accompanying her talk about the families of London. In the room adjacent, a rowdy party of young men was in progress. Helene entered the Vesta's iris portal, not bothering to take off her long black coat and riding hat, and walked down the great hall for the stairs. One woman in male dress passed her and tipped her hat. Helene merely nodded. She met Alice at the foot of the staircase.

"Good evening," she said.

"Good evening, Lady Helene!" Alice said. "If you'll follow me."

"I'd like to see Art first," Helene said as she and Alice mounted the steps.

"Yes, My Lady! She's in the Rouge Room."

"That was Harold's old room. Has Art been comfortable?" Helene said.

"My Lady, she seems quite content, and she is a joy to have."

Helene briefly smiled.

At the second-floor landing, Catherine Moore stepped forwards, a page by her side. Helene thought it interesting how quickly Catherine had been alerted to her presence. After civilities, Catherine assured Helene that Art's every comfort was attended to. Thus informed, Helene parted from Catherine and continued with Alice to Art's room.

Alice knocked. No one answered. She opened the door. Art could not be seen. Alice looked about and also inside Jim's study.

"I'm sorry, Lady Helene," she said unhappily. "I believe she may've—"

"Flown out, yes," Helene said. She found the note on the table that was addressed to Jim. "Who is Fiona Bell?"

"Oh. I'm not entirely certain, as I did not hear of this directly from Art," Alice said.

"Give me the hearsay, then," Helene said as she put the note down. She saw the shiny, silver bullet on the dresser top and went over to touch it curiously. She found Art's list and read it.

"My Lady, while working on her first case, I understand Art accidentally killed a man. He was bewitched and pole-axed her," Alice said. "Fiona Bell is his widow."

Helene looked at Alice gravely.

"Well," Helene finally said. "Now I'm in proper spirits to see Manon."

꩜

When Helene and Alice had continued to the third floor, the page with Catherine Moore received instructions from her mistress, parted from her side, and ascended the stairs for the fourth floor. There she saw Oleg standing before a room.

He bent to hear her whispered information. Surprised at her words, he asked her to repeat them. When the page left, Oleg knocked and opened the door.

Both Arlette and Manon were nude. Manon was rolled over, asleep, while Arlette sat at the bed's edge, reading the evening paper. Oleg gestured for Arlette to come outside. She folded her paper and tucked it under a pillow. Once Arlette was in her dressing gown and in the hall, Oleg closed the door.

"Coming now is new client," he said quietly. "Is named 'Lady Helene Skycourt'."

"*Quoi?*" Arlette said.

"'Lady,'" Oleg said patiently. "Is niece to earl. She is here now."

"I know who she is!" Arlette said. "Oh, Manon will not like this. Lady Helene is whom we're meant to please by pleasing Art! Delay, while I go in and—"

They noticed Alice enter the hallway with Helene. Helene's walk was quick and firm. She was upon them before Arlette could do anything.

"Manon should be within, My Lady," Alice said when they'd stopped before the door.

"And not flown off, we hope?" Helene said. She looked at Arlette.

Arlette found Helene's scrutiny unsettling. Helene peered through the spectacles perched on her nose as if to find some minute flaw in Arlette's visage. Arlette raised a hand to her face.

"I would like to be alone with Manon," Helene then said with a smile. "If you don't mind."

"But of course, My Lady," Arlette said. "One moment, while I inform—"

"Tut," Helene said, firmly setting Arlette aside. "Let this be a surprise." She slipped in and closed the door behind her.

Oleg and Arlette stood helplessly in the hallway. Alice, her duty done, left the two by the door.

Arlette turned to Oleg and looked up at him.

"She will scold you, later," she accused.

⤛

Manon was nearly fast asleep when Arlette left the room. As night fell, so did Manon's energies. She and Arlette allotted a small break in their schedule so that she could obey the directive of the setting sun and sleep. She only needed a little rest, and when roused, could return refreshed to her work. There had been long periods of her life where she could not act upon such body-instinct. Only at the Vesta did she finally come to trust this time in bed.

When someone entered the room, Manon thought nothing of it until that someone sat beside her. She smelled gunpowder and oil.

Manon sprang awake and nearly hit the bedpost in her attempt to get away. A woman who looked exactly like Helia Skycourt sat at the foot.

"Be not alarmed, though it's too late for that," Helene said, holding her hands up. She rose slowly from the bed and stepped back. "I can see that my idea of jest was not terribly smart."

Manon stared at Helene, trying to discern her intent. She'd never seen Helia's twin before. Helene did not appear to harbour anything eldritch in her face as her sister did.

"Catherine does not allow weapons," Manon said, her voice less steady than she liked.

Helene sat down on the bed again.

"It's not for you, silly," she said gently. "It's for the bad things out there."

"You still entered here with it," Manon accused.

"I couldn't just hand it over to the footwomen," Helene said. "It's rather delicate. They might shoot themselves in the foot."

Manon said nothing, her breaths deep.

"What revealed it to you?" Helene asked curiously. "Scent, perhaps? You've quite a nose."

Manon's fear rose again. Helia must have told her sister of Manon's true nature.

"Oh, very well," Helene said. "I was wrong to come in here armed. But there's a menace afoot, and one that may be a direct threat to Art. Were she here for me to protect, I could justify my actions."

"Menace?" Manon said. "The cruel doctor?"

"Yes. A very apt description. Please relax. For my jest, I do apologise."

Manon looked sharply at her.

"I am capable of apology," Helene said, grinning. "Now, tell me. Are you an Apsara? A daughter of Ishtar? A succubus?"

"*Non*," Manon said, offended.

"Then, what are you?" Helene asked, her gaze searching.

Manon did not answer. As with Helia's bewitched mask, she could see the sheen of sorcery on Helene's lens.

"We are off to a bad start, aren't we?" Helene said ruefully. "I do have that unfortunate effect. Let's talk of business, then. You know who I am, don't you? I am not Helia. I, being the more respectable Skycourt, am here only so Art's own respectability may be preserved. Though I can't see how, when Milly Sedgewick is lurking about, ready to wag that loose tongue of hers. But this is Helia's mad idea, and I am only pleasing her. Therefore, in the story as woven by her mad mind, I am a rather lustful admirer of Art and am gifting my Convenient, which happens to be you, to her. And generously."

"Yet somehow," she continued. "I'm incapable of seducing Art myself. Helia has conveniently forgotten to give reason for my strange shortcoming. Perhaps I'm perverse, as I'm sure will be thought, and I like to secretly watch the two of you. But I would like to think that I am merely shy. I'd somehow conceived of the queer notion of distracting her with you, until I mustered the courage to show Art the painfully composed love poems I hope to give her. Would you say that's a good story?"

Manon smiled despite herself.

"Since I'm incapable of verse, this liaison between you two will be a time," Helene said drily. "And Catherine is happy to support the ruse. She is also quick to tell me that Art is content with this arrangement. But I must hear it from you. *Is* Art pleased . . . with this?"

Manon bit her lip.

"Art is not pleased?"

"*Non*," Manon said. "But we've yet to have pleasure with each other."

"Really?" Helene said. "Which was far more than I needed to know."

"She is content to leave matters to me," Manon said. "She has given me choice."

Helene looked at her in surprise.

"'Choice'," Helene repeated. "That is . . . very much like her."

"*Elle est un enfant*," Manon murmured.

"What?"

"Pure of heart."

Helene stared at her.

"*Très bien*," Helene said.

Manon waited, uncertain. Helene grinned.

"Do as she wishes," she bade.

Manon's heart beat rapidly. She was surprised that she could feel such elation, twice, in only the span of a day.

"I am your Convenient," Manon said.

Helene snorted. She opened her hands. "Yes, and here I am, *in flagrante delicto*. I should have thought to bring a book."

Manon sniffed and tossed her head.

Helene turned away, hands on hips. She looked about the room.

Manon reached beneath the pillows and pulled out Arlette's newspaper. She held it out for Helene.

"The evening paper? Good," Helene said. She took it, rose from the bed, and walked over to an armchair under the gaslights. She did not bother to take off her coat or hat. She sat in the chair, her movements precise, and began reading.

"You will not remove your false spectacles?" Manon said.

Helene looked at her. She took the spectacles off.

"Just for that, you will explain how you knew," Helene said.

"Tell me why you wear them, and carry weapons for bad things," Manon said.

Helene did not reply. Manon pulled the bedcovers up. Helene resumed reading the paper and Manon kept one eye open to watch her. As the pages rustled, Manon fell asleep.

CHAPTER FOURTEEN

Fog descended and clouded the streets of London. An old man hunched in his coat drove a delivery wagon down Commercial Street. Six passengers rode within.

Two large men in overcoats sat with their collars upturned and gazed threateningly at the two staring men across from them. A man with a scarred face sat next to the men in coats. The staring men were also large, but the man sitting with them was small, slim, and had one eye. He never blinked nor bothered to shut his eyelid over the black gap. His staring companions didn't blink either. One had a slack mouth and drooled slightly.

"What's wrong with 'im?" one of the men in overcoats muttered.

As if in response, the drooling man stood and lumbered forwards, arms out. He nearly fell on the man who spoke. With a curse, the man shoved the drooling man back.

The scarred man briefly laughed as the drooling man fell into his seat again.

"He is dying," the scarred man said. His accent was German.

The wagon turned down a street across from Spitalfields' Metropolitan Free Hospital and came to a halt. Fog cloaked them.

The two men shed their overcoats. Underneath, they wore policemen uniforms. They reached beneath their bench, retrieved their constable helmets, and strapped them to their chins. The men disembarked, walked through the fog to the lit hospital, and entered.

The wagon continued on. It circled the block, passed the hospital again, and turned for the small street behind the building. An eight-foot-tall iron fence edged the back of the hospital grounds and light shone through the windows of a few rooms. The wagon slowed to a stop.

The men sat, silent and still. The dark, clouded street was empty.

A long, black carriage emerged from the fog, drawn by two large horses. Electric batteries were mounted on the undercarriage. Light leaked from the edges of the curtained glass. The door had no markings. The carriage came to a halt on the opposite side of the street.

In the wagon, the man with one eye slowly turned his head to look at the carriage. He then turned his head to look at the scarred man across from him.

"Your Serene Highness," the scarred man said, nodding.

꙳

The prince sat in his brightly lit carriage, one eye pale blue and his other brown, and stared through the eye socket of the one-eyed man at the scarred man. His pinstriped trousers was neat, his coat brushed, and his walking stick of human vertebra was in his hands. His manservant, seated opposite him, carefully dropped his second blue eye into the glass jar mounted on the carriage wall. Electrical wires ran from the glass. The pale blue eye floated.

The prince gestured to his servant.

Between the two was a small table with a cloth-covered tray. The servant pulled back the cloth. Three dry human hearts lay in a white rectangular dish, hooked to electrical wires. They pulsed rhythmically.

The prince listened as the scarred man in the wagon across the street murmured orders to the two large men and nodded to himself.

He watched through the one-eyed man's eye socket as the scarred man approached. The prince made as if to stand, but remained seated.

꙳

The one-eyed man stood up. The scarred man tipped

a chloroform bottle into a cloth and stuffed the cloth into the one-eyed man's pocket. The one-eyed man jumped out of the wagon and went to the hospital fence. He climbed it. The scarred man followed and quickly threw a heavy blanket over the iron spikes. As the one-eyed man climbed over and landed on the other side, the two large men climbed the fence and followed. The scarred man removed the blanket and returned to the wagon.

Within the hospital, nurses were dimming lights in private rooms or in wards. The policeman guarding the entrance to the orthopaedics ward watched in boredom as two nurses rolled a cart by the beds. They stopped intermittently to administer medicine or aid. At the ward's other end, another bobby sat in a chair by Felly Pritt's closed door. The policeman guarding the entrance touched his helmet's brim and smiled when the nurses rolled their cart out and exited the ward.

He saw two policemen walk down the hall and pass the nurses. He looked at them curiously, recognising neither of them.

"'Ello!" one of the new bobbies said, raising a hand. "It's our turn now. Off with you!"

"I heard nothing about this," the policeman declared. "On whose orders?"

"Risk needs you, not us. That's all I know," the bobby said. "You'll have to report in to find out."

"Very well. Good night to you," the policeman said. He straightened his jacket and left.

"Good night," the bobby said. His companion moved into the ward and accosted the policeman seated at the door. The policeman didn't bother to question the new situation, but rose and also left. He nodded to the new bobby at the ward's entrance and continued down the hallway.

The bobby firmly shut both ward doors as his companion entered Felly Pritt's room. He stood in the hallway with his back to the doors and stared stoically down the corridor.

Roger Flannagan sat by Felly's bedside and read the script for their next play. Felly, under the influence of morphine, was deep asleep. She didn't stir when he touched her hand. Her palm was warm. There was a knock at the door.

The door opened. Roger looked up, expecting the return of Dr. Lau. Instead, a bobby entered and shut the door. Roger rose to greet him. The bobby grabbed his arm, raised a blackjack, and swiftly hit him.

The false bobby hit Roger two times before he crumpled to the floor. He hit him one more time for good measure and wiped the blood and hair off his blackjack onto the man's waistcoat. He stuffed him beneath the bed. The woman in the neck brace didn't awaken.

He went to the window, unlatched it, and pushed the shutters out.

The one-eyed man and his two companions climbed in. They shambled to surround the bed, the one-eyed man staring balefully from the foot at Felly. The bobby exited the room and shut the door. Outside, he took the chair, set it where he liked it by the door, sat down, and folded his arms.

In the carriage, the prince stared balefully through the one-eyed man's eye socket at Felly Pritt. He watched as his two thugs held down the sleeping woman. The prince slowly lowered his gaze and focused on Felly's throat, stiffly encased in a neck brace. His hands ran from the femur-head handle of his walking stick down to the cervical vertebra. He stopped at two cervical bones and pressed his palms to the bones' sides. Heat formed between his hands.

Felly's eyes flew open. Her neck felt red-hot. She saw the two thugs above her and realised she couldn't move. A one-eyed man stood at the foot of her bed, staring at her. The air seemed to quiver, like gas fumes rising. She felt fingers around her neck, their touch searing.

"Roger!" she cried.

She couldn't break the hold of the thugs. She thought her neck might be on fire. She smelled sulfur. The hot sensation stopped. She collapsed.

Despite the lingering heat, Felly felt that somehow, her neck was no longer broken.

She saw the one-eyed man approach. He tottered, sweat upon his brow. His body trembled. He reached into his pocket and removed a cloth.

When he neared the bed, Felly raised a foot and kicked him, hard.

~

The prince fell back into his carriage seat. He sat, trembling, his brown and blue eyes wide.

~

Art spiraled down through the chimney smoke of London for the roof of Spitalfields' Metropolitan Free Hospital. She ghosted down through the building until she reached a floor where two nurses were pushing a cart through a ward. The beds were filled with patients, some shivering. One who was strapped down appeared to be hallucinating. Art saw the bottles of gin on the cart. One nurse measured out a dose; it was a detoxification ward. She materialised and gently hailed the nurse.

"Friend," she said. "I am Art, of the Secret Commission. Where might a woman with a broken neck reside? 'Tis a large hospital."

The nurse screamed and threw up her hands. The second nurse fainted. Patients exclaimed in fright. Art swiftly winked out of view.

Hoping she hadn't caused the sick more injury or trauma, she decided to remain invisible. She descended through the floors until she reached the ground floor. She flew to the front lobby and solidified. She removed her Secret Commission badge from her breast and walked to the reception window where a nurse was arranging papers.

"Friend," she greeted. She held her badge before her. "I am Art, an agent of the Secret Commission. Where might a woman with a broken neck reside? 'Tis a large hospital."

After being given the directions, Art walked on and turned invisible once more. She flew down the corridors until she found the ward for broken bones. A bobby stood stoically before the shut doors. She flew through him. Inside, she slowed and saw the patients in plasters and suspended in traction devices. Some moaned fitfully. But as Art floated by, wondering which was Felly Pritt, she sensed a vague disquiet in the air. Something was causing disruption, yet Art could not tell what that disturbance was, and what exactly was being disturbed. The patients in their beds fretted, oblivious to the cause of their unease. Art saw the policeman seated by a closed door at the end of the ward. He rubbed the back of his neck, frowning. Art raised her stick and drifted through the door.

~

The thugs forced Felly to sit up. The one-eyed man brought the cloth up again. She tried to kick him, and he caught her foot. She felt her head being grabbed by the hair.

"*Help!*" she screamed.

She saw the one-eyed man knocked aside. He fell heavily to the floor and didn't move. Felly saw a glowing woman, as tall as herself and broad-shouldered. The ghost woman grabbed the thug nearest her. She brought her stick down upon the arms that held Felly fast.

She hit the thug again, his grip on Felly still unshakened. Felly struggled. She saw the ghost woman swing her stick around and strike the man on the opposite side of the bed. He swayed. The woman brought her stick up higher and whipped it down a third time on the thug in her grasp. His grip broke. She pushed him to fall back and pulled Felly from the bed, the other thug still holding on, and used her foot to shove him off.

Felly was surprised to feel the ghost woman's solid, warm hands.

"Thee is Felly Pritt?" she asked.

"I am!" Felly said.

"I am Art, of the Secret Commission," she said. "These men, I think they are bewitched. Thee must—"

Felly saw the thug nearest her drive his fist into the side of Art's face. He grabbed Art's head and attempted to twist. His fingers dug into her flesh. Felly stared in amazement as Art ghosted out of his grip. The ghost woman swung backwards and struck the thug, and then struck him again. He lumbered forwards and grabbed for Art's neck. Felly heard the bed creak and saw the second thug stand on it, ready to fall upon Art.

"Art!" Felly cried in warning.

Art tossed Felly her stick and ghosted out of the man trying to strangle her. She kicked him back. Felly brought the stick up, but before she could hit the man on the bed, Art grabbed him and heaved. Felly watched as he flew towards the door.

~

The false bobby outside the door heard the commotion. The ward's patients looked curiously in his direction. When the scuffling continued, the man rose from the chair. He took hold of the door handle.

~

Art saw the door break off its hinges and crash beneath the weight of the thug. A policeman lay collapsed under the door. Felly turned for the broken entrance and then looked back at Art, the walking stick in her hands.

"Yes, go!" Art said. "I'll—"

Art jerked to an abrupt halt when the other thug wrapped an arm around her throat and began to squeeze. With a cry, Felly swung the stick and struck the fellow on the head. Art ghosted out of his embrace and solidified. The thug lunged and choked her again. Felly brought the stick down.

"*Oh!* Sorry!" she said, hitting Art.

~

In the hospital kitchen, Dr. Lau finished his tea. He sat by the hearth on a little stool with a china cup and saucer given to him by the kitchen staff. The smell of stewed ox and potatoes filled the air. Nurses sat at the kitchen long table and chatted as they ate their evening meal. Earlier, he had seen the doctors in their coats and top hats depart the hospital for their homes, taverns, or clubs. Lau packed tobacco into his pipe's bowl and lit it. He swung the little tobacco pouch back into his pocket, rose, deposited his teacup and saucer in the scullery, and exited.

He passed the front lobby. It appeared empty. He saw no sick people sitting within. A nurse was gently ushering out visitors. Lau saw the policeman who had been stationed at Felly's door walk in his direction. They nodded to each other, and the bobby continued for the lobby exit.

When Lau reached the hallway that led into the orthopaedics ward, he saw that the doors were shut and a policeman, burly and tall, stood before it, arms folded. Lau walked up to him and removed the pipestem from his mouth.

"I am Dr. Lau," he said. "Miss Pritt's doctor."

"No one passes," the man said, his expression stony.

Lau stared up at the man. He smoked, pensive.

"Go on, now," the man said.

Lau turned around and walked back the way he came. He headed for the front lobby. Two people hurried by him, a young African man and a woman wearing a half-mask and an azure coat. Dr. Lau puffed thoughtfully on the pipestem between his lips and continued out.

~

"The orthopaedics ward is this way," Helia said in a low voice to Perseus as they passed an elderly Chinese gentleman. "I don't doubt after the attempted kidnap that Felly Pritt's room is guarded.

I might be refused my chance to speak to her, even if I use my credentials as a journalist. Therefore, Perseus, you must distract the bobbies while I slip in."

"Distract! Well, I could—I guess, oh, here we are," Perseus said as they rounded a corner and entered the hallway to the ward. A large, imposing bobby stood before the closed doors. He stared at Helia and Perseus coldly as they approached.

"Hello, there!" Perseus hailed heartily. He brought his arm up in greeting. "I'm looking for a ward, and I've no idea where it might be. Perhaps you can show me. I'm looking for the dysentery ward!" Helia continued walking and slipped past the bobby.

"No you don't," the man said, catching Helia just as she opened one of the doors. It swung open. "None are allowed."

"But is this the dysentery ward, sir?" Perseus said.

"Unhand me, I've a right to visit!" Helia said. She struggled in the man's grip as he attempted to pull her away from the entrance.

"Sir! You heard the miss!" Perseus said. "That's no way to treat a lady!" He stepped forwards.

Helia heard a loud crash, and saw a broken door lying on the floor at the ward's end. A man rose awkwardly from it and re-entered the room. A policeman lay still beneath the door.

Helia wiggled out of the bobby's grasp. She ran through the ward's entrance and for the room, passing the bewildered and awoken patients.

The bobby ran after her and caught her again. Perseus followed.

"Let go of—*Oh*," Helia said, as he flung her at Perseus. They both fell to the floor. The man stepped forwards, picked up Perseus by the front of his shirt, and punched him. Helia crawled away. The man attempted to stomp down on her hand.

"You brute! You're not a true bobby, are you!" she cried. She scrambled to her feet and kicked him hard, missing his gonads. Perseus punched him, trying to loosen the grip at his shirtfront. The man picked him up and threw him down the hallway and out the ward's door.

Perseus skidded across the hall floor and crashed into a laundry cart. It fell on him, burying him in bedding.

Helia picked up a medical tray. Supplies fell, clattering. She swung at the man and missed as he stepped back. He grabbed her again and forced her to drop it.

"*Oh!*" she said as he roughly picked her up by the waist and tucked her under an arm like luggage. She hammered her fists against him as he walked into the hallway and opened the laundry chute door in the wall. Perseus regained his feet and straightened his hat just as Helia was forced headfirst into the chute. She shrieked as she slid out of view.

"*Arr!*" Perseus cried as he rushed at the man and punched him repeatedly. The man hunched, grabbed him, and ran Perseus backwards. Perseus struck the wall with his back. The man pulled him away, swung him around, and ran him into the wall again. Perseus hit it face-first, his bowler falling off.

The man picked him up by the seat of his trousers and the scruff of his neck. He shoved Perseus headfirst down the laundry chute. As Perseus slid out of sight, the man picked up his bowler and threw it down after him.

~

While the man dusted his hands off, two nurses fearfully poked their heads into the hallway. He ignored them and walked back to the ward. A doctor appeared and called out to him, demanding an explanation for the disruption and hurried to accost the bobby. The man ignored him as well and entered the ward while the patients looked on in apprehension. They pulled up their sheets. The bobby shut both doors firmly behind him, took a chair, and jammed it beneath the door handles. The doctor pounded on the doors.

The man walked farther down the ward, hearing the fight inside the room. He quickly knelt to look at the state of his companion beneath the collapsed door.

~

The thug Art had thrown into the door merely rose and shambled back in. Felly met him and hit him repeatedly with Art's stick. She danced back as he continued to advance. Art ghosted out of the man trying to choke her. She grabbed him and swung him into the wall, which shuddered at the impact. She grabbed the other thug threatening Felly and threw him into the wall as well.

She took hold of both men by the back of their necks and turned them to face the wall. With a mighty heave, she brought them back. She shoved their heads into the wall's plaster, which exploded and crumbled.

The men struggled. Art held fast and leaned upon them, driving their heads in farther.

Felly raised her stick and cheered. Behind her, the one-eyed man rose from the floor.

He stood unsteadily, touching the bed, and slowly swung his gaze around. When he saw Art, he fixed his gaze and lowered his chin.

～✕～

In the carriage, the prince lowered his chin. He focused on Art's back and ran his hand slowly down his walking stick to the lumbar vertebrae. His fingers found the large bone he wanted. He took hold and pushed against it. His hand trembled with the effort. He twisted it out of alignment.

～✕～

Art felt searing pain shoot through her spine. She lost strength to her legs. She didn't see Dr. Lau climb through the window just as she clutched at her lower back and fell to her knees. The men tried to pull themselves out of the wall.

"Dr. Lau!" Felly cried.

Lau shoved the one-eyed man aside, the man falling violently to the floor once more. He lay inert, like a ragdoll. Lau jumped over the bed. He landed beside Art. He swung his long–stemmed pipe back. With his other hand he felt for the misaligned vertebrae, right through Art's corset. Art looked back in surprise.

POW!

He hit the bone directly with his pipe and struck the vertebrae two more times. It popped back into place. Art felt as if a knife blade had been slipped into her spine and left to stay there, but sensation returned to her feet and legs. With a cry, she rose, pulled the men out, and shoved their heads into the wall again. Plaster dust erupted from the new holes their heads made.

Art saw Lau move quickly for the broken doorway.

"Let us go, Felicity!" he called to Pritt. Then he halted.

The bobby who had turned Lau away stood outside with a fellow policeman. The other man was holding his head. They stared at Lau. Lau glanced back at Felly.

"They're not good men, are they? We're a match for 'em!" Felly said, brandishing her stick.

Art ghosted swiftly through the wall and appeared in the ward's side. She solidified. She was briefly surprised to see two policemen. She grabbed them and banged their heads together until they both slid to the floor, senseless.

"Come now, Friends!" she said to Lau and Felly.

Felly moved to obey. The one-eyed man stirred on the floor. He rose and lunged.

He grabbed her. Felly cried out and struggled. The man dragged her back to the window.

Lau hurried in. The one-eyed man lashed out with his foot and kicked him hard in the middle.

"Dr. Lau!" Felly said as he fell back.

Art rushed in as a ghost, passed through Lau, and solidified once she reached Felly and her captor. She grabbed the one-eyed man's hands and with effort, broke his grip on Felly. Felly wiggled out from between them and whacked the smaller man several times on the back. He gave no response, and Art felt that his strength, like the two men previously, did not lessen.

With a great heave, she shoved him back against the wall. She took him by the shirtfront and slid him up so that his feet dangled. She heard more plaster crumble as the men worked to free their heads from the other wall.

"*Run* now, Friend!" she said.

"Felicity, come!" Lau beckoned from the doorway.

Felly stepped forwards. The one-eyed man in Art's grip turned his head and stared at the back of Felly's encased neck.

～

The prince stared at her neck brace. He pushed on the topmost vertebrae of his cane with all his might and twisted it all the way around.

～

Felly's head jerked. There was a loud snap.

"*Méiyou!*" Lau cried and caught Felly as she pitched forwards. Art's stick fell from her hands and clattered to the floor.

Art looked at Felly and Lau, baffled. The man in her grip convulsed. She returned to look at him. His head lolled and his one eye blankly stared. She heard a sudden kicking against the other wall and turned around quickly. Both men were in spasms. Then they stopped, arms dangling.

Art put down the dead man and swiftly knelt by Lau. Felly Pritt lay in his arms, her surprised eyes sightless.

"Can . . . can thee mend her?" Art whispered.

"No," Lau said in a harsh voice. "He *cut* the nerves to the brain!"

Art looked about her, and at the men who hung with their heads in the wall. The room was silent except for her desperate breathing. She returned her attention to Felly.

She gently closed Felly's eyelids.

～

The black carriage rumbled down the street, followed by the wagon bearing the scarred man. The prince sat with his hands out and open, the crushed remains of three shriveled, dry hearts soiling his hands. The pieces lay scattered on the carriage floor. A burst eyeball was smeared beneath his heel. His manservant wiped the prince's hands clean with a moist cloth. Once cleansed, the prince put his hands down. The servant reached into the liquid of the glass container and fished out the blue eyeball.

He carefully inserted it into the prince's empty eye socket. With a fresh handkerchief, the servant patted the prince's forehead of sweat.

While his manservant cleaned up the carriage floor, the prince turned his attention to his walking stick and worked to set the vertebra back into their proper alignment again.

~

Art sat with Lau and Felly's body and heard doors being forcibly opened down the ward. She picked up her stick, rose, and saw that the policemen she'd subdued outside still lay unconscious. A doctor rushed into the room. Seeing the dead, he quickly went about to confirm that each person's condition was so. He found Roger Flannagan stuffed under the bed, alive but in a serious state. Art helped the doctor place the bludgeoned man on Felly's bed. Helia and Perseus, both bedraggled, appeared at the broken doorway.

Helia looked at Art. She touched Perseus on the shoulder and murmured to him. He nodded grimly and quickly took his leave. Dr. Lau moved Felly to lie in repose at the side of the room, her arms folded on her chest and sat cross-legged by the body. Art decided that, like Lau, she would simply remain where she was and wait for the police.

Helia did not come to her side, but she appeared to keep an eye on her even as nurses hurried in to help the doctor treat Felly's sweetheart. Art watched Helia in turn.

Helia soon faded into the background of the activity and wrote down her observations. Art watched her go to the open window and look out, peer at the inert men whose heads were shoved into the wall, use her foot to poke open the hands of the dead, one-eyed man, and then look soberly down at Felly's body. All the while, Lau remained silent and still, and Art did as well.

Finally, Art heard the heavy, swift steps of men and Risk's voice giving orders outside. He expressed surprise at seeing the two policemen—strangers to him—lying on the floor. He had them seized. When Risk entered the room, Art saw that Jim was with him.

"Art!" Jim said. But he said no more, and Art briefly wondered if her countenance reflected her sober state. Risk asked her for an account, and Art gravely gave it as Barkley and Helia wrote it down. When Art finished, Risk and Jim looked at the three dead men.

"These men," Jim said. "Such show of strength and lack of pain! I'm uncertain if 'mesmerized' was the condition. We'll need autopsies, Risk, and have your man Barkley observe the procedures if you've no time to. I wouldn't be surprised if something might be found inside them—or not inside of them."

"They're already beginning to stink," Risk said. He ordered Barkley to get the bodies to the hospital's mortuary, and swiftly.

Risk enquired with the hospital doctor about the condition of Felly's unconscious sweetheart. Roger Flannagan was in no state to be revived and give his account right then. Risk and Jim turned to Lau. He simply rose from beside Felly's body and walked out of the room. Risk, Jim, Helia, and Art followed.

Outside, Lau gave his version of events, including his witnessing of the black arts attack that injured Art. He explained the circumstances of Felly's fatal injury to the police and agents. Helia listened and scribbled silently in her notebook.

"The spine is the house to all nerves," Lau said. "Very important are the ones which go into our brain, here." He pointed to the back of his neck, at the base of his skull. "From here, we are alive. We recognise the world, we know to breathe, we know to move, we make our heart work." He brought his hand around to point to his eyes. "He watched from somewhere. He used his faraway hands to touch the neck and *cut* the nerves to Felicity's brain."

"Which caused her to die, right on the spot," Risk said grimly. "Doctor, do you know how he did the watching and touching?"

"No," Lau said. "I cannot do it. Therefore, I don't know how."

"Thank you, doctor," Risk said.

Lau bowed. They heard plaster fall as Risk's men removed the men stuck in the wall. The policemen exclaimed, and the foul stench of decay reached the noses of those who stood outside.

Risk quickly rejoined his men, taking Jim with him. Lau looked up at Art.

"You will hurt, very much," he said. "But nothing permanent was done."

"Thank you, Friend," Art said. "I am Art."

"I am Dr. Lau," he said. He looked at Felly, still lying inside the room. He turned quickly away. Art watched as he walked down the ward and exited.

"Art!" Jim called. When she looked, Barkley held Jim aloft. She heard more exclamations as plaster fell inside the room.

"Just a word, Art!" Jim said.

Art glanced at Helia.

"I'll be here, Art," she said.

Art reentered the room. Two policemen picked up Felly's long and lanky body. They carried her out. The bed with Felly's unconscious sweetheart was being rolled out as well. When Art glanced to where the two men had been shoved into the wall, she saw that their bodies' decay had worsened. One man's head had started to tear off. The stench was overpowering. A bobby rushed to the room's waste bucket and vomited.

"Art," Jim said quietly. "I did learn more about our man. We've a time and place for his demonstration. It will be tomorrow."

Art looked at him.

"We'll get him, Art, don't you worry. Felly Pritt will be his last victim," he said.

"Aye, Friend," Art said. "My thanks. Please excuse myself. The one-eyed man is turning green."

"Yes. Odd, that," Jim said.

She turned and walked back out.

Helia came to her side. Art walked slowly away from Felly Pritt's room, leaning on her stick.

"Are you hurting, Art?" Helia asked softly as she walked beside her.

"Aye," Art said. "But my back will heal."

The tap of her walking stick echoed in the ward. The police were interviewing patients in their beds. Those who weren't preoccupied by the police watched the two as they exited.

"Thee sent Perseus away," Art said.

"Yes, Art. He brought me here in his buggy. And he tried to help me enter the ward when that false policeman was guarding it. I felt that Perseus shouldn't have to trouble himself with the police. It's bad enough he was tossed into a laundry chute along with me."

Helia touched the closed chute in question as they passed.

"Thee, in a chute? Is thee hurting?" Art said, stopping to look at Helia.

"No more than I usually do," Helia said. She looked up at Art, her gaze searching. Art looked away.

"Art," Helia said.

"I was told . . . that there is a place and time confirmed," Art said. "For the Bone Stealer's demonstration."

Helia gazed at her in surprise.

"Can you tell me, Art?" Helia said.

Art looked at her. "Thee is safer not knowing. And 'tis police work, a knowledge in confidence."

"I . . . yes, Art," Helia said, looking down.

"Had I known," Art said. She gripped her stick. "Had I been smarter, I would have let them take her, followed them whilst invisible to the surgery location. She would still be alive."

"Art," Helia said. She touched Art's hand. "Your heart would not have let you do that, nor would Felly have wanted it. You had described to Risk how she had helped in this fight. She also fought during her first kidnap. If taken this time, she would have surely endangered herself, due to such valiant spirit."

"He killed her from behind," Art whispered. "'Twas spite."

Helia slipped an arm through Art's and held it.

They were still arm in arm when Risk brought Jim to Art. She accepted Jim and bade the inspector farewell. With Helia by her side, Art walked out of the hospital and into the cool and foggy night. Perseus sat patiently in his electric buggy.

"Oh!" Jim said upon seeing the odd vehicle. Art waited for him to say more, but he didn't.

Perseus disembarked, and Art saw his bruised face. After introducing Jim to Perseus and expressing her concern for his injuries, she declined his invitation for a ride back to the Vesta.

"Were I to sit now, my back may protest the action," she said. "And Helia must be taken back to Westminster."

"Art, I intend to return to Helene's tonight," Helia said. "But we understand. Your injury needn't the jostling of a buggy."

"I am sorry about Miss Pritt, Art," Perseus said.

"My thanks, Perseus," Art said. She turned to look at Helia.

"I love thee," Art said.

Helia blinked. Her eyes darted madly, as if seeking the spaces where Art wasn't. Art thought Helia both euphoric and devastated, all at once.

"Have I expressed my affections for thee too soon?" she asked softly.

Helia shook her head rapidly. "I am only . . . overwhelmed. By the antics of my heart. For the measure of your affection, in so short a time, may not be the measure of mine," she whispered.

"Aye. I may say I love thee for thy companionship, dear to my need for friendship. And I may say I love thee for thy generosity and precious understanding. But my love can only grow. Thee wrote me thy declaration. Tonight, a woman died while her own sweetheart lay, unknowing. Important things cannot be said too soon," Art said.

Helia nodded, her eyes bright and wet. Art took a breath, her chest expanding. She had the sudden need to kiss Helia, and she thought that wish insensitive in its selfishness. An act of desire or even mere affection for Art would be a heartfelt intimacy for Helia, like prongs sent into the organ itself.

"I will see thee again. Be safe," Art finally said. "Thee must go!"

Helia quickly boarded the buggy. The gas lamps of the vehicle hazily lit the foggy dark. Perseus released the brake, stepped on the accelerator, and leaned on the tiller. The buggy jumped into motion and sped silently away.

"My," Jim simply said as they watched it disappear into the fog.

"I know thee wanted to enquire more," Art said. "'Tis an

impressive vehicle."

"Oh, I can express curiosity of such funny carriages another time. Art, you all right?" he asked softly.

"Running will clear the heart of sorrow," she said. "And of frustrations."

"Run then, my dear spectre!" Jim said. "Run, thou mighty Clydesdale!"

She hefted her stick and ran.

∽

At the Vesta, Helene fished out her small silver pocket watch, the cover engraved with an ancient Greek huntswoman scene. A hind bounded from a woman with bow and arrows in a moonlit grove. She popped the cover open and looked at her watch's crystal face. The inscription on the inside of the cover read: *Artemis Not Lost But Gone Before.*

Tiny onyx stones marked each quarter hour. After viewing the time, Helene clicked the watch closed. She took out her bewitched spectacles, unfolded them, and put them on.

Helene set the paper aside. She rose, went to sit on the bed again, and looked at Manon.

"I waken when kissed," Manon said, her eyes closed.

"You'll have to wait for another bestower. I'm usually the recipient," Helene said. "I must leave. Since no one has come to tell us otherwise, Art must still be away. I would like you to do something for me."

Manon opened her eyes and gave Helene her attention.

"I know she granted you free will in this, but if I might make a suggestion," Helene said. "Especially if it will keep her at the Vesta when she returns, and not larking about."

"You would like me to go to her room?" Manon said.

"Yes. And make her stay there, please. Until we all learn more about this Bone Stealer business, which will probably be by the morning. I will speak to Catherine about this arrangement."

"I am unaware of other plans for the night," Manon said.

"Excellent. And your extravagantly priced menu of services,

as explained to me by Catherine, are all to be made available."

"It is my understanding," Manon said.

Helene then looked at her, puzzled.

"However did you conceive of putting a price on kisses?" she said. "Women kiss all the time. It's absurd."

Manon sat up. "It is not absurd. Kisses, *elles sont importantes*. Matters of the heart. The kiss of friends is different from the kiss of intimacy. I will not have them made—how do you say—'trite'. Intimate kisses have no part in my profession."

"*Je suis d'accord*," Helene said.

"But if I choose to give them, they are free," Manon said.

"And if I had kissed you awake, even on the cheek?" Helene asked in curiosity.

"You, I would have billed."

Helene laughed. She rose from the bed and went to the door.

"Good night," Helene said, grinning. She opened the door and left.

～

Manon fell back on the bed and sighed. She covered her eyes. She recalled the many kisses she had taken when attacking Art.

Oleg opened the door and poked his head in curiously. Manon ignored him.

Matters of the heart, she thought ruefully.

Manon left the fourth floor, wrapped in her dressing gown, and went with Oleg to Art's room. She was certain that Catherine would approve of the arrangement. Catherine would profit more from Manon spending time exclusively with Art (or Helene), than performing with Arlette for any peeping or touching clients. She had her supper of fruit and flowers sent to her while she waited, and ate them on Art's bed. Arlette visited and brought Manon her drawstring sewing bag. Manon pulled out her embroidery frame, a needle from the pincushion sewn to the bottom of the bag, and a shimmering, blue silk thread.

"May I have Oleg with me, since you are here?" Arlette asked.

"*Non*, but once Art comes, then you and he can be alone,"

Manon said. "You are taking this time to read your many books, *oui?* That Russian one, with the woman."

"*Anna Karenina,*" Arlette sighed. "It is difficult *en russe,* but so very good."

"It will end badly," Manon muttered. She held her frame and stitched a blue violet into the linen handkerchief she was working on.

"Don't tell me the story's end, and how do you know, you don't even read!" Arlette said.

"It is a story *avec les aristocrates,*" Manon said. "No one may survive them."

"Ah! Ingrate! And after the generosity of Monsieur Blanc! We would not be here and under good contract if not for your rich master!"

Arlette left in a huff. Manon continued to stitch. Arlette was mistaken. Manon's old master had been a very rich man, friend to Catherine and her husband. But he had no title. Arlette, who had grown up among the Parisian poor, sometimes forgot that "rich" and "noble" were not the same. The nobility were, by blood, superior.

In Manon's long life, she had been a peasant, a kept woman, servant, and lone creature, and her attempts to live freely in forests—on soil somehow always possessed by remote, powerful humans—had been brief or disastrous. The nobility were what they were: an oblivious, privileged society who inexplicably owned everything and were immune to the concerns of those inferior.

She felt Art's and Jim's presences enter the Vesta. Manon breathed deeply and stitched more, intent on finishing the violet. Rather than disrobe right then and lie upon the bed provocatively, she assumed that Art would not mind her embroidering instead.

She heard Jim, Art, and Oleg speak outside the door. Then Art ghosted in. Manon smiled at Art's smile of greeting. Art floated by Manon for her dresser and materialised.

"Thee is well?" Art asked as she set aside her stick. She raised her hands for her hat, but Manon saw the slight grimace she made.

"*Oui,*" Manon said. "I am here for your company. Is it

agreeable?"

"'Tis," Art said. "This night is one that must be laid down."

Manon looked at Art in puzzlement. Her sober demeanor seemed in contrast to what sounded like a vague request for sexual intercourse.

"*Parle-tu 'qua qua'?*" she asked.

"*Oui,*" Art said, smiling. "'Tis 'duck' speech. I only mean, this night's happenings need putting to rest."

She slowly pulled off her gloves and unhooked her bodice. Manon placed her embroidery in her bag and rose. She stood before Art, her dressing gown untied, and undid each of the fastenings of Art's bodice.

"My thanks," Art sighed.

"Where do you hurt?" Manon asked. She helped Art out of her bodice and unfastened the skirt as Art explained the nature of the injury, and how she loss temporary use of her legs.

"*Le mal sorcier,*" Manon said darkly. She released the lacing of Art's corset. Art exhaled audibly. Manon lightly touched the lower back, discerning the injury, and loosened the lacing more. She helped Art with removal of her corset, boots, stockings, and petticoats.

"I ran to the Vesta to ease my heart and try my legs. In so doing, I've worsened this injury," Art admitted ruefully.

"This part of the back. Such hurt would also affect the penis," Manon said.

"'Twould?"

"*Oui*, it is from there that sexual organs work."

"I've looked, I've no male organ," Art said.

"Not even a very little one? No matter, I will discover the size of your pleasure later."

"Oh," Art said.

"It is easier to show than to explain," Manon reassured. She removed the last of Art's petticoats and knelt to pick up the fallen ones.

"Sight of thee does make me forget such discomfort," Art said. She wore a silly smile as she looked down at Manon, who rose with Art's petticoats in hand. Her opened dressing gown revealed her breasts and belly.

"Ah, *bon*. A client tonight was unaffected by my gifts," Manon said. "And I was wearing nothing. I thought it time to retire from this profession."

"'Twas a blind client?" Art said. Manon laughed.

She helped Art remove her chemise, which was the most difficult for Art in her condition, as it had to be pulled over her head. Once Art was nude, she placed her clothing on a chair. Manon admired the defined musculature of Art's back and legs. Art, she noted, had very long legs.

"*Tu es belle*," she said.

"My thanks," Art murmured demurely.

Manon looked at the ugly swell that was the injured area. She thought of a treatment. She left Art to go down to the kitchen and prepare a remedy.

When she returned, Art was lying facedown on her bed, just as Manon had earlier bidden her do. Manon carried a small iron pot filled with fragrant ginger slices, lightly roasted until warm in the kitchen's gas oven. She set the pot on Art's stove and retrieved a few pieces before testing their heat by placing them on her arm. She climbed on to the bed and laid the slices in a row on top of Art's injury.

"You will feel very warm there, *oui*?" Manon said. "*Le gimgebre*, it is fiery. These will draw away the bad in the wound, and bring healing."

"Oh yes," Art said, her eyes closed. "The heat, 'tis a wonderful sensation."

Manon lightly pressed the slices down and noted how they took on Art's spectral glow and paleness. The injured area, however, retained a darker colour, evidence of bruising. When the slices cooled, Manon went to the little pot on the stove and retrieved more. She continued to reapply the ginger poultice even as Art's bruising faded. Since it was an injury to the bone, Manon knew the ginger's fire needed its time to sink deeply.

"How was thy day?" Art murmured. "Besides business with

a blind client."

"As it always is. Except for attacking you." Manon fussed with the ginger. "I am sorry."

"'Twas no trouble."

"I flew at you because I was afraid," Manon whispered.

"Aye, thee was," Art said sleepily. "And angry." She yawned. "Thee did not try to beguile me, this night. Or has thee?"

"*Non*," Manon said thoughtfully.

Art fell asleep. Manon heated more ginger slices, applied them to Art's back, and pulled out her embroidery. She stitched until she thought Arlette and Oleg had been alone for a sufficient amount of time. Dawn was a few hours away. She ate all the ginger slices, picked up the pot, and departed.

But as she descended for the kitchen, Helene's words repeated in her mind. She should sleep by Art's side, she realised, making certain Art did not leave until Jim was roused in the morning. Yet Manon was reluctant to spend that time with Art; it would be a time shared without having to perform or give pleasure. As with her rule about kisses, Manon never remained in bed with anyone except Arlette, once duty was done.

"But this too, this . . . sleeping! It is our work!" she said to herself. She imagined Arlette saying so to her, with greater severity.

After depositing the pot in the scullery, Manon returned upstairs. She re-entered Art's room. Art still lay on her stomach, fast asleep. Manon disrobed and sat on the bed again. She took out the blue silk thread from her sewing bag and snipped a long length. She tied one end to Art's left ankle, the other to her own left ankle, and then pulled the sheet and coverlet up and covered them both.

She listened to Art's deep breaths and eventually slept.

CHAPTER FIFTEEN

Art woke in the darkness before daybreak and felt no pain. She saw Manon asleep beside her. Art pushed up and moved to slip out of the bed. Her left foot came to a jerking halt.

"Oh!" Manon said, her foot tangling with Art's. "Do not move! We are tied together."

When Manon drew back the covers, Art saw that it was so. Manon pulled the tie on the shimmering, blue embroidery thread around Art's ankle and released her.

"Ha ha. 'Tis a funny thing," Art said.

"I was told not to let you leave," Manon said, lying back down.

"By Helia?" Art asked curiously.

"*Bon.* But it was Lady Helene. You have discovered who pays for me," Manon said.

"Aye. 'Tis a strange generosity."

Art remained on her stomach and elbows and thought of Helia.

"Is it still agreeable?" Manon asked. "This arrangement?"

"Were I decorous, I would end this. Yet . . . 'tisn't the answer. Somehow, I need thee to learn Helia more," Art said in bafflement.

"And learn Lady Helene?"

Art looked at Manon in surprise. "*Oui,* thee speaks my mind.

Helene as well. For thee is playing her Convenient?"

Manon made a derisive sound. "'Playing', *oui*."

"A ghost, my human self, stands between myself and them," Art said thoughtfully. "I am newly returned, and therefore precious like a newborn. Yet, I wish to pursue, and in ignorance may cause damage and consequence. How may I engage them, learn those two anew, and they, my new self? Perhaps I can do so with thee. In this matter, thee is my *liaison*," Art said in realisation.

"I can be that," Manon said. "And we may have pleasure too?"

"Well," Art said, blushing.

Art looked at Manon as another understanding formed.

"Helia peeps," Art whispered in a conspiratorial tone.

Manon smiled.

"I will exercise!" Art said. She hopped off the bed.

~

Manon watched as Art left the bed and while still nude, flung herself face-first down upon the floor. Manon moved down the bed and lay on her belly to watch. Art tossed her long hair aside. She lay prone, nose to the floor, feet upon toes, hands flat beside her shoulders, and elbows bent. She raised herself by straightening her arms, her body rigid. She then lowered herself by her arms and repeated the process.

Art's back seemed entirely healed, Manon observed. As Art moved up and down, Manon admired the shape of her buttocks.

"Oleg also exercises in this manner," Manon said. "Would you like me to sit on your back?"

"Oh! 'twould help," Art said. She lowered herself again.

Manon rose and did not bother with donning her dressing gown. She seated herself between Art's shoulders and faced Art's feet. She held on to Art and with bent knees placed her own feet on Art's buttocks.

Art uttered something incoherent but continued with her exercise.

Manon stifled a yawn and watched the room go up and

down as Art steadily raised and lowered herself. She wondered how strong Art was, for Monsieur Harold was known to lift the Vesta's banquet table with twelve men standing upon it, much to Catherine's dismay.

After Art had long surpassed Oleg's own stamina, albeit with both Arlette and Manon standing upon him, Manon began idly tracing a toe along one of Art's buttocks.

Art made a sound. When Manon began tracing her other buttock, she bucked.

"Thee may dismount, now," Art said raggedly. "I will change to another exercise."

Manon smiled ruefully. She resumed her previous position on the bed. She supported her head on her hand. Art crouched, placed her hands on the floor, and with her knees against her elbows, slowly rolled forwards and raised her legs into the air.

"Ah, the handstand," Manon said.

"Aye," Art said. "My first since—whoop!"

She fell, rolled on the floor, then returned to a crouch and tried again.

"This feat of strongmen, Oleg can also perform. And walk on his hands. For Arlette, he tried to walk up the stairs. He is a wrestler too, not just a strongman," Manon said. "He is flexible." She bit her thumb as she smiled at a recollection.

"Oh! Stairs, 'twould be hard!" Art said as she slowly rolled her legs up again. "I will try a walk, but I wish to lift."

Manon watched as Art did just that. Once she had her legs up in the air, she bent her arms and lowered herself down until her nose nearly touched the floor. She raised herself up again, straightening her arms. She continued the exercise, her legs wobbling for balance. When she seemed about to fall, she stopped and walked about on her hands until she was steady enough to resume.

Manon ran her gaze up and down Art's body as Art maintained her balance and continued with her exercise. Manon hung her head.

"*Quel dommage*," she said in regret. "I am so tired."

"I am keeping thee awake," Art said. "Please return to sleep."

"Sleep is not what I want," Manon said. She looked up again and admired the way Art's heavy breasts swayed as she raised then lowered herself once more.

"Such breasts," Manon said. "Oleg's penis also sways so."

Art fell on her head.

~

When Art was upright again and seated on the floor, she looked at Manon, who was propped on her elbows, her head resting on a hand. Perhaps it should have occurred to Art that Manon, Oleg, and Arlette were in an aberrant relationship, but it had not been apparent until Manon mentioned Oleg's sexual organ.

"Is thee in 'free love' with Oleg and Arlette?" Art asked.

"'Free love'?" Manon said.

"'Free love'," Art repeated. "'Tis a movement of radical individualism, discarding the social control of marriage and having love and sexual intercourse a matter of free choice. And it advocates women's pleasure." She thought a moment. "My, what I remember. Perhaps 'tis through study I know these things. To know my beliefs, I should know those of others. And perhaps, as a sapphist, I needed to know. 'Free love' comes from the anarchy movement."

"Such ideals," Manon said. "I do not want Arlette to start reading about anarchy."

"But thee is in such life-companionship?" Art asked.

"One with many lovers? That is not easy to do," Manon said. "It is difficult work, or else everyone would do so. In matters of love, humans are too possessive. Oleg, Arlette, and I are together, how do you say, making a household. And the companionship is made easier because I am a creature."

Art looked at her in wonderment.

"You will learn more with your human women," Manon said. "It will be confusing, *oui*?"

Manon leaned on her hand and sighed, her mood resigned.

"But better you should learn, now," she said. "The conventions of mortals do not matter if you wish to love more than one. Death comes too soon for them."

Art nodded solemnly. She thought of Felly Pritt.

Manon yawned again, but instead of lying down as Art expected her to, she suddenly raised herself on her arms and stared at the curtains. The dawning sun was brightening the thick fabric. Sunlight peeped, and Art thought Manon's eyes grew bright and pale.

Manon's lips parted and she unleashed a sound. Art felt as if flowers burst from buds inside her, that leaves unfurled and plants rose, yearning for the sun. Art reached up to touch the warmth.

The sensation faded and the flowers disappeared. Art sat with a hand outstretched and saw Manon's eyes shutting.

"Your day begins, and I must rest," Manon said.

She slowly rose. Art did as well. She watched Manon don her dressing gown and pick up her sewing bag.

"You will stay, and not leave?" Manon said.

"Aye, I will stay," Art said.

She looked down and saw the blue embroidery thread, still tied around Manon's ankle. Art knelt and took Manon's foot. She pulled the thread loose.

"You may keep it," Manon said with a smile when Art attempted to hand it to her. She laid her hand over hers.

Art looked at her. Manon's smile faded. Art saw no beguilement in Manon's eyes but a rapid succession of emotions: curiosity, fear, doubt, fondness. Art nearly said aloud: *I see thee, as thee art.*

Manon took Art's face in her hands and kissed her. Then she quickly left.

Art carefully wound and tied the blue silk thread and laid it atop Helia's card. A maid gently knocked and entered, carrying new clothes. As they greeted each other, Art saw the dresses. One was in Montebello garnet with a lighter trim, and another was of chartreuse yellow, pinstriped with black.

Art was slightly appalled at the stripes. Perhaps Charlotte had forgotten her request for no stripes, though they only appeared — as revealed when the maid hung the dress — on the bodice front, skirt front, and in gathered material in the back. Art knew she could no longer make a pretense for plain dress, but she still liked simplicity in her worldly clothing.

"Miss, shall I help you dress?" the maid said. She quickly laid down the rest of the new clothing — undergarments, stockings, and a dressing gown — upon the bed.

"Oh! I've a dressing gown! But I will dress. My thanks," Art said. She selected the chartreuse yellow. As the maid brought it to her, Art hoped her spectral aura might bleach out the stripes.

Booted, laced, dressed, hair done, and her Secret Commission badge back on her breast, Art felt physically fit and no longer suffering the effects of last night's injury. Looking in the mirror, she saw that the pinstripes were of the same spectral tone as the rest of her dress. The maid drew back the curtains, put away the rest of the new clothing, made up the bed — though Art tried to help — and left. A page arrived and rolled in Art's first meal for the day. After she set it on the table and departed, Art sat down. She gave silent thanks and removed the lid of the dish before her. A bundle of blue violets lay on the plate.

Art felt her heart beat fast.

She picked up the flowers, touching the petals to her lips. She closed her eyes at the fragrance.

"Aye, I will know thee," she said. She ate them.

There was another knock on the door. Delphia poked her blonde head in. Art saw with surprise and delight that she wore a boy's coat and lady's top hat. She tipped her hat to Art.

～

In the room above the Society of Friends' meeting place, Helene watched the light of the dawning sun slowly brighten. She sat cross-legged and barefoot in a yogi position. She was dressed in a short-sleeved Indian bodice, a sari wrapped around her waist and tucked between her legs *kaccha nivi* style, forming pantalettes. Her breath misted in the early morning air. Helia snored on the small bed, buried under blankets. Her half-mask was tossed on the floor. Another of Helia's portable typewriters sat at Helene's desk, folded closed and surrounded by balls of paper.

Through the thick glass of her window, Helene saw a rolled newspaper hover into view, held aloft by a wooden staff it was wrapped around.

Helene smiled and shook her head. She rose, unhooked the window, and swung it open. She saw Ganju below, grinning and holding the staff. Helene untied the paper and saluted him. She carefully shut the window and latched it again.

"Be as wolves, take their throats!" Helia said savagely and shook herself awake. She sat up and put a hand to her head. Her hair was in disarray. She was dressed only in her chemise and stockings.

Helene grabbed her spectacles from her desk, put them on, and came to kneel by Helia.

"Oh. Good morning," Helia said, rubbing her eyes.

"Good morning," Helene said softly. She stared at the side of Helia's face that had its spidery pattern of light, white scars. With her bewitched lens, she saw the black thing that lived inside Helia's flesh. It drew back its tendrils, folded in upon itself, and glowered.

Helia tutted, bent, and searched about the floor for her mask. Helene found it and handed it to her.

"My story, is it printed? My teeth are dirty! Have you *miswak* for it?" Helia said crossly as she put the mask on.

"I'm sure your story is printed and reads well," Helene soothed. She opened a hidden cubbyhole above the bed, put her hand in, and retrieved a twig. She presented it to Helia.

"There. Is this not considerate of me? I've given you a fresh one," Helene said.

Helia took the Indian chewing stick, gnawed on the end, picked off the bark broken by her bite, and chewed a little on the exposed white wood. Bristles formed from the wood fiber, and she began cleaning her teeth.

"Deadlines, deadlines. I wished I'd gone back to the Vesta with her!" Helia whispered fretfully around the stick.

"Hush, no regrets, now. But to this surgery demonstration tonight, that the police know about," Helene said, unrolling the paper. She saw the note Ganju had wrapped with the newspaper. It read: *Barkley knows nothing.*

"Art told me nothing," Helia said, eyes downcast as she moved the twig about in her mouth.

"I think she just didn't know, dear. Ganju's sergeant friend has no information, either." Helene sighed and folded the paper. "Risk is being exceedingly protective. I'm tempted to seek out that awful Milly Sedgewick at this point."

"Where is our very tall, stricken girl? Yes, where is she?" Helia said. "Tucked in a hidden wing. Locked inside a private sanitarium. Seen to by foreign doctors in strictest confidence. One day is not enough to break that silence. And such a confidence, if betrayed, should mean death. Milly is not stupid."

Helia pointed her chew twig, its wet bristles wildly bushy.

"And you're not supposed to talk to anyone, Countess Skycourt," she said. "Not even a cat."

"I more prefer dogs, and stop calling me that," Helene said. "Auntie *is* still alive. What do you intend next?"

"I shall speak to Arthur Fellows," Helia said. "Right away. He is invited. He must know this demonstration's whereabouts by now, and if not, I'll remind him that he's meant to tell me."

"Let Arthur eat his breakfast first," Helene said. "And I'll have Ellie escort you into the Black Market. Now." She rose and removed her spectacles. "Come and perform a Sun Salutation with me before the sun becomes any older."

"I wonder what Art is doing," Helia said, tossing her twig aside. She swung her legs out of the little bed and stood. Helene was already standing and facing the windows, her palms together in a position of prayer.

"Oh, it's a silly supposition, but she might be enjoying something," Helene murmured. "Like food, perhaps?"

"If it's Manon, I wish I'd been there to see," Helia complained. She put her palms together.

Helene turned red and grunted.

"Sun!" Helia cried. In unison, they stretched their prayer hands above their heads and arched back, beginning the yoga exercise.

Delphia arrived by omnibus near the Vesta's Whitechapel location. She ran down the steps from the rooftop seats to hop off at her stop. Once she reached the club, she heeded Elsepeth's advice and sought its back entrance. The alley, at the break of dawn, was already alive with activity. Amid steam rising from basement grates, a driver and his hackney carriage waited patiently, a woman and her children peeled potatoes around a basket, a man unloaded a crate of live pigeons from a delivery cart, and an older woman hurried past Delphia, carrying a basketful of flowers. The woman entered the scullery of the Vesta. Delphia followed.

Scullery maids were washing, stacking, and drying dishes, while another unloaded a dumbwaiter and walked the dirty chinaware and utensils to the sink. Delphia passed the pantry where a cook's assistant was storing flour sacks, and then passed the steel doors of the icebox, which an iceman was neatly loading with blocks of ice. In the large, bustling, hot kitchen, the cook—a chubby short fellow with rosy cheeks, small hands, and a penchant for skipping about—milled with his assistants.

Delphia thought of the celebrated English cook, Robert May, who wrote *The Accomplisht Cook* and of the French court chefs who refined their country's cuisine and were of influence in the great hotels of England. She wondered if this man was a chef as well, trained in France. One of the kitchen assistants addressed him and called him "'Cook". Delphia nodded to herself and waited patiently until she could make introductions. Breakfast of broiled fish, toast, potatoes, sausage, ham, eggs, bacon, and jars of jam and marmalade were being laid on silver trays. She watched as an assistant whisked two of the trays away for a second dumbwaiter. With a whistling jet of steam, the dumbwaiter quickly ascended. When she returned her attention to Cook, he was speaking with Manon.

Manon was barefoot with hair down, and wrapped only in a dressing gown. She carried an ivory-coloured, silk drawstring sewing bag, intricately embroidered with the leaves and stalks of wildflowers. Delphia had never seen such needlework. The level of skill and time spent spoke of aristocratic indulgence.

Manon turned, saw Delphia, and stared in curiosity. Delphia raised her hat. Manon gave a small smile, picked up the edge of her dressing gown, and departed. Cook noticed Delphia and waved her to come forwards. He quickly arranged freshly washed blue violets on a plate, placed it on a silver tray, and covered it. An assistant promptly fetched the tray and sailed past Delphia for the dumbwaiter.

After introductions and a welcoming grasp of hands with Cook, Delphia joined a footwoman reading the paper and a maid polishing silverware, at the servants' dining table. She was served a cup of tea with toast, a boiled egg, and a plate of sausage, ham, potatoes, and bacon. She could not believe her good fortune when she saw the slice of ham. She nearly refused it, thinking it too extravagant.

Breakfast done, Delphia made her way up the back stairs for the gentry's area of the Vesta. Maids in white caps, aprons, and black blouses descended en masse, their buckets, cloths, and other cleaning tools in hand. They had just finished the early morning polishing, sweeping, watering of plants, cleaning of grates, and dusting.

Delphia was about to exit the servant stairs at the second floor when she saw Alice come down with an armload of clothing from the third. At the landing they greeted each other. A few items slipped out of Alice's grasp and Delphia bent and helpfully picked up a soiled male garment. Then she realised how it was soiled.

She gingerly handed the item back to Alice, and after a few

cheerful refusals from Alice for her help, followed the page to the Vesta's laundry room in the basement. She saw the locked up wine cellar and machinery rooms—with their water heaters, pumps, and boilers—and finally the steam machines of the laundry room. There, the launderer and laundress, with their extended family of helpers, were diligently pressing, ironing, starching, folding linen, hanging clothing, churning wash, and steaming. In the basement was another dumbwaiter, but it was utilised, as far as Delphia could tell, to send fresh linen and bedding up to the maids servicing the rooms and for them to send used linen down. She retrieved Art's napkin—used for her tea parcel—from her pocket and added it to the used linen pile.

After Alice dropped off her armload and wrote out a client's ticket for it, she gave Delphia a quick overview of the Vesta's design.

"Yes, the fourth floor is for residents and clients," Alice said as they walked back to the stairs. "The attic is for the more important staff. Manon and her partners live in one of the attic garrets, as does Cook, for he does need the exercise, and our housekeeper Mrs. Cribble and her husband. Though she may eventually move down to the wing we servants are in, as Mr. Cribble is starting to get on and his legs aren't what they used to be."

"You live here at the Vesta, Alice?" Delphia said. "Do you mind it? I mean, despite the . . . bawdy aspects."

"Oh yes, I am so happy to be here! I can dress in trousers, cut my hair, and I needn't be feminine, and . . . and I needn't marry," Alice declared. "Unless with another girl. And if that can't be done, then I just won't."

"Alice, I believe it can be done, no matter what church and government think," Delphia said. "I've just learned that women form marital contracts with each other and I think it a wonderful idea!"

"Oh, I know it's possible, Delphia, and such marriages are very respectable. They've property and money," Alice said. "But were I to love . . . "

Alice paused on the steps, and Delphia looked at her expectantly.

"I've a betrothed, you see," Alice said. "I come from a very good family. And he is from another. But now I've run off, and they're still waiting. I'm doing my best to end the engagement. It seems it doesn't matter how many letters I write them. I'm still of marriageable age, and for a good while yet! I don't care about my family's money, I just don't!"

"Goodness! How adventurous your life is! But . . . we've only this life, haven't we?" Delphia said and touched Alice's arm in encouragement. "Oh, do the best for you, Alice! Even if your family doesn't understand. You'll have your girl, you'll see!"

Delphia hoped her attempt at cheer gave Alice courage. She saw in Alice's eyes what she had often seen in Gavin's—a desperate unhappiness. It was one that finally drove her brother to sail far away for the elusive freedom he sought.

When she and Alice parted, Delphia entered the gentry's second floor and looked about the hallway with new understanding. She was no tom, but she currently enjoyed the exciting liberation that came with wearing male garments. Though deviancy was still an aspect of the Vesta, the club was becoming, to her sense of comfort and admiration, a worthy haven.

Delphia thought it time to attend to her employers and went to Art's room on the third floor. When she knocked and entered, Art warmly received her. She was having her own breakfast. Art enquired about her new coat and hat, and Delphia was happy to show her the new shillelagh, dangling by its leather cord at her wrist. Art held the wood and remarked on its virtues. Delphia thought she smelled of violets.

"'Tis a loaded stick," Art said, weighing the large knobby end in her hand. She balanced it in her palm with the long end straight up, and Delphia made a mental note to try that herself.

"It's leaded? My, I should have known," Delphia said.

"The Irish stick is clearly a weapon," Art said as she handed the cudgel back to Delphia. "It will invite challenge."

"Oh, Art, you are right, and I am ill-prepared to use it on a person," Delphia said.

"Thee will be taught. But until then, do what's simplest. Hide thy stick in thy coat."

"I shall. And if we were in the midst of conflict, as what happened at the Black Market? Should I try my stick's use?"

"Until thee is skilled, I say thee should run instead."

"That, I can do," she said.

"Has thee broken fast?" Art asked.

"I have, Art. I had my breakfast in the kitchen, and Cook was generous!" Delphia said. "But Art, I believe I'm to retrieve Mr. Dastard as part of my morning duties. Where would he be?"

"I'm here, I'm here!" Jim called from behind his cabinet in the study.

"He is awake," Art said, smiling.

Delphia entered the study, drew back the curtains, and opened the cabinet Jim resided in. It was filled with cabinet cards of female performers, tintype portraits that Delphia believed were of other Secret Commission agents, and odd curiosities. She brought Jim out, picked up his top hat, and set it upon his head.

"Good morning, Bloom! My, you've a hat too! And a fine coat and cudgel! I approve. Is this the work of Miss Thackery?"

"It is, sir, and good morning," Delphia said. She relayed Charlotte's words regarding Jim's desired design.

"Well, I rather like this; it's discreet and good for meeting all manner of folks in our business. It'll do. Bloom, I've need for a breakfast cigarette or four. Much has occurred since we parted company. Time for your briefing!"

"My . . . yes, sir!" Delphia said. She set Jim down, found his cigarettes and match safe in his hat, lit his breakfast for him, and listened gravely as he related the events of the night.

"Oh, dear Miss Pritt," Delphia finally said. "Yet she was valiant to the end!"

"Perhaps too valiant, but I won't fault her spirit," Jim said. "I only hope you will know when to fight, and when to flee."

"I've a great sense of self-preservation, sir," Delphia said. "I've fled from Hettie O'Taggart countless times."

They rejoined Art in her room. Her tea and breakfast plates were still at the table. Art was hanging by her fingertips from the doorframe of the washbasin's closet door. Her legs were bent and crossed at the ankles beneath her skirt. She was slowly pulling herself up, head back so her chin nearly touched the frame. Then she lowered herself. She repeated the action.

"Ho! Strength enthusiast! Well recovered, we see! Bloom, you could do with performing a few of those yourself," Jim said.

"Er," Delphia said.

"You want muscles like Art, don't you? You're an utter Slim-Jim!" Jim said.

"A . . . 'slim-Jim', yes sir," Delphia said, baffled. Jim twisted in Delphia's hand and looked towards the breakfast table.

"Ah, the paper! Art, have you read Miss Skycourt's account of last night already?"

"I hadn't interest, Friend," she said. "More for the events endured, not for lack of enjoyment of her writing."

"Shall I read it to you, sir?" Delphia said.

"Ah, no! That's quite all right. Just hold up the paper and I shall read, thank you, Bloom."

Delphia seated herself at the table and held the paper for Jim, turning the pages when asked. While Jim muttered to himself, Art ceased her lifting and came to sit with them. She enquired if Delphia would like tea, poured a cup when she accepted, and then poured one for herself. Delphia eventually turned the pages for the editorial and letters section.

"Art, I'll have you know, Miss Skycourt writes like a fox, as always," Jim said.

"Aye. She is clever," Art said, before sipping her tea.

"Hm. In light of our recent loss, that of the valiant Miss Pritt, the black arts practitioners are getting quite the drubbing, and the scientific men are looking like saints," Jim said as he read the editorial section. "But by fortunate contrast, the anti-vivisectionists are equally drubbing the scientific men, blaming them for inspiring such heartless crimes. Reasoning that the cruelty of vivisectionists begat that of another, our notorious Bone Stealer, may not be a factual argument, but it is a heart-wringer."

'*Heart-ringer*'? Delphia thought. It was the oddest term. She looked at Art, who seemed thoughtful, but Delphia was uncertain if the words had perplexed her too. She returned her attention to Jim.

"The Surgical Academy announces once again that they are closed due to the anti-vivisectionist demonstrations," Jim said. 'Well, at least they're not getting any vivisecting done."

"The kept animals. A trouble I'd forgotten," Art murmured.

"What's that, Art? Feel like rescuing something again? Well, there will be plenty of that tonight. After our victory, you may join your plain and bonneted brethren with their signs at the academy."

Art coughed and put down her cup. Delphia felt concern for Art's sudden discomfort but frowned at the realisation that while the Bone Stealer crimes were happening, animals were being harmed. She thought she might join in the demonstrations too, once they'd captured their evil quarry.

"Friend, as to this rescue tonight. Miss Pritt is dead, but we must assume they may have another woman?" Art said.

"We must. Or, they're still on the hunt, which means you're still in danger. So I must ask that you stay with me here, at the Vesta," Jim said.

"Stay with thee? Thee would forego adventuring with Delphia?" Art asked, her tone light.

"Dear partner! I wouldn't think of it," Jim said. "And how I miss being held aloft at thy impressive height. I've been a rather short person lately."

"Well!" Delphia muttered into her cup.

"A thought has occurred to me in exercise, and perhaps to thee too," Art said.

"Yes, I do lift my brows now and then. What is your thought?" Jim said.

"The recipient of the anticipated surgery," Art said. "We have yet to discover her."

"Indeed, our mysterious, young aristo. The girl must already be a well-kept family secret, being a cripple and all. In such a scenario, doctors, family members, and servants would be the only ones to know of her. Risk has given all medical bone specialists a thorough shakedown, but none has spoken up yet. And, I bet, never will."

"'Tis a matter of waiting, then?" Art said. "Or hiding, in my case?"

"Well, we can't have them take a stab at you, can we?"

"'Twas a thought," Art said. "Then thee and Risk may follow, were I to be kidnapped."

"A horrible idea! No, no, no!" Jim said.

"Friend," Art said.

"*No!*"

Delphia watched as Jim and Art argued. She folded and put the paper away. After reading Helia's story about the second Pritt kidnapping attempt, Delphia didn't think it wise to have Art let herself be captured. There seemed more chance of something going wrong in such a scenario rather than going right, which was the point of Jim's dissent.

"Art, it is a bad idea and that is all! Must I demand a solemn affirmation that you will stay with me?" he finally said.

"'Tisn't needed, I will stay with thee," Art said begrudgingly.

"Good! Then it's settled! Our work, my young friends, is often as much waiting as investigation and the apprehending of quarry. Though we may tap our toes, rest assured we *will* take the offensive, and soon. Now!" Jim said. "I must apologise for excusing myself, but I still feel rather vulgar after that morphine attack. I've need of a good bath and internal brushing. Bloom, if you would summon one of the staff, please? Whoever comes will know how to bathe me."

Delphia pulled the cord by Art's bed and returned to the table. A maid and page answered the call. While the maid took Jim into the washbasin closet, the page gathered Art's breakfast and rolled it out.

"If thee could bring me a length of string, as is used in wrapping packages, three feet long," Art requested of the page before she left.

"Ho ho! Hee hee!" Jim said from inside the closet. Water was heard being poured by the maid, and the two amicably chatted.

"Art," Delphia said in a low voice. "I don't wish to insult, but I feel that the better I understand the unique natures that are you and Mr. Dastard, the better I might serve."

"What is it, Delphia?" Art asked gently.

"Mr. Dastard has a strange way with words," Delphia said. "He once said 'dog-house' when I believe he meant 'kennel'."

"'Dog-house'. Aye, that does sound like an Americanism," Art said thoughtfully.

"Oh, is that what it is?" Delphia said in relief. "For a while, I rather suspected he might be from a distant colony, and therefore peculiar in meaning and use of the English language, like New Zealand, or British New Guinea."

"Not Canada?" Art asked curiously.

"Well, we met Canadians yesterday," Delphia said.

The page brought back a spool of white cotton twine and a pair of small scissors. Art thanked her for the generosity and bade Delphia doff her coat and hat. Art laid string in a diagonal from Delphia's shoulder to her opposing hip.

"Why, is this to be a simple holster for my stick?" Delphia said excitedly. "Just like carrying a quiver!"

"Aye," Art said. "'Twill do until thee finds a belt to wear." She doubled the length, snipped a hand's width longer than she had measured, tied off the long loop to be worn across Delphia's body, and tied another much smaller loop to hang at the side, where the cudgel would be slipped in.

Delphia tried the makeshift holster when done, and found her shillelagh's large head stayed secure in the small loop end. It hung by her side without discomfort. When she tried on her coat and left it unbuttoned, the stick's presence was not terribly apparent.

"There," Art said. "Now thee is ready to give another an unwelcomed surprise."

Delphia chuckled. Art looked at her, her kind eyes serious, and Delphia sobered.

"Harm to another is a matter of choice," Art said. "But with such threats as we face, whether bewitched men or things that only look like men, thee must choose preservation of thy life. When fighting, fight hard. When fleeing, fly fast. Always live."

Delphia nodded. "May I share something that happened to me?" she said.

Art brought Delphia to sit at the table.

"Of course, Delphia," she said.

"Now, it isn't . . . that," Delphia reassured. "I've been very fortunate to not have that happen, despite how adventurous and unescorted I've been. I mean to tell you of the first time I had to kill things. Horrid things. It was when the Devil Dogs overran East London."

"Five years ago," Art said. "I've knowledge of this event."

"Then you may remember. They were the red river worms that were infected by the tainted sewage from the Krike & Sons Organic Chemicals Factory. The worms grew horns and mouths with teeth. They were nearly as big as my forearm and moved very fast. First, the mudlarks and coal bargemen were killed, and then the tanners on the shore, and finally the Thames flooded, sending the Devil Dogs into the streets of lower East London. But it rained as well, and they were able to swim through the tunnels system all the way to Bethnal Green."

"Thee had to kill them?" Art asked. "Thee at twelve years?"

"You weren't a very small twelve years, were you, Delphia?" Jim said.

Delphia turned and saw that Jim sat on Art's bed, swathed in two white towels, one about his base and the other made into a turban on his head. The maid was shutting the door behind her.

"Sorry, Bloom," Jim said. "Please continue!"

"Yes, sir. Well, I . . . I was left to watch over my smaller sister and brother, who were no more than babies, at the time.

I guess one could say I wasn't quite grown yet. Not like Hettie
O'Taggart, who was allowed a stick and joined the others of
the street, my parents and brothers included, to meet the Devil
Dogs. And they did come. It rained so and there was so much
shouting and screaming!

"They came inside through the kitchen's sink and I'd only
time to put the little ones up high on the cupboard. Those
horrible worms, they liked to fling themselves. They bit me.
They were everywhere. I nearly thought myself done. Aengus
screamed and he threw down our plates! One hit me on the
head! Then I became angry. The rabid monsters, scaring the
babies! I would be rabid in turn. I grabbed the nearest thing and
hit the beasts, and when I did, they burst, like rotted fruit."

"What did you use, Delphia?" Jim asked.

"Oh! It was grandpapa's polo stick. I may've hit myself more
with the long end with all my hammering . . . splattering. It was
strange. They never ceased to come. And I was hitting for such
a long time that I believe my perceptions, the very senses of my
head and heart, somehow rose and resided in a different place."

"Thee was in warrior's grace," Art said.

"Or berserker's rage," Jim said.

"Mummy was the one who finally grabbed the polo stick from
me. Papa held me until I understood to stop fighting. Calliope
and Aengus were safe," Delphia said.

Delphia felt Art take her hand. Though she was a ghost, in
solid form her hand was warm, strong, and firm. Art smiled
reassuringly.

"I might have developed hysteria if not for my good fortune
of seeing the new Blackheart," Delphia said. "We had all taken
refuge on the roof, even in the rain, and saw the new Nick
come, riding on her black horse. My, what a sight! She wore a
black tricorne and black cape, breeches and a black mask. What
long boots she had! She swung her strange, flexible sword, the
blade that was long and thin. It slashed through the air like a
whip! Papa said it was a weapon of India. No other Nick but
her wielded such a thing! She slew what seemed like hundreds

of those worms with just one blow. And then she threw us all fishing nets and told us how to catch the Devil Dogs and beat them in the nets. It was wonderful. When I saw the Blackheart that day, I knew my wounds would heal, my terror would fade, and the danger would pass. My heart swelled."

"Huzzah!" Jim said in a hushed voice. Art smiled broadly.

"I've yet to strike another human being, however," Delphia said. "Well, with any great effect. Hitting Hettie O'Taggart is quite like punching the side of an elephant."

"Boxing will come," Art said with firm assurance. She rose. "But for now, I will show thee dirty tricks of fighting. Best suited for one of thy slender frame, when against men or stronger women. Or Hettie O'Taggart."

Delphia eagerly stood, removed her coat and string holster, and joined Art in the center of her bedroom.

"Delphia, the Blackheart . . . had she dark hair?" Art asked as they stood before each other.

"Dark hair? Why, it's been five years. I can't say. She was dressed all in black," Delphia said.

Art smiled and directed Delphia on what their exercise would be.

~

The Black Market echoed with the sounds of hammers and saws as workmen repaired the damage wrought by Art. The atmosphere was more tense than usual. Residents and attendees stood about, nervous and short-tempered. A fight broke out while Helia and Ellie Hench made their way down Sawbones Row. They sidestepped the altercation. Ellie put her stick out and tripped a man hurrying to the fight. He fell, the empty bottle he held by the neck shattering.

They passed the storefronts of the corpse-sellers and mounted the steps for Arthur Fellows' office. Helia knocked. There was no answer. She knocked again.

"Ellie, can you feel him, inside?" Helia asked. "Arthur doesn't mean to be rude, but he's such a recluse."

"Door's shut, windows're shut, and it's all blocked orf with paper," Ellie said.

"Well, can't you press yourself against the glass, Ellie? Can't you feel anything else? Him hiding, perhaps?" Helia asked. She fished about in her pockets.

"I feel paper," Ellie declared, standing by the windows with her nose against the glass. "And I smell 'is sulphur. Perhaps more rabbits lie dead inside."

"Doesn't feel like his sort of work, that . . . darkness." Helia touched the masked side of her face. "I guess Arthur's tried a new sort of working. It's very powerful."

"You kin sense such with yer taint, and I'm the one pressin' 'gainst the glass?"

"Oh, hush."

Helia knelt and put her pick to the door's lock. She suddenly shuddered and dropped the pick. She held her gloved hand, her fingers like claws.

"*Oh!* Electrocution is so painful! How I hated when they did that to me in the asylum!"

"A booby trap?" Ellie said. She tapped the door curiously with her blackthorn. "That, 'n all the veils."

"Those, yes, so odd how many layers. I feel Arthur has added even more wards than before," Helia said. She rose in frustration and pocketed her tool.

"There're two watchin' us, right across, 'idden behind the open winder," Ellie said softly. "We can't stay."

"Nor wait outside in the courtyard," Helia said miserably. "Oh, Arthur."

Helia and Ellie descended the stairs. Helia glanced up one last time at the office and its papered windows, then left with Ellie.

~

In Medicines Row behind the office, where the wigs- and false teeth-sellers conducted business, Arthur Fellows walked slowly up the steps for his back door. His manner was grim and thoughtful. He absentmindedly waved his hand before the doorknob and inserted his key.

He stopped and swallowed. His stomach dropped. Horror gripped him, almost as debilitating as when he discovered Emily would die from her defective heart. He sensed the power of another, disrupting his own carefully placed wards and waiting within.

He turned his head. A man in a slouched cap mounted the steps below him, his eyes cold. The door opened.

Another man stood inside, holding the door. His face was scarred.

Arthur stilled the tremor of his hand that held the key. He straightened and slowly stepped in. The scarred man closed the door behind him.

Seated in Arthur's office was an impeccably dressed man, grey-haired, with a small moustache. His pale, blue eyes were devoid of emotion. A large, crystal fob hung from his watch chain. Within the glass orb floated a human eyeball. His gloved hands rested on a walking stick made of human vertebrae. Two other men flanked him. A manservant stood behind him.

"Arthur Fellows. Are you attending the demonstration, tonight?" the scarred man asked. He stood behind Arthur. His accent was German.

Arthur said nothing. His skin felt clammy and his limbs bone-cold. Dread resided in the pit of his stomach.

The men in the room watched him. The grey-haired gentleman looked away. His pale-eyed gaze rested upon an empty silver platter that was laid on a small table before him. He stared at it absentmindedly.

"Your presence," the scarred man said to Arthur. "Is no longer needed."

The thugs on either side of the gentleman moved forward. They went to Arthur's desk and tore down his pinned-up work. They ripped his books, threw them on the floor, and shattered vials.

"And your work," the man said amid the clatter, "is already

forgotten."

"You can't take what I've already lost," Arthur said.

The scarred man grabbed him and covered Arthur's mouth.

The silver platter rattled. The scent of sulphur suffused
the room. Arthur felt his insides gripped by an unseen hand.
Something severed neatly within. He screamed against the man's
hand.

When his scream turned to silence, the man let him go.
Arthur saw nothing but red. His head grew light and his tongue
thick. His body became heavy like lead, and he fell to the floor.

He curled up in agony and stretched his mouth wide. He put
one hand to his chest. His fingers clutched around his jet pin.

The prince stood up. His manservant adjusted the fit of the
prince's long, brushed coat at the shoulders. Arthur stilled on the
floor. When the servant stepped around the prince, he picked up
the silver platter.

A bloody, red liver lay upon it.

The prince glanced at it briefly. He spoke, his voice light and
quavering.

"Sauté it," he whispered.

Chapter Sixteen

Art decided that perhaps she was not a very social person after all, or had lost, in her second life, all understanding of what good manners required. After some exercise with Delphia, Jim insisted that they descend to the dining room and see who was about, enjoying the late-morning buffet. Art carried Jim and with Delphia in tow, the group made an impressive entrance. Jim was delighted.

Miss Eustania Dillwick and Miss Lizzy Fesque, the visitors from Canada, seemed especially fascinated with Art. They hovered and stared enrapt up at her, delighting in the few answers she gave to their questions. Several of the toms, mandrakes, and ladies also looked at Art with curiosity, their plates forgotten. Milly rose from her breakfast to greet Jim and address Art.

"Art, your exquisitely unique physique impresses us, so!" she said. "We can't help our admiration. But forgive me for saying. Today, your arms seem . . . bigger!"

"'Tis the swell from exercise," Art said. Her sleeves did feel tighter, especially on the flexed arm holding Jim up.

"We must ask Mrs. Moore to provide an exercise room," one of the men said. He wore earrings and was dressed in silks with a turban on his head. Art thought he might be playacting, or was an artist.

"So that you might enjoy the swelling of male muscles?" a woman said, laughter in her voice.

"Those would not be the only objects swelling," the man

answered provocatively.

"Tut, you've the men's gymnasium to do that at," Milly said. "And there's the Exercisium for both sexes nearby."

"Exercisium?" Art said.

"Yes, but they admit all classes of people too," Milly said, lighting a cigarette. "I'd prefer an exclusive establishment."

"Art, you may like the equipment," Jim said. "I hear they've the latest mechanisms from Sweden."

"A machine may break, where the lifting of a cement sack would do. But we'll tarry here no more, Jim. Thee are all in the midst of breaking fast," Art said, addressing the room. "We will leave thee to enjoy thy meals."

"You'll bring your hymns later to the drawing rooms, perhaps?" Milly said, smiling.

"I will not proselytize," Art said. "Thee is safe from sermons."

As Delphia followed her downstairs, Art thought her abrupt withdrawal had been unseemly, but she could not help her restlessness. Her limbs, awaken by exertion, were ready for action. Since last night's debacle, things felt undone. Art wanted her chance to meet the Bone Stealer again.

Jim sought to preoccupy her with the playthings that could be found in the ground floor rooms—billiards, cards, musical instruments (at Jim's query, Art discovered that she did not know how to play the harp nor the piano), books, paintings, cabinet cards, stereoscopes, microscope slides, astronomical instruments, automatons, wind-ups, phenakistoscopes, zoetropes, and simple thaumatropes. They dallied in the Curiosities & Mechanical Room.

"Why I know this toy," Delphia said. She put down an ornate brass astrolabe with Arabic letters and picked up a thaumatrope. "You simply wind the strings and pull them between your hands—oh my," she said, when the illustrated thaumatrope she spun revealed a naked man being animated.

Art looked over her shoulder.

"'Tis a well-formed physical culturist. He is only exercising. If thee views the stereo photo cards, be sure to pick the boxes marked 'Anatomy', 'Beauties of the World', or 'Classical & Ancient Scenes'."

"Otherwise, I might receive an explicit education?" Delphia said, putting the thaumatrope down.

"Aye," Art said. "A very pornographic education."

"Art, must you shock young Bloom here with your typical lack of discretion? Come and have a look at this fine praxinoscope!" Jim said. "You spin it like you do the zoetrope, but gaze into its mirror, within, to see the animation play."

"'Tis another pretty, nude female frolicking?" Art said, spinning the brass praxinoscope. The pictures of a nude, jumping girl could be seen moving up and down. "'Tis."

"And your enthusiasm flags! Perhaps all you need to keep you busy is a real woman," Jim said in mild exasperation.

"Or embroidery," Art said. She put another strip of illustrated paper inside the praxinoscope. As she spun the devise again, a girl dressed only in a black domino mask cracked a whip. "I like sewing. Would the Vesta have kegs I might lift?"

Jim persuaded her not to seek out any kegs. Art also declined the offer that they procure Manon for her. They then moved to the library, where Delphia distracted Art with readings of Elizabeth Barrett Browning's poetry. Just after two in the afternoon, Inspector Risk visited the Vesta.

"Well," Risk said, when Art, Jim, and Delphia had settled in the Vesta's waiting room. He sat with his hat resting on his knee. "A girl's been kidnapped, a giantess from a sideshow twenty miles outside London. Same method as happened to Miss Pritt, with men in gas masks and a wagon. This time, the witnesses present couldn't act quickly enough to save her. We'll assume our quarry has his victim."

"And the location and time of the coming event?" Jim said.

"Still the same," Risk said. "Those police impersonators we arrested at the hospital didn't mind speaking up, once faced with the prospect of being hanged for murder. They confirm the information Livus has been giving."

He reached into his coat pocket and removed a note. He

unfolded it and showed it to Jim and Art. It read:

Curtains Theatre near Whitechapel Church. 7 o'clock.

"Have it?" he said.

"We do," Art said evenly.

"Won't be long, now," Jim said.

"Meet us at the church, ten before the hour," Risk said. "We then storm the theatre, together."

"Should I not go in first, unseen?" Art said. "To secure safety for the giantess."

"There's a thought," Risk said.

"We could," Jim said. "Though one fell swoop may ensure nabbing the Bone Stealer and halting the crime. If we see to rescue first, there would be a window of escape for him."

"If we enter all at once, then allow me first engagement with the sorcerer," Art said.

"You may have that," Risk said, "and the agent's privilege that comes with it." He rose, and Art and Delphia did as well. "Oh, and those men Art fought in Felly Pritt's room. Hospital mortuary made some sense of the remains even as they were turning into soup. Doctor believes each man was entirely missing his heart."

The information was met with silence. Risk put his hat back on.

"We'll see you then," he said.

———

Delphia had the collywobbles, but they weren't of the exciting kind, like when trying a ropewalk for the first time. The dreadful feeling was more reminiscent of when she knew the Devil Dogs were coming. After Risk had told them of the missing hearts, she wondered what more to expect of this dark arts surgeon and his strange, living-dead men. She would need to keep ears, eyes, and her mind open for anything, as her brother Philo would caution.

Therefore, when Jim dismissed her so that she might have tea before they departed, Delphia felt uncharacteristically without hunger. But remaining in Jim and Art's company made her more nervous. Art was agitated, and such agitation made her restless. Delphia didn't mind leaving Jim to argue once more with Art about how she needed to remain at the Vesta even though she was no longer in danger of being kidnapped.

Delphia forsook the sumptuous teas laid out in the drawing rooms and descended for the staff's dining table. She obtained a cup of tea and a biscuit there. The kitchen staff bustled, assembling tea trays to be delivered to the rooms upstairs. Delphia watched as an assistant stacked delicate cakes on a tiered silver server and set it in the dumbwaiter. She sipped from her hot cup and could not help sinking into a grave mood.

While Delphia debated the number of sugar cubes (molded with an ornate V, for Vesta) to drop into her cup, Cook looked over from where he was overseeing the cutting of crusts from tea sandwiches.

"Oh, must it be *that* expression!" He waved his small hands. "I know that face well. Something is about to happen."

"Oh, sir! I didn't mean to upset you, but I may not say what the matter is," Delphia said.

"You needn't say anything," Cook said. He tutted and moved around his working assistants. "Here." He briskly mounted a stepping stool, reached up to a high cabinet, unlocked it, and removed a gentleman's leather-covered, glass flask. The dark, burgundy leather was shiny and worn. "You will need this."

"Sir," Delphia said when Cook came to the table and stood the flask before her.

"Take it. Harold's gone and I'm sure he would want you to have it," Cook said. "It's filled with the best of its sort. Smooth, strong, and with backbone! Remember it when you need it most, which may be often." He looked at her. "It's for courage." He hurried away to where one of his assistants was pulling a sheet of baked pastry from the oven.

"Thank you, sir," Delphia said in awe. She took the flask in both hands. A window in the leather showed the liquid sloshing within at the half-bottle increment. A silver chain kept the screw cap in place. The embossed monogram read: HJM.

She put the flask in an inner coat pocket and patted it.

Evening found the three finally departing the Vesta by hackney carriage.

While Delphia was enjoying her cup below, Art and Jim had been invited to tea in the room of Miss Dillwick and Miss Fesque, who were such pleasant and unassuming company that Art found herself finally relaxing. Both women were indeed spiritualists or at least scholars of, for they were in London to research a book they were writing on the subject. When Delphia joined them (after Alice had fetched her), the Canadian couple was happy to share parts of their book and the gathered research. Jim brought up certain aspects that might further their knowledge on supernatural subjects, which Eustania and Lizzy wrote careful notes on. In the couple's company, the trio's time of departure came rapidly. When they took their leave and descended for a hackney carriage, Art was calm and Delphia was in good spirits.

Whitechapel Church was within easy walking distance from the club—or in Art's case, running distance—but Jim advised a more discreet approach. He sat in Delphia's hands while Art sat opposite them in the carriage, her stick set to the floor.

"Friend, I recall something Risk said that made me curious," Art said. "He spoke of 'agent's privilege'. What did he mean by it?"

"Ah, and to think I never had trouble explaining such before," Jim said. "But Quaker thou art. Somehow you must reconcile with the knowledge . . . for all our sakes. You've permission to kill, Art."

Art stared at him.

"Consider this: what if our Bone Stealer was, in actuality, an archbishop? What do you think would happen were the police to find out?"

Art said nothing and frowned.

"Yes, exactly. But when His Royal Highness created the Secret Commission it came with a unique benefit. For we are creatures. We are not of class. And we are known, whether in truth or no, for acting as creatures do. Passionately. The Blackheart is not alone in her effectiveness."

"When the Secret Commission agent, Mr. Hands of Thunder, strangled the Breath-Eater Killer in a fit of passion rather than wait for the police, I must admit that we Blooms cheered. As well as all the people of my street," Delphia said.

"Thunder couldn't help that," Jim said. "A girl was involved. Poor wretch."

"And the Secret Commission?" Art asked. "How did they treat his action?"

"With their usual silence," Jim said. "But Art. Despite this privilege given us, we agents can't risk misbehavior. Do evil, and Fall need only undo us. It's as simple as that."

"The agents don't run amok, at least to my awareness," Delphia said. "Though your detractors like to write their opinions to the papers of your unnatural character. But such is written about the Blackheart too, and she's never acted the loose ship's cannon. When she shot the Living Gargoyle out of the sky with blazing fire, killing him, we cheered then too. He may have been a man once, perhaps deserving of capture and imprisonment, but he used his eldritch wings to snatch us children."

"When he successfully corrupted his body into that of a flying beast he developed an appetite for tasty children, yes," Jim said. "But in that situation, I believe ole Nick, as those Nicks before her, could only choose the action she resorted to. She often chooses well."

As Art listened to Jim and Delphia converse, she soberly recalled her conversation with Helia at the Blue Vanda.

"Without knowledge of his name, then you and Mr. Dastard may act as agents do, and all that is about identity may be known after."

"After . . . that we should have him?"

"If that is the result."

Art heard Jim speak again.

"Tonight, we must make certain that this man, whatever his title may be, does not leave. He may give himself up and save us the trouble. Or, he may attempt escape, which is the most likely. And that, we cannot let happen. Not only is he both powerful and cruel, but possibly untouchable. It is up to us to see to his apprehension. Or, if such unfortunate circumstance should arise, to his end. England needs only one Dr. Fall."

Half a mile from the hackney carriage that carried Art, Jim, and Delphia down Whitechapel Road, Risk sat with Barkley in a similar vehicle driving down Shoreditch. In the seat opposite was Livus, a white bandage wrapped over his missing eye. His shirt and waistcoat were stained with old blood, and his hair was in disarray. He didn't blink.

"I don't know why I'm here. I was safer where you had me," he said.

"You're to point the Bone Stealer out to us," Risk said. "And if you've been wrong all this time about this demonstration, we can then take it out on your hide."

"Believe me, it is what I know," Livus said.

"Then we'll know soon enough," Barkley said.

Livus touched his chest. "My heart. I have a heart, haven't I?" He pressed his hand over the spot. "I can feel it beating."

"Now why mention that?" Risk said. "You think it's gone missing?"

Barkley chuckled beside him.

"No, I feel it. I still have it." Livus dropped his hand. "And the Secret Commission agents—they will join us?"

"Well, two of their sort no doubt will. They're all busy, those agents," Risk said.

Livus pushed at his bandage. He forced it up until the black gap of his eye socket was revealed.

"What are you doing?" Barkley exclaimed.

Livus sat and stared.

"It needs to breathe," he said.

Within the bustling and cacophonic Royal Aquarium, gaslights were slowly being lit. Early diners were settling into reserved tables or awaiting seating. Members of the evening string quintet—none blind—were arranging their chairs, stands, and instruments. People stood about, turning the pages of the papers they purchased from the aquarium newsagent. They avidly talked about the contents. The Bone Stealer was the topic of discussion.

Helia Skycourt sat at her Blue Vanda patio table, a look of irritation on her face and a lit cigarette brazenly dangling from her lips. She ignored the veiled looks of disapproval from women and men and randomly typed words on her typewriter.

Bone specialists Swedish sanitarium seaside mountain city orthopaedic correctional device brace fitting girl age 22 height 6 foot 2 affliction bone leg spine neck hands arthritic condition spinal curvature malformation paralysis poliomyelitis child of baron viscount knight merchant manufacturer /////// (strike) *Prince Duke Marquess Earl*

She believed she'd exhausted what suspicions she could think on and follow. It was too much to sift through, in too little time, and no one—not even Milly Sedgewick, seemed to know anything. Or refused to acknowledge that they did. She and Ellie visited Arthur Fellows' home and his office at the Black Market a second time, to no avail. Helia knew without looking at the great clock face that adorned the French building façade that she had already run out of time.

Gentlemen seated themselves at a table near her and promptly opened papers. She saw the title of their newspapers and overheard the men's discussion: the Bone Stealer. Helia snorted and tapped ash from her cigarette.

The Standard was a good paper, especially with regards to foreign affairs, but their local journalist on supernatural events, by Helia's estimation, was an unapologetic sensationalist. Though hers was the more lengthy, thorough (and truthful), reportage on the hospital events of last night, his was the story that people were currently discussing in hushed, excited tones, merely because he'd used the word 'zombi'. There it was in bold, thick black and white upon the front pages of *The Standard* which the gentlemen held up in plain view: ATTACK BY ZOMBIS.

"Utterly misleading, to call those men's condition 'zombiism'!"

she muttered to herself. Her editor at *The Times* would no doubt harangue her later for not leaping to that farfetched conclusion herself, but Helia had read the doctor's mortuary report on the Bone Stealer's henchmen, acquired right after her failed visit to the Black Market, that morning. She had felt no need to type up new findings for the afternoon edition only because she had yet to understand what manner of men Art had fought.

Those unfortunate thugs had been living 'undead'; that conclusion, she was certain of. But their rapid decay was a unique circumstance, unlike what might occur with defeated, reanimated corpses or a possible zombi. And, they had been missing their hearts. She suspected that this German prince had applied a combination of black arts and science that was either of his own superior formulation or of a forgotten supernatural application that no one, except perhaps Dr. Gatly Fall, could be aware of.

But such speculation, Helia thought in irritation, was neither here nor there. Her most pressing concern was as swiftly slipping from her as the sky was rapidly darkening above. She needed to know where Art might be, tonight, and she wondered again why she hadn't just hidden herself at the Vesta, eavesdropped, or merely followed Art from the club.

Helia stopped randomly typing. The cigarette sagged from her lips. She knew the answer to those foolish questions.

A server approached and held out a silver tray. On it was an envelope and a letter opener. Helia snuffed out her cigarette, accepted both items, and looked at the envelope's markings. There was no other address except the Blue Vanda's, and the letter had been posted. Helia frowned, noting that the handwriting was vaguely familiar. Many who knew her habits were aware that they could easily reach her at the Blue Vanda by messenger or telegram. Though the post was reliable, the sender had apparently not been anxious about having the letter arrive with more immediacy.

She cut the envelope open. A black ticket fell out. It had no marking except for a single number written in white: 6.

Helia pulled out the accompanying letter, unfolded it, and read:

Dearest Helia,
Please understand that what happens to me is what I want. I no longer see any other way. I want to be with Emily again.

Helia paled and dropped the letter. She turned to her typewriter, quickly fed it a new sheet, and typed a telegram:
Helene-Sky. Arthur Fellows immediate danger Black Market. Save him. Helia-Vanda.

She summoned a server, pulled out the paper and gave it to him. Her heart beating frantically, she returned her attention to the letter.

My doom was sealed the moment I received the black horror that is now in your hands. I've since been writing letters and concluding all my personal affairs. Please do not feel you could have saved me. Please do not think I could have fled, or sought protection, or gone to the police. Truly, do you believe even the agents of the Secret Commission, who serve a German prince themselves, will mete final justice to this man? Even if he were apprehended, a prison cannot hold him. Only death can. Were I to flee now, in constant fear of my life and with him free to find me, it would only delay the inevitable.

I told you once that the matter of transference is dependent on both the donor and recipient being compatible, in body and age. We who attempt supernatural transplanting rely on measures. What this man has done is not conceivable, to insert a full skeleton or even just the foot bones inside another and adhere afflicted skin, muscle, tissue and nerves to an entirely new frame. But somehow he has that power, one that fools our realities, attains manipulations that present the impossible, and not once but four times. We all know that his triumphs are enjoying their changed bodies, even now.

But I believe he is not here to help the afflicted, even for the excessive sums, which he—as a prince!—accepts! Nor is he here to share his secrets. I am certain of this! We in this dark craft do not always work in isolation. I'd been in correspondence with three colleagues in Germany. They are now dead. I thought their deaths were due to the unsavory aspects of our profession. But now, I understand better.

This Durchlauchtig has invited every English dark surgeon practicing transference to his wicked event. We are but a handful, but just that many is enough for sacrifice; for blood. I am perhaps the only one willing to express the suspicion—no, the belief!—that we are sought out only to feed his power, and for him to remove any who could remotely rival him.

My dear Helia, you who have borne such a horrible affliction for so long. Emily always had love for you, even at your darkest. I'm sorry that when you came to me years before, I hadn't the knowledge of how to remove that awful infection that plagues you. I've still discovered nothing, nothing that can't kill you, and yet this man, this villain, he could be your savior, and perform the exact procedure your illness needs.

It became clear to me, as I studied more and more on how I might perfect supernatural transference, that the longer I practiced such arts, the more corrupt I can't help but become, and then, I would be no better than the man coming to murder me, and my hopes for rejoining Emily would be lost.

Dear Helia, I am and will be at peace. I will go to Emily without further corruption and having avoided the more severe judgment for the darker path almost taken. In God's light, may you and I see each other again.

With profound love,
Arthur

The letter crumpled in Helia's grasp. She took a breath and turned the letter over. It was blank. She picked up the black ticket and looked at its back. On it, Arthur had written in white chalk pencil: *Curtains Theatre, near Whitechapel Church. Seven o'clock.*

Helia folded her typewriter closed, put on her coat and gloves, and ran down the steps of the Blue Vanda. She sped across the pavilions and by the great aquarium exhibits. Once through the exit doors, she sought her wheel. She saw by the fading light that Perseus had parked his electric buggy nearby. He stood on the walk and jovially conversed with three young women and their older chaperone.

Helia jumped into the buggy, released the brake, stepped on the accelerator, and leaned on the steering tiller. The buggy jumped and sped away.

~

As the sun neared setting, Art and Jim's carriage came to a stop near Whitechapel Church. Delphia watched Art become invisible. After a minute, she rematerialised. Art seated herself across from Delphia once more.

"Friend Risk is not yet here," Art said. "But his plainclothes men are gathering."

"Sir, since we're about to enter a sorcerous situation, perhaps it's time you share your abilities with me," Delphia said to Jim.

"My abilities?" Jim said.

"Yes, sir. Like that time in the Black Market when you made yourself glow."

"Well, yes, I can do that. And set myself on fire."

Delphia looked at him expectantly.

"I can't blow myself up, Bloom," Jim said.

"Oh," Delphia said. "A fire, then."

"Just the fire," Jim said. "I can keep it alight for a few seconds. And I can eject marbles."

"Marbles," Delphia said.

"The ones your siblings are playing with now, come to think of it. Oh! I can spit pennies."

"That will be handy, sir."

The driver rapped on the roof. Art touched Delphia on the knee, and she and Jim quieted. They quickly disembarked and joined Inspector Risk, standing with his men before Whitechapel Church. Two buildings down, unmarked wagons concealing policemen sat near a theatre. Dusk had fallen, and the unlit street was swiftly shrouding in darkness.

"So. Livus," Jim said, seeing the man standing by Barkley. Livus merely stared, his missing eye uncovered.

"Another time, Dastard. Let's go, men. Art will lead," Risk said.

Art ghosted and flew ahead. Policemen left their wagons and followed. The group moved quickly for the old, dilapidated Curtains Theatre. It was an abandoned penny gaff, the playbills on its walls faded and tattered. Art passed through the doors, and Risk pulled them open and entered. Delphia, Jim, and Barkley hurried close behind him. Livus followed, escorted by a plainclothes man.

The entry hall was dirty and filled with debris, but the gaslights were lit. A man's voice could be heard, droning in a lecturer's style, and the whining of dogs accompanied him. Art continued on. Like many makeshift penny gaffs, there was no lobby. A passageway led into the theatre proper. She flew through the entry with its torn-down curtains into the seating area. Tiers of chairs led down to a theatre stage, brightly lit with gaslights. A handful of young men stood around an older man. He was speaking loudly and cutting open a dog strapped to a table on the stage. Surrounding the table were several dirty cages containing more dogs. The dog on the table howled.

Art swiftly descended while Risk and the rest ran down the tiers after her.

"You there! *STOP, NOW!*" Risk shouted.

Art solidified by the older man and pushed him aside. The dog had not been sedated. The animal shook and gave a long, painful cry.

"What are you doing?" the older man asked. He held a scalpel. His apron was splattered with fresh blood. "This is a medical demonstration!"

"Vivisectionist!" Jim cried. Delphia put a hand to her mouth as she neared the stage. The dog on the table continued to howl. Art laid a hand upon it, torn on what to do. Its skin along the back had been laid open to reveal the spine. It was bleeding freely. She looked at Risk.

"This animal needs—"

The assistant next to the older doctor suddenly plunged a knife into the dog. Art punched the man. The howling stopped. Art looked down in horror. The dog shuddered its last and stiffened.

"*You*—all instruments are to be dropped, *now!*" Risk yelled.

Policemen took hold of all the observers roughly. The older man and his woozy assistant loudly protested, as did the young men, who insisted that they were merely medical students. Amid the commotion and the barking of dogs, Risk turned to Livus, his face wrathful.

"Nice trick," Risk said.

"He must be here! He must be!" Livus said.

They heard the church bells ring the hour.

Art stepped back from the dead dog. She stilled her anger and ghosted. She spun slowly around, regarding the theatre. Policemen passed through her, including Delphia, whose shocked gaze was still fixed on the dead dog. Jim was speaking calmly to her. Nothing could be heard but the protesting and the barking.

Art looked for who might be watching them.

~

Livus watched Art. He trod on something lying on the floorboards. He looked down and picked it up. It was a theatre prop; a broken tomahawk.

"Here," he said and tossed the prop to Art.

Surprised, Art solidified to catch it.

Something sailed through the air from a theatre wing. A pop sounded as a projectile struck Art in the chest and exploded. The remains of a glass ampoule lay shattered on her bosom, its liquid contents releasing pungent fumes. Another glass ampoule smashed against her chest. Then another. Livus turned and ran. Art staggered. She flickered briefly, attempting to ghost away. She materialised and collapsed.

"*Art!*" Jim cried.

Men in gas masks appeared in the tiers and from the pit, hoisting glass bottles. They threw them down, shattering them against the floorboards. The sickening, sweet smell of chloroform rose. The dogs barked and whined. More bottled chloroform was thrown. Policemen shouted and slowly succumbed. A medical student fell off the stage. The men in gas masks moved forwards and pulled out clubs.

Delphia turned and ran.

She bounded across the theater floor, her coat's collar pressed against her face and with Jim in her hand. She leapt over a stricken policeman's body and rapidly climbed the steps, ahead of the rising fumes.

A man in a gas mask came quickly down the steps with a blackjack raised.

On the theater floor, another man in a gas mask stepped forwards and threw his club. It hit Delphia in the legs. She fell and tumbled down the stairs, Jim held tight to her. Chairs toppled. When she stopped falling, she crawled painfully up the steps. The chloroform fumes rose.

The man who threw the club neared. Delphia suddenly collapsed on Jim and stilled. The other man on the steps descended, blackjack still raised. When Delphia didn't move, he lowered his arm. Jim watched from beneath her arm as the man studied them, breathing noisily through his respirator.

The man stepped over Delphia and continued down the stairs to join his companion.

Jim heard the men shuffle out. His eye sockets stung. The air was thick with the foul odor of chloroform. He was pressed to Delphia's forearm, and his jawbone wedged by her fingers. He tried to move his jaw.

"Del—fee—ah!" he attempted. "Del!"

Delphia's arm muffled his sounds.

If you're feinting having succumbed, now's the time to get up! He thought. he agitated himself trying to rouse her. Delphia didn't respond.

Jim saw the air cease to distort. He hoped that most of the fumes had risen and evaporated. The overwhelming scent of something rotten remained. There was no sound from the animals and policemen. He worried about Art. He began to worry that he could not hear breathing. The theater was completely still.

Someone ran through the entry hallway above and down the steps. The rapid, light sound of heels indicated a woman.

Jim twisted in Delphia's arm, hoping to free himself. He remained trapped, but could see beyond the fallen chairs for the other set of stairs. Helia Skycourt appeared, descending rapidly. She stopped, coughed, and retreated a few steps.

"Oh, these poor—where's Art? *Art!*" Helia cried. She pulled her handkerchief and put it to her nose and mouth. She ran past Jim's line of sight. He could hear the clatter of her heels on the floorboards.

Jim heard Helia run back up the stairs. She carried Art's hat. Art's stick was beneath her arm.

"Oh no, oh no! *Art!*" Helia cried, shaking her fists.

Jim tried to call. No sound passed that could reach Helia, far across the theatre.

"That horrid—well if I were you, what then? Yes, what then?" Helia suddenly snarled, nearly mangling Art's hat. Jim gaped; he thought he saw a darkness come over Helia's face, on her masked side.

"I would, what? What?! Where would I be? Yes, *where!* I'm the best at what I do, aren't I? Why, I'd do my surgery where only the most lauded may show off their skills! And I'd do it where no one can ignore what I've done, won't I?" Helia laughed. "Because I'm a *Durchlauchtig!*" she cried. She ran up the tiers and exited the theatre.

A. . . a Serene Highness? Jim thought. *We're dealing with a prince of Germany?!*

Minor prince, minor prince! Jim reminded himself. *Even if related directly to Prince Albert, well . . . our man could be from one of the houses that's no longer! That's right. A destitute noble. The very reason then, why he's in England, and earning a despicable living!*

Now . . . 'Best at what I do', she said, 'best at'. . . Jim mused. *Where would I go, Durchlauchtig that I am? What theatre? Where's the best? Why, I'd go to—Yes! Of course! Science's hallowed Coliseum! He's at the Surgical Theatre in the Royal Surgical Sciences Academy!*

Jim opened his mouth as wide as he could. He bit down on

Delphia's fingers.

Delphia didn't respond. Jim bit her fingers again, right on the tips.

"That . . . doesn't hurt!" Delphia said thickly. She tried to rise and Jim hopped, freeing his mouth.

"Ah! Since you're numb, I'll bite you again, you needn't your pinkie!" Jim threatened. "And I can have the Commission pay recompense!"

Delphia rose off Jim. She fumbled and nearly fell on him again.

"Ggh," she said and slapped herself.

The smack echoed in the still theatre.

"Did you feel that?" Jim said.

She attempted to crawl up the stairs, dragging Jim with her.

"That's it, Bloom! Fight it!" Jim said. "Fight hard! Our hats, Bloom!"

She reached back and grabbed his hat and straightened hers. She kept crawling. They passed tier after tier. She knocked chairs down as she stumbled up the final steps for the topmost tier. She fell.

"Well at least when you fall, it doesn't hurt!" Jim cried, Delphia on top of him. "Mind the hat! Keep going, girl!"

Delphia pushed herself up and crawled forwards. When she reached the hallway and the fresher air, she breathed deeply. She put Jim down and sat with her back to the wall. She pulled out the flask and unscrewed it.

"Why, that's Harold's!" Jim exclaimed. "Good girl! Claret is for boys, port for men, but he who aspires to be a hero, must drink—"

"Brandy," he and Delphia said in unison. She took a swig.

"Ah," she said, heaving. She coughed and her face grew red.

"Fire in the belly!" Jim said happily. "The chloroform can't numb that! Is it clearing your head? Is it?"

"Not . . . yet, sir, but I'm more awake, now," Delphia gasped.

She capped the flask, picked up Jim, and forced herself to stand.

"We must awaken the men," Delphia said. "So much chloroform will cause harm."

"That's true! More of your medical reading, eh? But you saw

how the men were doused. I don't think you can stand another round in that contaminated pit. We must get to their drivers, outside. They'll summon help for Risk and the others while we rush to Art's rescue!"

"Yes, Art!" Delphia said as she stumbled down the entry hall and out the theatre doors. "They'd wanted Art all along! Where do we go, sir?"

"To where we can give anti-vivisectionists reason to storm the surgeons' castle! Find us a cab, Bloom! *You men*, yes, you!" Jim shouted to the drivers of the wagons. "Hurry in, but beware the chloroform! The raid has gone awry!"

Delphia ran down Whitechapel Road, past the blocking wagons that had kept loiterers and cabmen away and for a cross street with its corner gas lamp. She waved at the lone hansom cab traveling down the road.

Once she and Jim were seated and the driver urging his horse to a swift pace, she set Jim down beside her and pulled out the flask again.

"You all right, Bloom?" Jim said. "Can you feel things now?"

"Somewhat, sir. I hope to burn away the last of the fog in me," she said. It was more than a fog affecting her. She still felt dull, and the chloroform's effects were causing her senses—touch, sight, and hearing—to stray from her body. She dearly wanted to rest her head and obey her eyelids' need to shut until morning. Unlike the other factory girls, she never took to drink, but the likelihood of becoming drunk seemed better than being insensate.

"*Bloom!* Wake up, girl! Take a swig, you'll be all right!" Jim said.

"Yes, sir! Yes," Delphia said. She didn't realise that she had nearly passed out again.

Fear of being maimed was what roused her when she felt something happening to her fingers. Her first thought had been of rats. She'd only managed to get out of the theatre because of what Philo would lecture to her and Gavin, especially to make her understand how she might escape a burning factory, and Gavin, a sinking ship: if her head stopped working for whatever reason, her body—like a headless snake—could still move. It only needed the memory of what it had to do, even if it were one last command from her perhaps non-functioning brain.

And she would move, Philo had said. Because life was better than being dead, no matter what was praised of Jesus and heaven.

She unscrewed the flask's cap and put the bottle's mouth to her lips. With a grimace she managed a swallow.

Even as she gasped from the brandy's effect, feeling her face and stomach afire, she heard Jim speak.

"That's the best of Harold's stash you have there. May it bless you with his strength."

～

Helene kicked in the backdoor of a sawbones on Medicines Row and quickly stepped in. Her tricorne sat low over her eyes. Her hands were bare and loose by her sides. Ganju took a position next to her. He wore no hat over his stiff, black hair. His sleeves were rolled up. In a leather holster at his belt sat a sixteen-inch *khukuri*, the handle prominent against his waistcoat.

The astonished doctor straightened from his work. He was a balding, wet-lipped fellow with sharp-browed eyes and pupils like pinpoints. Arthur Fellows—or what was left of him—lay on his table. The skin of his nude body was splayed open from throat to crotch, his rib cage cracked and pulled up, and his organs removed. His head had been scalped. The sawbones had been pulling Arthur's teeth while his assistant held the bowl.

Two thugs present in the room stood and reached into their coats.

"Do that, and you're dead next," Helene said. "That's Arthur Fellows. We're here for him. Put him back together, now."

"I bought this!" the doctor sputtered. "A German fellow sold it to me! And his scalp is already with the wig-maker!"

"Don't play the businessman," Helene said. "You're that sawbones who boasts of providing the freshest corpses, aren't you?

You specialise in women. Died young, never buried, and too recently and suddenly dead."

The doctor licked his lips, the whites of his eyes round and nearly bulging.

"How did one of your customers describe it?" Helene said. "'Still warm to the feel'?"

He threw his forceps into the ceramic bowl his assistant held.

"No one cares about prostitutes," the doctor said.

"We do," Helene said.

He reached beneath his apron and pointed a six-shooter.

Helene stepped aside and snapped her right arm up. A blue barrel, percussion derringer popped out of her black sleeve into her bare hand. She pulled the folding trigger. A gunshot sounded.

The doctor's head snapped back. He fell on the trolley behind him and rolled. A perfect hole leaked blood between his wide eyes.

Helene flicked her arm down. The derringer disappeared into her sleeve. Ganju held his *khukuri* high in his hand. His curved blade flashed in the gaslights. The thugs quickly put their empty hands up in surrender.

"Get out," Helene said. They hurried out of the backroom for the front of the office. "But not you," she added, addressing the assistant. "You're to put Arthur back together."

"I'll—I'll try, miss," the assistant said. He was a tow-headed young man who looked incapable of growing a beard. He put the bowl full of bloody teeth down and opened Arthur's jaw. He turned and pushed the trolley that bore the doctor's body out of the way.

"How did he die?" Helene said.

Ganju moved forward, *khukuri* in hand, to investigate the front room. Helene inspected the pile of clothing that had belonged to Arthur. She found his jet mourning pin still attached to his waistcoat's front.

"His liver was missing, miss," the assistant said as he worked. "But . . . he hadn't been operated on. His liver was just . . . missing."

Ganju returned. His *khukuri* was sheathed.

"I know where his scalp is," Ganju said. "A simple request will have it returned to us."

"Good. Stay here and make certain this boy makes Arthur tidy again. And you," Helene said, addressing the young man. "Go work in a mortuary from now on. I don't want to hear of your master's business resuming."

The assistant shook his head and then nodded vigorously. "I only—I just helped make them pretty," he said, looking down as he inserted a tooth.

Helene turned to Ganju and murmured, "I'll return to his office and see if I can find anything more."

"Even if you don't, you must still leave," Ganju said in a low voice.

Helene took a breath. "Damn her. And she's left me with nothing but this. Will you see to it that he reaches a mortuary? Then I'll notify his parents."

Ganju nodded. He then nodded pointedly to her arm that concealed her spring-loaded rig.

"Strange choice," he said. "A single shot, muzzle-loader. Yet, I approve."

Helene's brief smile held no humour.

"If I must take up the gun again, a single shot must mean everything or not at all."

Ganju nodded once more and turned to face the young man working on Arthur's body. Helene left by the back door.

She walked down Medicines Row, her long black coat wafting behind her. Denizens and customers stepped back. Helene ignored them but noted who might be trouble. Her rigged derringer was presently useless, but she had other concealments at her disposal.

She saw a boy emerge from a wigmaker's storefront and hurry towards her. As he passed, she saw Arthur's thick, black hair and the skin of his white forehead, sitting in the bloodied newspaper the boy held open.

CHAPTER SEVENTEEN

Helene departed the Black Market by hansom cab, empty-handed. Her gaze darted, surveying what could be viewed from the open cab, as if she might spot some lingering clue on the darkened streets. Male pedestrians stared, unused to seeing a respectable woman ride within an open cab, but Helene ignored such attention. She'd learned nothing about the Bone Stealer and his impending demonstration. No one had intelligence to share though there was much discussed about the ghost agent, Artifice, and the recent havoc she'd wrought.

"She was shot, you say?" Helene had said in surprise, speaking to a group of prostitutes fanning themselves outside an obstetrician's shop.

"Much good it did, she is a ghost," the prostitute had sniffed. Her face was heavily painted. "And wouldn't you take a shot yourself? Ten guineas are still ten gold coins, little pastor."

Her friends had tittered at her jest and eyed Helene and her ascetic dress.

"I am no more pious than you," Helene had said. "But men will pay three hundred pounds to take a child's maidenhead. Ten guineas for a life is nothing!"

"Very true," the woman said, and her friends laughed more.

Helene rode back to Whitechapel in a state of frustration.

She didn't know why she was peeved; perhaps it was from learning that Art had been shot again. Or perhaps it was because she knew Helia's entire inheritance had been spent to bring Art back.

She entered her tenement building in darkness. She hurried up the steps, keyed the code for her entrance, and walked into her darkened room, expecting another telegram from Helia. Instead, she tripped over what she discovered was—after lighting a gas lamp—an explosion of clothing all about her living space. Black garments were everywhere. Her closet door was ajar. She saw a note in Helia's hand, stuck in the wall with a hatpin. It read: *The Surgical Sciences Academy.*

Helene swiftly unbuttoned her coat and doffed it. Strapped to her forearm was her spring-loaded rig, her derringer attached. She unbuckled it. Reaching inside her closet, she toggled a switch. The closet suddenly lit. She entered it and closed the door.

Southwark's night sky was clear, the Thames' wind having beaten back the smoke curling in from the tanneries on the shores and the factory stacks of East London. Office clerks rushed for home and dinner. The more well-to-do prepared for an evening spent at restaurants, clubs, and theatres. Southwark's residents avoided the area around the Royal Surgical Sciences Academy, leaving it absent of traffic and curious onlookers. It was a Saturday, and those in nearby homes shut their doors and curtains to enjoy their night and ignore what went on outside.

In the square before the Academy, tiny lights floated in the dark, and white signs waved. The anti-vivisectionists stood with their candles, linked arms, and sang. Others were seated eating paper-wrapped sandwiches. They tended a billycan over a portable kerosene stove.

"Quite a chill tonight!" a woman activist said, huddled in her coat.

"It's chilly enough that the bobbies have stopped watching us!" her companion declared.

"Well, that's hardly right; our policemen shouldn't be frightened of a little wind!" the activist replied. They shared a cup of smoky billycan tea and laughed.

A horn honked down the street. When the protesters looked, two gaslights bobbed in the darkness. A red and black horseless buggy appeared, its wheels clattering on the stones. In the driver's seat, a young gentleman in top hat and coat rattled about. He wore a steel half-mask.

The masked driver slowed his electric buggy. The protestors paused in their song and sandwiches to gape at his vehicle. As he passed around them and stared back, some could see his small handlebar moustache and his long dark hair, combed back to hide beneath his top hat.

The "fellow" honked her horn again, waved, and continued on her way. Helia trundled into the small street that ran alongside the Academy.

She drove the buggy by the side gate she and Aldosia Stropps had squeezed through where a bobby stood on guard. At the end of the campus, gaslights were lit, brightening the building that housed the surgical theatre. Helia rounded the corner for the back gate. It was wide open, and on the pavement and lawn several carriages and broughams were parked. Here more bobbies stood guard. Helia slowed her buggy as one beckoned to her. The policeman's uniform had buttons missing, and his belt hung below his belly. He walked out into the street to meet her.

"Wot strange thing is this?" he said, looking at the vehicle and then at her masked face. His breath smelt of gin. He peered closely.

"Are you from music hall?" he exclaimed.

Helia pulled out the black invitation and held it up for him. When the false bobby tried to take it she held it back.

Without a word, she stepped on the accelerator and steered the buggy past the flustered bobby and through the gates. She honked the horn. Several gentlemen who had disembarked from their carriages hurried out of her way. She drove the buggy up the lawn, obstructing horses and vehicles. She brought it to full stop, pulled on the hand brake, and hopped out.

She adjusted the black lapels of her long tan men's coat and retrieved her walking stick. The derby silver handle was of a deer's head. With Art's ironwood in hand, Helia sauntered across the lawn for the building.

A long black carriage sat near the building's back entrance. A young man emerged from the carriage door, bright light shining from the interior behind him. He shut the door, cutting off the light. In his hands he carried an old, locked wooden reliquary box, painted black and paneled with thick, black crystal glass. The young man stopped in surprise at the sight of Helia.

Helia stopped as well, a hand on her hip. She returned the young man's gaze. His regard dropped a fraction to study her chest, and she deduced from his formal bearing that he was a gentleman's valet. She looked at the reliquary box.

Helia raised a gloved finger to soothingly stroke the steel of her mask.

With a flourish, she smoothed her little handlebar moustache. She walked on, following the other gentlemen for the front of the building. The young man gave a minute shake of the head. He continued on his way and entered the back entrance.

As the door closed behind him, Helia turned around and walked quickly for the door he had disappeared into.

"Sir!" a man said. "You're to go this way!"

Helia turned again. The helpful man who accosted her waved in the correct direction. Another false bobby, far too short to fulfill the required height of five feet ten inches for a Metropolitan policeman, stood on the lawn and looked on. Helia obeyed the summons and set Art's stick to the grass.

She walked down the path leading to the building's front.

～

Inside, the manservant made his careful way through the backroom of the surgical theatre. He passed trolleys, tables, washed surgical instruments, and hanging surgeon gowns to where the prince stood before porcelain sinks and an ornately framed mirror. The manservant came to stand behind him.

The prince looked at himself in the mirror's cracked surface, his regard absentminded. His eyes moved and saw the reliquary box's reflection.

"Make certain all is precise," he said. "Then fetch the women."

The prince returned his attention to his own reflection. The manservant departed. He passed the trolley Art lay upon, a steel chloroform mask strapped to her face. The men guarding her looked at the box with curiosity. The servant stepped through the open door leading to the operating floor and entered its brightly lit space. Gentlemen were filling the seats, and their voices echoed about the theatre proper.

Tiers above, Helia stood at the theatre entrance with other gentlemen while an usher inspected their tickets. She gazed down at the surgical floor, noting the two steel tables meant to hold patients or subjects of dissection. In the sawdust covering the floor, five Xs had been traced, as if with a stick. The marks lay at equal distance from one another in a pattern that circled the tables. Helia watched as the manservant walked onto the floor. He carefully laid the reliquary box on a pedestal between the two tables.

As he stepped away, Helia saw that the box rested at the very center of the theatre's circular floor, equidistant from all five Xs.

And since it stands at the heart, where will you *stand, you heartless man?* she thought.

"Your ticket, sir?" the usher said to her.

Helia offered her ticket. The usher took one look at the number and escorted her down the tiers to six chairs lined on the edge of the operating floor itself. Gentlemen occupied five of the seats. Helia gracefully adjusted the tails of her coat and took the sixth seat. All the gentlemen but the one in the first seat noticed her. That young man, dressed in a grey suit, sat on the edge of his chair, excitement in his face and posture. He scanned the surgical floor. The portly gentleman nearest Helia tipped his hat to her.

Helia ignored the gesture. She raised her chin and turned

her attention to the operating floor. The manservant walked the perimeter, using his stride to check the distance between the five Xs. Helia looked at the back entrance's open door.

Black, blackblackblack, she thought, sensing the eldritch power of another. She had considered rising and merely walking towards that entrance and into the back room, but that chance had passed. The source of that black presence slowly appeared at the doorway and stepped through.

When the prince emerged, the young man in the first seat exclaimed in enthusiasm.

Helia stared at the prince and watched how he made his slow, diffident way onto the floor, glancing without interest at the manservant's preparations. He carried a walking stick of vertebrae bones. At his waistcoat, a large crystal fob hung on a silver chain, a human eyeball floating within. The prince slowly swiveled his head, as if he'd heard a tiny sound that intrigued him. His gaze came to rest on Helia.

The young man in the first seat turned to say something to the man next to him and noticed her. He leaned forward to brazenly look her up and down.

"Why, you're a music hall performer," he said with an American accent. "Yes, I've heard of your sort! You're a queer bunch, you impersonators. Well let me tell you, that moustache, it doesn't suit at all!"

"I beg your pardon. Neither do your shoes," Helia sniffed.

The young man looked at his brown shoes.

"Please forgive that young man, there," the portly gentleman next to Helia said in a low voice. "He is an American." He fished within his waistcoat's pocket. Across his belly was a heavy gold watch chain. He handed Helia his card.

"Dr. Horst Pendlecraft, at your service," he said, raising his hat again. "I also specialise in sex transformation. I can help with that voice of yours." He nodded knowingly.

Helia pocketed the card and merely returned her attention to the prince again, her chin raised and her hand resting on the handle of Art's stick. She put a hand on her hip.

The prince was speaking to a scarred man. His eyes didn't look at the man but stared elsewhere, as if in mild distraction. Helia scanned the floor and noted the five Xs again. At each mark, the manservant was laying down a silver serving dish.

Helia turned to the gentlemen. She leaned forward and attracted their attention.

"Gentlemen, you must all leave," she said softly to them.

The men looked at her in surprise.

"Arthur Fellows is dead," she said. "By the hand of that man, there. You are all next, and if you look at the floor and the manner of its preparation, you can guess as to the reason why you'll die. You must leave, now."

Helia saw in the wary eyes of several of the gentlemen that they understood what she was speaking of.

"Nonsense!" the young man said. "What you're inferring— would anyone do such a thing before *all* these people? Really? Why, I bet it's chickens he'll use. Or pigs. If you think we should leave, you go first! Perhaps you want all his knowledge for yourself."

Before Helia could answer, the young man turned away and scoffed.

"Try again, you weak charlatan!" he said.

The faces turned to her lost fear and turned cold. The portly gentleman cleared his throat and averted his eyes. The men returned their attention to the operating floor. Helia leaned back in her chair.

She drew out her cigarette case. She chose a cigarette, shut the case, and then fished for her match safe. Once she picked a match and lit it, she put it to the cigarette at her lips. She sucked in breath and raised her gaze to look at the Bone Stealer.

The prince was staring back, fixed in quiet fascination on her steel mask.

Come, have a closer look, she thought to him. *Talk to us. Have us taken to the back room.*

The scarred man approached while Helia smoked. He carried a chair. He smiled, set the chair next to Helia, and sat down. He placed an elbow on his knee and looked at her.

"My master wonders who you are and why you are here," he said.

"Why, I'm here to witness greatness, of course," Helia said. The prince's gaze was still on her, studying her face. She noticed the manservant's departure for the back entrance.

"After the demonstration, he wishes you to remain. He would like to speak with you."

"I'm sure he does," she said.

The scarred man straightened. Helia exhaled smoke and saw that he had a knife laid on his thigh. His resting hand concealed it. His attention remained on her. The prince turned away and pensively walked to stand by one of the tables.

Helia heard the sudden slam of the theatre doors and the rattling of a heavy chain being threaded through the handles outside. A padlock hit the doors, the sound echoing in the theatre. Someone laughed nervously. Another man made a jest, and more men laughed. The gentlemen beside Helia looked at each other.

Helia smoked and watched the back entrance.

A matronly, upper-class woman emerged. By her dress and bearing, Helia assumed she was titled, but she didn't recognise the woman. A nurse followed the matron, leading a very tall girl with hunched shoulders onto the operating stage. The manservant walked behind them. The murmuring of the spectators died down as the three made their way across the theatre floor to the table nearest the Bone Stealer.

The girl wore a steel corset. Helia didn't think it odd that she wore her spinal aid atop her clothing; if she were required to remove it for the procedure, she needn't undress before the male spectators to do so. The corset was hinged in the back and fastened shut with locks in front. Despite the devise, a hump— not yet terribly prominent but significant enough to be noticed— protruded from between the girl's shoulders.

Consumption of the spine, Helia speculated.

The girl caught Helia's look. Helia thought her sad and resigned. The girl's gaze fell away. Helia wondered, due to the girl's passivity, if she might already be drugged.

Run, child, Helia thought to her.

But the girl was not a child; no more than Art was. Her skirts were long, her hair pinned up. Helia was certain the girl was aged twenty-two, the same as Art. She only saw this young woman as a child because there her mother stood, a proud stern matron who had kept her darling daughter helpless by helping too much. Helia looked into the girl's downcast luminous eyes and thought that she was not simpleminded. She was merely frail of will.

While the prince looked on, the nurse and his manservant helped remove the girl's steel corset. Her body bowed, the weakness of her sick spine made evident without the supportive device. They helped her onto the surgical table. The nurse arranged pillows beneath her while the manservant took cotton and a glass ampoule from a tray to prepare a chloroform mask.

Helia looked away when the mother kissed her daughter. A few tears left the girl's eyes.

When Helia glanced to her side, the scarred man still watched her, his hand over his knife. Helia exhaled smoke. She returned her attention to the prince, who came to stand in between the surgical tables, his back to the reliquary box. He faced the tiers. The manservant applied the chloroform mask to the girl's face and once done, stepped away. The nurse and mother stood by the girl's side until her eyes closed. They then took seats in the first tier before her table.

The prince stood before the filled seats, not quite looking at anyone, his stick in his hands. The spectators of the theatre fell into further silence. He began to speak.

His voice quavered, the sound weak. He spoke in German.

Helia heard the scattering of whispers in the crowd, expressing their displeasure. A gentleman beside the American hurriedly shushed him when he tried to protest. The prince continued speaking and Helia listened. Like Helene, she was fluent in five languages and familiar with three more.

"What I do tonight, I do because I can and because I like to," he began. "You are here only to witness. I have learned that not only is superiority a part of our natural world, as animals are superior to insects, as men are superior to animals, but that there are men who are superior to men. I am that kind of man.

"And I say this not because I am of blood and title, but because I know I simply am. I was born with more than what mere men have." He looked at the gentlemen who sat next to Helia.

"You have all come to witness my secret," he said, turning to face the tiers again. "And some of you have come here to learn it. Imitate it. I will tell it to you. The secret is myself. Only I can do what I can do. Here I stand, by birthright and blood, a royal being. But titles and possessions are nothing. They can be seized. What is inside myself cannot be taken away or relinquished. I am the gift itself. I am the secret."

The prince smiled.

The smile stretched the corners of his mouth, causing wrinkles like cracked rubber. His smile faded as slowly as it had appeared. His pale eyes lost focus. He moved to stand near the slumbering girl's table. He turned and gestured abruptly.

"You may think: he needs to look there or stand there or face there, to do this. No. I know where each platter is. I know them like I do each of my fingers. And there is no ritual. I don't even use my stick."

He looked at the five men next to Helia.

"It's very simple, really," he said.

The young man in the first seat doubled over, clutching himself. The men next to him shook. They contorted, gave strangled cries, and collapsed, their chairs falling over. Horst Pendlecraft grabbed Helia's arm. He looked into her eyes as he tipped, a hand pressed into his shaking belly.

I'm sorry, Helia thought.

He fell in a heap on the other stiff men.

Helia removed each finger of Dr. Pendlecraft's claw-like grasp. Behind her, the spectators sat in frightened silence. The smell of fresh blood permeated the air, warm and thick. Helia glanced at the floor as she dropped the last of Dr. Pendlecraft's fingers and saw a bloody human liver lying on the silver platter nearest their seats.

The scarred man beside her was grinning. The prince stood with his eyes closed and his hands resting on his walking stick. He trembled slightly. Helia heard the sound of trolley wheels.

A trolley emerged from the back entrance, bearing female boots. Then the long body of the woman those boots belonged to emerged. Two thugs wheeled Art in. A steel chloroform mask was strapped to her face. As they brought Art next to the empty surgical table and lifted her, Helia flicked away her dwindling cigarette. She reached into her pocket.

The scarred man placed a hand on her arm. Helia looked at him. She drew out her cigarette case despite his firm grip. She also brought out her match safe. He slowly withdrew his hand as she lit another cigarette.

Drawing breath, Helia looked at the table and saw the thugs secure Art with leather straps across her chest and legs. When the two men finished they moved to stand near the back entrance. The prince opened his eyes and stared at Art.

"Harvesting and putting bones inside another is a different matter," he said. "I can only describe it as myself taking a precise photograph of the interiors of both subjects with my mind. It is a photograph that sees everything, right down to the nerve endings. This is the secret. I take and I insert everything precisely into the body, like puzzle pieces placed into the gaps. I do this at the same time I remove the corresponding pieces from the recipient." He turned to look at the sleeping girl on the other table.

"This process causes pain. The recipient should be in pain. But this girl will rise and walk away, feeling perfect in body. Why? Because by my action will these women experience a gift. A rare gift, sought by hedonists and fanatics alike. The highest known euphoria of the body. It is an elevation beyond base pleasure or the so-called touch of God. I've the power to cause this in their bodies. I will give the woman receiving perfect health a state beyond pain, just as I will give the woman going to death her state of perfection."

Helia stood up. The scarred man stood as well, grabbed her stick-wielding arm, and drove his knife into her ribs. The blade snapped. Astonished exclamations rose from the spectators, and the scarred man froze in surprise. Helia wrenched away and kneed him in the groin. When he doubled over, she brought her stick down on his neck. He collapsed to the floor and remained still.

As some of the spectators stood up, Helia ran to Art's table. She pressed the lit end of her cigarette into Art's hand and snatched off the chloroform mask. She shook Art by the chin.

"Wake up, Art!" she cried. "Wake up!"

The two thugs rushed forwards and grabbed her. One grabbed the stick. Helia struggled as they dragged her back. She shouted at Art, and the prince looked on in curiosity.

"No," he said, when the thugs attempted to force Helia into the back room. They paused. Helia met the Bone Stealer's gaze, seeing the interest in his eyes.

"You must watch," he said and smiled.

The murmuring of the spectators died away. Those who had stood slowly sat back down. The manservant entered the circle and picked up the dropped chloroform mask.

"No," the prince said again. The servant held the mask and looked at him. "She'll have no need for it."

The servant obeyed and walked off the operating floor. He resumed his position near the seated nurse and the girl's mother.

"Art!" Helia shouted. "*Art*, wake up!"

One of the thugs hit Helia, silencing her. The prince stood by the girl's table, his hands resting on his stick. He stared at Art's body.

~

Art swam slowly to consciousness. She became aware that she was sleeping. She felt that she was suspended somewhere very far away, even though she knew that her body was surely lying someplace tactile, real, and still of God's Earth. In her state of suspension, she drifted back into sleep and dreamt of when Jim was in her hand, summoning his flame and searing her to rouse her out of Madame Chance's trance.

My hand, 'tis burning, she finally thought, recognising the sensation in her palm yet feeling no pain. She woke up.

Light, strangely grainy in its appearance, met her eyes. She smelled cigarette smoke. She heard Helia's voice, faintly shouting. Her body tingled yet was numb. She felt an encompassing touch like the clamping of a great dark cloud-hand. It thickened around her. Its touch chilled, straight to her bones. She tried to rise and found her body restrained. Art swiftly ghosted.

In her ghost state, the cloud became a pulse, hard and powerful. It sounded in the fabric of her Fourth Dimensional reality. It gripped her, and like horses galloping in every direction, it pulled.

She felt her ghost body rent asunder.

~

A hansom cab ran smartly down the quiet streets of Southwark. It turned for a road that led to the back of the Royal Surgical Sciences Academy. Delphia breathed deeply of the night air that blew, and pulled out her cudgel.

"This street runs alongside the Surgical Academy," Jim said. "On our last visit, Art pulled the bars apart on a side gate. You can easily squeeze through, and then we'll fling the main gates open and let the demonstrators in. With such numbers on our side and by sheer confusion, we'll disrupt the surgery and challenge that prince's thugs, whether they be of the living or of the undead variety."

"The Bone Stealer has many men working for him, that's true," Delphia said. "A 'prince', sir?"

While Jim explained who the Bone Stealer was, the cab slowed and they saw the lights of the academy's campus. Inside the back gates was a congestion of carriages and broughams, their drivers loitering. Bobbies stood in the street, feet planted and clubs in hand.

"Delphia! Hide me! Driver, keep going, don't stop!" Jim said.

Delphia hastily placed Jim at her feet as the driver slid open the cab roof's trap door.

"Sir?" he said, glancing down. "But one of 'em waves to us, sir."

"Those are false policemen, man!" Jim said from Delphia's

feet. "Ignore them, keep driving!"

"Quiet, Mr. Dastard, we're being hailed," Delphia said. She straightened her hat and coat and looked up at the driver. "Sir, if you would. Let's obey this bobby, and then be on our way."

"Yes, miss, I can do that," the driver said. He left the trap door open as he slowed his horse down for the bobby who waved to them. Delphia placed her stick to the dash of the cab, hand on the knobby end, and raised her chin. They came up beside the policeman and halted. The policeman stared at Delphia through her open cab.

"Wot's yer business?" he asked suspiciously.

"The stage, though that's no business of yours!" Delphia retorted. "I'm here to join my factory girls in protest, sir! Once I'm at the front gates I'll be raising sign and candle and leading my girls in song! Those you guard inside will see God's judgment for their cruel actions, mark my words!"

"Feh! Actress. Git on with you, then," the bobby said. He brusquely motioned. The driver quickly drove his horse forwards and away.

"We're clear of him, sir," Delphia said as their cab ran past the academy's fenced grounds. "But I mustn't pick you up yet."

"That building where the carriages were gathered, it's where the surgical theatre is!" Jim said at Delphia's feet. "It's all happening now!"

"I see the side gate you mentioned. Another bobby stands by it," Delphia said.

"Driver!" Jim shouted. "To the front, my good man! We'll join the demonstrators!"

"Yes sir!" the driver said.

Delphia picked Jim up, and the sound of singing reached their ears. The cab entered the square where the demonstrators gathered, dotting the space with lit candles. A woman in suffragette sash stood on a crate before the academy's gated entrance and led the song. When the cab came to a stop, Delphia reached up to pay the driver and disembarked with Jim.

At Jim's urging, she made her way quickly through the singing crowd and approached the woman on the crate. She held Jim up.

"Madam!" Jim addressed, interrupting the singing. "Good woman, a most dire crime is about to be committed, and all you good demonstrators must be told!"

"Good gracious," the suffragette said. "Well—take the box, then, sir!"

One of her members helped her down from the crate, and Delphia hopped up. She placed Jim on the head of her cudgel and held him high.

"Glow, sir!" she said.

"Right!" Jim said. He did so, his skull becoming a beacon as bright as a torch. The demonstrators exclaimed and gathered closer to witness his light.

"Friends!" he cried. "I am Jim Dastard, agent of His Royal Highness' Secret Commission! Help us! My partner, Art, the artificial ghost, is being held by the Bone Stealer, *inside* the academy's surgical theatre! Six foot two, she is, and even now, like our animal friends, may be cruelly harvested!"

An alarmed murmur ran through the crowd.

"What do you need from us, sir?" the suffragette said.

"Help us break down the gates! Storm the castle with us!" he said. "Together we can overwhelm the Bone Stealer's undead men and rescue my partner!"

While some cheered heartily, Jim saw the hesitance of the rest. Demonstrators looked at their pastors and leaders.

"*Friends!*" Jim shouted. "Do not fear the law or reprisal! Do you see the police here? Where are they, who once watched your vigils, day and night? When the valiant Felly Pritt died, she was guarded by false policemen! No doubt the villain *inside* has made certain no true lawmen be present tonight! Therefore, as agent of His Royal Highness, I *am* law! I deputize you all! Can we stand by and allow another woman to die tonight, *vivisected*, by a surgeon who defies common decent humanity? Who has already *murdered* five good men and women?"

"No! No!" came the cry from the crowd.

"Tonight, I give us the right to strike! No longer will the surgeons ignore us and continue their cruel practice! Tonight, we save my friend and we will *save the animals!*"

A great cheer rose, and the demonstrators advanced, signs waving. Several men pressed themselves against the gates, others urging them on. The heavy tall gates barely budged.

"Shall we try to climb?" a churchman said.

"Let's get a rock! Break the locks!" a woman said.

"My hat for a battering ram!" Jim said. He tilted to look down at Delphia.

"Can you pick the locks?" he called down to her.

"What?" Delphia said.

"Well, your brother was a thief!"

"Sir!" Delphia said indignantly.

Amidst the fervor of the crowd, they heard the far-off sound of hooves, thunderous and fast approaching. Jim spun on Delphia's cudgel to see.

"A lone 'orse?" a workman declared. Demonstrators turned their heads to look down the street. "'N racin'? None rides a lone 'orse like that in the very street unless—"

"Unless like times of yore!" a churchwoman said excitedly. "In tricorne and black cloak he rides!"

"With silver pistols at his sides!" a factory girl cried. "It's the *Blackheart!*"

The sound of hooves grew louder. Into the square galloped a black-garbed rider, her black steed huge and muscular. A black cloak billowed behind her. She wore a black tricorne and black mask. She reined her horse in at the edge of the crowd, and he reared.

"The Blackheart!" a man shouted.

The crowd took up the cry. The demonstrators surged forwards, trying to catch a glimpse of the Blackheart as her horse trotted back and forth on the edge of the gathering. It reared again, and the crowd drew back.

The Blackheart pulled out a large blunderbuss slung on her back. The barrel gleamed.

"The gate! She—*make way for her!*" Jim shouted. "Can't you

see? She needs to get to the *gate!*"

The Blackheart set the weapon to her shoulder and aimed.

Women screamed, and the demonstrators swiftly parted, creating a clear path down to the academy gates. Delphia retrieved Jim from atop her cudgel, jumped off the crate, and ran. The Blackheart galloped forwards.

"*Flying lead!*" Jim yelled as Delphia backpedaled, pushing back the crowd.

At fifteen feet, the Blackheart fired. With a boom, the locks flew apart and the twisted metal of the gates screeched as they parted. The Blackheart turned her horse and rode back through the crowd. She swiftly galloped away.

Once the Blackheart disappeared into the darkness, the protesters looked at each other.

"Will she come back?" an old woman said.

"Good ole Nick! Thank you!" Jim shouted. He glowed brightly. "Everyone! *To the gates!* We've *lives* to save!"

The demonstrators cheered and shook their signs, parasols, and Bibles. They moved forward—suffragettes, workers, church members, and activists. Delphia kicked the gates farther open and ran ahead, placing Jim back on her stick and holding him aloft so that his glow may be seen.

As the demonstrators poured into the campus, leaving the street littered with signs, food wrappings, and melted candles, the Quakers stood in uncertainty. One among them, a wizen vegetarian whose shoes were woven sandals and whose hat and clothes, lacking dye, were made of cotton free of slave labour, raised his cane. He pointed at the broken gates.

"Not violence, but action!" he cried.

In silent agreement, the Quakers thrust their signs to him. They hurried to follow the crowd inside.

The Blackheart trotted her horse back to the square and watched the Quakers enter. She urged her steed on. She galloped past the old Quaker and rode for the back of the academy campus.

The protesters weaved their way down the paths, following Jim's glow towards the building that held the surgical theatre. A false bobby, upon spying the crowd, hurried inside the building and closed the doors. The male demonstrators ran up, put their shoulders to the doors, and forced them open.

Delphia hurried in and led the way inside, cudgel out and Jim in hand as he directed her down the proper hall. The demonstrators chatted excitedly with each other, both nervous and emboldened as they glanced at the medical displays and cases in passing. No one noticed the dank sea scent in the air.

En masse, they noisily entered the hall leading to the theatre. In front of the shut and chained doors of the surgical theatre, four large men stood, armed with clubs. The look of them, with their blank stares and stiff bearing, gave the demonstrators pause. They halted in their advancement.

"Are they the zombis?" a woman said, looking at her fellow demonstrators.

"We're many, 'n they're only four!" a workman said, balling his fists. He and his fellow workmen and women moved forwards. Suffragettes held their parasols up and followed. Once they neared the silent men, an ugly clash ensued. Fists and sticks met flesh, and thuds and groans sounded.

"Bloom!" Jim said above the fighting as Delphia, along with the church folk and spinsters, held back. "They'll never defeat those men if they're the sort Art fought! But if they can hold them aside, then we may get through!"

"But the doors, sir!" Delphia said. "Chained and locked, and we've nothing to break them!" She and the others searched about the hall for something to use. They heard the sound of hammering. When they turned to look down the hall's other end, the Quakers were using a large rock to break the locks on the double doors there.

"The animals!" Jim said.

The lock broke. The Quakers swung the heavy doors open. The scent of stale seawater filled the hallway. They heard the sound of tapping, echoing. Delphia and the rest rushed forwards to see what the Quakers stared at.

Cages of various animals lined the cavernous lab. The animals cried. Dogs yapped at the sight of the demonstrators though some lay still, their bodies curled. In the centre of the room stood the source of the overpowering salty scent.

A large rectangular tank of thick glass, six feet high and wide and twelve feet long, rested on a low steel trolley. Within floated an adolescent, colossal squid. Its huge round eyes stared.

Its body was six feet long and its tentacles longer. It tapped the glass. The amputated tentacle that tapped was fitted with a segmented and hinged steel appendage imitating its original limb. It curled into a simulated fist. As the squid slowly moved, it revealed severed arms, also fitted with segmented steel limbs which flexed. Crude metal devices were embedded in the scarred flesh of its body.

The squid continued to tap. The sound echoed above the sad sounds of the animals.

"You . . . great and mighty creature!" Jim said. "I'm sorry you won't grow to the magnificence you deserve. And for what we've done to you, we will always pay. But we *will* give you vengeance! C'mon! Everyone! We'll break the theatre doors down with this tank!"

Delphia ran forwards and looked beneath the tank. She kicked out the stops that locked the wheels in place. The others rushed in to put their shoulders and bodies against the glass.

POW POW!

"Ah! What man would shoot at demonstrators?" a pastor cried. He rushed out of the lab to see.

"C'mon!" Jim urged the protesters. "That sounded like it was in the theatre, not in the hall! Now, more than ever, we must get inside!"

They resumed pushing. Slowly, the demonstrators set the huge tank in motion.

The squid turned its immense eyes to regard each person who gripped the glass. The protesters straightened the tank's path and rolled it out the doors for the hallway.

At the hall's end, no one lay from bullet wounds, but workers and suffragettes were flagging before the stoic undead men who beat upon them. Demonstrators leaned on walls or lay aside, injured. The tank rolled loudly down the hall and gained momentum.

"This will surely do!" a spinster cried as she ran after the tank and the demonstrators who pushed. "Faster, faster!"

"Stand aside!" Jim shouted. "Let the undead men face *this!*"

The other protestors abandoned the fight and pressed out of the way. The four silent men resumed their positions before the doors as the tank rushed forwards.

～

Just as Art felt her bones ripped from her, the deformed bloody bones of the sleeping girl clattered to the surgery floor. The girl's body lengthened and straightened. She and Art screamed. The prince stared at Art as she lay in a transparent state. When she did not collapse into a heap of flesh, his eyes slowly grew.

As Art screamed, she felt herself in two places. She saw two ceilings. She screamed from two mouths. Her sense of reason and self fled. She was merely two bodies, instinctual, mindless, and in unfathomable pain. Just when she thought death should release her, her perceptions catapulted to another plane. Pain resided in her screaming bodies but her awareness flew straight into a dream state of euphoria. She still knew things were wrong. She sat up, and in ghost form, began to float off the table like a person-shaped balloon.

The girl sat up. Her mother stood and shouted. Art lashed out. The girl's arm shot out, and she grabbed the prince by the neck. He broke the grip and stepped back, frightened. Art, still rising in the air, leaned forwards. The girl left the table and stood.

Art lashed out again. The girl did the same, and her hand clenched the prince's throat. She throttled him.

Helia watched Art float, her body slowly losing shape and becoming insubstantial. She resumed her struggle against the men who held her. The scarred man staggered to his feet, peered up at Art in astonishment, and pointed at her.

"We must kill the ghost!" he shouted. He took up a chair and flung it.

The chair passed through Art and crashed against the other wall. She continued to thrust her arm out. The prince choked in the girl's grip. One of the thugs who held Helia let go and drew out his revolver. He aimed at Art and fired.

A spectator seated in the topmost tier jerked backwards, an eye shot out. The thug fired at Art again. The spectators yelled and abandoned their chairs, trying to flee.

"*Dummkopf!*" the scarred man cried.

Helia kicked the thug nearest her in the groin, grabbed back Art's stick, and shoved the thug into the one shooting. The pistol wielder stumbled and his gun went off, shooting the man who collided with him. Helia leapt for the stand between the tables. She brought her stick down and struck the reliquary box square. Instead of breaking it, she succeeded in knocking it to the floor. The little door opened. Out popped a beating, black human heart.

The prince trembled, his eyes wide. Art's ghost form suddenly rushed, as if sucked, into the girl's body. The girl convulsed and she gave a bottomless cry.

"*Amalie!*" her mother screamed.

Slowly, Art emerged in ghost form from behind the girl. Within Art's transparent body was her skeleton. She landed gently on her feet and solidified.

The girl deflated like a pricked balloon. Blood poured from her eyes, ears, and mouth, splashing the prince. She collapsed into a pile of skin, hair, and tissue. Her mother screamed, long and shrill.

The theatre doors crashed open, rocking the walls. The tank rolled in, its glass shattering. It tipped, crushing an undead man trapped beneath. The steel lid slipped off and tumbled down the steps. Water cascaded down the tiers. The squid flopped out and rode down the spilling water.

It lashed out, grabbing men and flinging them. Its serrated suction cups tore off clothing and skin—blood sprayed as a tossed man's face ripped away. The squid slapped its steel limbs and smashed bodies and wood floors. It tumbled down the tiers for the surgery floor, bringing people and chairs down with it. The scarred man ran for the prince. The squid headed straight for Art.

The squid grabbed her. She grabbed back. Its open beak slammed into her abdomen. She pressed shoulders and chest to its immense body and refused to be lifted. The squid slapped a fleshy tentacle to the side of her face, the cups suctioning. Its steel arms flailed and broke the flooring. Sawdust rose in clouds. It grabbed the table Art had lain upon, held fast, and forced her to totter to one side. The squid then grabbed the prince. It slammed him against the edge of the table the girl had lain upon. When it released him, he lay front side-up on the table's edge, back snapped and bent at a severe angle. His head hung over the side. He wheezed for air as his manservant and the scarred man stared.

They looked at each other and then ran for the back entrance.

Art held tight. The squid wrapped all ten of its limbs and squeezed. Art shook in its grip. She began to compress. The squid's beak broke through Art's corset with a loud rip.

Art sucked the entire beast into herself, and its metal parts clattered to the floor.

The room stilled except for the moans of the injured. A hoarse, high-pitched wail emitted from the girl's mother. The broken prince struggled for breath from where he lay.

Art convulsed. She heaved. When it seemed she might vomit, she became translucent. A large beak dropped from her chest and landed noisily on the wet floor. A tentacle burst from her midsection. With a sucking pop, she absorbed it back in.

Delphia ran down the wet, smashed tiers for Art, Jim and cudgel in hand. Art stumbled, her translucent body revealing the immense squid squished inside of her. It slid around like wash being slowly churned.

"Art! You're so, er," Jim said.

Another tentacle poked suddenly from Art's belly. She smacked it, trying to push it back in. Delphia hopped and held Jim out of the way.

He spied the reliquary box lying on the floor. The black,

shriveled human heart lay beside it, beating rhythmically.

"Bloom!" he said. "That thing down there! It must be destroyed! Step on—"

Art stumbled backwards, and her heel landed on the heart. It burst with a sickening pop.

The prince gave out a long pained gasp, his lungs expelling air. He collapsed and hung still.

"Well," Jim said, when Delphia had spun to witness the prince's expiration. "Good riddance."

～

From the skylight above the surgical theatre, the Blackheart crouched, a hole smashed in the glass and her silver pistol aimed. When the prince expired upon the table, she withdrew her weapon. She watched as the demonstrators cautiously descended into the theatre, finding the injured. Several demonstrators laid hands on those who looked suspicious and held them firmly. Spectators who survived the squid's attack attempted to leave and loudly protested when accosted. In response, the demonstrators sternly blocked the doorways with their parasols, Bibles, and sticks in hand.

The Blackheart watched as Delphia and the disguised Helia gently helped a very unsteady Art to the door that led to the theatre's backroom. Once they exited, the Blackheart left the skylight and swiftly climbed down the building. The lawn below was littered with the unconscious bodies of thugs and false policemen. Several carriages were hastily departing, trying to find passage around the electric buggy that blocked their way. But the prince's black carriage stood dangerously tilted, the electric batteries beneath revealed. Its interior lights flickered. One of its rear wheels lay shattered by a blunderbuss' blast. The driver stood, reins in hand after detaching his horses from the broken carriage.

He balked at the sight of the Blackheart. She jumped into the saddle of her waiting horse and rode through the academy grounds. She galloped out the broken front gates and past the wizened Quaker man.

The moon shone on London through drifting clouds. The pea-soup fog cleared along the Thames as the night winds fiercely blew. Coal barges with lantern-lit windows glided down. An electric buggy sped across London Bridge.

Art lay with her head in Helia's lap and her legs folded on the seat while Helia drove. Delphia and Jim sat in the rumble seat behind them. Helia had put her walking stick between Art's uncooperative hands, and Art found the touch of her ironwood comforting. Wind from the river blew into her face, and she smelled the Thames. She thought Helia's trousers beneath her head were of a nice material, not at all scratchy. She could see the stars, but mostly she looked at Helia.

She still experienced the odd euphoria that manifested from enduring extreme pain. She knew at any moment that feeling would fade and the truth of her body's condition would make itself excruciatingly known. Perhaps because of such trauma she lacked recall of what had just happened. She remembered waking because her hand was burning, and then her body's rending. She had stared out of someone else's eyes into that of the Bone Stealer's, her fingers around his throat.

Then what happened? she thought. She had wrestled the squid. But between that and her rending, her memory was a wiped slate. She decided to let the matter lie. She looked at Helia's steel mask, her funny mustache, and the fit of her gentlemen's attire.

She thought: *Helia is far too pretty to be a gentleman.*

The squid rumbled inside of her, and its tentacles poked her ribs, desiring to lash out. One did, bursting through her chest and waving. She drew it forcibly back in, and the wound in her chest swiftly healed. Her bodice showed a gaping hole.

"Oh," Art said belatedly.

Helia laid a gloved hand upon Art's chest as she drove.

Art smiled, but she felt as if her lips and face were in another place, and her teeth and jaw perhaps one increment in the opposite direction. Her nose might be where it should be, but it felt more as if it lay just a dash out of alignment from her jaw. She was uncertain if she were really splitting into pieces or merely coping with the remaining sensations of having existed as two torn parts at once. Like a violin string, she might be vibrating. Concentrating on Helia's very real touch and the fabric of her men's coat seemed an appropriate way to ignore the effects of her body's sundering.

She stared up at Helia's chest and realised something.

"Where is . . . thy bosom?" she asked.

"It's still here, Art," Helia answered, smiling. The buggy ran over a bump and Helia steadied her. The jostling caused a part of Art to lag. She wasn't sure what part exactly; it seemed her whole body might be a smitch of a second in need of catching up to the rest of her.

"I am . . . in two places," she said. Helia's hand soothed her chest.

"Art, you're a sight!" Jim said. "We can still see what goes on inside of you. Brr! How about we give the beast a shot of Harold's brandy?"

Delphia suddenly twisted in her seat and retched over the side.

"*Ho!*" Jim said. "Bloom, is Art's digestion disturbing you? Those huge, staring eyes of the squid are unsettling!"

"Ah, sir," Delphia said. She put Jim on her knee and took her handkerchief out.

"I apologise for my driving, Delphia," Helia said. "I'm being terribly reckless, but I mean to get Perseus' vehicle to the Vesta before the battery is depleted."

"Oh, M'Lady! It isn't your driving," Delphia said. "And Art, it isn't your squid's eyes. I've only now identified the sad mass of horror I'd seen on the surgical theatre's floor."

"There were many of those," Jim said.

"Very many, sir," Delphia said soberly. "I'll see them again behind my eyelids tonight."

Art wanted to raise her hand and reassure Delphia, but her arms were of their own mind while separated from the part of her body that still housed her brain. She hoped her arms wouldn't turn into tentacles. She wanted to say something too, but she couldn't think right then on what could comfort. She herself sometimes recalled the reanimated children she'd destroyed, during moments when she was most unguarded.

"You must tell someone of your nightmares, Delphia," Helia said. "Right away. Not those that come with sleep, but the ones you saw tonight. Relinquish them. It's the only way to be rid of them."

In the dark street before the Vesta, beggars slept in a doorway. A few women slowly walked. A drunken man made his way with a heavy step, looking up at each building to see if it was the right one that had his room. Into the street, the Picnic-hicle appeared, its gas lamps brightly lit. Helia walked beside it in her shirtsleeves and waistcoat, hands on the doorframe. She pushed the vehicle forwards. Delphia, coat and hat doffed, pushed from the back.

When they neared the Vesta, Helia hopped into the front seat and steered. The buggy bumped along as it ran up the walk. She pulled on the hand brake and the vehicle came to full stop, parked in front of the Vesta.

"That was fun!" Jim said in the rumble seat. "Let's do it again!"

"Sir, if I might have your admittance key," Delphia said tiredly when she came around to stand by his seat. She held her hand out.

After retrieving the key Jim spat out, Delphia went within the portico, Jim in hand. Helia looked down at Art, who still lay on the front seat.

"Are you still everywhere, dear?" she asked softly.

"I am," Art said. "I float."

"It's the sort of place one goes to after a great hurting," Helia whispered. "You'll descend soon enough. Then you must take something for the pain."

"Thee knows such hurting?" Art asked.

"I do," Helia said. She looked up at the sound of footsteps approaching. Delphia and Jim had fetched the footwomen.

"Art can stand, but not yet manage walking on her own,"

Jim said. "So if you two will be so kind as to help her to her room, as you did for Harold on nights like these."

"Yes, sir!" the footwomen said. The squid slowly spun inside Art, but the women paid it no heed. They each took firm but gentle hold of her arms.

"On three, we shall pull you up, miss," one footwoman said. "One, two, three."

They had Art sitting up in the buggy, but before they could tug again and pull her to her feet, she reached behind and grabbed Helia's arm.

"She comes with me!" Art said.

One of the footwomen peered at Helia.

"Why, that's—"

"With me! With me!" Art said, brandishing her stick.

"Quaker tantrum!" Jim said. "Art! She'll join you briefly, yes. We'll send her up another way, all right? In a manner Catherine would approve, and she may arrive at your room before you. Not a word, you two," Jim said, addressing the footwomen. "Is that understood?"

"Sir, we only strive to see Art comfortable," a footwoman replied.

"Then to it!" Jim said. Art let go of Helia, and the women pulled her to her feet. They placed each of her arms around their shoulders and began walking her forwards.

"We'll see you inside, Art!" Jim called.

"Helia is very pretty," Art said to the footwomen as they helped her through the iris portal. It spun closed. Delphia, Jim, and Helia departed quickly for the back alley.

As they hurried down the walk, the Blackheart trotted her steed out of cover of a building. She watched them disappear around the corner. The drunken man, still looking for his room, bumped into her horse. He looked up.

"Oh!" he said, raising his cap. "Sorry, Miss 'Eart."

———

As Jim had promised, he, Delphia, and Helia were waiting in Art's room long before she arrived. Two maids joined them, ready to prepare Art for bed. A page informed Jim that a doctress had been summoned.

Art's translucent body with its squished giant squid caused a stir in the floors below, but eventually Art bade the Vesta residents good night and climbed the stairs. With jaw set, she forced herself to take each step, not wanting the footwomen to carry her.

"The squid and I may be twenty-four stone," she told them.

When she reached her room, the maids set about undressing her. Her ragged clothing was removed, and each article, once off her body, lost translucency and became solid. Their damage was apparent. Art saw that her pinstriped, chartreuse yellow dress was completely ruined. Her corset had two huge holes, the plating and boning burst outwards. She looked at Helia. Still in gentleman's dress, she had her top hat in one hand and her coat in the other. She smiled at Art, eyes twinkling.

"Art, your organs can't be seen at all," Jim said. "You're all squid."

"Thee sees no kittens?" Art said.

"Kittens? Er, I—oh, ha ha!" he said.

A maid searched Art's dresser for a nightgown. Art told her she had none and was content to sleep nude. The maids helped her into bed and brought the covers up.

Delphia set Jim on the nightstand and the maids departed. One footwoman remained at the door, and Helia stepped forwards. She leaned over Art's bed.

"I'm allowed just this minute," Helia whispered. "Then I must go." She bent and kissed Art on her forehead.

"Silly moustache," Art said, grinning.

"Rest now. I will see you soon."

"I want thee," Art said.

"I want thee too," Helia whispered. "Always."

Helia straightened, and the footwoman escorted her out. The door closed behind her.

"I should live elsewhere," Art said mournfully. "I should have a balloon as my home and invite her to it."

"Art, you haven't had any morphine, yet," Jim said. "Where is that doctress? Our ghost is in delirium and already babbling!"

"No more medicines," Art said.

"It will help you sleep. That untidy thing moving about inside of you could do with a bit of morphine, as well."

"No more," Art said. "I'd my fill of chloroform."

"Well then, some laudanum?"

"No."

"Bah! Physical culturalist!"

"Art, would you like a sip of something, at least?" Delphia said. "I know you're Quaker, but I do have brandy."

"No need, Delphia, but my thanks," Art said, smiling. "Sleep is what I'll have."

Delphia nodded and watched Art close her eyes. She tucked the blankets around her. Jim swiveled on the nightstand.

"Bloom, you've been above and beyond!" he said in a low voice. "As it's very late, would you like to stay or return to Bethnal Green? We can make arrangements!"

"Sir. I'd like to be with my family, if you haven't further need of me."

"Very well!" Jim spat out some coins, and Delphia picked them up. She turned for the door.

"We'll see you in the morning!"

Delphia didn't answer. She also forgot to tip her hat.

~

Delphia closed Art's doors, made her way down the hallway, and descended the staircase. A rowdy gathering could be heard on the ground floor, with piano playing and lusty group singing. The song was bawdy. She thought that such an upper-class establishment shouldn't tolerate such lower-class antics, suitable for gin palaces, but she wouldn't be surprised—by the quality of singing—that a few music hall performers were among those enjoying themselves in the gathering below.

Two men, drunk and in evening dress, weaved their way up the stairs as Delphia descended. They held each other and kissed.

Their fine clothes reminded her of the men she'd seen, fallen on the surgical theatre floor, bodies stiffened in contortions of pain and with eyes frozen in gazes of horrified surprise.

Delphia hurried down the hall for the portal entrance as gay laughter sounded.

～

The doctress who arrived to tend to Art was a tiny African Jamaican woman wearing gold spectacles. Her name was Judith SeaJane. After listening to Art's heart and lungs, checking her pulse, eyes, her tongue, and taking a good look at the squid, slowly swirling and staring out of Art's translucent body (this gave Dr. SeaJane a hearty laugh), she prescribed that valerian tea be ingested for pain and a glass of milk stout for sound sleep. A page delivered both items. The page carried a vase of lavender as well, which she set on Art's nightstand with the liquids. Art absorbed the valerian tea and felt that it relaxed her, much as the chloroform had to such an overwhelming degree.

"The beer is a fine thought, but I still can't drink it, no more than cow's milk," Art said when Dr. SeaJane had left.

"But it's made of hops, with just a bit of cow added," Jim said. "'Tis medicinal stout, Art. Never mind that it's evilly alcoholic. Can you eat the lavender?"

"Nay," Art said. "I've too much squid. But I can smell it, and the glass of beer. 'Tis pleasing." She yawned.

"Harold loved his milk. He drank pails of it," Jim said.

He quieted, but Art thought his silence solemn. She turned her head to look at him. He sat by the glass of beer, his hat doffed.

"Harold," Jim said quietly.

"Friend."

"I watched him die," Jim said. "Harold. Deck, my partner after Harold, died without my witnessing it. His death was a suicide, and for those women he cared for as wives, Risk was the one to tell them. Billy died in foolish bravado, tricked by a girl. He'd other sweethearts, too, but they ended up learning of his death from the newspapers.

"For Harold, I came back to the Vesta to tell Catherine.

She had a huge dinner laid for him. She had been waiting. I don't believe I said . . . I don't believe I could," he whispered.

"It was . . . we had been beset by golems, Harold and I. Huge monsters. Such fists! They felt nothing. At least with undead men, when you take them apart they eventually stop moving. Not so, with golems. And Harold, on that night, he had been distracted! As if a terrible thought disturbed him. What went through Harold's mind that made him falter? Was it really a mistake? Did he really tire?

"He slipped," Jim said softly. "And I knew it was the end. I had to watch as they beat, and beat, and beat him dead and then beyond dead. Nothing left that Harold could come back from or Fall could bring back, if he cared to. Just blood, smeared. Catherine had nothing to bury."

Art brought her hand out from beneath the covers. It was unsteady. She reached to touch Jim but stuck her finger into his eye socket instead.

"Ow, Art."

"My apologies, Friend," Art said. She put her disobedient hand back beneath the covers.

"I've helped today, haven't I, Art?" Jim asked fearfully.

"Thee did," Art said. She smiled. Her teeth, cheekbones, and nose bones were beginning to ache. She felt her euphoric state finally fading.

"Oh, is that all."

"Any more, Friend, and thee will call me flirtatious."

"Aha!" Jim emitted, sounding pained.

Art's eyes closed of their own accord.

"I called him Ford," Jim suddenly said.

Art's eyes opened again.

"Harold. I called him Ford because Fall gave him a ghastly name. I wouldn't use it. We didn't know he was Harold Moore until his mother finally revealed it to him. I don't know why I called him Ford. Somehow I was endeared of the name. And I loved Harold, so very much."

"Fortunate was he, to have thee as beloved Friend. And I,

as well. My forever thanks," Art murmured.

"Sleep, my young friend," Jim said. "Sleep. I'll be here. Watching over you."

Delphia sat gingerly in a dirty cab seat and scowled. She had the misfortune of riding with a recalcitrant cab driver, one who was reluctant to take her further into Bethnal Green and insisted she disembark several streets away from her own street. Patience at an end, she made the man drive her right up to the front door of her home. She thought she might regret using the Secret Commission's name to bully the man, but her guilt, in the morning, might also be fleeting.

When she quietly entered the house, Gaiety sat fast asleep in the rocking chair, covered by the quilt. It was something she often did when Philo would disappear at nights. Delphia took off her hat, removed her cudgel from its holster, and checked to see if her coat had any frightful stains. She gently kissed her mother awake.

Gaiety woke. Delphia led her to bed with assurances that she would soon follow suit. Once Delphia made certain that her mother was laid beside her snoring father and fallen back to sleep, she picked up her stick and went to sit on the front porch.

She sat staring down the dark street. It was silent and empty. A lone, female figure appeared, walking. Delphia thought it odd, and not just because of the late hour. The girl's attitude was leisurely and confident, like one at home in the darkness. She carried no parasol or purse. She wore no hat or shawl. With her hands by her sides, there seemed no caution or timidity in any aspect of her feminine silhouette. The girl walked towards her. By the dim light of the moon, Delphia could discern her identity. It was Elsepeth.

"Elsepeth, this is very late for you to be out!" she snapped.

Elsepeth stopped short, startled.

"Delphia! I was worried about you," Elsepeth said. "You're doing very dangerous work, now that you help these agents. Since I was near, I thought to see how you were."

"Elsepeth, are you prostituting?" Delphia asked.

"Oh, Delphia! You are so horrid!" Elsepeth said, but she smiled in surprise.

"That was wicked, I'm sorry. It's just that I've noticed your clothes, Elsepeth. They're much finer. You must not work at the boot-making factory anymore. And you've never explained how a girl like yourself, who speaks so well and is mannered, happens to be slumming! Perhaps someone's caring for you, and I don't mind it, as long as you're happy.

"But no matter," Delphia said. "He really shouldn't let you wander alone and so late; it's just not safe."

Delphia swallowed suddenly. Her hand went to her mouth.

She suppressed the sobs that came. Elsepeth urged her to her feet with surprising strength and pressed Delphia to her shoulder. Delphia felt Elsepeth fold her arms around her tightly. Thinking that somehow the world might not hear while Elsepeth smothered her, Delphia allowed the ragged sounds to come.

Delphia hoped she didn't wet Elsepeth's jacket too much with her tears. When she finally stilled, Elsepeth let her go.

"Delphia . . . what has happened?" she gently asked.

"Mother might wake, and then hear," Delphia said, her voice raw and tired. "But we can talk on the kitchen rooftop. I used to share there, with my brothers." She pointed to the sloped, shingled roof of a one-storey addition. The moon had brightened, and its light sharply showed the roof's edge. "We walk the fence and then climb up the wall for the roof. Do you think you can follow?"

Elsepeth looked up at the roof and smiled at Delphia. "I will try."

Elsepeth's step on the fence and up to the roof was timid, but Delphia helped and showed her how to stand on the sloped surface by bracing their feet against the gutter. Once Elsepeth was safely seated and they were looking down on the dark street, Delphia arranged her skirts. She sighed.

"I'll begin with Miss Felly Pritt, who had a broken neck," she said.

When she reached the part of her narrative where she saw the dead men who lay with surprised eyes in the surgical theatre, Delphia heard her own voice quaver and she covered her mouth again. But the sobs that came were very few, and she shed no tears. When she spoke of the pile of bloody skin and hair that she had seen, remnants of the poor girl who had died, her voice was dull and solemn.

"I've shared such horrible things," Delphia finally said. "All the more horrible because they are not just stories we read in the papers and magazines, or that are in those penny dreads. I've told you things that happened to *me*—terrible, fresh visions, which will burden your mind's eye and give you nightmares. I am trying to transfer my horror to you."

Elsepeth took her hand, and Delphia covered the clasp with her other hand, seeking to warm her friend's cold fingers.

"Transfer if you must, you are welcomed to try again and again," Elsepeth said. "Don't worry about me. Nothing much greatly horrifies, it seems. I've been through my own sorrows. And caused some. I'll tell you what I think. You've seen more tonight than people might in a lifetime. Therefore, it's much like your having volunteered for war. Like the nurses. Consider this your first, bloody battle. If you've the steel that some women do, and I believe you do, you will survive what you have seen.

"You aren't conscripted," Elsepeth continued. "You can leave this work at any time. But always keep in mind what I'll tell you now, Delphia. Whether you stay on or decide to leave. You faced terrible things tonight, yet made certain someone very powerful will no longer commit horror again. In this way, Delphia, you have won and *will* be stronger."

"Perhaps I did help 'good' win tonight," Delphia said softly.

"I believe you did," Elsepeth said.

They sat holding hands in silence. After awhile, Delphia looked at Elsepeth and smiled gratefully.

Elsepeth began humming. Delphia found it an odd tune. It was European in sound, but not like what the Italian street musicians would play. Finally Elsepeth sighed.

"The night is not done," she said. "You should be in bed. And

I must go."

"To your gentleman?" Delphia said.

"You insult me so," Elsepeth said.

They rose, and Delphia helped her down from the roof. When they reached the street, she hugged her friend.

"I feel I've talked myself dry. Now I've a thirst," Delphia said, smiling.

"Thirst," Elsepeth said, staring at Delphia. "Yes."

This time, Delphia did not walk with Elsepeth to find a carriage or cab. She accepted that Elsepeth intended to wander the night whether Delphia liked it or not, and as Elsepeth reminded her, it was not uncommon for women to stroll about in the darkness. Elsepeth bade her farewell at her door. Just as Delphia was about to shut it, she glanced at the sky and the position of the moon and thought of how many more hours of night remained. When she looked at Elsepeth, her friend had not turned away.

"What is it that you do?" Delphia said thoughtfully.

"It's a foolish girl who asks questions," Elsepeth said.

"Good night, Elsepeth."

"Good night, Delphia."

~

At the Vesta, late night festivities wound down. Hallway gaslights were darkened and the drawing room hearths lit to bring warmth and intimacy. Couples who sat in cozy divans before the fires enjoyed books and each other's company. Helene stood in the library, an austere figure in black, and received word on Art's condition from the page on duty. She saw the doctress, Judith SeaJane, departing. Helene accosted her to discuss Art. Satisfied finally that Art was well, Helene exited the Vesta.

When the iris door spiraled shut behind her, she saw Ganju standing in the darkened street, staring in perplexity at the Picnic-hicle.

"Good," he said, noticing Helene. "I was going to enquire next if you were here. Arthur Fellows' body has been mended. It's at Billingsgate Mortuary now."

"Thank you," Helene said. "It's been a long night. Have you seen Helia in passing?"

"I haven't."

"The Bone Stealer is dead."

Ganju nodded his approval.

"And yet more needs to be done," she said.

Ganju looked at the inert buggy and then askance at Helene.

"Yes. It, too, is dead. At least Perseus' workroom is not that far," she said cheerfully.

Ganju's response was a tolerant expression. While he loosened his tie, Helene removed her coat, tossed it into the buggy, and rolled up her white sleeves.

CHAPTER EIGHTEEN

His name was Heinrich; the scarred man believed he had never been addressed as such since growing up a hall boy in his prince's house. He couldn't recall the manservant's name either, not that he cared to. The prince had always referred to Heinrich as 'Scar' and to the manservant as 'Servant'. Such designations seemed always to echo in their minds in the prince's voice, made truths set indelibly into their brains like chiseled stone. Only when the prince lay broken and his black heart on the floor did Heinrich think: *I am free.*

The manservant had the same thought as Heinrich. They stole a carriage, fled the academy, and in silent agreement headed back to the Regent Park home their prince had resided in.

Right then, they were ransacking their prince's bedroom. Heinrich found the money, and the manservant retrieved a valise with his prince's documents and notebooks. In unison, they turned for the door and saw their prince's host, a minor baron, standing in their way.

"What has happened?" the baron demanded, stepping in. "Isn't His Serene Highness returning? I was hoping for my son's trans—"

Heinrich picked up the letter opener and stabbed him. They had no time for the baron's talk, nor could they leave him to think on contacting the police. Heinrich rolled the stricken gentleman beneath the bed, knowing he would die slowly. The servants were not fond of the baron and they were especially wary of entering the prince's room. They would not come looking for their master until the morning, which was an hour away. Heinrich shut the door and locked it.

In only half an hour, Heinrich and the manservant were seated in the first-class compartment of a train bound for Dover. Heinrich grinned. He was becoming comfortable with referring to himself by his own name. He enjoyed it. While his companion looked over sheets of paper that listed his prince's contacts, Heinrich opened the valise. There were his prince's worn notebooks, tied shut with ribbons. He ran his hands through them, counting them all, and pulled out one to flip through the pages. It was full of meticulous, tiny handwriting with diagrams and other drawings. Heinrich grinned more, put the book back, and looked at the manservant.

"I regret that we could not sell his stupid stick too," he said. "Do you see any likely buyers?"

"*Doktor Gatly Fall,*" the manservant read aloud from the list.

"A good choice." Heinrich rubbed his eyes in fatigue. The night's excitement was wearing away. He scratched his hands. "But I want several to bid. We should contact generals. They would want undead men."

"Only *he* could make that work," the manservant said.

"They don't have to know that," Heinrich said, grinning. He then rubbed his face. His eyes felt irritated. He blinked the itchiness away.

Dawn crept up behind the night sky, its light still too far away to be known. The world turned a deep blue. In that blue, a hackney carriage swiftly rode. It carried Helia. Her destination was Westminster and Victoria Station.

After leaving the Vesta, she'd returned to Helene's, changed back into feminine dress, left her sister a new note, and flagged down a carriage. She had a notion, as she often did, that she needed to pursue. She might be too late, too early, in the wrong place, or she might just be very wrong. All she knew was that when a thought needed pursuing, it had to be seen to its end.

"It's a terribly obvious choice, simple as a turn in the plot of a penny dread," she said to herself as the driver swiftly drove his horse. "But I know you. I know your kind, and the like of that young valet too. You'll flee."

She stretched uneasily, feeling her ribs sore, though her corset's plating had broken the knife that caused the ache.

"If your prince has an airship, would that crew help you?" she mused. "I wouldn't. I'd fly and leave you to rot. Nor would you choose a passenger airship. Passport papers would need to be shown and if later recognised, might mean a wire sent to the aeroport destination, alerting the police there. And if the papers were falsified? Would you really risk it? If I wished to exit before ever having to show papers, I'd cross the Channel. Now . . . the gamble. Which train station?"

The massive ornate façade of Victoria Station greeted her as her carriage pulled aside cabs and other carriages in queue to let off passengers. Helia disembarked, paid her driver, and told him where to wait for her. She removed the eighteen-inch wheel she'd taken from the boot of Perseus' electric buggy. He'd placed the little invention there, in case the Picnic-hicle ever ran out of power. It was an electric unicycle measuring twenty-eight inches from the wheel when extended, which Helia did right then, turning the knob to fix it in place. It had a high seat and pedals for leaning the body on to either advance or to stop. Above the wheel and pedals, an electric battery was fixed.

Helia pulled up her skirts and with the wheel at a distance before her, set the seat between her legs. The drivers and pedestrians stared at her, aghast. She jumped up and forwards. The wheel rolled beneath her, adding a foot and a half to her height. With her arms out for balance, she firmly stood up. She arranged her skirts, leaned on the pedals, and zipped down the walk of the station and into its doors.

The vast station proper was already milling with people headed determinedly in every direction for every conceivable destination and platform. The great space echoed with the sounds of footsteps and people calling to each other. Many watched in astonishment as Helia rolled swiftly by, standing head and shoulders above everyone and with a wheel visible beneath her skirts. She weaved through the streams of human traffic and zipped directly for the ticket windows selling passage to Dover.

Helia hopped off the wheel and made her enquiries at each window. She found her answer at the last window.

"I did, sold two first class tickets to two German fellows," the ticket agent said. He was a tall, gangly older man with bags under his eyes and a bushy, white mustache. "And those two were just as you described. Dover train doesn't leave for another fifteen minutes."

"That's not enough time for the police to arrive," Helia said. "And we've yet to tell them these men are here. Summon the stationmaster. The engineer must delay the train's departure so that your conductors can apprehend these men."

"Well, yes, certainly," the ticket agent said reluctantly. "What newspaper did you say you worked for?"

"The *Times*," Helia said. "Hurry, there isn't much of it."

"Yes, certainly, certainly," the agent said. He stood, walked over to another man standing within the ticket office, and began conversing with him.

After five minutes of the men having discussion, Helia moved to the next ticket window.

"May I have a ticket to Dover, please," she said, smiling at the man behind the window. "Any class will do."

Once she gained admittance to the open-air platform meant for Dover, she mounted her unicycle again. The massive black train stood, steam puffing from beneath the locomotive. Last-minute boarders ran for the train. Others who stood on the platform waved goodbye or walked alongside, carrying trays filled with buns and refreshments.

A stationmaster and his assistant hurried through the admittance gates to join Helia.

"What's all this about stopping the train?" the stationmaster said, looking up at her.

"The Bone Stealer's men are on this train," Helia said as she wheeled around him. "I've just confirmed with your ticket agent. He sold tickets to two Germans, one scarred on the face and the other a young man. You must apprehend them at once, but be careful lest they try to flee or fight you."

She watched the stationmaster order his assistant to summon the police. He then straightened his coat and hat and walked calmly to the train. He called to one of the conductors within. As the conductor stepped out and walked with the stationmaster, they conversed. They approached the locomotive, where the engineer looked out of his window curiously.

Helia rolled for the cars designated first class. She came by the side of the train and wheeled through the venting steam. She gazed at the car windows as she zipped by. Several people opened their windows to look at her.

"Blackblackblack," Helia finally said, sensing a familiar dark taint, emanating from one window. She didn't bother to peer in. The glass showed only her reflection. Steadying her wheel, she smiled and rapped on the glass.

～

Within the compartment, Heinrich looked out and stared at Helia in astonishment.

Curious as to why Helia stood at such an unnatural height, he slid the window open.

～

Helia's eyes widened upon seeing the eldritch taint on the man's face and hands. She sniffed.

"Wretched scent," she said.

"You were that masked gentleman," Heinrich said.

"I am glad you chose to flee by train rather than airship," she said, "else we'd have quite a disaster on our hands."

"What do you want," Heinrich said. He blinked rapidly,

grimacing.

"I thought to distract you. But now it doesn't matter. Don't waste your last seconds," Helia said, no longer smiling. She hopped off the unicycle and held it, her gaze never leaving the face of the scarred man's. She took a breath as if to say something. Instead, she turned around and walked away.

～

"What?" he said. Heinrich brought his head back in and looked at his companion. "*Was ist sie—*"

The manservant suddenly coughed. His stiff hands dropped the list. Heinrich saw the blood seep from his companion's shaking fingers that had touched the paper. More blood dripped from the manservant's mouth as the young man's eyes closed in agony.

"Inspection!" a conductor called from the compartment's door. He rapped loudly. "Inspection, if you please. Open the door!"

Heinrich turned and looked at the opened valise from which he'd handled his prince's notebooks. His face and hands began to burn. He saw smoke rise from the books, and the scent of sulfur filled his nostrils.

"*Nein—*" he cried. Smoke rose from his burning eyelids.

～

Helia continued to walk away. She looked to the distance and thought of nothing as the train compartment erupted into flames.

～

Art woke up.

And then she wished she hadn't. She remembered that she was at the Vesta. She could see the ceiling moulding. She remembered some of what happened last night. Her body, from top of the head to toe, was screaming rather vehement testimony to those traumatic events.

"Art!" Jim said from the bedside table. "You're awake! How are you?"

"I," Art uttered, "hurt."

"How so?" he said. "You're entirely solid! Was the squid disagreeable? You made the oddest sounds last night."

Art raised her arms.

"Ahhhh!" she cried. Her arms felt on fire.

"*Ahh!*" Jim said in alarm. "What's happening?! What are you doing?"

"I . . . must . . . move!" Art said. She grimaced as she tossed the covers aside. She attempted to sit up.

"*Ahhhh*," Art said. Her entire self felt electrocuted.

"*Gahhh, Art!* Have mercy on yourself! Please, lie back down!"

"Nay, the body . . . must move!" Art said through clenched teeth. She placed her feet upon the floor.

"I can see that! And such a sight it is! If you're trying to prove it all still works, the screaming rather answers that, yes? Art don't—"

"*Arrrgh!*" Art said when she finally stood.

"*Ahhhh!*" Jim cried. "Oh please, Art, stop! But if you insist on—"

"*Aagh*," Art said when she reached for her walking stick.

"—this torture, *gaaahh*, at least throw on your dressing gown!"

Art managed to do so, amid many pained exclamations. By the time she had taken a few steps around her room with the aid of her walking stick, Jim was babbling nervously.

"Oh, look at you!" he cried as she stiffly hobbled. "And listen to you! Damn physical culturist! Must you test your body already? You'd get shot, pole-axed, nearly eaten alive, beaten down by Ellie Hench, and not once let the slightest murmur pass your lips! Yet *now* you must alarm me with your vocal sufferings?"

"Thee was not there," Art said through gritted teeth. "When my bones were ripped out. My lungs gave same, most heartily."

"Oh . . . that was you?" Jim said.

The door suddenly opened. Manon and Arlette entered, wearing hats, boots, and gloves. On her arm, Manon carried a wide basket filled with greens and roots. Her cheeks were rosy from being out in the cool morning air. Oleg followed and closed the door behind them.

"Art, *bon jour!* Please excuse us, Manon is such a creature, she is always rude!" Arlette said as Manon came near Art. "When Manon heard what happened to you, we went in search at dawn for these. Covent Garden *et le marché chinois*. Manon insisted on the herbs *exotique!*"

Manon smelled of the morning chill. She took the basket from her arm and showed the contents to Art. Inside were laid large green onions, garlic heads, thick ginger roots, and curling red and green chili peppers.

"*Manger de tout*," Manon demanded.

Since Manon insisted, Art did. She raised a pained hand towards the basket. The herbs, roots, and vegetables sailed into her body.

Once absorbed, the fire and spice of the mixture lit a furnace within. Warmth shot from Art's center to her extremities. Her fingers, toes, and head felt aglow. Art let out a long gasp and blushed.

"My," Jim said. "You look like you'd quite the shot. A potent glass of spiced mulled wine might have done the same."

"'Tis stimulant of the blood," Art said in surprise. The heat continued to grow within her, a steady climb in temperature. She felt herself radiate like a sun. She began to sweat. She sniffled.

Manon studied her closely, pleased. She laid a hand on Art's chest, as if gauging her state.

"Now. You must eat what Arlette has," Manon said. Arlette stepped forward, and in her small basket was a pile of fresh tumeric leaves.

"This is for the pain, Art," Arlette said. "And it works very well. I should know."

Art ate them. Though she was still overcome with the sensation of spicy heat, she felt the tumeric lessen her pain, much like the valerian tea had done, though with greater potency. She looked at Manon happily, but Manon was glancing at Arlette.

"*Plus de gimgebre*," Manon said to Arlette.

"But of course." Arlette sighed. "Let us sleep first. Cook can provide more ginger, *oui*? He knows your preferences; such herbs and vegetables will be very fresh for Art."

Manon nodded, seemingly satisfied with the answer.

She removed her hat and gloves. Arlette followed suit and handed her articles of clothing to Oleg.

"May we sleep here?" Manon asked softly, staring up at Art. Art watched Manon's slender hands unfasten her coat, then her bodice. When Manon pulled the clothing off, Oleg took them.

"Please," Art said. She slowly followed when Manon approached the bed's edge.

Manon presented her back to her and removed the pins of her hair. The long, blonde locks fell free. Manon moved her hair aside and reached behind to unhook her skirt.

Art dropped her walking stick and forced her sensitive fingers to undo the lacing of Manon's corset.

"Art, your hands all right? You're all thumbs, like a school boy," Jim said when the last lace was loosened. Manon began shedding her petticoats.

"I've the touch of a babe. I may need a giant rattle," Art said.

Arlette laughed. She was also undressing. Oleg pick up both Arlette's and Manon's petticoats. Art held the corset as Manon sat to undo the buttons of her boots. When those were removed, she stood again. Manon pulled her chemise over her head. Art saw Manon's buttocks and pale back slowly reveal. Art smiled, the expression hurting her face.

"At least you've stopped grimacing, Art," Jim said.

"The pain recedes by degrees," she said. She watched as Manon scooted nude up the bed until she reached the pillows. Art helped to pull back the spread and covered Manon.

Arlette fell beside Manon and pulled the covers over herself. She was also nude. She placed a hand over her mouth, yawning widely.

"*Merci, Art,*" she sighed. "*Bonne nuit, Monsieur Dastard.*"

"Goodnight, girls!" Jim said.

"Oh, monsieur," Arlette added. "Did all turn out well? You caught the bad doctor?"

"We did, and it's only a matter of seeing his legacy destroyed."

"*Bon,*" Arlette said. She settled next to Manon.

Art picked up her walking stick, stifled her exclamation of pain, and slowly paced once more. Oleg laid out Arlette's and Manon's clothing on a chair. He left with their hats, coats, and boots. Arlette and Manon slept. A page knocked, entered, and admitted Dr. SeaJane. After a brief, whispered discussion with the doctress (and a stern admonition from her to rest), Art and Jim bade her farewell.

Art resumed her slow pacing. The page returned with another cup of valerian tea prescribed by Dr. SeaJane, which Art absorbed. The page cleared the nightstand of the glass of untouched stout and left. Finally, Art paused in her exercise, shoulders stooped.

"Losing the effect of the chilies, Art?" Jim softly asked.

"Aye." Art yawned tiredly. "Thee must be bored. I will dress and take thee downstairs, then return."

"No need, Art, just come to bed. Oleg will poke his head in soon. And Delphia! She's sure to arrive! Either one can take me below. Then I can hear how our recent adventure is playing out in the drawing rooms."

Art set her stick aside. Manon had taken the center of the bed with Arlette to the right. There was room for Art on the left. She slowly removed her dressing gown, grimacing as she did so, and mounted the bed.

"If you should engage in naughtiness with these angels, I hope to be long gone by then," Jim said.

"If there be naughtiness, I will most likely be snoring."

"I meant to ask. Before your exercise in agony and torment, did you have a peaceful sleep?"

"I'd a deep rest," Art said. She recalled fragments of a dream; her great body and many long limbs sleek, powerful, and graceful, far beneath the ocean surface and swiftly swimming. She had found a whale and given it a deadly embrace.

"You made the strangest sounds at one point."

"'Twas the squid."

As if in response, the tentacles within stirred, gripping her insides. A rumbling sound emitted.

"Ha ha, it still tries to kill me," Art said. She glanced at Manon and Arlette, who continued to sleep, undisturbed.

"It is?" Jim said curiously. "Still thinking? Plotting? Extraordinary."

"'Tis dead. I ate of its brain and organs," Art said. "But the limbs have memory."

"Ah. Still executing the command given. Anyone within a mile would know you ate the thing. You smell like the sea."

Art's eyes closed. Manon was warm beside her.

"When you wake later, perhaps Manon's herbs will have healed the funny suction marks on your face," Jim said.

~

An omnibus wound its way through East London, laden with passengers. Delphia sat in her rooftop seat and looked at the advertisements for Hershey's, Bovril, and other billboard signs as they rode by. Once the omnibus lumbered to her Whitechapel stop, Delphia ran down to disembark. She weaved through the beggars, ragged boys, workwomen, and costermongers and found the alley for the Vesta's back entrance. Steam rose from the vents and grates. The woman and children whom Delphia had seen before were peeling potatoes. A fishmonger handed salmon to a kitchen assistant at the scullery door, and Delphia wondered if his cartload of fresh fish might be meant for Art.

But then, Delphia thought, *Art did just eat a colossal squid.* She squeezed by the assistant inspecting the fish and entered the scullery.

The first thing she did once inside the bustling kitchen was greet Cook and thank him for the flask of brandy.

"And did you find use for it?" Cook said.

"I had need, thank you, sir," she said.

"Well, good. Good," Cook said. He turned and hurried away.

Delphia seated herself at the staff's dining table with a page and the maid polishing silverware and helped herself to the breakfast laid out. Having had no appetite the night before, she found that this morning, she had plenty. Alice entered the dining area and they exchanged greetings.

"Alice, is Art well?" Delphia said.

"She's asleep, that much I know, and Manon and Arlette are with her. We'd no cause for alarm or vigil, so I'd say that she's well, Delphia."

"Thank heaven."

"Mr. Dastard's presently in the ladies' drawing room," Alice said, "but he would like to see you in his study, once you've finished breakfast, for your 'beefing'."

"My . . . 'beefing'?" Delphia said.

"Or do I mean, 'breathing'?" Alice said.

"I believe the word you seek is 'briefing'," Delphia said.

"Oh, yes," Alice said, flustered. "I don't always have his odd words right."

"Don't worry, Alice, my father is a scholar, and even I don't understand Mr. Dastard half the time!"

When Alice left, Delphia finished her meal, cleared her dish and utensils from the table, and bade Cook a good day.

Once on the third floor, she paused before Art's doors, recalling Alice mentioning an "Arlette" along with Manon. She assumed Arlette was also a prostitute in residence and hoped their companionship made Art feel better. She entered Jim's study, opened the curtains, took off her hat, laid her stick aside, and sat down to wait.

Before she'd left home that morning, the family had already risen and eaten a simple breakfast. Gaiety needed to pick up more saddlery to mend, and Aengus was up and dressed so that he could watch Calliope and father. Though Aengus was seven, he could already read very well, and it was his task, whenever Delphia had a position to go to, to borrow the morning paper from the retired soldier who lived in the room above and read it to father.

Delphia had been happy to depart right then, because though Gaiety would not be present to hear the lurid stories that would be shared of the previous night's events, Aengus was certain to excitedly describe them to her later.

This was the reason, Delphia mused, why Philo never shared his secret life as a thief, even in sibling confidence. She had resented his secrecy but she was beginning to understand his actions. She could never tell her family all of what had happened last night—of what she witnessed, experienced, and in the future, of any actions she may have to commit. Even here, at the Vesta, Cook and Alice wisely did not express curiosity. These were things no sensible person would want to hear about.

Delphia tipped her riding hat up. Inside the crown, secured by a strip of ribbon her mother had helpfully glued for her, was the "leech" invitation to the Black Market. Whenever she should be free of duty, she intended to show Elsepeth a kindness in return.

The door opened, and Alice stepped in, carrying Jim.

"Squire!" Jim exclaimed.

"Sir," Delphia said, rising. "A very good morning to you."

"Good morning! Did you manage a peaceful rest?"

"As well as could be managed." She accepted Jim from Alice, and the page took her leave.

"How is Art, sir?" Delphia asked as she set Jim on the table.

"Asleep again, and deservingly so. Her nervous system is protesting the abrupt removal and return of her skeleton. But she is healing, and I won't be surprised if we find her strolling amongst us later. Bloom! Now that you've breakfasted and I've smoked, here is your briefing!"

He then shared news about Inspector Risk and his men, who survived their chloroform dousing, though with head injuries and some with need of medical attention. Jim described a recent conflagration at Victoria Station and the demise of the prince's remaining organisation. The giantess, abandoned by her kidnappers, had found police to help her and was returned to her sideshow. There had been no intention by the Bone Stealer to use her in the demonstration. As belatedly shared by her sideshow cohorts, she was a woman nearly seven feet tall.

"And the animals at the academy, sir?" Delphia asked.

"Oh, what a glorious mess that is! They were rescued by our stalwart anti-vivisectionists, yes, but not before documentation and visual accounts were taken and shared with the newspapers, and I'm very certain, soon with Parliament. *The Strand* promises some very revealing illustrations! I've a copy requested.

Would you like one as well, Bloom, for your scrapbook?"

"Why . . . " Delphia thought of Aengus and her father. "Yes, I believe I would."

"The medical men will have much to explain, especially their cruel experimentation with artificial limbs. And even if they were to hide behind their intellectual rationalisations their own, more humanist peers will surely call upon them to take their actions into account."

"I liked that the Blackheart came to our aid and helped open the gate, but she left perhaps too quickly!" Delphia said.

"Yes, but remember the state of the theatre grounds when you and Lady Helia walked Art to the horseless buggy? Wasn't that something?" Jim said gleefully. "I'm very certain that was Nick's doing. You know as well as I do, Bloom, it's the style of our heroine to be swift and mysterious. Having never laid eyes upon her until now, I wonder if that was still the fifth Nick. It could have easily been a new woman."

"Sir, she seemed the same person I saw five years ago," Delphia said. "Though perhaps shorter."

"Well, fifth or the newly minted sixth, I am glad of her finally emerging. Perhaps now I can take that seaside holiday! But to turn the matter back to our departed Bone Stealer. I have heard more news not entirely unexpected whilst tarrying with those breakfasting. Baroness Sedgewick has given me quite the earful. But like all gossip, I must have it said from the horse's mouth."

"The horse's? Very well, sir," Delphia said.

"If you'll pick up the paper, please. And turn to the obituaries section. We will know what we must know there."

Delphia found the section and started to read about a young gentleman named Arthur Fellows. Jim interrupted and directed her to find the obits for a baron, viscount, and young lady instead. Delphia looked the page through and began reading again.

"So abruptly did the Baron Algoron Fenk depart this world at the home of his Scottish friend, the Right Hon. Hunter McLeary, this night of the Saturday, 13 March, he has left behind a freshly widowed young bride to mourn the severing of his bloom of life, yet celebrate his early admittance into the Providence that would bestow upon him the rewards of his pious life. Baron Fenk was recently blessed with the miracle of health in the complete recovery from a spinal affliction, and in attaining such perfection on our Earth, had earned him the sacred call before the Throne of Mercy."

"Died just last night," Jim said. "That one was our hunchback."

Delphia nodded and continued reading.

"The Viscount of Igliff passed in Paris this night of the Saturday, 13 March, in the *Palais Garnier*, whilst in the company of a good many female acquaintances, who may not shed tears for this righteous act of God but will for the cessation of the viscount's generous expenditures. The viscount, once known for his bedridden state and the issue of his poisonous pen from such, had found mysterious relief from his miserable conditions. He then, to our gratitude, inflicted such newfound health on our continental neighbors rather than upon England's daughters, and in the indulgences of such sins, as so cynical, venomous, and perfectly mediocre a writer should deserve, expired quickly and grotesquely, but without further trouble to the world."

"Ha!" Jim said. "The living stabs the dead, indeed."

"This was the arthritic viscount, sir?" Delphia said.

"Indeed, yes."

Delphia returned her attention to the paper.

"On the *Oceanic*, bound for the port of Philadelphia, this Saturday, 13 March, the Hon. Mary Mellowings expired from a self-inflicted wound, having suffered the severe and intolerable return of a former foot illness. She leaves behind two parents, Lady and Lord Mellowings."

"There you have it," Jim said quietly. "Their bodies were never meant to have another's bones."

Delphia clenched the paper, her knuckles white.

"Is your last hope for your father gone?" Jim said.

Delphia lowered the paper to stare at him.

"How did you know?" she said.

"One doesn't repeatedly brave the wrath of secondhand

booksellers and read their wares under their noses just to research a simple procedure like transfusions," Jim said. "I am sorry."

"No," Delphia said. "It's still possible. This surgeon we defeated, he was evil. He may have intended these horrible ends, after all. There are those in the Black Market who want to help—"

"Delphia," Jim gently said. "I know the market well. What happened to these gentry has been happening for a long while. When the lower classes suffer such fates, no one cares to write about them, and of course, no one wants to admit they resorted to the Black Market. The unfortunate results die with them. The money is paid and the patient long gone, in more ways than one. Transplanting is the most difficult of processes, whether by science or black arts. It does not end at the transference. Not only might new eyes not succeed in working properly, but they may kill your father."

Delphia looked away.

"But I will give a very cautious assurance," Jim said. "Transplants *will* become successful. It will take much learning, and much care. Just be patient, and until then, help your father learn what his new life will be."

Delphia wiped her eyes and nodded.

～⚬～

By midday, Manon was awake again, and she watched Art sleep.

She studied the subtle, spectral glow Art gave and wondered about the true colour of her eyes and hair. The creatures of the Secret Commission were so odd, Manon thought. Here was a woman of human form, warm of body and capable of breath, her strong heart beating, yet Art had the abilities of a phantom. Manon idly wondered when the remnants of Art's human side might war with her creature side. Manon preferred the queer mix.

There was a gentle knock at the door. Manon turned to look, and Alice poked her head in. Seeing Manon awake, Alice entered and approached the bed. She offered her a piece of paper, and Manon reached over Arlette's slumbering form to accept it.

It was a telegram. Across the top was a stern note, written in

Catherine's hand:

She is not to step foot beyond the servants' wing.

When Manon read the telegram, she understood whom Catherine referred to.

Moore—Vesta. Must come speak with Manon. Please confirm. Helia—Sky.

Manon looked up and nodded. Alice took back the paper and silently left the room.

Once Helia received Manon's response, she would be at the Vesta's back door. Manon chose not to prod Arlette awake in case she verbally protested. She gently kissed her on the forehead.

"Oleg," Arlette softly moaned.

Manon rolled her eyes. Clearly, she was not Oleg. She had no moustache. She pushed Arlette until she was forced to rouse and slip disgruntled out of the bed.

They dressed and silently left Art's room to fetch Oleg. He was not resting in their quarters but exercising, bare-chested, with his wooden Indian clubs. After Manon pulled Arlette away from Oleg and he had dressed, they descended.

Alice met them at the foot of the servants' stairs.

"The scullery maids have left the area for your meeting. Lady Helia suggests that you greet her . . . in the manner in which I'll instruct," Alice said. After listening to Alice, the three did as she advised.

Thus, when they went to meet Helia in the dim scullery while Cook and his assistants noisily went about their business, it was Oleg who entered first with Arlette beside him, and Manon behind Oleg. With Oleg's broad back before her, Manon could only view Helia by peeking beneath his arm.

Helia waved to her. She looked tired. Her clothes were wrinkled, as if she'd slept in them. A crack in the scullery door let in a sliver of light that lit one side of her face.

"How is she?" Helia asked Arlette.

"Art is sleeping well," Arlette said cautiously. Manon had barely time to warn her and Oleg that Helia had an eldritch presence secreted within her; one she could not predict the behavior of.

Manon, with her hand on Oleg's back, could feel the tension in his muscles.

"Good," Helia said. Her eyes closed briefly. "I would see for myself, but I just needed a word, Manon. Would you say that everything is still agreeable about our arrangement?"

Arlette looked at Manon. Manon nodded.

"Art is content, *oui*. Though we have yet to play cards," Arlette said.

Helia sniggered, apparently deeply amused. She clasped her hands in glee.

"Oh, Art. I love how she—"

Helia suddenly snarled, leaping forward. She grabbed wildly for Manon.

Oleg swiftly pinned Helia against the scullery door. She wrapped her right arm around his. She did not fight his grip but seemed to hold on for dear life.

"St—stop it! *Stop* it, stop me!" Helia said. Oleg held her fast.

"Stupid—was tired—!" Helia said desperately. Her left hand clawed for Manon.

Manon watched the infection inside Helia's face sputter and seethe, stretching black tendrils. It spat eldritch fire. Slowly, she reached beneath Oleg for Helia. Oleg grabbed Helia's left arm as Manon touched her chin.

Manon released the sound meant for the morning sun, slowly and steadily into Helia. She gave the song of water, pouring like a waterfall, rushing like the flow of creeks and streams—cool, steady, pure. Helia sagged, and Manon watched the infection fold in upon itself, numbed by cold and resentfully lulled.

"It doesn't like you," Helia whispered, her eyes shut.

"I do not like it," Manon said.

Helia smiled wearily, and Oleg cautiously let her go. Manon stepped to stand beside him, but Arlette held her back.

"We understand each other," Manon said.

"Good. For I understand nothing," Helia said. "But I believe it agrees. Yes." Helia patted Oleg on his chest.

"You see why I ask that you take care of her?" Helia said to

Manon. "For I know you can. Even when hired to do so."

"Art deserves better than the care of a whore," Manon said.

A slow smile grew on Helia's lips. Manon watched the masked side of her face darken.

"Oh, you weren't *always* that," Helia said.

Manon stiffened.

"I will give her what you wish. We will play more than cards," Manon said.

Helia's smile faded.

"Good! Good," she said. She took a deep breath. "That is all I needed to know." She reached for the door handle behind her. As the door opened, sunlight spilled within. Helia dashed out, grabbed her penny-farthing, jumped into the seat, and sped away.

Oleg sighed. It was a heavy sound. Arlette took his hand.

"The English are *stupide*," Arlette said. "But . . . if something were queer about myself, I might do the same."

"*Nyet*," Oleg said.

"But wouldn't Manon be a proper substitute?" Arlette teased. The three passed through the kitchen for the servant stairs. Manon saw Oleg's waxed moustache crook as he suppressed his initial answer.

"A substitute is only that," Manon simply said.

Humans complicate things, she thought as they walked up the stairs. Alice waited to inform them of their schedule for the day. While Arlette and Oleg listened, Manon's thoughts drifted to Art, whose presence still burned, a low fire, in her room above. Manon trusted Art would eventually resolve the triangle in the manner creatures often did.

~

Before the broken gates of the Royal Surgical Sciences Academy, dustmen swept up debris and loaded them into their dust carts. A locksmith inspecting the gates scratched his head beneath his cap, shrugged, and brought out chains with a padlock. Before he ran the chain through the gates, Inspector Risk walked through with Barkley following. Both wore a white bandage beneath their hats.

With a grim gesture, Risk summoned their waiting hackney carriage.

"Quite the carnage," Barkley said. "Too bad we couldn't join in, on account of being clubbed and chloroformed, but our man is dead."

Risk sighed heavily.

"And his men burned in Victoria Station," Barkley added as their carriage came to their side. "Well, we weren't there either, and HQ might have a word about that, but good work, I say."

As they boarded their carriage, an undertaker's wagon slowly trundled by. It carried five plain wooden coffins.

"We'll have a lot to investigate once all the bodies are identified," Barkley said, watching the wagon from the carriage window. "I'm not sorry the seizing of the animals was bungled. We've still enough of the poor beasts for court evidence. That is, if they live long enough." He turned to Risk. "By the way! Did you hear? The Blackheart finally showed herself last night!"

Risk rubbed his forehead as Barkley went on to describe what he'd heard. Their carriage rumbled down the street running alongside the academy. As they passed the building that held the surgical theatre, another mortuary wagon departed. Curious visitors stood outside the building, chatting and looking on.

Inside the building, Helene walked pensively amidst the wreckage of the surgical theatre, a black book held to her chest. The bobbies on guard were busy preventing casual visitors from entering, but allowed certain people to pass. Walking the theatre proper were journalists, photographers, several curious gentlemen, and illustrators. Helene nodded to a respected gothic novelist and his playwright companion, both friends to Helia, who were contemplating the theatre setting. A man stood on the topmost row, his drawing board propped on an upturned chair. He rapidly sketched the scene below. Sunlight poured down from the skylights, clearly illuminating the steel surgery tables and the huge, dark stains on the sawdust floor. The air smelled of dank seawater and spilled blood.

"Looks just like a slaughter floor," one photographer remarked as he carefully positioned his camera and tripod to focus on the thick blood that had pooled and congealed near one of the tables.

Helene mounted the damp steps and exited the theatre.

The members of the Royal Surgical Sciences Academy, perhaps because of the newspaper attention and the presence of the police conducting investigation, had not bothered to secure their campus and expel visitors. Anti-vivisectionist demonstrators still remained, intent on standing vigil within the laboratory that had kept animals captive. A mixed group of activists and Quakers were sat down in the room when Helene entered, eating a midday meal of cheese-and-onion sandwiches. When two journalists also entered, a spokesperson for the group rose and gave testimony about the events of the night before. The spinster activist led the men around the room, showing them the various sites of vivisection and the tools.

Helene turned from the picnic scene and guided tour. Some of the cages still held animals, mostly dogs. They appeared fed and wagged their tails at the sight of her. Aldosia Stropps, the illustrator for *The Strand*, was stroking a black cat lying purring within one open cage.

"I'll be taking her," Aldosia said when Helene approached. "She hasn't long, this ball o' fluff, *fork* them all."

Helene saw the ugly scar along the shorthaired cat's side.

"Yes. Fork them. Aldosia, may I see your sketchbook?"

Aldosia pulled it out of her satchel and handed it to Helene without looking at her. She continued to pet the cat.

Helene opened the book. Aldosia had meticulously recorded the location, date, and time on each drawing, right down to the seconds. Aldosia's first illustration of last night noted that she had been present at the Academy by 12:07 a.m. and twenty-two seconds. Helene studied the elaborately detailed drawings that showed the dead surgeons, the pile of flesh and blood on the floor that had been a girl, the scattering of her bloody bones, the human livers on their silver platters, a giant squid's beak, and the broken, dead body of the Bone Stealer.

Helene took special note of the pages that illustrated gentlemen who had been made to stay within the theatre, their class evident in their dress. Some obscured their faces with hats and hands. Helene looked for who of the nobility might have been present — and perhaps related to the dead girl — but she could discern no recognisable faces.

The following pages illustrated the lab they were presently in, with the cages still full of animals. Aldosia had recorded many of their vivisection injuries, including amputations.

Helene glanced from an illustration of a table laid with metal artificial appendages to the same table the demonstrators were calmly eating at. The photographer from the theatre was setting up his camera to photograph the table's collection of artificial devices.

Helene returned the sketchbook to Aldosia and found the plainclothes sergeant on duty.

Half an hour later, Helene was disembarking from a hackney carriage before the stables her Rama resided in. She lifted two bulldogs out of the carriage. They snuffed and wagged their tails happily. One had a single eye and a scar around its cranium; the other was missing a hind leg. They trotted about the yard while Helene spoke to the stablemaster. He nodded, and they both led the dogs into a small fenced pen.

After a brief visit with Rama, Helene left the stables and walked on. She arrived shortly at her tenement building. When she glanced down to the open door of the Society of Friends meeting room, she saw their neatly stacked demonstrations signs lying against a wall. An elderly Friend sat by the signs. He wore rough sandals and plain clothes lacking dye. He was concentrating on penning a letter.

Helene mounted the steps for her room. She keyed her combination, opened the door, and saw Helia lying in her bed amid the still scattered clothes. Her face was buried in her arms and she murmured fretfully. Her bewitched mask was cast on the floor.

Helene's heart raced.

Helia rarely removed her mask when awake; it kept her eldritch virus asleep. When Helene approached, she saw why the mask was set aside. Helia was weeping.

"What has happened?" Helene whispered. She knelt by the bed.

"Nothing, oh it's nothing, nothing," Helia said. She sobbed wearily.

"This is not 'nothing', unless—Art?" Helene asked, her voice rising.

"No, Art is safe. And for that, I'm glad. So very glad!" Helia said.

"But?" She pulled Helia up and embraced her.

"So much she doesn't know," Helia said. "Too much. And if only I weren't. If only. But that's neither here nor there . . . nor anything."

She wept more, and Helene, at a loss, simply held her.

CHAPTER NINETEEN

Art rose at midday, or so the time seemed to her when she hobbled to the windows and noted the length of shadows on the street below. Manon, Arlette, and Jim were gone but she didn't mind their absence. Jim had left a note for her in Delphia's hand, saying that he would be with his typist and would return shortly.

"Typist?" Art said. Typing reminded her of Helia, and she wondered where she might be. She suspected Helia rarely took rest, being too busy with investigation and writing.

Why, she might be typing e'en now. The memory of Helia at the Blue Vanda warmed her.

She donned her dressing gown, finding her bodily state still fragile but tolerable. She spied an envelope slid beneath her door and retrieved it. It contained a note from Charlotte Thackery, informing her that her hat (delivered by Helia to her shop) was repaired. Charlotte also requested that Art visit so that she might discuss the bullet-riddled outfit. Art hadn't noticed that her hat had been missing and a quick look around the room proved it so. She read the note again, touched by Helia's thoughtfulness.

She went to the armoire, chose another hat, and placed it on the dresser.

In all sentimentality, she favoured the currently missing one above the others Charlotte had provided. She'd woken in that hat when resurrected at the Secret Commission and she'd worn it ever since.

She slowly retrieved clothing to wear. The armoire contained one remaining outfit; the dress in Montebello garnet. She took it down and held it against her body. Its colour immediately bleached away. She then noticed something peculiar about her face in the full-length mirror.

Art traced the raised circular scars the squid's suction cups had made on one side of her face and sighed.

"But I am thankful. 'Twasn't ripped off," she said.

While she donned her stockings, a page knocked and entered, carrying a serving platter laden with ginger roots and tumeric leaves. She laid the platter on the table. To Art's surprise, the page left as quickly as she'd come but she soon learned why. Just as Art was absorbing her meal, Catherine Moore politely knocked and entered with Alice and a maid. After exchanging greetings, she and Catherine conversed while the maid helped Art with her boots.

"I wanted to make personally certain that you were mending, Art, and to see what further assistance we could bring. Have Manon's plants been of help?" Catherine said.

"Aye. Her herbal lore has lent correction to the body. And she has lulled me to needed slumber on more than one occasion. I rose to second life resistant to rest," Art said. She felt stimulated by the heat of the ginger roots.

"Splendid. Harold—my son, Harold—was the same when he first rose. And his nature! So like when he was a little boy, utterly passionate and fiery! When needing calming, he always benefited from Manon's mesmerist skills."

Art nodded, busy with the maid and the donning of her undergarments, but she thought it interesting how Catherine guised an aspect of Manon's eldritch nature as a human ability.

"'Tis a gaze that could tame lions," Art said.

"How apt. Who knew there was so much power in such a simple stare?" Catherine said. She learned forwards. "I appear to be immune to its effects."

Art smiled as the maid laced her. Catherine clasped her hands.

"It's good to see you standing, Art. Harold was also a regenerative. Your gift must have surmounted the trauma of being separated from your bones."

"Aye, 'twas also fortunate that my ghosting ability granted myself a living state, though one close to fleeing," Art said in contemplation.

She recalled how she floated, her mind losing coherence and her body losing cohesiveness. A moment longer and she might have evaporated like so much mist.

"We are very grateful that was not the outcome," Catherine said. The maid hooked Art's skirt and buttoned and hooked the bodice in place. She took up the brush to put up Art's hair.

"Friend," Art said to Catherine as she sat before the dresser mirror for the maid. "I've been asleep much of the time and have no knowledge of the latest happenings. Have you heard, by chance, of what befell a giantess who was kidnapped by the Bone Stealer's men?"

"Oh! That was quite a development, Art! I'll be happy to share what I've learned!"

Alice moved the armchair for Catherine to sit in and stood alongside while her mistress spoke. Art saw the enthusiasm in Catherine's face as she related the latest particulars, read in three different newspapers, of the Bone Stealer case. Supernatural events seemed to be of keen interest to her as much as male impersonators delighted her. Throughout her narrative, she brought up various observations on Harold's own escapades and feats, whether similar or dissimilar to Art and Jim's recent case.

She misses her son, very much, Art thought.

"Even Helia's story gave no specific reason for the Bone Stealer's demise," Catherine said. "True, there was a colossal squid involved, but . . . failing to share that particular detail was very remiss of her. I thought it rather shoddy reportage."

"He has expired?" Art said. "My. I wonder how it happened."

"Oh! Please don't concern yourself, Art. You've had a very trying night, and his passing should be the least of your concerns. I've now told you all I know, really. Mr. Dastard will certainly have more to share."

"Thee has been of great help," Art said. "And much that I've learned of thy son has given me inspiration towards my work. Harold has my admiration."

Catherine smiled, the corners of her eyes wrinkling. Art thought that if not for the streak of grey in her dark hair, she did not seem very mid-aged.

"I'll leave you, then. You need your rest," Catherine said, rising.

"I will rest further after suitable exercise," Art said, smiling.

When Catherine had bade her farewell and left, the maid exiting with her, Alice remained behind. She moved the armchair back to its original position, retrieved the silver platter, and turned to Art.

"Will there be anything else, Art?" she said.

"Aye," Art said, smiling. She was warmed by Alice's use of her name. "Can thee tell me of the Exercisium nearby? And if it has a bath."

～

When Alice had left, Art tested her legs and ability to remain upright with a few circles around the room. Though she felt an overall soreness and slow burn, right down to the soles of her feet, it was not the excruciating fire that she had woken to earlier that morning. Hopeful that she was rapidly mending, as seemed the nature of her eldritch body, Art went to her dresser to retrieve her gloves and hat. She heard a soft knock at the door. Art turned and Delphia poked her head in.

"Well, is she awake? Is she?" she heard Jim say.

"I've risen, Friend, please come in," Art said.

When Delphia entered, Jim in hand, they exchanged warm greetings.

"Your glow is subdued but can only grow, Art!" Jim said. "At least you've ceased grimacing! Del' and I were at my typist all this morning. Miss Adella Pepper is most adept with her machine. She types for barristers and doctors, but she's always willing to lend me her services. I've finished giving my reports and feel terribly accomplished."

"Friend, a typist and thee feeling accomplished," Art said. "What mystery might this be?"

"Oh, I apologise, Art. I've been remiss in your further instruction as an agent. You must give formal statement on our case. Or cases, as it were. We hadn't time to do so for the re-animationist investigation, but now that the Bone Stealer has been taken care of it's required that we see to our neglected paperwork."

"Then we've two reports to write, Friend?" Art said.

"Well, you do! I've finished both of mine!" Jim said.

"His dictation is quite swift," Delphia said.

"As is Miss Pepper's typing," he said.

"Oh," Art said. "I wonder if I've enough paper. I should forego hydropathy at the Exercisium."

"Art, your recovery comes first! But I don't recall Dr. SeaJane prescribing water therapy."

"'Tis mine own notion, Friend," Art said. "Water can cause no harm, only betterment."

"When jumping into ice-cold pools, I'll take your word for it," Jim said.

A page knocked and entered, bearing a tray with a teapot, a light midday meal for Delphia, and Art's prescribed cup of valerian tea. Delphia set Jim at the table and at his encouragement, sat down to enjoy her chicken leg, cheese, sliced apple, and crusty bread. Art joined them. She hadn't seen this particular page before and thought the young woman nervous in her company. When she opened the door to leave, she fumbled the tray and the doily fell. Flustered, the page knelt to pick it up.

In the hall, a woman laughed gaily. Art saw a well-dressed lady run within view of the open door. Another woman garbed in dark men's clothes, black cape, black tricorne, and wearing a black mask, caught her and the two merrily tussled. The lady screeched as the masked woman attempted to undo her bodice.

Art rose quickly and shut the door once the page exited. She looked at Delphia.

"Did thee witness that?" she said.

"I did, Art. My, such playacting," Delphia said, munching.

"Thee is becoming a woman very quickly," Art said. "Aye, 'twas for an erotic game."

"Ah," Delphia said around the slice of bread she bit. "Oh."

"*Art!* Ha ha!" Jim said. "Dear Lord. What just happened?"

Realising that Jim hadn't a view of the door and therefore had not seen the costumed woman and her companion, Art returned to the table and briefly explained.

"I see!" Jim said. "The Blackheart's reappearance would inspire such, er, celebration!"

"The Blackheart . . . appeared last night?" Art said.

"Yes! Delphia and I saw her!" Jim said excitedly. "Riding on her big black horse. What fun! She blasted open the academy gates for us. If Delphia and I hadn't rescued you in the nick of time, I'm certain Nick would have! Ha ha!"

"I am sorry I missed her emergence after so long an absence," Art said thoughtfully. She poured tea for Delphia, set the pot down, and turned her attention to her own cup. "She must have looked daring."

"And here I thought you might be her," Jim said.

Art paused in absorbing her valerian tea to stare at him in surprise.

"Well, it was only a notion, but her being gone these many months and you dead during the same time—of course, we've yet to know when you really died! But if you died when she disappeared, it rather works out for Fall. He has only so much time to design his resurrections before the body's no longer suitable material, and with you, he had certainly taken his time.

"You also cut quite the formidable figure, Art, rather fitting for a warrior of the night. And you confessed that though you'd knowledge of Father Christmas and Punch and Judy, you hadn't heard of ole Nick at all. As I've told you, only our personal memories are excised by Fall."

Delphia looked at Art curiously.

"I," Art said, flustered. "How extraordinary, Friend. Yet thee and Delphia saw the Blackheart last night."

"True, but I've never laid eye sockets on her until now, and she could very well be a new Blackheart. The sixth."

"And myself, the fifth? Friend! I died a criminal."

"You must remember, Art, you weren't hanged dead, you were shot," Jim said.

"Yet Helene confirmed I was imprisoned," Art said. She recalled Helene's words.

"Imprisonment was an easy way to torment those who loved you. And I know, for I was one of them."

"I died 'a victim, a cruel joke'," she repeated softly to herself.

"Art?" Jim said.

They heard a polite knock at the door.

"Ah," Jim said. "That must be Miss Fesque and Miss Dillwick! I promised to join them in their room for further consultation on their book."

Delphia rose to answer the door while Jim hopped, catching Art's attention.

"Art, can you straighten my hat? Now don't fret about my fanciful notion, it was only that. Delphia has been well instructed on the proper approach to writing an agent's report. She'll remain here, finish her meal, and teach you what must be done, won't you, Bloom? Then come join me! Art, do you still insist on seeking out your frigid baths and hydropathic stimulations?"

"I do," Art said, smiling. She straightened Jim's hat.

"Perhaps we'll rejoin each other by evening. Bloom and I have tasks to take care of!"

Delphia let Miss Dillwick and Miss Fesque in. After the couple exchanged pleasantries with Art, they escorted a jovial Jim to their room across the hall.

Delphia quickly finished her meal while Art sat in wonderment, her valerian tea grown cold. Delphia moved her dishes out of the way, laid out paper and pencil for Art, and began writing a list. Art watched her write: *date, day, time, event, summary, words of witnesses, evidence found, details observed.*

"Delphia," Art said. "Dost thee think I could be the fifth Blackheart?"

"Art, when Mr. Dastard said he suspected the Blackheart might be you, I then considered the thought myself. It may have been five years since I saw her, but really, I did believe the Blackheart was bigger."

"Bigger? As unsexed as myself?" Art said.

"Oh, not like that, Art. The Blackheart I remember was not so broad! But I thought her taller. She rode such an impressive horse last night, perhaps that's why she seemed not so very big." Delphia leaned forward. "Why, I might be taller than the present Blackheart!"

Art smiled as Delphia resumed writing.

"Thee might be," Art said. "Delphia, I am curious. What manner of woman is this Blackheart? That I might picture her. She sounds very dashing. Has she green eyes, perhaps, or brown eyes . . . or blue?"

Delphia paused in her writing, considering the question.

"Art, I cannot say," she said regretfully. "She was all in black. And well . . . very intent on shooting the gate. I saw nothing but the muzzle of her great blunderbuss. For myself, I'll only know if she's the Nick of my childhood if I see her slash about with her flexible sword again!"

Art imagined wielding a blade and wondered if she knew swordplay.

Delphia looked at her.

"If you hadn't your spectral glow, Art, we'd know the colour of your hair and eyes," she said, smiling.

Art smiled in return and turned to Delphia's list of instructions.

～

Smoke grew thick in the afternoon air of London. Airships sailed, one after the other, in the skies above the fog and ash while the streets below congested noisily with omnibuses, cabs, and wagons. Newsboys shouted about the death of the Bone Stealer.

Ellie Hench strolled down a tenement street in the East End, her chin high and her hat, with its long, stiff pheasant feathers, low over her nose. Her opaque, black spectacles reflected nothing, and passersby who turned and noted her blind state, moved to give her room. All the while she smiled a strange half smile and tapped her blackthorn.

She followed a little ragged boy who ran ahead of her. When the boy stopped before a building with a deep portico and round, iris portal, Ellie gave him a coin. She sauntered up to the entrance and stood before it.

"Bell," she mused, and with her bare hands searched the entryway. She felt nothing resembling a bell or knocker. She rapped on the portal with her walking stick. She rapped again. She kept rapping until she heard gears and hydraulics come to life, turning and hissing. The blades of the door spiraled open.

Two women were inside, standing at attention. Ellie sensed their life energy in the fluidity of their world. Glow-fires shaped them, right down to the planes and valleys of their eyelids. Ellie stepped in and with nose raised, turned her head this way and that. It was a big space, she thought. Grand and hoity-toity. She could sense by "fluid-flow" the location of the staircase at the end of the hall and the measure of each polished, carved step.

"Ellie Hench for Mr. Dastard." She smiled to no one in particular, though she well knew that one of the footwomen was standing right before her. The footwoman held a silver tray in her gloved hand. Ellie reached into a pocket, found one of her calling cards, and pulled it out. Her name was stamped on it in Braille. She'd punched it herself and even punched a rather decent border too, of periwinkle flowers. She dropped it into the tray.

"If you'll follow me, miss," the second footwoman bade, indicating a waiting room.

"Wot's in 'ere?" Ellie said, motioning with her stick to the open doors that were to the left. She smelled leather, ink, paper, and glue with her own nose just as their fluid world gave back to her the shape of books. Many books. Unless they were Braille or embossed, books had no interest to her. For her, words needed to be felt.

"That's the library, miss—"

"And 'ere?" Ellie said, waving her stick as she moved on to the next room. *Ah, playthings,* Ellie thought. Moveable things, instruments, objects, and devises. She walked inside the Curiosities and Mechanical Room even as the flustered footwoman answered her. She reached out for a contraption sitting on a table.

If Ellie were educated in matters of moving parts, she might understand what manner of toy she was presently handling. Etched brass balls and smaller orbiting balls, all mounted on wires, went around and around and caused a brass dial on the bottom to click. Ellie gave the entire contraption a spin and waited for something to happen. One of the balls popped off and rolled on the floor.

"Oh, Venus!" an occupant of the room exclaimed, and the woman put down her own toy to chase the ball on the floor.

"The goddess?" Ellie said, confused. To her perceptions, she was certain the ball was a ball and not a figure of a woman.

She stood, and "read" more of the room, wondering what she might next put her hands on. For Ellie, the flowing world gave her the whole of the room and its contents from top to bottom and all around with a precision and awareness as if she'd eyes all over her body. And to call them "eyes" was not exactly correct. Her ability to know the world was more as if her body-eyes took in the fluidity with a gigantic inhale, a fully dilated sniff of the pupils, and then exhaled back to her the measure and nature of what she swam in. It was as easy as breathing, or blinking. Or sleeping.

Of course, her brain could only breathe in so much of the knowledge; she was content with just knowing what was immediately around her. She had heard people talk of how they could see things far off with their eyeballs, such as an airship or a mountain. She couldn't perceive at that distance but she knew when odd things were in the wind, when a shift most unkind was about to happen in the world around them, and when things uncanny broke the soil. Living things affected the fluid world too, when trees, people, and animals all died at once in an accident, or flood, or in a building or stable fire. Ellie felt such things, but they didn't greatly upset her. As a London orphan, she'd had enough poverty, death, and suffering to have some good humour about them.

Ellie caused more apparatuses to make noise or animate, then turned her attention to what she understood was a very large painting. Paintings, like pages, had content she could not perceive, not in its entirety. Strokes of paint and the marks of ink on paper said to be letters, like her Braille, those she could feel. But unless she spent hours on it, which she didn't care to spend — as she'd rather be dancing — the strokes and marks never came together to make immediate sense. They needed embossing. Like daguerreotypes, tintypes, postcards, glass slides, carte de visites, and magic lantern projections, pictures did not work with flow-perceptions.

Once, at an exhibition, Ellie met a toff who helpfully suggested that she try distinguishing the content of a painting by its colours. Ellie thought the accidental knock of her blackthorn into his groin had been well deserved.

She had no perception of a painting's subject matter but she could still appreciate what it was made of. That stuff, paint, that was applied to the canvas in strokes — it was such rich, and rather tasty, stuff.

Ellie put her blackthorn under her arm and reached out for the painting on the wall.

"Oh! I hope you won't do that. I don't think the canvas can withstand the placing of your hands in such a manner," the woman who had rescued Venus said.

"I want to feel it," Ellie said, her hands still raised.

"Oh, but must you? It would be a shame to ruin such a lovely painting."

"Is it of somethin' naughty?" Ellie said.

She felt a movement in the fluid.

"Oh, it's the big one!" Ellie said. She dropped her hands, ran her right hand down her blackthorn as she set it to the floor, and turned to face the doors with a grin. In the hallway outside, Art slowly strolled by and noticed her. After a moment, she entered the Curiosities and Mechanical Room.

Ellie felt that Art's glow-self was less powerful than usual. She had a funny pattern on the side of her face, the skin raised like scars, but so neatly done that Ellie thought Art might have had her face embossed. Her subdued life-pulse indicated that the strongwoman was in a rough state. Ten guineas had really not been a worthy bounty for a body like hers, but for Ellie, it was right then neither here nor there.

"'Ow's yer nose?" she greeted.

Ellie grinned more as she felt Art bristle.

"How is thy chin?" Art said coolly.

"Oh, me teeth seem corrected, I can eat meat on the bone now," Ellie said, tapping the side of her jaw.

"Thee has business at the Vesta?"

"Aye, simple business. I was askin' 'bout this painting. What's the picture of?"

Ellie felt Art turn her head briefly.

"'Tis an allegory, told with naked women," she said.

"Ah," Ellie said in the direction of the painting. It was always intriguing what eyeballs put together and somehow perceived. "Are there any naked men?"

And that was the gist of the matter, Ellie thought. Why have flat things when one ought to be seeking what was real and often right there? To taste, touch, smell, and make ripples with in their flowing world. Especially after a fun night of dancing.

"There's a very fine example in the men's drawing room," the Venus-saving woman said.

"Men's drawing room?" Ellie said. She tried to imagine it, hoity-toity men smoking, drinking, and looking at other naked men.

She stepped for the doors to find out more.

"Ellie!" Jim said as Delphia brought him through the doors.

"Mr. Dastard," Ellie greeted. He was a peculiar energy to her senses, a glow-life contained in such a tiny vessel. Vibrant and alive, yet confined. To Ellie, it was almost as though he was never meant to be, yet was.

"Miss Ellie Hench, may I introduce my assistant and fighter-in-training, Miss Delphia Bloom," he said.

"How d'ye do," Ellie said.

"How do you do, miss," Delphia said, and tipped her hat.

"Art, I hired Ellie to give Delphia stick-fighting lessons," Jim said.

"The stick learned first, Friend?" Art said. "Before Delphia knows the skills of the body?"

"Rest assured, she'll have pugilist skills taught by you," Jim said. "And strength exercises! After you've mended more."

"Yer unwell?" Ellie asked in Art's direction.

"The stick should not be a dependency," Art said.

"No, no. I want Delphia's martial arts well-rounded," Jim said.

"He would also like me to shoot," Delphia said.

"Arrows?" Art said in alarm.

"Pistols?" Ellie said curiously.

"*Tin cans!* I meant it as a surprise!" Jim said.

"Please don't worry, Art," Delphia said. "I intend to continue my better skills at cunning, hiding, and fleeing."

Ellie grinned.

"Those, I can teach ye too," she said. "Well, to it, then."

Delphia walked with Jim to the door, and Ellie stopped before Art.

"I remember yer kindness at the Black Market," she said in the direction of Art's chest. "Expect the same. Next time." She tapped her blackthorn lightly against Art's ironwood.

❧

Art tried to be receptive to Ellie's participation in Delphia's training. It would be advantageous for Delphia to learn from a foe as formidable as the one who broke her nose, she rationalized. And Ellie, Art grudgingly conceded, was considered no foe where Jim was concerned.

Jim had thought it appropriate for Delphia and Ellie to practice at the same Exercisium Art intended to visit. Despite her protests, they all boarded a hackney carriage for the very short ride to its location. Art suspected Jim of mollycoddling her. When they disembarked, she encouraged the three to enter the staid stone edifice ahead of her. They disappeared within, and she slowly followed. In the stones above, the etched letters read: HOMINUM SUNT EXERCISIUM.

"'Mended more'," Art muttered to herself. "I am better than needing more mending."

Three young men suddenly emerged from the entrance, intent on catching the omnibus just then departing from the walk. Two bumped Art, causing her to totter. With profuse apologies, they steadied her and ran after the omnibus.

"Oh," she said, leaning on her stick. The effort to keep her balance had sent her limbs burning. If she were to collapse and curl up in agony right then, it seemed an eldering deserved.

She gritted her teeth and resumed her careful pace into the Exercisium again.

She progressed down a hall and into the Exercisium proper. The air was filled with the sounds of various machines working. The three-storey space had a second-level walkway. At the railing, visitors and class attendees dallied or looked down. Skylights brought in sunlight, and Art thought the space well ventilated. Several tall potted plants dotted the floor.

She saw the Swedish exercise machines Jim had mentioned. Art smelled the machine oil, leather, rubber, and steel that accompanied repetitious mechanical movements. She spied all manner of people engaged in mechanotherapy. The fully dressed participants who sat, stood, lay, or were strapped to their machines stared at her in turn as their pelvises, trunks, arms, legs, and feet were rolled, raised, lowered, rocked, bent, or gently rotated. To Art, it seemed an odd yet sedate dance of bodies manipulated by equally rolling, spinning, squeaking springs, gears, and pulleys. She realised then that since the human body itself was a machine, one of muscles acting on bone, the apparatuses and their occupants were, when positioned correctly, purposed to move as one.

Though she thought nothing surpassed the benefits of

weightlifting, she recognised that many kinds of bodies and ages were utilizing the machines with their personal needs in mind. In one machine was a male laborer, his hands thick and face weathered, slowly receiving rotation in an arm-massaging machine for what appeared to be a shoulder injury. In another machine, a pregnant woman was mindfully pulling against resisting straps, her pulley-weights locked at a percentage suitable for her condition.

Art warmed at witnessing such human healing in practice. It was a welcomed sight after her dealings with black arts surgery and violations of the body. She nodded her approval as she walked by.

Facing the area of the machines were administrative offices, one of which was an examination room for the patients partaking of mechanotherapy. She stepped onto the last part of the floor, an area of free exercise. Here she saw wooden barbells and large Indian clubs stacked or hung in long rows on the walls.

Girls were engaged in pugilist activity, their space containing a hanging, stuffed canvas punching bag swinging from a frame, and a balloon-shaped punching bag mounted on a pole with a spring base. One girl punched the balloon-shaped bag while two others took turns giving blows to the hanging bag. Two more girls sparred with each other, their fists up and waving as they circled. All the girls appeared to be Delphia's age. They were rough looking, their hair unkempt and their brows sweaty. They wore no boxing gloves but had their hands wrapped in dirty white bandages. One girl sported a black eye. Art paused to observe them, and thought that the skill they exhibited exceeded mere exercise.

Beyond the boxing girls, a supplies counter filled with remedies and small exercise equipment stood. The counter clerk, an older woman with a bored expression, slowly folded a towel. Art saw the white towels stacked in shelves behind her. Doors beside the counter had a sign above that read: BATH.

Just as Art stepped for her destination, she heard a woman cry out a maneuver. She turned her head and looked past the boxing girls for the opposite corner of the Exercisium.

Jim, Delphia, and Ellie stood among spectators facing a large practice area. A team of ladies in dark blue middy blouses, sailor caps, and bloomers executed drills with their Indian clubs. One woman led them and called out the maneuvers. When Art saw Ellie scratch her nose and yawn discreetly in boredom, Art surmised why the three were waiting patiently. The area the club-wielding ladies occupied appeared to be the only large space that might soon be freed for their stick-fighting practice.

Art turned her attention back in the direction of the bath. The boxing girls had gathered and were watching her.

She looked at the hard edges of their youthful faces. Their rolled-up sleeves revealed old bruises. As they stared, she felt recognised. But unlike the Friends, the eyes upon her weren't scared or shocked. The gazes varied from intense, curious, bold, hungry . . . to menacing.

She stepped towards them. They ran from her in a rush, sending the punching bag swinging. The balloon-shaped bag fell over. One girl grabbed her comrade who still stared at Art and pulled her to follow. Art spun and watched them flee for the offices of the Exercisium and run up the stairs that led to the upper level. They moved along the second story walkway until they reached a spot overhead where they could watch her.

Art looked up. She stepped into the vacated boxing space, flipped her stick, and hooked the fallen bag, righting it. The girls smirked.

Art set her stick to the floor and considered the young ones above. She was in no condition to pursue them. Before her was the entrance to the bath. Within, she would find therapeutic hot and cold pools and machines dedicated to hydrotherapy. She decided that the girls could wait while she saw to her body's tendering.

She resumed walking to the supplies counter. The counter woman watched her, pale-faced and still, with a pile of unattended towels beneath her hands. As Art neared, she realised that the woman's wide-eyed gaze was both hateful and terrified.

"You!" the woman said.

Art stopped short.

"Friend," Art said.

"You—you're not welcomed here," the woman said, her voice rising. "And you've no business here! Be gone!"

Art stood in wonderment. She watched the woman's mouth twist, her teeth like tiny stones, grinding.

"*Be gone!*" she ground out.

"It *is* you," Art heard spoken behind her.

She turned. A young gentleman stood before her, slim of build and pale of face. His clothes were dark. At his tie, he wore a tiny onyx-and-gold mourning pin. His dark hair was neat, short, combed back, and curly. His nose was arched and his moustache small. He had large brown eyes, framed with long dark lashes. The lost manner in which he stared belied his composed face.

"They resurrected you," he said, his hushed tone bitter.

Art stared into his eyes, wishing she could recognise him.

"How dare you return?" he said.

"I remember nothing, Friend," she gently said.

She glanced at his pin. The center was an amethyst stone. Gold letters in the onyx said: IN MEMORY OF.

The man's slim hand fluttered as he covered his pin from her gaze. On his hand he wore a matching mourning ring. When Art met his gaze again, surprise, anger, and grief warred in his eyes.

"I am the assistant director of the Exercisium," he said. "You were once in our employ here. And then. You did something."

His throat worked.

"If there's any decency left in you, please leave," he said, his voice strangled. He turned abruptly and rushed for his office.

Art felt hollow. The counter woman peered at her, sharp and calculative as she rested her hands on the counter. Art slowly turned. She thought briefly of speaking to Jim, and then dismissed the thought of remaining further. She walked back the way she had come.

Above her, she heard the girls giggle. In the far corner where the club-wielding women were concluding their exercise, spectators applauded.

Art walked past the Exercisium's offices. She didn't know which one the assistant director had fled to. Inside the exam room, a girl was raising her arms while the examiner studied her back. She saw the examiner trace the crookedness of the girl's spine with a pointer.

Correction of the scoliosis, Art thought. She gripped her stick. The memory of the Bone Stealer's eyes as she strangled him came to the fore.

When Art passed the exercise machines, a Quakeress in plain dress was working the straps of the pulley-weights machine the pregnant woman had stood in. She wore spectacles and a receptive smile, her greying hair uncovered. Her bonnet hung behind her neck. Their eyes met but Art only nodded. She was in no mood for further attentions.

She was nearly down the hallway for the entrance when she realised the Quakeress had abandoned her exercise and pursued her. The woman fell in step by her side.

"Thy face is still marked by the sea creature," the woman exclaimed.

Art stopped. She turned to look at the Quakeress, who smiled.

"Thee . . . was at the surgical theatre?" Art said.

"Aye, I was in the demonstration and then joined the rest within the building to partake of rescue. There's more to be done for the freed animals. 'Tis First Day, and we've a Meeting for Worship, Friend, would thee like to attend?"

Art said nothing. Her heart was half in yearning to join and half in quavering fear of rejection.

"I am foolish," the Quakeress said. "Thee knows me not, though I know thee. I am Sarah James, Art. The Friends learned during a visit to the Secret Commission that thee has no memories. And here, in my excitement, I had forgotten. I've now lost memory myself!" she exclaimed and laughed.

Art watched how Sarah's spectacles flashed in the light as she tilted her head back in mirth, and marveled at her ease.

"Did we know each other well, Friend?" Art asked.

"Oh, two years nearly, perhaps. Thee came to London not very long ago. We are not close acquaintances, but thee guided me to come here to lift weights for my back pains, and such advice so resolved the problem, I've heeded thy words since!"

"The Friends know me, then," Art said. "And thee went to the Secret Commission."

Sarah smiled and looked at her kindly.

"Aye. We knew thee was new, like a baby born. We only wanted to understand how best to welcome thee, for our previous knowledge affected our behavior. Thy ghost state caused unneeded alarm. By our words and actions we did cause thee harm, didn't we?"

"'Twas no trouble," Art said, though her voice caught.

"Come," Sarah said. "Let us attend the meeting, Friend."

～

When they exited the building, Sarah saw a wagon driver she knew and asked the favour of a ride in back. Art would have protested but she felt that her legs and sore feet could do without further exercise. As they sat, backs against the stacked barrels of pickled fish the driver transported, Sarah explained the Friends' visit to the Secret Commission. A meeting with an assistant to the director was arranged so that the Friends could hear instructions or ask questions. It seemed that with resurrections, the problem of dealing with the amnesia of the risen was a more common one than Art or the Friends had realised.

"Then thee will not address myself by mine old family name?" Art said.

"'Twould cause confusion to thy newborn identity, the Commission said, and the Friends are in agreement. Unless thee wish it, we'll strive to not impose thy old life on thee."

"Until I am ready . . . and willing to learn more," Art said.

"Aye. I hope our silence does not cause thee pain!" Sarah said. "The sudden hushing of words, I mean, when realising such words are more than should be shared with thee! If I were to ever censor myself, know that it is only that!"

"I understand the dilemma, Friend," Art said. "For I censor myself in turn, with those who loved my human self too well."

Sarah nodded. "Know that not all the Friends consider such

silence, if held overly long, beneficial to thee. Thy old life, if truly flawed, should not be tainted with shame or judgment by our refusing to speak of it."

"My thanks, Sarah," Art said. She recalled the hostility of the counter woman, the grief of the Exercisium's assistant director, and the strange familiarity the boxing girls had exhibited towards her.

"Friend, was I so very violent, before?" Art said.

Sarah took a breath, hands in her lap as the wagon rolled.

"Here, I speak of we Friends needing to help thee more, yet I worry to tell thee more!" Sarah said. "To confuse matters, to give thee assumptions unhelpful or even untrue. For 'tis only what I know, tidbits and hearsays, and thee and myself were not so very close as acquaintances!"

"No need to answer, then. I will try not to fly into imaginings," Art said. "For such had me flee the previous meeting, and since then I've learned that mine is a complex story. Thus, I can only surmise that there is too much to explain, and thee feels inadequate to the storytelling."

"'Tis truly that. Thee has explained it," Sarah said.

Art held her stick and sighed.

"Patience," Sarah said, giving Art's gloved hand a pat. "As way opens, thee will learn all soon enough. And then perhaps thee could tell the story to me."

They disembarked the wagon at their destination, and both thanked the driver. Art saw Helene standing before the tenement building. Two bulldogs circled her, afflicted with injuries and bearing surgical scars. The three-legged bulldog hopped about comically, seeking to please Helene with his attempts at leaping. She gave him and the one-eyed bulldog vigorous rubs around the head and neck. A penny-farthing leaned on the wall behind her.

'Tis Helia's wheel, Art thought. She and Sarah walked up to Helene and greeted her.

"Sarah James, dost thee know Friend Helene?" Art said.

"I do. She is our generous landlord."

Helene owns the building, Art thought. She looked thoughtfully at Helene as Helene and Sarah amicably chatted. Her gaze traveled from her spectacles down to the trim figure she made in her buttoned black attire. Helene wore no hat right then. Art imagined her wearing silver pistols and smiled at the thought.

"Well, I seem to amuse you today, Art," Helene said, apparently noticing Art's appraisal.

"Thee is very pretty, Helene," Art said.

Helene blushed, looking flustered. She reached down to pet the bulldog by her side.

"I believe I've seen these faces!" Sarah said, petting the one-eyed bulldog. "Weren't thee at the surgical academy?" she said to the dog. "Thee is far happier now than when I saw thee there, aye?"

"If he could answer in our speech, it would be in the affirmative! I've taken these boys as my own," Helene said. "They'll reside with Rama for the time being. I've brought them here to perhaps cheer someone up." She glanced briefly up to her room's window. "Art, after your meeting, won't you stop by my room and visit?"

"I would gladly, Helene," she said.

"Thank you, Art. And I apologise for mentioning, but you've the most interesting scars on your face. I haven't seen the like, even in Africa."

"'Twas the captive squid I fought at the academy," Art said. "Released, it ran amok. Its suction cups sought to take my face off."

"Sounds like a tremendous battle," Helene said. "I hadn't time to read Helia's story. I was more concerned about the liberated animals and what was being done for them. How did you defeat the creature? With your bare hands or with a weapon?"

"Well, I—"

"Improvised weapon, I mean. I doubt your stick would have done much damage," Helene said. "Surgical theatre . . . did you use a table? A beam? Strangled it?"

"It near strangled me," Art said.

"I would have collapsed a roof on it," Helene said.

"Thee would not use thy sword?" Art asked.

"My what?" Helene said.

"I ate it," Art said.

"Oh," Helene said. "You . . . began eating it."

"Aye. It ate of myself first. So I ate of its insides, and then I put the whole of it inside me."

"You put the whole squid inside of you," Helene repeated.

"'Twas very queer to witness," Sarah said.

"Aye, 'twas large," Art said. "Eighteen hands tall, not counting the tentacles. 'Twas a tight fit."

"Yet thee managed it," Sarah said. "What a struggle! So big it was!"

"Very big," Art said. "Oh! And it's inside me, still."

Helene's mouth twitched.

"And how it moves! In and out, and around—"

"Yes, of course," Helene said.

"And its beak I had to spit," Art said.

"Eating your opponent would be rough," Helene said. "But it intended the same for you, wouldn't you say? It's what animals do. You did what was in your nature."

Art remembered the whale from her dream. "Aye," she said slowly, realisation dawning. "'Tis the way of we creatures."

"Like lion and unicorn," Sarah said as Art stared thoughtfully at Helene. "Friend, our meeting, 'tis starting."

"And 'tis the starting that matters," Helene said, smiling as she returned Art's gaze. "Go inside, Art."

Thus dismissed, Art had no choice but to turn away. Helene slapped her thigh and commanded the dogs, which obeyed and returned to her, tails wagging excitedly. Helene gave them treats from her pocket. Art followed Sarah and mused on Helene's use of Quaker speech.

When she descended with Sarah into the meeting room, dread nearly made the remains of squid perform flip-flops inside of her. She swallowed her temporary nausea and entered the room, finding many Friends within conversing quietly. When they looked at her, their eyes were kind. Others bore a sense of grave acceptance, especially in their nods to her. She nodded in turn and felt a little more at ease.

Soon, all moved to sit, and Art did so beside Sarah.

While Art sat in the silence of the Friends, her head bowed and her heart focused on listening to her still voice within, she eventually became aware that the energy of the meeting place seemed different. Or somehow, different from what she anticipated. She looked and saw that Sarah gazed upon her with an expression of pleasant expectancy.

When Art glanced about her, she saw that the Friends hadn't their heads bowed or their regard inward, but were looking at her. They were waiting for spoken insight, and it appeared that they assumed Art had already touched her spark within and was then moved to speak.

She thought that very little time had been spent in silent listening, but she already knew the words of her heart, and such words had questions, needing counsel. While exercising, flying, or merely standing in her room at the Vesta, Art had devoted her quiet time to deep listening. But what she heard felt like incomplete truths, and her Light would not give up more.

Right then, with all faces turned to her, it appeared that the Friends had anticipated her need.

'Tis odd, she thought, looking back at those who looked at her, that the Friends should change the nature of meeting to give focus to one need above the rest. Though she wasn't certain, due to lack of memory, if the occasional meeting was sometimes conducted so. She took the Friends' silent encouragement to have her speak first amongst them as a gift; the gift of community.

Art stood, hands around her stick. With all eyes upon her, her voice was slow to come, but eventually it did.

"I have taken a man's Light; his name was Dennis Bell. He was not evil nor a criminal, only someone used by another, and in my vigor I slew him.

"I raised my fist to reanimated children, sixteen of them, and made certain they did not rise again.

"I had beat upon many, too numerous, who attacked me, and some of whom I may have wounded grievously. I've hit a blind woman, though she was most deadly in martial skill. I struck a man for killing a dog, and I spoke no word first. I merely struck him.

"I am newly risen. I accept my eldritch state. But in becoming mere instinct and less a woman, will my love of man be also lessened? With each death caused by my hand, I fear the loss of my heart and of my Light.

"As servant of the Commission, I am tool and weapon, and e'en now, I was meant to kill the Bone Stealer myself had he not perished on his own. I had power to end him. This—this 'freedom' given me, without my having to fear consequence or punishment! Who am I, then, as Quaker woman? Who am I, if not that?"

She looked at the faces turned to her.

"Am I executioner? " she said fearfully.

One woman rose.

"No. Thee is 'protector', " she said.

Art stood in silence, gazing into the woman's eyes. The woman's hands, clasped against her skirt, shook in earnest.

"Believe," she said.

A bearded man stood. His face was lined, his eyebrows thick, and his eyes calm. He had one blind eye with a scar that ran beneath.

"Let thy life speak for thee," he commanded.

The man's voice was rough, a deep rasp that cut. Art felt it like gravel upon her soul.

"Let thy life speak, for conscience can only be tested," he said. "Thee cannot live, protected. When conscience faces trial, thee must not look away. Heed thy Light and live. Thee is a Quaker woman."

~

When the women's Indian clubs drill team finally vacated their section of floor, Delphia and Ellie claimed the space. Ellie moved in and bumped some of the lingering chatting women with her stick, driving them further off. Jim discovered Vesta acquaintances among the spectators—two women in dapper male dress who had been watching their sweethearts on the drill team. Jim elected to go back to the Vesta with them, and Delphia handed him over to the women.

"I know you'll do well, Bloom!" he said. "I'll remove myself so you'll concentrate better during your maiden session. Meet me back at the Vesta, won't you?"

"Yes, sir!"

Jim departed with the two toms, speaking loudly of how he was dying for a cigarette since smoking wasn't allowed in the Exercisium. Delphia doffed her coat and hat, laid them on a shelf, and drew her cudgel. Several people gathered to watch.

Ellie showed her how to hold her short cudgel and how to dedicate her entire body to the application of the weapon so she wouldn't suffer from the vibrations of impact. Delphia didn't understand what that meant until Ellie encouraged her to try a hard swing—only for Ellie to merely raise her stick and block Delphia's blow.

Delphia felt the impact ring painfully through her arm on contact.

Once she shook the temporary injury away, Ellie demonstrated three blocks with the stick and corrected Delphia's positioning until the stances felt familiar to her. Then the real lessons began. Ellie hit her repeatedly, only pausing to signal that she was changing the direction of her attack, and Delphia valiantly blocked. But it was the way Ellie swung her stick, with such grace, precision, and economy to her long, lean body that had Delphia quite in awe.

Ellie moved as if she were water; that was the only way Delphia could describe it. When her stick connected, it was as if she flowed right into the blow and then right past Delphia, which was an effect that made Delphia feel the impact that much harder. Delphia recalled the more practiced stick fighters who'd come to angry blows on her street. The men would beat right on each other. Ellie beat right through. Delphia was mere flotsam in the thrust of her rushing stream.

Delphia was out of breath and flagging in a short while.

Keeping her stick up was hard work, and Ellie allowed a brief break so Delphia could gather her wits. While the spectators murmured their opinions of Delphia's performance to each other, and Ellie had sauntered to the side to poke at exercise equipment with her stick, Delphia noticed the woman at the supplies counter watching her.

The woman didn't observe her as the others did, by merely looking on or viewing with the intent of being entertained. She looked at Delphia on the sly and ducked her head whenever Delphia glanced her way. Delphia had thought she'd felt the woman's gaze during practice, and her actions confirmed it. The covert attention irritated her.

Ellie wandered near and suddenly engaged Delphia again. Though she was refreshed, Delphia's attention suffered. Whenever she and Ellie rounded on each other, Delphia could spy the counter woman. The woman watched Delphia sharply, and then ducked away again.

Ellie's stick knocked Delphia's from her hand.

"This won't do," Ellie said as Delphia pursued her clattering stick. "A snail gives more attention."

"I'm sorry Ellie, I'm distracted, and—"

"Take this moment to clear yer 'ead," Ellie said. "Or I'll knock you black 'n blue."

Delphia nodded. She wanted to ask Ellie if she had noticed the attention of the woman at the counter. Right then it wasn't just the counter woman watching her, but the girls who had been boxing were gathered together and staring in her and Ellie's direction too. She thought their collective gaze resembled the looks of mocking challenge she'd seen from the likes of Hettie O'Taggart.

But as she turned to Ellie to mention it she remembered that Ellie couldn't see—if whatever Ellie did could be called any kind of "seeing". It was then that Delphia realised what she really wanted to ask her.

"Ellie, you're blind," Delphia said.

"Aye," Ellie said patiently.

"But you can see."

"Oh, I don't 'see', I feel," she said. "Like yer supposed to be learnin'."

"No, I meant . . . I've a father who is becoming blind."

"Time he came to the Institute for the Blind, then," Ellie said.

Delphia turned away. She really didn't want to get upset right then, in front of the entire Exercisium.

"'Ere." Delphia heard Ellie say. When she looked, Ellie handed Delphia her card.

"I've seen this. Mr. Dastard said it was your calling card," Delphia said, studying it. "What are these embossed dots, are they a sort of code?"

"It's Braille," Ellie said. "It's our alphabet 'n it's 'ow we read. We've books at the Institute."

"Books?" Delphia said hopefully. "The blind have books?"

"Well not many, and we fight over 'em."

"I can learn this," Delphia said in excitement, feeling the card. "And Papa will too. I can help transcribe more books. He must do this too. He will be wonderful at it."

"Good," Ellie said. "Make 'em excitin' books."

She struck Delphia on the shin with her stick.

"Oh!"

"That's for not concentrating," Ellie said. "Keep the card."

Delphia fared better when they resumed practice. She performed the series of blocks Ellie had taught her with more and more ease, repeating them until her body gained memory, and in the ending exercise, performed three blocks in succession to Ellie's impromptu attack. Relieved that her knuckles came away without suffering a bruising blow, she curtsied to the applause the observers awarded her.

"I'll have sore arms tomorrow," she said, rubbing both her biceps.

"But you'll raise 'em lest yer wanting a rap on the 'ead," Ellie said lightly. "Same time tomorrow, then?"

"Yes, Miss Hench. Thank you," Delphia said and curtsied again.

Ellie immediately left her side. She sauntered across the Exercisium floor, nose high and stick tapping. People hurried out of her way. She tripped one fellow who was not so swift and just like that she was out the doors and gone.

Delphia holstered her cudgel and retrieved her coat and hat. Her spectators had dispersed and returned to their activities. As she walked across the floor past the patrons focused on exercise routines or operating their machines, she neared the supplies counter. The counter woman fussed about. Delphia paused to put on her coat. The woman then looked at her, eyes wide.

"You'll be coming back tomorrow, then?" she said pleasantly.

"Why yes, I'll be returning," Delphia said.

"Oh, good, good," the woman said, smiling.

Delphia adjusted the fit of her coat and moved on. She saw the boxing girls hovering around their punching bag, watching her. One stout girl with hair in pigtails had an elbow resting on the shoulder of another. She grinned at Delphia, her front teeth missing.

Delphia put her hat on, ran her fingers along the brim, and walked for the exit. She felt the girls' gaze follow her.

～

Taking Art's example, Delphia took further exercise by walking back to the Vesta. She strolled into the back entrance. The bustling kitchen was in the midst of tea preparation. She sat with pages and maids, had two cups with sandwiches, cakes, cut fruit, and biscuits, and then sought out Jim.

When she knocked and entered his little study, a chambermaid was seated at the table, entertaining him by manipulating a small, nude ivory female figure with a crystal round belly and hinged limbs. The maid spread the doll's legs, and a tiny ivory baby that looked very much like a kitten, fell out.

"Ha ha!" Jim laughed.

The maid put the kitten figure back inside the doll's crystal belly as Jim and Delphia greeted each other. After the maid stored the figure in Jim's cabinet, she picked up her feather duster and left the two to converse at the table. Delphia brushed some biscuit crumbs from her coat front and removed her hat.

"How went your first exercise, squire? Ready for the tilting at windmills, mayhap?" Jim said jovially.

"Windmills can always be fought, sir, I just won't be ready yet for the dragons," Delphia said as she rubbed the sore shin that had received Ellie's blackthorn.

"A most clever mind is what impresses dragons. That and shiny things," Jim said. "Much like what I now have the pleasure of bestowing upon you. I've a box! And it's for you, Bloom. Do me the kindness of accepting and opening it."

"Sir," Delphia said. A small, white gift box wrapped in paper and red ribbon lay on his table by his pile of newspapers. She picked it up.

"Open! Open!" he said.

When Delphia had carefully unwrapped the box and put the folded ribbon and paper into her pocket, she removed the lid. Inside, laid in tissue, was a cast-metal badge of a skull in top hat, side-by-side with a deer's head.

"That's my skull but they insisted that the deer be in the design! Its head is like the one on the handle of Art's stick. A silver hind. It's meant to represent her, or so they've written me."

"'They', sir?"

"Oh! I mean Miss Thackery, who speaks also for Art's patroness, Lady Helene. Now, Bloom, we should wait for Art to pin that on you to make it official, but I dearly want to see it on your chest. As my acting hands, I do bade you to represent myself as you pin that on yourself."

Delphia pinned on the badge.

"Thank you, sir," she said, saluting.

"Salute returned! Congratulations, Bloom!"

"This is a great honour. And I hope my service will do this badge justice. But sir, the awarding of this badge reminds me of a question which my parents wished to share with you. Do I also work for the Secret Commission while in service to you and Art?"

"A good question from Mr. and Mrs. Bloom. No, Bloom, you are exclusively our squire. We are your sole employers. And if the Secret Commission should, oh, attempt recruitment of your services, you must refuse."

"Sounds ominous, sir."

"I may work for them—owe them my second life," Jim said. "And they certainly pay my expenses! But I don't trust them any farther than I can throw myself. I'd been spied on, you see, and such covert behavior soured my faith. My partners, except for Harold and Art, had all been told to record anything I said, whether I liked it or not. And I didn't like it. I'm sure you've noticed by now, I've a most unique command of the Queen's English."

"A very creative command, sir," Delphia said thoughtfully. "Rest assured, I've not been approached to spy on you. My parents were hoping that were I in government employ, I might earn pension."

"Even we agents have enquired about pensions. But most of us never seem to live long enough to merit a firm answer from the director."

"Oh," Delphia said.

"No time like the present!" Jim said. "The director is elusive when it comes to appointments. Like chasing a fox. Now that Art is here, I'll formally initiate the query of pensions once again on our behalves, with a written letter."

Without further prompting, Delphia turned for Jim's cabinet, retrieved a portable, wooden writing box from one of the drawers, and sat down at the table. She slid open the box's lid and laid out the dip pen, uncapped the inkwell, and pulled out a sheet of paper.

"Ha ha!" Jim said. "As the eldest surviving agent of the Secret Commission, it always seems to fall to me to make these repeated queries. Must keep the ball rolling."

Keep the ball 'up', Delphia thought, realising that she was mentally correcting Jim's Americanism.

"Another thing, sir. Father had noted that our supernatural cases don't occur often," Delphia said. "And there are pairs of agents around, though some are now assigned to other cities. Mother rather anticipates that I'll help more at home when there's no work to be had."

"True, we've lulls when not heroically defending England.

But there will be a task needing us. You'll be investigating more, soon enough."

"You anticipate something, sir?"

"I do, but only when Art is ready. Then, you shall be my most helpful legs and fingers, Bloom, for that time when Art finally asks for our help in finding the answers to her past."

Delphia gravely nodded and moistened the metal pen nib with her tongue.

~

At the waxing of teatime's hour, Art arrived back at the Vesta in a manner she was unaccustomed to. For the first time she rode a hansom cab—alone—and took that solitary time to gaze out the open front and enjoy the scenery. Men and women, whether in their own vehicles or walking the street, looked at her in surprise, curiosity, and some in disapproval, but Art thought the reactions were inspired by the spectral glow she emitted.

She would have been running or flying among the folk of the street right then, if not for her mending state. When the one-eyed Friend at meeting had ceased speaking and sat down, Art had sat too. The rest of the hour was held in silence without more Friends being moved to vocal ministry. An elder at the head of the room then shook the hand of the Friend next to him, and in this gesture of heart to hand, Art turned and shook the hand of Sarah James, her heart full.

Afterwards, she had walked painfully up to Helene's room, only to find no answer to her knock. She saw no dogs and Helia's penny-farthing was also gone. Her disappointment made the taxing of her still healing body acutely apparent.

With every nerve protesting and the bottoms of her feet feeling on fire, she realised that she needed to seek specialised professional treatment for her nervous system. She hailed her first hansom cab of the day and rode it to Billingsgate and its Black Market.

She ignored the man minding the market's curtain entrance and walked into the warehouse. She would have preferred to ghost, but considering the cause of her present state—the splitting of her body from her skeleton while in ghost form—she was wary of a return to the Fourth Dimension. She felt askew, and the pain seemed evident of such misalignment. Were she to ghost and then regain solidity, she might cause further error in the whole of her body.

None of the market's denizens confronted her, though their glares and sullen stares were plenty. Art wandered through without incident and found the shop and shingle that had the cartoon of a body with red circles drawn on it. She knocked on the doorframe.

Dr. Lau pulled back the curtain. He stared up in surprise, his lips slack around his pipestem.

"I've need of thy healing, Friend," she said.

Lau's lined face broke into a broad smile. He nodded and waved for her to come inside.

Thus began her first treatment, with the application of pressure and of steel needles (much to Art's surprise). He even had a machine, which, when attached to the needles, sent electricity into the body. Art declined its use for this healing session. Once the visit was concluded and she had in her possession a parcel of smelly herbs to apply as instructed, she felt far less askew than she had before.

She then caught her second hansom cab outside Billingsgate Market and rode to Cheapside and Robin Hood's Row to retrieve her mended hat.

Art was eager to have it back. She was presently wearing one of the remaining hats Charlotte had provided, but for Art, it didn't feel the same. Like her stick, she was irrationally fond of her first hat and thought it might improve her spirits more to have it on her head again.

Her visit at Charlotte's dress shop was not overly long; the place bustled with customers being attended to. A new set of clothes and undergarments was being wrapped and boxed for her as well, in preparation for delivery at the Vesta. One dress had a long coat draped over the bustle. At the waist was a belt sash with ornamental pom-poms dangling. Black lace with a pattern of flowers decorated the bodice front.

"Oh!" Art exclaimed, admiring the dress's colour. 'Tis like chocolate!"

"It's aubergine, Art," Charlotte said.

"'Tis . . . aubergine! And . . . it has a bustle, Friend," Art added in dismay.

"Oh, but it's a little one, Art," Charlotte said.

According to Charlotte, Parisian designers were reviving the bustle design (to appease the French silk trade). Art pointed out that Helene and Helia wore no bustle (nor did Charlotte), which Charlotte dismissed with a wave.

"Well, I have to sit most of the day, Art, unlike you! Yours will be padded, not metal this time. Think of the things you can hide in it!"

When Art saw the wide vertical stripes of Cremorne red and Florentine yellow of the second dress, running down the curves of the outfit, she held her tongue. It had black velvet cuffs and collar, ruffles that flowed down to the waistband, skirt layers of ruche, and a bow-tied bustle.

It was very pretty, but Art thought it would make her look the very gaudy prostitute among her Quaker brethren.

Charlotte invited Art into her office to discuss the circumstances that led to her bullet-riddled outfit, query whether any new garments had been ruined (Art affirmed that the striped, chartreuse yellow dress was irreparably damaged due to the colossal squid), and to give Art her newly mended hat.

But the hat was more than mended. As Art rode her third hansom cab back to East London and to the Vesta, she amused herself by rapping on her newly reinforced and hardened crown. She found the hollow knocking sound the top of her hat made terribly satisfying to her ear.

When she entered the Vesta, bearing her packet of smelly herbs, she felt in far better spirits than when she left.

Vesta patrons greeted her from the two drawing rooms. After some pleasant and even jovial interactions regarding her fragrant and mysterious herbal package, Art took her leave. Alice greeted her at the foot of the stairs, and at Art's request for help with some medicinal application, promised to send a maid. Once she was back in her room, she began to undress just as the maid arrived.

The maid Alice had sent was one Art had met during the re-animationist case. She had been a nurse in the second Afghan War. She'd also just returned from attending a relative's funeral in the country. When Art related her recent adventure and traumatic injuries, the maid tutted. She didn't mind being called "Nurse" by Art, either.

Nurse helped Art undress, and while Art lay front first on the bed, her paper and pencil by her head, Nurse expertly mixed warmed oil and the packet of herbs to make the paste. She applied it all along Art's spine. A liberal dose was smeared near her tailbone ("the most important working spot," said Nurse). Once she made certain Art was comfortable, she promised to return in forty minutes and remove the paste.

"Seems a long time for absorbing medicinal herbs," Nurse said, her voice skeptical. "But you're hardly an ordinary woman, and after what you've suffered, such a long application does seem right! But summon me the moment you've discomfort, miss."

Art assured her that she would, and Nurse left.

Whatever was in the herbs heated her flesh to the bone and made Art relaxed and drowsy. She managed a few sentences to begin her report on the Bone Stealer case before deciding to set the pencil down and rest her head.

When she heard a knock and bade that person enter, she felt she might have dozed twenty minutes. Alice entered with Jim in hand.

"My! Smells like an Italian warren in here!" Jim said. "Apologies, Art, I should leave you to your herbal healing. Or soup, I'm not sure which."

"'Tisn't soup, Friend," Art said sleepily, turning her head. "Thy company is welcomed, if thee doesn't mind the smell of the herbs. If I feel whole after this treatment, I shall try ghosting."

"Glad to hear it! I'll add my 'baccy scent to this pervasive fragrance. Then we'll really be homey!" Jim said.

Alice placed Jim on the nightstand, prepared and lit a pipe for him, and after seeing that Art was well, departed.

"And where is Delphia, Friend?" Art asked. "Perhaps thee sent her home to care for family?"

"What a womanly thought!" Jim said as he puffed on his pipe. "It's an early day, yes, with no case. She's to go home, but after one more task. I'd asked her to mail a letter to the Secret Commission for me, but she insisted on taking a cab and delivering it herself! Truly a budding adventuress. I think she's never been to the West End and wishes to see the Strand and the workings of the Secret Commission building itself."

"She's a girl alone," Art said.

"And she's a smart girl," Jim said. "A swift learner. Every adventure in independence shall teach her more."

They discussed her wage, which Art learned Catherine would deduct from Art and Jim's Secret Commission salaries and then pay Delphia. It was news to Art that Catherine was the one handling their money, but she didn't mind it since banking was the least of her concerns when only eight days living, and she'd yet to figure out who was paying for what. Namely, where her own expenses began, and where Helene, as her secret patron, ended them.

Nurse returned to cleanse Art's back of the paste and help her dress as Jim explained Delphia's new badge. She commended him on the gift. When Nurse left, Art picked Jim up, set him at the table with her pencil and paper, and resumed work on her report again. Soon, the only sound in the room was of her pencil scribbling and the rustle of paper.

"Ha!" Jim murmured, breaking a long silence. He puffed on his pipe. "'Keep the ball up.' Bloom didn't know I saw her lips move."

"Friend?" Art said. Her pencil was at its dullest, and she had nothing to sharpen it with—not even a penknife.

"Oh, nothing. I spoke an Americanism today, and I saw Bloom correct me silently. 'Keep the ball up,' you see. Not 'rolling'."

"Aye, the ball 'up' is how 'tis said."

Art enquired if he had a penknife, and Jim did, in a drawer in his study. Art took Jim in hand and went to fetch it.

"I've need of a smaller penknife to keep in my hat," Jim said. "Lost the last one on a case with Billy. I should give Delphia this one."

"Friend . . . if I might note, Perseus Kingdom is an American," Art said after she retrieved the knife.

"I don't sound anything like him, do I," Jim said.

"True, thee does not. I also heard other Americans whilst at the aquarium. Thee is a mix of accents at times."

She brought them back into her room and set Jim down. She sharpened her pencil.

"Yes, it's very likely that Fall designed my voice. It's admirably masculine, but undetectable as to cultural origin. Humph! Would be a great jest on his part if I were, in actuality, a woman's skull! But no, I've a man's mind, and therefore have retained a male voice. Though time spent amongst the mandrakes and toms of the Vesta has me wonder what lends gender to a mind. Say I were a woman's skull, yet given a deceptively manly voice, and my sensual appetites most deeply sapphic."

"Friend, that's a complex consideration," Art said thoughtfully. "In that regard I might have formerly been male and am now in a female body."

"Indeed! But Lady Helia recognises you for the female specimen you were before, and still are, so that speculation is moot. With regards to your mind, I still think it quite sexless, Art. Until a skirt distracts you, of course."

"Though I am a sapphist, I've no inclination to be a tom," Art said.

"I do prefer you queenly and not kingly. Nor have you any preference for male company?"

"It has not come to mind," Art admitted. "Despite having been in the presence of men pleasing to mine eye."

"There are women and men who can partake of both," Jim said. "And then there's the inexplicable. A man happily wed with his wife may suddenly discover his true happiness with another man. A tom of deep sapphic interests might suddenly decide she would rather have a husband. I'm sure you would say—"

"Love is love," Art said. "God is love."

Jim chuckled.

The light from the windows began to fade as evening approached. Art's new clothes arrived with a maid who helpfully hung and stored all the items away. Jim exclaimed over the striped dress with the skirt layer of ruche, believing it was her prettiest yet. Art assured him that Charlotte would return to designing plainer outfits.

"'Tisn't just for meetings, but for the work," Art said.

She laboured more on her Bone Stealer report. But there came a point when her account became vague, and words failed her in describing her bone-harvested state. Right then, her words took on a surreal tone and hardly seemed factual as she read them through. She decided to set the report aside. She wrote a few notes for the re-animationist case and then set that paper aside too.

"Art, don't tell me you're already done?" Jim said.

"I am not, but I have run out of paper," Art said. She stood and deposited her unfinished reports and pencil on her dresser.

"Ho! With your duties done for the night, thee is smiling," Jim said as he smoked. "I know that smile."

Art turned translucent, disappeared all together, and then returned to solidity. She grinned.

"Never had there been a more pleased Cheshire Cat!" Jim exclaimed.

Art put on her newly mended hat and gloves. She looked in her full-length mirror and made certain her hat was straight and all buttons and fastenings were tidy. She fussed with her hair. The suction marks on her face appeared to be fading. She was glad she had the dress in Montebello garnet to wear because Helia had not yet seen her in the outfit.

She rapped on her hardened crown and grinned.

"Ah. 'Tis time for your skirt-chasing?" Jim said.

"Aye," Art said, smiling. "For now I feel fit enough to fly." She went to her dresser and found the prettier of the smashed silver bullets. She carefully tore paper from her re-animationist report, folded the piece around the bullet, and placed it in a pocket.

She turned to Jim, suddenly recalling what he had mentioned when speaking of Harold's death.

"Friend, thee had said that Deck, thy former partner, had wives."

"Mm? Yes, Deck was a polygamist," Jim said. He blew pipe smoke from one of his eye sockets. "Not on the sly, and no, he was of no faith that excused such behavior. He just tended towards it. He was honest to a fault and the women knew of each other."

"And Billy Black, thy last partner. Thee said he had sweethearts. One assumes . . . at the same time?"

"Yes. Attentive boy, Billy. He lacked good judgment, however."

"Are the other agents so amorous?" Art asked.

"Well, to a degree. Deck lived two and a half years. I can't say that other agents had time to make things work. Harold . . . oh, but he was a rogue. Too much the sensualist. Deck was the marrying sort, and I'm certain had Billy lived he would have been too. Probably would have married all the wrong ones. But to answer your question somewhat, we are what we are, Art. Aberrant."

Art smiled. She approached the table and picked Jim up.

"I've Helia to see. Where would thee like to be, whilst I'm gone?"

"Merely pull the cord," Jim said. "I will shortly be transported to the merriments of below by a helpful page."

Art did so and set him on her bed.

"Thee be well," she bade. She ghosted and flew through her window.

~

Jim watched her swift departure and refrained from bidding farewell in return.

He was afraid that a merry "adieu" would not leave his teeth, but that fearful call of parents instead: *Do be careful, now.*

CHAPTER TWENTY

In the darkening sky over Westminster and Big Ben, Art spiraled down for the Royal Aquarium.

The Palace Hotel and Pleasure Gardens adjacent to the great building were lit for the coming night. Gaily dressed patrons emerged from the Palace doors for cabs or disembarked from carriages to enter the hotel. A small band played a leisurely tune in the gardens. Couples danced before them. But the aquarium building itself stood bereft of people, its courtyard empty and its glass dome dark. Art descended for the shut doors and while floating, read the sign listing opening and closing hours.

SUNDAY, CLOSED, it read.

"Oh!" she said in dismay.

It was First Day, a day of rest after all, but Art rather wished an attraction—especially one Helia lived in—remained open. Through the glass, she could see a man slowly ride a steam-powered polishing machine along the floor. As he steered, he pushed a treadle bar with his foot that kept the wheels turning. Steam blew from the exhaust pipe behind him. Art righted herself and turned invisible. She passed through the doors.

The lights of the aquarium were low, the waters of the tanks casting blue reflections that rippled on the ground. The polishing machine whirred steadily. Two more maintenance men stood on ladders and worked with sponges and wipers to cleanse the glass of the tank housing the giant crab and clam. The performing divers were present, practicing their routines. Art heard the water splash repeatedly as they dove in.

She flew down the corridor of tanks for the pavilions proper and the great dome filled with airship and balloon replicas.

Restaurants, cafes, storefronts, and carts were all closed. Chairs were stacked or upended and resting on tables. A man seated on a slow-moving, steam-powered mopping machine stepped on the accelerating bar and steered while another man drove a vigorously whirring drying machine after him. Art floated through the drivers and their vehicles as they leisurely wound around the displays and saw the fountain in the lounging area. It sparkled and splashed, the coloured glass at its gas-lit base turning the water blue, red, and green.

The French café was dark, their display tank empty of creatures. But when Art looked to the Blue Vanda, the patio lights were lit. Helia sat at a table and typed.

Art flew near and circled her.

～

Amalie Swinstock knew herself to be trapped in circumstance, Helia typed. *That of an unyielding mother's desire to make her whole, and the knowledge that her own lifelong illness was destined to end her. When or how soon, she did not know. The option of surgery, even of the conventional sort, was known for questionable outcome. Therefore, she did what she felt she could only do, then aged twenty-two and without strength in will or fragile body to defy a parent's resolve, even when she knew such resolve meant another would die for her. She gathered all that was hers, precious words and paintings brought to life by her imaginative powers alone, and bestowed those stories upon her brother for safekeeping. In this manner did Amalie Swinstock bid final farewell to our world.*

Helia paused in typing and sighed. She turned to the chair next to her and removed a leather portfolio from the large open valise that sat there. She carefully flipped through the sheets of watercolour paintings within. One was of a night-blooming garden of evening primrose, four o'clocks, night gladiolus, and moon flowers surrounding a cracked fountain and sunken glowing stepping-stones. A silent house with a single lit window sat in the distance, cloaked in enveloping darkness behind an overgrown crumbling wall. The next painting was of a warm yet shadowed sitting room, lit aglow by an unknown source, with small lattice windows opening upon strange starlit skies and dark hulking trees. The third was of a corridor with stone columns and arched windows, stretching into darkness. More starry skies could be seen beyond the windows, and statues stood in the dark foliage and looked within.

"You hadn't an interest in bunnies and hedgehogs, did you?" Helia murmured as she glanced at more mysterious and ethereal landscapes and settings. "Inside your heart, you were this great and infinite night."

Helia briefly closed her eyes and shut and secured the portfolio. She returned it to the valise. Within were many notebooks, wrapped attentively with paper detailing the number of each volume and the date created. Helia had opened the last one to see the final sentences Amalie had written. She then carefully wrapped the volume up again. Those words were enough for Helia to understand what kind of creation was placed in her hands.

Earlier that day, while recovering from her self-pitying fit at Helene's apartment, Helene had stepped out briefly. She then received a telegram at Helene's desk from their Aunt Juliet, wife to Uncle Cadmus. Countess Skycourt had been made confidentially aware that her old friend, Lady Swinstock, who had recently lost her daughter to circumstances of black arts surgery, had threatened to have Art arrested.

Then Lady Swinstock attempted suicide.

Aunt Juliet, not terribly proficient at dictating a simple, and therefore effective telegram, sent a garbled message, but Helia surmised the intent. When Helene returned with her two new bulldogs, there was only time to give their funny faces a hasty kiss, have Helene return them to the stables, and rush to the Swinstock residence on her wheel. Helene departed for the Skycourt home to fetch their brougham marked with the family crest in order to arrive in a more respectable manner.

At the Swinstock home in Regent Park, Lord Swinstock was too upset to receive Helia. Lady Swinstock was insensate from an overdosage of laudanum. But their son Robert, grave and sad, received her and Helene when she arrived, twenty minutes later. He reassured them that no real trouble would be brought against Art. His father had never supported his mother's plan for Amalie though he had reluctantly agreed to pay for the procedure. And because of the surgery's outcome, Lady Swinstock had been driven quite mad.

Helia thought she'd been summoned so that the family could demand she not write of their complicity with the Bone Stealer (a fact she might have discovered later, if not for their revealing it to her first). But surprisingly, that was not the case. If Lady Swinstock was presently mad, so it would seem her husband was too. He had no desire to protect the family's reputation from law or society.

"You will be ruined," Helene said in a matter-of-fact tone to Robert.

"We've no real concern for the police or courts. But of our society?" Robert said flatly. "Yes. We expect to live in hell."

Lord Swinstock had bouquets of forget-me-nots laid all about Amalie's bedroom. Helia then, was not surprised when the son pressed upon her the responsibility of the valise's contents.

"Though I will try to explain these to you, I have also given what I know in an enclosed letter," he said quietly, showing her and Helene what was inside the valise. "Only because my sister's work, her passion, was of such complex creation that even the thimbleful of understanding that I have of it is inadequate to convey what her magnificent inner eye could discern . . . that of a Kingdom deeper, richer, more beautiful, and more right for her than our own world could ever be." He handed the valise to Helia. "You must have these published."

When Helia left with Helene in the brougham, her wheel stored in the back, Helene glanced at the valise at Helia's side.

"Those are not her diaries, then?" Helene said. "They're . . . stories?"

"A world, Helene," Helia said. "Like *The Blazing World*."

"Like that? A visionary's fantasy? But you haven't looked inside the books yourself to know this."

"I only had to see the paintings, Helene."

Helene turned and stared out the window.

"Rather like what you used to do," Helene abruptly said. "Except with . . . voles."

"Why . . . that was so long ago. How funny you should remember."

The brougham rolled on, only the sound of hooves and wheels apparent to Helia's ears.

"Odd how we'd never met this family, Swinstock," Helene finally said. "Though I believe I've heard their name now and then."

"They're never in London," Helia said. "Did you see the collection of novelty seashells in Amalie's room?"

"Yes. From every seaside resort imaginable. Yet Auntie knew the family. We should have met the son at least once."

"Perhaps Auntie and Lady Swinstock were good friends as girls, once upon a time," Helia said. "Perhaps when Lady Swinstock saw how terribly sick her youngest was, she preferred Amalie . . . protected. From the pity, if not the scrutiny of our society."

Helene looked at Helia.

"We were never ashamed of you," she said.

"How guilty your face is," Helia said, but she smiled.

She smiled more when Helene grasped her hand.

"And how glad I am that you were never like Amalie Swinstock," Helene said. "You escaped what was thought best for you. You had the audacity to defy us all."

~

Helia dearly desired a cigarette but she didn't dare smoke. Not when so precious an item sat next to her, still smelling of the girl who apparently was fond of the scent of jasmine, and which scent permeated her books. Helia herself had shilling shockers published (of a sword-wielding, creature-fighting masked woman), under a fictitious name, but collecting and transcribing an intimate and artistically unique body of work would take more editorial and curative expertise than she possessed. She would seek help for the project. But until then, she could give Lord Swinstock and his son some peace by writing of the circumstances of Amalie's life and how she ended up in the hands of the Bone Stealer.

Helia looked up. The pavilions proper was empty and still except for the mopping man, his drying partner, and their machines. But Helia was certain she'd felt something.

Like the electrical shocks she endured when she was an asylum inmate, supernatural presence crackled on her skin in the same manner. Her eldritch awareness was like a great bubble all around her with a spinning diameter of twenty-four feet. Unlike Ellie, who needed unobstructed open space to feel things, Helia's ability to sense queer energies could pierce walls.

Thus, she felt a beautiful warmth fly by, swooping around her like a kite taut on a string from her hand. She laughed, but before she could speak, she felt Art's spectral presence depart and disappear.

"Oh! Must you?" she said aloud, looking around. She tamped down her disappointment—and irrational fear. If she hadn't understood that Art had merely left briefly, she might have given herself up to the frightening thought that she'd lost her all over again.

Helia secured the valise, placed it at her feet, cleared some of the debris of her table away, and resumed typing. After a while, she heard what she had been expecting: the tapping of a walking stick. Helia rose to look for the source.

From the direction of the Palace Hotel, Art walked down a corridor adjacent to the pavilions proper, a restaurant server in his black coat and long white apron by her side. He carried a serving tray bearing a teapot, cups, and a small, covered ceramic bowl.

Helia clapped her hands in delight.

"Oh, Art!" she said.

~

When Art and the server reached the patio and mounted the steps, she saw Helia seat herself again. They warmly greeted each other as Art sat down too. The server set out tea and placed the bowl before Helia. He bowed, bade them an enjoyable dinner, and returned to the Palace Hotel.

When Helia removed the bowl's cover, she laughed.

"Porridge!" she exclaimed.

"'Twill warm thy vitals," Art said. "Thee looked cold sitting here!"

"Why, I guess I am, Art! I don't notice, not when I'm writing," Helia said, rubbing her chilled gloveless hands. Without the presence of visitors, the temperature of the aquarium had dipped a few degrees.

At Art's urging, Helia ate her hot porridge and drank her tea. There was honey and cinnamon to add to her porridge, a dish with a dab of butter, a slice of bread on another, and for Art, a glistening, raw portion of salmon filet.

"Has thee been well since thy handsome self parted from my delirious self last night?" Art said.

"Oh, I'm always well when you're near, Art," Helia said, smiling.

"Thy wee handlebar made thee a very fetching gentleman," Art said. "But how much fonder I am of thy feminine countenance."

"Helene berated my choice of moustache!" Helia said. "She prefers the pencil moustache."

"To wear?" Art said.

"Oh, yes."

Art imagined Helene in a pencil moustache. Male impersonators, if she had appropriate recall, never donned facial hair. The appeal of female cross-dressers was their emulation of the beauty of beardless youths. Their female admirers attested to their success. Art determined that Helene and Helia chose to cross-dress for adventuring purposes rather than to attract attentions from either sex.

While Helia ate (her spoon making no sound in her bowl, Art

noted), Art shared her day. She told of how she'd been welcomed back by the Friends, taken Dr. Lau as doctor, visited Charlotte in her shop, and how she enjoyed riding about in hansom cabs. She mentioned meeting Helene and her rescued dogs. Helia apologised profusely for being absent when she discovered that she and Art had nearly seen each other earlier.

"Thee and Helene had departed for more investigating?" Art said.

"It was that, Art, yes," Helia said. "Oh, how sorry I am we couldn't wait for you."

"'Twas no trouble. Our meeting now is made sweeter."

When Helia ate her last bite of porridge, Art absorbed her filet of salmon.

"Your lovely glow!" Helia said. "Was it very good, dear?"

"Aye," Art said. "'Tis pleasing sustenance, the salmon!"

She refrained from mentioning that she still felt the weight of the slowly digesting squid within her.

She had also, in the recounting of her day, omitted her visit to the Exercisium. Any desire to seek answers from Helia disappeared at viewing her solemn face when she had been typing. Art knew her questions could wait, especially when she had the option to query others, such as Helene.

Art moved the dishes to another table and fished in her pocket. She gave Helia the paper-wrapped, smashed silver bullet.

"For thee," she said.

With a delighted smile, Helia accepted the tiny parcel and carefully opened it. The silver bullet rolled into the middle of her bare palm.

"Oh! Look at it! The dear thing!" Helia cried.

"'Twas vomited by myself," Art said.

"Did it make you very ill, Art?" Helia said as she examined the bullet. Even in the dim lighting, it sparkled.

"Aye, so uncooperative was mine body with it inside me. Is it enchanted, Helia?"

"Oh it is, naughty thing! We don't like it, do we? No we don't!" Helia laughed. She put the bullet against her mask. "Ouch!

My, what a perfect little blessing it has! Oh!" She handled the bullet as if it burned her mask.

Art watched, fascinated. She saw a darkness coalesce in the masked side of Helia's face. It gathered like a black scowl.

"Well if I swallowed it, what then, eh? Yes, what then!" Helia suddenly said. Her lip curled in a snarl.

Art placed her hand over Helia's.

"'Tis a blessed bullet?" Art said. "By the Catholics?"

Helia laughed again, her snarl gone and the darkness no longer visible to Art's perceptions.

"Those Catholics! They've the most fun things. Blessed water hurts too." Helia held the bullet up. "This has, or had, an intention written upon its ball. I can't tell what words since they're obliterated now, but I can feel them. It's meant to harm a creature, like yourself, Art. And like myself, who har—harb—who is flawed."

Helia's stutter was brief, but she seemed to pay it no more heed than a mild cough. Art watched her regard the bullet between her thumb and forefinger, moving it across the air. Helia shut her eyes and slowly brought the bullet down until it gently struck her masked temple. She cocked her head at the feigned impact and smiled.

Art picked up Helia's hand and pressed her lips to it.

"Oh, Art, have I said something?" Helia said, opening her eyes. "Your beautiful mouth! Yet it's so sad."

"'Tis nothing," Art said softly. "Nothing but mine ache for thee."

Helia's lips parted, still upturned in a smile. Her gaze fell away.

"I need to explain to you," she said.

"No need," Art said.

"I've a—a—I'm. It. *It.*" Helia's eyes closed and her throat worked. She took back her hand. She secreted the bullet in the folded cuff of her sleeve and began typing.

"I've had a long time in asylums, balloons, and boxing rings," she said. "People die. Yet violin strings, they are lovely things."

She pulled out her typed paper, folded it, and handed it to Art. Art accepted and unhooked her bodice. She tucked the paper into her front while Helia watched with wide eyes.

"Why dost thee live in a balloon?" Art asked as she refastened her bodice and made herself presentable again.

"Oh, why does Diogenes wander?" Helia said. She looked down at her hands.

"After Mama and Papa were . . . died, I ran away from asylum and stowed away in our airships, all around the world. Helene fled to the sea. When you died, I ran to here, to this balloon. Helene ran to your . . . to where she could be poor. It's what we do."

"Thee should no longer be poor, of heart or spirit," Art said. "For I am here. Thee can both go home."

"I can't!" Helia whispered franticly. She raised her fists. "Not yet! Oh, I can't."

Art moved her chair closer and hugged her. Helia's body gave within her firm clasp, and Art held her tightly. Their hats knocked awkwardly. She felt Helia's tension lessen, her fists loosen. Art's embrace gentled until she rocked them both.

Art thought of families and of parents. She recalled the daguerreotypes she had seen on Helene's desk.

"You mustn't mind me, Art. I'm noise," Helia said against Art's shoulder.

"Thee is the noise I wish to hear in my silence," Art said.

"What does your silence say to you now?" Helia whispered.

Art kissed the masked side of Helia's face.

"Have I parents who miss me?"

"No, Art," Helia said gently. She moved away from Art's arms to look at her. "You told us you were orphaned."

"Like thee?" Art asked.

"Yes. Like us," Helia said.

"Did thee and I know each other very long?"

"Not very long," Helia said.

"Yet thee and I loved . . . I, who was such a violent Quaker?"

"No, dear," Helia said, smiling. "You weren't so, at all."

"I did not ride about on a great horse, then, and bring terror among creatures?"

"Ha ha!" Helia laughed and clapped her hands. "Oh!"

Art smiled, delighting in the renewed sparkle of Helia's eyes. Helia's response had been neither affirmation nor denial. Art was unsure what to make of it. Her smile lessened when she thought of Helene.

Helia's own mirth faded as she looked into Art's eyes.

"You've another question, Art?" she gently asked.

"'Tisn't so much a question as a truth, needing further understanding," Art said. "Oh, but to cause thee pain! Yet, I must know. Helene said . . . I died a victim, a cruel joke."

Art saw Helia's face shadow. Her gaze grew distant. Her eyes were pale blue lights in the shuttering of her face.

"I'll kill her," Helia whispered.

Art grasped Helia's hands firmly.

"Who, Helia?" Art asked.

"That twin of Medea," Helia whispered. "That scorpion. Why did we let her live? Because Helene was devastated, that's why. And I was . . . I was busy gone all mad again, wasn't I? She ruined us so effectively. Slipped away. Last laugh. Ha ha."

"Nay, Helia," Art said. "If laughter means happiness, then 'tis we who laugh now. In thanks. Rejoicing."

Helia looked at her. Art watched as her face lost grimness and slowly lightened. A smile blossomed.

"You are my wonder," she said.

"Let us talk no more on past happenings," Art coaxed. "'Tis time thee rested, aye? Put away thy writing."

"But—" Helia said. She abruptly yawned. She turned and put her hand to her mouth. "Oh dear!" she said when the yawn ended.

"Thy body gives the message! Which balloon is thine?" Art asked.

Helia smiled. She looked up and Art did as well. Helia pointed to a Skycourt airship replica high above. It was a pale yellow with bright, gold detailing and the crest of Skycourt on its ribbed body. Art could see the gleaming engines with propellers protruding from the sides and back, along with spread blue wings and the rudder tail. The replica car beneath with its tiny brass porthole windows was of wood, painted blue.

"I can mount it from here," Helia said. "A detailed model of one of our best hard shell ships, and Uncle Cilix built this model especially. *The Helios.*"

"Mount it? Thee can leap from here to there?" Art said.

To her eye, the model hung nearly four stories above. It was a secure spot to retreat to, she thought, if lonely.

"Had I a long enough pole to vault from, perhaps!" Helia said. "But never mention that to Helene, she just might try it. I'll show you."

Helia folded her typewriter shut, stored it in its case and shut it as well. She rose, picked up the valise, and placed it by her typewriter case.

"'Tis heavy items thee is bringing. I've still not discovered how to ghost and carry such at the same time," Art said in concern.

"When flying, Art? Not to worry, dear. I can manage," Helia said. "We'll store my typewriter inside the café. But the valise must come with me. Now, for my key."

Art helpfully carried the valise and case, her stick beneath her arm, while Helia produced a key from her pocket and unlocked the Blue Vanda doors. She led Art inside. They weaved through the tables and upended chairs for the office. She unlocked the door and showed Art the shelf where she stored her typewriter. She then opened a desk drawer and retrieved a devise. It was a small, flat mahogany box with a round brass housing stood on top like a mantle clock. A tiny lever with a mahogany knob emerged from the slot on the housing's head. The knob was inlaid with a gold letter 'S'. The housing itself had a round empty space where a clock face would be.

Once outside by Helia's table again, Helia produced a gold-coloured pocket watch and showed it to Art. But the watch face had no hands or numbers, only small words—UP, DOWN, RELEASE, START, and STOP—spread in increments on one half of the face. Helia placed her pocket dial in the housing and pushed it in. It locked in place with a click.

"It's not yet engaged," Helia said. "So I'll show you the function."

She moved the lever with its tiny knob and demonstrated how

each movement clicked an arrow back and forth upon the dial face, switching from UP, DOWN, and so forth.

"Have I seen such a devise before?" Art asked.

"Does it seem familiar, Art? It's the look of the EOT of our ships, the 'Engine Order Telegraph'. You've not been to a true airship yet. We promised you your first viewing but . . . hadn't the chance."

"We've that chance now," Art said.

"Indeed! Helene would love to take you up into the sky."

Helia looked above, and Art did as well.

"I will activate it by flipping its switch, and . . ."

She pointed the box upwards and toggled the lever to RELEASE. Art heard a click from Helia's box and then a responding sound echo from the airship replica above.

A hatch popped open beneath the airship's car, the door hanging. It was large enough for a person to pass through.

"Oh!" Art exclaimed. "Thee did that? Thy devise is a . . . wireless? Or magic?"

"'Tis the magic of Hertzian waves, used in wireless telegraphy, Art. This devise created by Uncle Cilix can give electric orders. Whichever I choose on my dial will transmit a unique message to the receiving devise, up there." Helia pointed to her airship. "The receiver operates the tasks of an engine within my ship. When my engine order is received, the action is performed."

"'Tisn't known technology, this remote ordering," Art said. "Or . . . is it?"

"Not yet," Helia whispered and winked.

She toggled the lever again. Art heard something whir. A rope ladder descended from the hatch, rapidly falling until it dangled outside the railing of the Blue Vanda.

Helia leapt with surprising agility to the top of the rail, stepped off, and landed with a foot on the rope ladder, her free hand catching a rung. The ladder swung, and Art glanced up in panic. The airship remained firmly in its wire-and-rope moorings.

Art returned her attention to Helia and gave her a look of mild disapproval.

Helia smiled in response as the ladder swayed back and forth. She wrapped the arm carrying the box around one side of the rope ladder. She reached back with her free hand.

"Won't you hand me the valise, Art?" Helia said.

Art set the valise down. She also set her stick on Helia's table and removed her hatpin and hat. She placed her hat by her stick and smoothed an errant lock of hair.

"Oh, Art!" Helia said, laughing. "For what occasion do you remove your hat, dearest? Is God here?"

"God is, for God is in every man," Art said. "E'en as a Quaker, I would doff it to call upon thy tiny home."

"Such an honour," Helia said with a smile.

Art picked up the valise and approached the railing. She took hold of the swinging ladder and stilled it. Helia squealed as she came to an abrupt stop, bumping her.

Art gave the valise to her.

"Can such a suspended vessel take my weight upon the ladder?" Art said as she gripped the rope.

Helia dropped her head to giggle. They were so close, the owl feathers of her cavalier hat tickled Art's nose. The brim knocked her when Helia raised her head again.

"If Helene can ride with me, I believe you can," she said, her eyes twinkling.

Art looked at her skeptically. She ghosted and passed through the railing.

With Art floating and still holding the ladder, Helia put her teeth to the lever. She toggled the switch to UP.

The ladder jerked and ascended. Art heard the polishing vehicle slowly pass by the Blue Vanda. She smelled a whiff of pipe tobacco as the driver laconically smoked. She and Helia left behind the lights of the patio for the darkness of the dome above. The black of its glass held the tiny twinkling lights of the night sky's stars. Art watched the airship near, looming like a whale in frozen suspension.

She let go of the ladder as Helia entered the hatch. She heard the whirring machinery stop and Helia's boots land with a smack within the airship as she jumped off. Helia then peered from the opening.

"Art, won't you come in?"

"Nay, 'twould be improper."

"Come to my porthole window, then," Helia bade. She closed the hatch.

Art floated to the side of the ship, hoping she picked the correct side. She saw no human-sized porthole in the ribbed sides. The polishing machine made leisurely circles below. The airship suddenly lit with tiny lights at the tail, sides, and nose.

Electricity, Art thought.

She saw a round hatch crack open and swing its shutter out before her, spilling light from within the airship. Helia leaned out, her hat removed and her hair in disarray.

"'Tis a pretty little home! Solid enough, I think," Art said.

"Oh, it is! I can jump up and down in it, it's very solid!"

"Please don't, Helia," Art said.

"And Uncle Cilix outfitted it with electrical lighting. No worries of gas lamps tipping," Helia said.

"What do the aquarium patrons think when thee descends from thy secret home?"

"If the aquarium is in attendance, I walk the girders above, Art! But sometimes I forget my little box and leave it on the ship. Then I must walk the girders to return home."

"Thee be ever vigilant in thy step," Art said. "Thee does not tipple, I hope?"

"No, Art. Not since meeting you."

Helia reached for her. Art flew near.

Helia took hold of Art's face. Her fingers passed through. Art alighted on the ribbing of the ship and solidified, her body translucent. Helia's fingers found purchase and drew Art close. Art gripped the ship and she and Helia kissed.

Helia's lips were soft and warm. Art felt fireworks ignite within her.

After an endless while, their mouths parted. Art breathed Helia's breath and wondered if she felt just as solid and warm to Helia in return. She was floating, her hands on the airship. She vaguely heard something creaking.

"You rocked the balloon!" Helia said, laughing.

"What?" Art said fearfully.

She had pulled the airship closer during their kiss, tilting it. She gripped the airship harder as she allowed it to slowly settle back.

I am a ghost, yet can hold Helia's ship! she thought.

"It's meant to move a little. It's more than a model," Helia said. "Dear Art."

Art raised one hand from the ship and cupped the masked side of Helia's face. Her ghostly thumb ran along the cheek and near the delicately painted forget-me-nots.

Art thought that then was the time she should act the gentlewoman, though a greater part of her wanted to hover forever and steal every moment possible. She took Helia's hand in her own ghost hand and pressed her lips to Helia's palm.

When the kiss ended, Helia's hand slipped away. Art straightened.

"Fare thee well, Helia," Art said. "Until our next meeting."

"Dear, dear Art," Helia said. "Adieu."

Helia withdrew inside the airship, her eyes shining. She shut the porthole.

Art stared at the shut porthole, and then spun. She zigzagged all about the dome and around Helia's ship. She dove and swept up her stick and hat. She sped past Helia's ship and rocketed through the dome for the bright face of the moon.

When she finally flew back to the Vesta and landed silently within her room, she unhooked her bodice and pulled out Helia's typewritten note. She read it and her euphoria ebbed. Her eyes grew solemn.

Heed me. It thinks. It strangles my tongue. It can move my hand. Beware me.

~

The breaking dawn saw London slowly open doors, windows,

and curtains to the rumble of vehicles, the fast step of pedestrians, the call of sellers, and the smoke of coal barges, trains, and factory stacks, clouding the sky and the view of serene airships sailing above. Delphia disembarked from her omnibus at a stop far earlier than the one near the Vesta. She hopped off before the Exercisium.

Its doors were already open. Inside, patrons were partaking of the machines per their prescribed therapy. Others were exercising before departing for work or other duties. Once past the machines, Delphia saw well-muscled men in gymnastic outfits occupying the area where she and Ellie had practiced. She thought they might be physical culturists like Art. They performed all manner of repetitive maneuvers with barbells, sacks, heavy rope, thick chains, and Indian clubs. Some exercised in the manner Art did, by using their own body weight to exert their muscles. Fascinated, Delphia was nearly tempted to stop and rudely stare at the men performing squats or pushing up from the floor using only their arms, but she had a purpose for visiting.

She looked towards the spot where the boxing girls had been. The punching bags were gone. A man juggled Indian clubs in the vacated space.

At the supplies counter was a young woman, red-cheeked and bright-eyed. She was busy issuing towels to two elderly male patrons. When the men had departed the counter for the doors marked "BATH", Delphia approached. She looked with interest at the remedies and small exercise equipment on display inside the case.

"May I help you, miss?" the counter girl said, smiling.

"Oh! Perhaps you can, miss," Delphia said, tipping her hat. "My first visit to the Exercisium was yesterday, and when I saw this counter, why . . ." Delphia pointed at an item. It was a spring-operated hand exerciser. "This caught my eye. I spoke briefly to the sales clerk. My, what was her name again?"

"Oh dear, that I wouldn't know," the counter girl said. "I'm newly to this position, you see. How lucky I am! The woman who held it abruptly gave notice! I happened to be available to fulfill it, so here I am, praise our Lord!"

"Then you've just started this morning, miss? Congratulations!" Delphia said.

They chatted more, with Delphia casually enquiring about martial arts lessons given at the Exercisium that might include boxing. When the girl found the itinerary sheet, detailing classes offered, no boxing could be found. Delphia promised to return later and bade the counter girl good day.

Forgoing another omnibus ride, Delphia made quick time for the Vesta. During her walk she mused on the situation and wondered what Philo would have made of it.

~

Jim woke in his cabinet to the familiar sight of dim light leaking through the lattice panels of his doors. But this time he smelled a fondly familiar scent and chortled in delight.

Stood up before him was a gleaming box of apple-flavoured Turkish cigarettes from the Palace Hotel's tobacconist.

"Ah," Jim said.

He shouted vigorously for Art until she came to open his cabinet and retrieve him. He then bestowed upon her, to their great amusement, a description of his phantom hug as she held him to her.

"Pat, pat, pat!" he said, giving phantom pats to her back.

They returned to Art's room just as Delphia arrived.

"What a face, Bloom!" he said. "Bright-eyed and with blushing cheek! Art and I must have a positive effect on you. Like seaside air, we are! Art especially."

"Thank you, sir," Delphia said. "You are, indeed, the best employers a girl could desire. So many meals a day due to your and Art's generosity is making myself a most content and agreeable assistant."

She then stepped aside for the page rolling in the cart bearing their breakfast.

Jim enjoyed three Turkish cigarettes while Delphia and Art dined. He thought Art's spectral glow was significantly brighter.

If she were still ailing, she did not let it show. Her face had cleared of scars too.

The conversation he had anticipated happened sooner than he expected.

"Friend," Art said after Delphia ate her last slice of bacon and set down her cup. "While we are free of work, I would ask a favour of thee."

Jim and Delphia listened attentively as Art solemnly asked for their help in uncovering her past.

Jim was glad of the speed of Art's decision because from the moment he first met her at the Secret Commission, he had been curious as to what sort of woman (and Quaker), should end up dead and chosen for resurrection. But he had dismissed his curiosity, believing—erroneously—that she wouldn't last a day as an agent, being that she was Quaker. Yet she did last the day, and impressively so.

Was she a Nick Blackheart? Jim pondered. That, he admitted, was a fanciful thought, but in their line of business, fancies were not far from the fantastic realities they regularly faced.

"Do you know what you'd like to learn first, Art?" Jim said.

"Aye," Art said. "Helia says I'm an orphan. Therefore, learning of family is not the pressing issue. Nor are the details of my death, just yet. What I wish to learn I would have investigated myself, but I am currently not welcomed at the Exercisium."

When Art explained the circumstances of her ejection, Delphia spoke up.

"Art, I'll be happy to look for that counter clerk and those girls again," she said.

"'Again', Bloom?" Jim said.

"Yes, Art and sir," Delphia said. "I'd noticed her and the boxing girls whilst in practice with Miss Hench. Their behavior was peculiar with regards to myself. I thought to pay them a visit this early morn, but their equipment was all gone, and the employee herself apparently having served notice on her position."

Jim put Art's mind at ease as quickly as possible. She needed to know the matter was entirely in his and Delphia's hands and to apply herself to less mysterious matters—like skirt-chasing.

Though once breakfast was concluded, Art deigned to visit the widow Bell's family instead. Jim had an opinion about that, but he knew his young friend would have to learn for herself where generosity ended.

With Art indulging in her tendency for "rescue" and Delphia on a task to deliver Art's completed reports to Miss Pepper to type, Jim had time for a mental inventory of past events.

He recalled when he was morphine-addled that he'd a list of things to ponder. He believed all that had given him concern had been attended to except one, and this he then gave his attention to. Thus, with the aid of a page, Jim went to Manon and Arlette's garret quarters for a visit. Once Manon had received him and the page had left, Jim posed his dilemma.

"My sweet, I've a particular observation, not well-formed, in need of your wise assurance," he said. "If I may ask, have you ever gazed upon the countenance of Lady Helia Skycourt?"

Manon seemed to hesitate. Jim watched her expectantly. She rose to look out her window.

"Is the answer out there?" Jim asked.

Manon briefly smiled.

"Then you have looked at her?"

He watched Manon nod.

"She's written about the Secret Commission and our antics since my own awakening, but in these past five years I've never gazed upon her until now," Jim said. "And I feel, having now seen her a few times, that I understand why. Yet I've no firm knowledge; I sense nothing in her face that is different than say, in Delphia's. I've been of the belief that so heavily a bewitched mask must be to soothe her brain madness, or the ravages of an illness kept secret. For she goes to the Black Market, after all, for treatments, and once mentioned that she was cursed.

"But I must trust my phantom gut, which feels that something *is* there. And how I know this, or not really know this, is because, well . . . it has *looked* at me. I feel that something has. And of course when I look back, I see nothing there."

Jim waited as Manon gazed out her window.

"Should we be worried?" Jim finally said.

Manon did not answer.

"Ah. Shall we just wait and see?"

Manon turned and slowly nodded, her eyes solemn.

"Thank you, my sweet, then it's what we'll do. How very infuriating you otherworldlies are," he said drily. "I really must remember to bring offerings next time."

Manon smiled. Jim went on to discuss the surprise celebration he had arranged for Art that afternoon until Manon thought it time to pick him up and take him downstairs.

"Manon," he said as she descended the servant stairs. "If I might ask, will you be revealing your true nature to Delphia? I know she is newly in our employ, but she's fast becoming indispensable."

Manon paused on the steps, and Jim wondered if he'd overstepped himself. Beings like Manon—remnants of another time or world where humans hadn't held dominance—protected their anonymity above all else.

"I cannot prove to her what I am," she finally said.

"Oh! Has she the blindness to your powers that Catherine has?"

Manon put a finger to her lips.

"I know," Jim whispered in humor. "That you've led Catherine to believe she has such blindness."

Manon smiled and continued their descent.

"But you could show Delphia how you sprout things in your own hand, like an acorn, yes?"

"*Oui*. But . . . I shall when I think the time is right," Manon said.

"By all means! Yes, when you think it right," Jim said.

Manon handed him to a page on the second floor who then escorted him down to the drawing rooms. Right then, Jim felt that all matters under his stewardship were progressing well.

～

As afternoon approached, Manon had Arlette and Oleg dress respectably—he in coat and bowler hat and she and Arlette with properly fastened frocks, jackets, and hair swept up. She pinned a small black hat with iridescent plumes cascading down the back into her blonde hair. She wore a pair of ivory, French heeled silk shoes with bows and embroidered with flowers.

"Oh, *c'est jolie!* Why did I never purchase shoes equal to yours, mine are not nearly as pretty!" Arlette said, raising her skirts to show her silk striped shoes.

"But of course you should not. Save your best purchase for your wedding," Manon said.

Arlette looked at her in surprise and blushed. Oleg grinned broadly, his waxed moustache upturned. Manon tied his blue tie for him. She told Arlette not to bring her fan, and then told her she could bring it. She made Arlette carry her gloves. After more fussing where she chose which hat for Arlette to wear, they finally descended the stairs. In Oleg's hands was a small, gaily wrapped rectangular box tied with a green bow.

When they reached the third floor, Manon leading, Miss Dillwick and Miss Fesk entered the hallway. Arlette exchanged polite greetings with them. Both ladies smiled and complimented them on their dresses. Manon wondered if they were women of temperance—religious, perhaps, because though their own frocks were reflective of class, they did not seem the sort to dress for fêtes. As the Canadian couple departed, the trio reached Art's doors and Manon prepared to knock.

Millie emerged from Jim's study, walking stick in one hand and cigarette in the other. She carried a men's overcoat and top hat. As she strolled past Art's doors, she eyed Manon and Arlette.

"Playing a role, I see," Millie said.

Manon paused, her hand raised. She did not look at Millie.

"Your Ladyship," Arlette said, giving a slight curtsy.

Millie leisurely continued down the hall. Manon knocked.

Delphia opened the door, gazing down at Manon with a pleasant expression. She was dressed in what Manon assumed was "Sunday best" attire for a working-class girl of her age (though Manon thought Delphia was ready for her transition from girlhood to womanhood). Delphia wore a green jacket and a bow in her hair. She let the trio in.

"I apologise for not being introduced; I am Delphia Bloom," she said.

Jim called loudly from his study, whereupon Delphia fetched him. He apologised for his neglect in introductions and introduced Arlette, Oleg, and Manon to Delphia. Oleg removed his hat, Arlette made the proper noises, and Manon merely nodded. Delphia and Jim accepted the wrapped gift from Oleg and placed it on the table with other gaily wrapped gifts. While Delphia stood with Jim and chatted with Arlette, Manon openly studied her.

When Jim had jested about Catherine being led to believe she was immune to Manon's powers, that ruse had been true. If Catherine, as Manon suspected, was the sort who would be uncomfortable with beguilement, it would be prudent to give her a reason not to experience it. Then Manon needn't prove the extent or effects of her abilities to her employer.

Delphia was another matter. She had that quality Manon had heard whispered of but never encountered before. She seemed genuinely immune to bewitchment. Upon their first meeting, Manon's attempt at beguilement had failed. Fault hadn't lain with her own ability, she believed. She'd seen the clarity in Delphia's eyes, like one who could only view truth and for whom the effects of illusion did not gain admittance but merely slipped away, like drops down a windowpane.

Could Delphia pierce glamour? Manon wondered. Banish enchantment? Or was her ability merely armour, perhaps even impervious to curses, to more cunning spells? The implications, if Delphia was not just a girl deaf and dumb to magicks but one blessed with abilities (bestowed or otherwise), gave Manon trepidation. But that feeling, she knew, was present only because she was in the habit of being fearful.

Manon was no seer, and if she eventually discovered such gifts in that regard she would sooner dismiss them. But when she looked at Delphia she sensed the sword, the shield, the oath, and the clash of battle. Manon disliked soldiers, but the sensation was not so much that. *Guardian*, Manon thought. Delphia's ancestry had possibly intertwined with otherworldly folk. Perhaps in cohabitation (sexual or otherwise) with such entities as the *sidhe*, the "Fairy", or however such folk were called which Manon had been mistaken for too often to count. Being physically closer to the girl might reveal more, but Manon knew Delphia hadn't any great desire for her own sex. It was there in her attitude, both oblivious and indifferent.

A page entered the room, pushing a teacart. Alice followed and after shutting the door, addressed them all.

"If it pleases you, may I announce that Art has entered the Vesta," she said.

"Everyone, hide!" Jim said.

"Hide, sir?" Delphia said.

Art ghosted through her shut doors.

"Surprise!" Jim shouted.

～

When Art heard Jim shout "Surprise!", she was indeed, surprised. Having just returned from Whitechapel Market and its secondhand sellers (while accompanying Fiona Bell's family), she was ill-prepared for the sudden joviality, but her heart welcomed it. She saw that Manon and Arlette were respectably dressed and realised—especially by the presence of wrapped presents on the table—that an intimate celebration was in progress. From Jim's hearty explanation as she greeted everyone, it appeared the celebration was for her.

Alice and the page departed, leaving the laden teacart, while everyone welcomed Art.

"When I said I should have put an announcement in the paper, heralding your rebirth, I thought to rectify the neglect," Jim said. "Happy Rebirth, Art!"

"Jim and everyone, my heartfelt thanks," Art said warmly. She glanced at Manon, thinking how beautiful she looked with her hair up. "How grateful I am to have thee all present to share joy with me."

"Please enjoy such events while you are able, Art!" Arlette

said. "There will come a time when you will wish no one called attention to it. Like Manon does."

Arlette and Jim laughed as Manon looked at them with indignation.

"Art will have a while yet!" Jim said.

"Today, I am nine days living," Art said.

Jim invited her to join him at the table to open her presents. She laid her stick and hat aside and bade everyone sit, as it appeared she'd several gifts to open. Oleg remained standing behind Arlette and Manon as they seated themselves in the armchair. Delphia took a seat at the table with pencil and paper to note down which gifts came from whom. The first that Art picked up was a small silver-coloured wrapped box the size of her palm.

"That's mine!" Jim said.

Art unwrapped and opened it. Laid in the tissue was a silver pocket watch and chain, the cover engraved with a skull. Blue enamel the colour of lapis lazuli was laid beneath the cut-out eyes, nostrils, and teeth. Art picked up the watch and popped the cover open. Beneath the beveled crystal was an eggshell-white watch face set with tiny sparkling red, green, and blue inlay at each silver-number increment. The inside cover bore an inscription:

ART reborn Sun, 7 March 1880

"Friend, 'tis a dear gift! I thank thee," she said.

"It's an eternal chronometer, Art," Jim said. "A mechanism that can never die."

At Jim's urging, she played with the watch a little, then ran the chain through a buttonhole and secreted the watch inside her bodice.

"You tuck it there, no pickpocket shall ever budge it," Jim said.

Art opened more presents. From Delphia, she received a copy of *Black Beauty* autographed by Anna Sewell. From Manon and her partners, her gift was an oak keepsake box carved with flowers, leaves, trees, and peeping deer, owls, and rabbits. The interior was lined with red velvet. It was large enough to keep letters, and Arlette demonstrated how to unlock the secret compartment beneath.

Two more presents lay on the table, one the size of a book and wrapped in rose-red paper with a black ribbon, while the other was a box wrapped in blue with gold ribbon.

"From the Ladies Skycourt! Can you guess which is from whom, Art?" Jim said.

"This, 'tis from Helia," Art said, touching the red present. "And this, 'tis from Helene." She touched the blue-and-gold box.

"Well, golly!" Jim said.

According to Jim, Helia could not attend the celebration due to her being banned from the Vesta, and Lady Helene was previously engaged. Both sent their deepest regrets and well-wishes. But Art could not quite contain her disappointment as he spoke. She saw Manon rise from the armchair and approach while he and Arlette engaged in a conversation about Skycourt Industries. When Manon neared, she laid a hand on Art's shoulder, causing Art to smile.

"Lady Helene is an ascetic, denying herself fêtes and good company," Manon whispered to her. "She is also shy."

"She is?" Art said.

"Art, which will you open first?" Jim asked.

"I will open both at the same time. Manon may help me," Art said and proceeded to pull both ribbons.

With Manon lending a hand, Art unwrapped both presents. Helia's was of a tooled leather journal dyed a deep red with engraved silver caps at the corners and a carved border of intertwining moons, trees, and flowers. Helene's box contained a tin with a gold lid and red lettering. Above the illustration of a massively muscular arm holding a weight were the words:

VOLCANA'S WEIGHTED SPRING GRIPS

"Oh!" Art said. "'Tis the spring-grip dumbbells of the strongwoman, Volcana!"

"Really!" Jim exclaimed. "Well, now we know that you've recall of your performing strongwomen, Art."

She opened the journal just as Manon opened the tin for her, revealing the dumbbells. Each dumbbell was split in half with springs embedded between them. When gripped in the hand

and squeezed, the springs compressed and the two halves came together. Art picked up one and demonstrated the action to Jim while she opened the journal and silently read Helia's inscription. The dumbbell's tension bars squeaked loudly in her grip.

Dearest Art, Helia wrote. *Happy Birth—*

An abrupt inkblot marred her words.

I fell! continued the note.

She wrote this whilst on her wheel! Art thought.

My dearest Art, I give you this:

First, you came to us, then a second time.

By this gift are we made new,

for we were halved without You.

In grateful Love, we rest our hands in thine's.

Art took a breath, feeling her heart swell. Manon laid a hand on her shoulder.

"Good God, someone take her toy away from her!" Jim exclaimed. "What is that supposed to do, besides kill us with its noise?"

"'Tis for strengthening the palm and fingers," Art said, realising that she was still squeezing. She compressed the dumbbell rhythmically. Each time she did so, the devise squeaked loudly. "'Twill make the hand's grip unshakeable."

"And myself un-droppable!" Jim said. "Art, give your toy to Bloom. Bloom, it will aid in your pistol grip!"

Delphia accepted the dumbbell exerciser from Art and attempted to squeeze it. She then tried with both hands, Jim encouraging her. Finally, she put it on the table and leaned on it, using the weight of her body.

"Oh, you jest!" Arlette said, standing. She approached the table, Oleg following, and took a turn trying to make the springs compress.

"*Regarde*, Lady Helia has given you a pen and inkwell too," Manon said.

She drew Art's attention to an oak wood penholder with a finely engraved steel nib, sat in a box with an ink bottle.

Art broke the wax seal on the bottle, removed its stopper, dipped her new pen, and opened the journal to its first blank page. She wrote:

On the seventh day, First Day, of the third month of this year, 1880, I, Art, was reborn.

She put the stopper back on the bottle and cleansed the pen tip. She stared thoughtfully at her first diary entry.

In rereading her words, she could only think: hers was a life starting, just when two other women, similar to herself in age and body, had their lives end.

"What manner of devilry is this? Has no one the means for conquering this Gordian Knot?" Jim exclaimed.

Oleg was compressing the spring dumbbell between his two palms, his arms and chest straining. Finally, a slow squeak emerged from between his palms as the dumbbell's halves met.

"*Bravo!*" Arlette said.

"The strength of the tension is set high," Art said. "Helene was most thoughtful."

"Lady Helene seems to know your measure," Jim said. "Oleg wins the carnival game, ladies! Three tries, and you've both lost at ringing the bell! Your consolation prize will be to escort me to the Exercisium to purchase a set of those for Del'—the meek set."

"I'll surely be unsexed soon," Delphia said, collapsing back in her chair.

"You can count on it," Jim said.

Art stored away her gifts, wrapping, and ribbons. Arlette pulled the cord to summon a page. Two arrived, carrying a table with two more chairs, which they added to Art's table. They laid out the tea as well as—

"Christmas crackers, Friend?" Art said in surprise, picking up a bright green paper tube twisted on both ends.

"Oh, but why not? They've paper hats, Art, and what better hats to wear during your rebirth celebration! Bloom, pick me up and I'll help Art pull her cracker!"

The pages rolled the cart out and departed. While in Delphia's hands, Jim took hold of one end of Art's cracker with his teeth, and they both pulled. At the loud snap and dropping of a trinket, a joke on paper, a novelty item, and a tissue paper hat, everyone applauded.

They pulled apart more loudly snapping crackers, all participants donning a paper hat and enjoying the surprise contents. Even Manon carefully placed a bright green tissue-paper crown on her head after removing her *chapeau*. When Art donned a yellow one, her spectral aura rendered it ghostly pale. Jim had Delphia and Arlette read the printed jokes and heartily laughed at each one. They sat down to tea, Manon near the windows as sunlight touched her back. Art sat next to her and glanced to where she knew the peepholes were, wondering if Helia would come.

She felt Manon take her hand and Art returned her attention to her.

"Helia would enjoy a cracker," Art said. "Dost thee think?"

"*Oui*, we will have one saved for her. And for Lady Helene too."

Art nearly commented that perhaps the cracker would need a very loud bang for Helene to enjoy when Manon leaned in to speak into her ear.

"Lady Helia will come at night," Manon softly said. "And peep, even if you are sleeping."

Art felt giddy at the thought.

"Oh! And . . . when thee and I are playing cards?" Art said.

Manon's eyes grew warm with mirth.

"*Oui*, she will peep while we play cards," she said.

With Manon still holding her hand, Art absorbed her raw haddock, herring, salmon filet, mussels, oysters, whelks, and watercress (she thought it all quite extravagant, but didn't want to slight Cook by sending anything back). She offered to share some of her meal with her guests, who declined. Manon munched on her pile of flowers and herbs. Jim led various topics of conversation, and Art saw that everyone at the table was enjoying their tea.

At tea's end, Jim had cigars produced, which he and Oleg lit and puffed on. Arlette discarded propriety and sat in Oleg's lap, her arms draped affectionately around his broad shoulders. She and Jim continued an animated conversation in which Delphia participated but which Art had already lost the thread of.

"Surely, *monsieur*, you would agree that as Tolstoy depicted," Arlette said, "great events are nothing more than the result of many smaller events, accidents, and individual purposes, and not as one is led by historical account to believe, engineered by the will of great men?"

"His depiction of Napoleon in *War and Peace* was quite a revelation to myself," Delphia said.

"Of course, of course!" Jim said. "Just as any simple death of say, any of us can be hardly simple! Illness, for one. One does not simply die because one is sick, nor does one end up simply executed at the gallows. We die due to a million decisions and consequences, cumulating to that one effect."

"Even a death by accident?" Delphia said curiously.

"You're not one for predestination, are you, Bloom? Ah, good! Yes, even so!"

Art watched Manon sidle nearer to the fading light of the windows.

"Jim's room is well lit during this time of day," Art said.

Manon rose, taking Art by the hand. She followed, though it seemed impolite to rise from the table without word to those present. Yet, strangely, no one seemed to mind. Arlette and Jim ignored them as they continued to discuss philosophical matters. Oleg smoked contentedly. Delphia merely smiled at Art and Manon before returning her attention to the conversation.

Jim's study was bright with sunlight. Manon led Art to the armchair, bade her sit, and then slipped into Art's lap. Her arms clasped Art's neck. Art felt her grin grow, knowing it made her look silly, and gently placed her hands at Manon's waist.

She raised her eyes to look at Manon and saw Manon gaze down. Art saw and felt butterflies flutter.

"I shall break thy beguilement," Art said. "And see thee as is: Manon."

Manon looked surprised, then pleased. Art felt the sensation of butterflies disappear.

"You understand," Manon said.

"To say I understand gives me much," Art said. "I only know

that thee is a truth beyond thy glamour. Were I to know thee, 'Manon', and not by thy sex or beauty, would that not be thy greater pleasure?"

Manon smiled warmly. She lifted Art's chin and kissed her.

Art's tissue paper hat slipped off. It fluttered to the ground. When the kiss ended, Art saw Manon look at her.

"I should have asked first," Manon said in a tone of self-chastisement. "Arlette would have told me so. Especially now, when you have spent more time with Lady Helia. Are my kisses still agreeable?"

"Oh," Art said, still affected by the kiss. "I must think."

"Do you think of Lady Helia when we kiss?" Manon asked. "Or are these guilty kisses for you? You may answer, I will not be offended."

"Nay, I think of thee when I feel thy lips," Art said. "The scent of thee and the touch of thy body. 'Guilt' is not the word, for Helia knows of what we do, and has bade me to accept thy company. I . . . I only come to quandary when I wish to know ourselves as free women together and not thee as chattel."

Manon looked at her thoughtfully, her fingers running along Art's hair.

"How may I help?" she said.

"Would thee be my friend?" Art said. "'Tis asking much, aye? For 'tis of thy work to separate heart from the body. Thee should think of this as business. Yet, were we friends how happily would I kiss thee, knowing 'tis thy free will. 'Tis much to ask."

Manon smiled, the greens and browns within her eyes catching light.

"I will give you my friendship," she said. "But you may not enjoy it. Arlette says I am *un poisson froid*. And I am, how do you say . . . very dull, and I do not understand many things. But if you can forgive my ways, we can play together, *oui*? And kiss."

Art picked up her hand and kissed it.

"We can ride in hansom cabs," Art said.

Manon looked at her in surprise.

"Jim was right, 'tisn't done among women, is it?" she said.

Manon laughed softly.

"What does it matter, the conventions of the sexes," she said. "I will be happy to ride with you."

Art felt giddy once more. If Manon would be her friend then they could do more together as women do. Manon could accompany her to the Royal Aquarium. She remembered Helia typing alone at her table and her smile faded.

"I've recall of the girl who died—the one meant to take my bones," she said. "Long did I not remember the happening of it, and then it came to me as I wrote my report. And there was also Felly Pritt. In thanks will I enjoy thy friendship. For now, more than ever, I wish to live up to the Light. Not for what may be given me, but to remember those who could not."

"How I wish I could think so. For such a long time that would be," Manon said. "Forever remembering."

Art looked at her curiously. Manon slipped from her lap to approach the windows. Bathed in full sunlight and her paper crown aglow, she gazed out, her regard faraway.

"Survive, and you will live a very long time," Manon finally said. "And perhaps you will do well in living, better than myself. For you are stronger. A fighter. A phantom. And perhaps you will learn after a long while that you can live without others. Queen of the sea."

The thought of longevity was like a stone that sank in Art, for she knew Manon was speaking of time beyond mortal lives. She could not fathom life without the people around her: Jim . . . Helia. Everyone.

"'Tis my ninth day of living," Art said in small voice.

Manon returned to her and gently embraced Art to her chest.

"*Tu es l'enfant*," Manon said softly. "Forgive me. Think nothing. Just live."

Art's throat was tight. She nodded.

The sun fell upon them, and Art felt Manon's warmth and the beat of her heart against her cheek, steady and strong. She pressed Manon to her.

"'Tis the starting that matters," Art whispered.

❧

On the thoroughfares of London, streams of carriages, buses, and hansom cabs weaved, mingled, tangled within intersections, and then flowed on. Into the narrower arteries of East London, the roads congealed with laden delivery wagons, carts, and costermonger barrows. But as the roads wound farther down past ramshackle buildings where women peered from dirty windows and sailors loitered, the wheels and horses became fewer. By water's edge, no cart or barrow rolled. Ragged boys dove from a dilapidated pier for coal fallen from the river barges while two mudlarks, a wizened woman and small boy holding a sack, picked bits of wood that floated to the sandy edges of the embankment. An old man sat with a long bottle held to his breast and snoozed in front of a gin shop's open door that faced the meagre road. In the weathered building across, a woman's diaphanous and shredded red shawl flapped from a window.

Hearing a racket within the building, the diving boys and mudlarks paused and turned to look. Brutal blows sounded.

Hands, discoloured green-and-black, suddenly shoved a large, muscular man out a window, his head dripping red. The man fell limp into the water with a splash and then floated, facedown.

While the ragged boys and mudlarks gaped, a figure in a gentleman's dark overcoat burst from the building's front door. The figure ran wildly down the little road and disappeared.

The ragged boys swam to the floating man as the wizened woman held the little boy to her.

"Billy's dead!" one boy exclaimed, touching the body.

They heard the door slam again and both boys and mudlarks swivelled to look.

A woman stood before the building, her clothes in disarray and her loose hair obscuring her face. She slowly shambled towards the gin shop, her hands out before her and shaking.

The brothel-keeper, a stout, red-faced woman, stomped out of the gin shop's door and accosted the woman with a threatening finger.

"Wot's all the noise?!" she shouted. "And where's Billy? You whores know better than to come out! Git back in there, before I—" She looked at the other woman's face and screamed. The old man woke with a start.

"Wot's happen to *you*?" she shrieked.

She scrambled back to the gin shop's porch as the other woman shuffled forwards, reaching. The brothel-keeper grabbed the long bottle clutched by the old man and threw it.

The bottle shattered against the front of the shuffling woman, sending her reeling. The old man cried out in terror upon seeing her. When she approached again, he fell off his chair in his attempt to scurry away. The brothel-keeper took hold of it, raised it above her head and heaved.

The blow from the chair forced the other woman to spin around. The boys and mudlarks saw her face, one half appearing as if asleep, the eye and mouth shut while the other half was mottled green-and-black, the staring, white iris-less eye crisscrossed with tiny lines like a diamond. The discolouration ran down her chest and was forming on her reaching arms and hands, rapidly turning them green-and-black. The spots turned into sores that pulsated. She stumbled down to the embankment as the boys and mudlarks looked on in horror.

She fell into a half-sunken rowboat, moored despite its leaking state. One of the ragged boys climbed up the embankment, ran to the rotting rope, and flung it free. He pushed the boat as hard as he could. It floated away as the woman slowly rose. Hunched and trembling, her body made rumbling sounds.

The woman's arched back erupted into lumps of flesh and oozing blood, splitting her dress. Her hands fluttered.

The wizened woman pointed at the bobbing boat.

"*Diseased!*" she cried.

The End

RISEN'S
Illustration Plates

Art by
Elizabeth Watasin

More men in bloodied aprons, wielding
bone saws and cleavers, ran at Art.

The "Picnic-hicle" rattled on stones as a horse carriage did and was driven by Helene with as much recklessness as a racing coach-driver.

Then Helia turned, balled up a piece of paper,
and threw it at the head of the conductor.

"Is it still agreeable?" Manon asked. "This arrangement?"
"Were I decorous, I would end this. Yet . . . 'tisn't the answer.
Somehow, I need thee to learn Helia more," Art said in bafflement.

First portrait sketch of Art.

Additional
Content

Character Key
Places Key
Flower Language
Jim Dastard's Bon Mots
The Dark Victorian Timeline (thus far)
Author's Notes
and,
a *SUNDARK* Preview
(an Elle Black Penny Dread)

CHARACTERS

(In order of appearance).

Inspector Risk

Dr. Speller

Esther Stubbings (Deceased)

Art, "Artifice"

Dr. Gatly Fall

Jim Dastard

Lady Helia Skycourt

Alice (page working at the Vesta)

Manon and Arlette (French sapphic prostitutes-in-residence at the Vesta)

Oleg (Manon and Arlette's bully)

Mrs. Catherine Moore (The Vesta Club owner)

Harold Moore, "Ford" (Deceased; Jim's first partner)

Nick Blackheart (defamed by Helia as Nick Blaggard)

Lady Helene Skycourt

Ganju Rana (Helene's assistant and a Gurkha)

Rama (Helene's horse)

Baroness Millicent Sedgewick (A cross-dressing toff and gossip)

Olivia Hill (Music hall male impersonator)

Aldosia Stropps (Illustrator for *The Strand* and suffragette)

Horfinch (Owner of the Anatomy & Medical Curiosities Shoppe)

Ellie (Ellen) Hench (A blind woman and stick for hire)

Livus (Black Market sawbones)

Delphia Bloom

Elsepeth Fidd (Fidatov) (Girl who introduces Delphia to the Black Market)

Lucius Blanc (Manon's old master)
Gaiety Bloom (Delphia's mother)
Peter Bloom (Delphia's father)
Philosophy Bloom (Delphia's eldest brother, transported to Australia)
Gavin Bloom (Delphia's older brother, a sailor)
Calliope and Aengus Bloom (Delphia's younger siblings)
Hettie O'Taggart (Delphia's nemesis)
Tom Frye (Hettie O'Taggart's sweetheart)
Felly (Felicity) Pritt (A theater actress)
Dr. Lau (Felly's doctor)
Roger Flannagan (Felly's sweetheart)
Perseus Cassius Kingdom (inventor and mechanician)
Arthur Fellows (Black Market surgeon experimenting with transplants)
Emily Fellows (Deceased; wife of Arthur)
Miss Eustania Dillwick, Miss Lizzy Fesque (Canadian visitors to the Vesta)
Charlotte Thackery (Dressmaker, tailor, and outfitter)
Cairenn (Fiona's mother)
Fiona Bell (Widow of the slaughter man, Dennis Bell)
Dr. Horst Pendlecraft (One of five doctors invited to the demonstration)
Dr. Judith SeaJane (African Jamaican doctress who attends to Art)
Miss Adella Pepper (typist)
Sarah James (Quakeress at the Exercisium)
Countess Juliet Skycourt (wife of Cadmus, Earl of Skycourt)
Lady Amalie Swinstock (girl with consumption of the spine)
Lady Swinstock, Lord Swinstock, Robert Swinstock (brother to Amalie)

PLACES KEY

The Vesta Club (Whitechapel)
Royal Surgical Sciences Academy (and its Surgical Theatre)
(Southwark)
Anatomy & Medical Curiosities Shoppe (Southwark)
Billingsgate Market and the Black Market (Billingsgate)
Metropolitan Free Hospital (Spitalfields)
Royal Aquarium Exposition Palace and Pleasure Gardens
(Westminster)
Thackery Fine Dressmaker, Tailor, & Outfitter (Robin Hood's
Row, Cheapside)
Victoria Station (Westminster)
The Exercisium (Whitechapel)

❖

Flower Language

Dill (eaten by Manon): Lust
Violet, purple (eaten by Manon, referring to Art): Modesty,
Chastity (Virtue), Fondness
Violet, blue (eaten by Art): Love's Faithfulness
Orange (eaten by Manon and Art): Eternal Love, Marriage
Carnation, white (worn by Olivia Hill): Sweetness, Innocence,
Love's Purity
Daisy (Jim's Latin recitation): Love's Loyalty
Forget-Me-Not (painted on Helia's mask): True Love
Jasmine (Dr. Lau's pipe tobacco): Grace
Blue Vanda (Hindi for 'orchid'): Beauty, Cultivation
Gardenia (Manon beguiling Art into sleep): Rapture
Periwinkle (white, on Ellie's calling card): Happy Recollection

❖

JIM DASTARD'S BON MOTS

"Always on the ball", 1939
"She doesn't mind spilling the beans", 1908
"But to cut to the chase", 1927
"Keystone cops!", 1912
"Just don't poop out on me", 1932
"Your having sprung from the head of Zeus, fully formed. And how.", 1924
"The Academy's a belly up for us.", 1920
"Oh what the hell, it's a place for weirdos.", 1955
"An underbelly I must expose you to", 1942
"You hardly seem the chaste type with all that skirt-chasing you do.", 1942
"Good show, Art!", 1916
"Door! Door! Once outside we'll be all right", 1893
"In the doghouse before we've yet to really put you in there!", 1926
"Time for your briefing!", 1910
"You're an utter Slim-Jim!", 1889
". . . may not be a factual argument, but it is a heart-wringer." (unknown; nearest is: "to put (something) through the wringer", 1942).
"given all medical specialists of bone a thorough shakedown", 1914
"That's the best of Harold's stash, you have there", 1914
"Bloom, you've been above and beyond!" (American Medal of Honor, "above and beyond the call of duty", phrase in use possibly back to 1862, Civil War period).
"Ow, Art" (as an exclamation of pain), 1919
"I must have it read from the horse's mouth.", 1913

The Dark Victorian Timeline

(Thus far)

Sunday, 7 March, of this year 1880, Art is reborn.

Monday, 8 March, Art remains at the Secret Commission.

Tuesday, 9 March, Art partners with Jim. Art gets pole-axed.

Wednesday, 10 March, Art meets Madame Chance, battles the undead children, and visits the Vesta for the first time.

Thursday, 11 March, Art and Jim conclude the re-animationist case.

Friday, 12 March, Art and Jim receive the Bone Stealer case. She meets, Rama, Ganju, Perseus Kingdom, Delphia Bloom, and goes to the Blue Vanda. Art laughs for the first time.

Saturday, 13 March, Art battles the Bone Stealer.

Sunday, 14 March, Art goes to Meeting, visits Dr. Lau, and sees Helia's balloon.

Monday, 15 March, Art celebrates her ninth day of living.

＊

Author's Notes

"The stick, from brass ferrule to the femur-head handle, was a long stack of human vertebrae bones."
There is such an antique walking stick existing from the Victorian era, but of shark vertebra, and with no human femur bone. The shark vertebra was tightly stacked together (with a rod possibly running up the center). I happened on the shark vertebrae walking stick while researching on eBay.

"Children, hold your buttons!" the teacher said. "Do so, now!"
Holding one's button was what one usually did (as a Victorian mourning superstition), when a funeral procession approached, because it's bad luck to meet one head-on. The teacher decided to protect the children the same way when faced with the approaching spectre of Art. For more information, see: http://friendsofoakgrovecemetery.org/victorian-funeral-customs-fears-and-superstitions/

"Art returned Helia's smile, her walking stick tapping, and Helia thought of sweet-smelling flowers that floated like Handel's notes, down a sparkling river."
This is an overt reference to Leo Delibes' opera *Lakme*, specifically the "Flower Duet" or "Sous le dome epais", sung by Lakme and her servant Mallika. This score won't be written until 1881–82, and then performed in 1883. I would have liked to openly reference it, regardless, but the opera is the usual tragedy of doomed lovers. Art and Helia's nascent romance could do without that allusion, I thought.

"Aye. She is unique of Light. And she is of God's first temple, the grove, known without words and immutable. 'Tis an aspect that can terrify me."

"God's first temple, the grove", is a thinking of the Romantic Movement of the first half of the nineteenth century, when a great appreciation of nature developed in the face of rising industrialization. (Thomas R. Lounsbury, ed. (1838–1915). *Yale Book of American Verse*, 1912. William Cullen Bryant, 1794–1878. "A Forest Hymn".) Also see http://www.bartleby.com/102/18.html and *Victorian Views of Nature Revealed in Majolica*, by Jeffrey B. Snyder.

"Your gaze is a joy to me. Your smile uplifts me. Your voice is a gift to me!"
These lines by Helia were inspired by a twelfth century poem attributed to Judah Halevi, which begins:

> 'Tis a fearful thing
> To love
> What death can touch.

"The life you now have is the Victory that overcomes the World!
This next line by Helia refers to an inscription seen in a mourning brooch (c. 18th–19th), archived at the Art of Mourning online site. The inscription reads: "This is the Victory that Overcometh the World, Even Over Faith". (http://artofmourning.com/2012/06/22/hope-of-eternal-life-sepia-mourning-brooch/). The victory spoken of is death itself. The "victory" of which Helia types is Art's resurrection.

"Why, that's Harold's!" Jim exclaimed. "Good girl! Claret is for boys, port for men, but he who aspires to be a hero, must drink—"
"Brandy".
This quote is by Samuel Johnson, writer of *A Dictionary of the English Language* (1755).

"I called him Ford," Jim suddenly said.
This line, for better or for worse, is a hint as to what kind of man Jim was before he became "Jim". If you've read *The Dark*

Victorian: Risen, then you know that the medium Madame Chance gave Art information about Jim's past (or, technically, his future). If you are a science fiction geek, reading the name "Ford" may possibly not make you think of "Henry".

Art's Food:
Most every food item Art chooses or favours is food of the poorer classes. Periwinkles and whelks were favourite meals purchased often on the sly from barrows and stalls by women. (*London Labour and the London Poor,* 1851, by Henry Mayhew). They'd eat the meal on the spot, sometimes using their hatpins to pull out the creatures. Appetite satisfied and still respectable, the ladies would continue on their way. Haddock was, and still is, a hearty and reliable fish for the lower masses, while turbot, salmon, and trout were the fish of choice for those richer (*London Characters and the Humorous Side of London Life,* 1870, by W.S. Gilbert). Watercress was also a staple of the poorer folk and often eaten as is (*Life in the London Streets,* 1881, by Richard Rowe), and not always in sandwiches (or "between bread", as was said when the word "sandwich" was not commonly used).

Ellie Hench:
Ellie's unique perceptions are based on the possible abilities of blind fish. ("Fluid Flows Help Blind Fish Sense Surroundings," *The Journal of Experimental Biology,* November 15, 2010. (http://jeb.biologists.org/content/213/22/i.2.full)

The paintings and writings of Lady Amalie Swinstock:
Amalie's work was inspired by an imaginative blog entry written by Dave Walker at The Library Machine blog (for the Royal Borough of Kensington and Chelsea Library), introducing us to "The Secret World of Marianne Rush" (June 14, 2012):
http://rbkclocalstudies.wordpress.com/2012/06/14/the-secret-world-of-marianne-rush/
The original purpose of Marianne Rush's mysterious and very

private watercolours is no longer known, but I hope you'll enjoy her work (viewed online in colour, for the first time) and Dave Walker's accompanying narrative. Amalie's work is in homage to this "Secret World" and other such lost and unknown works by forgotten or secretive creators.

Victorian female marriage and other unconventional relationships:

Classifications like "lesbianism", "homosexuality", and the stigmatization and criminalization of such had yet to be invented and be of scrutiny until after 1890 (Havelock Ellis published his book on "sexual inversion"—what we call "homosexuality"—in 1896, and Freud and his work came into prominence after 1896). Such terms to create an "unnatural" individual, a person separated from and outside of society, were applied once situations like Oscar Wilde's trial played out publically. However in the decades before, from the 1860's on, women who wanted to live in "marriage" with other women—in order to keep their own money and property, combine resources, live with a trusted friend, or establish a love/sexual relationship with a significant other—made legal arrangements for such unions without any great community condemnation or social judgment (*Between Women: Friendship, Desire, and Marriage in Victorian England*, by Sharon Marcus, Princeton University Press, 2007). As long as such couples (usually well-to-do or upper class), maintained a respectable presence in society, there seemed no great reason to object (far poorer women, on the other hand, might have found such unions an unaffordable luxury).

The intention of *The Dark Victorian* series is to continue that thread of history, to explore what our world will become had the opportunities of contractual female marriage been advanced to such legal and cultural precedent that the accepted existence of homosexuals and their legal rights could no more be challenged than the accepted legalised right of former slaves and people of colour to be the equal of white men. In effect, *The Dark Victorian* will not be about having to hide, disguise, suppress, and practice in subculture for one hundred years the life-right of being homosexual.

What else could this mean? It may mean dismissing the Labouchere Amendment to the Criminal Law Amendment Act of 1885 (which criminalised "gross indecency" between males in public or in private), or strike down the Comstock Law (1873) in America, which obstructed the Free Love Movement's ability to provide literature and contraceptives via the mail. It may mean that despite the 1877 obscenity trial of Annie Besant and Charles Bradlaugh for publishing a six-penny book about contraception that the mechanical and industrial future would see couples prudently (and openly) curtailing large families by just such means.

Bigotry and inequality would continue to exist in the world of *The Dark Victorian*, but such attitudes would, in the progression of a hundred years from the year 1880, be the minority of cultural and social understanding in some well-to-do countries, rather than the prevailing majority.

The word "sex", and other terms for copulation:
"Sex" (meaning "sexual intercourse") is first referred to as such in writings by D. H. Lawrence, 1929, according to the Online Etymology Dictionary (http://www.etymonline.com). However, in my own research of Victorian Era accounts, people may not make direct reference to the act, but were very well aware of it and the naming of it, especially the cruder terms (*My Secret Life* by "Walter", 1888). In an autobiography published in 1908, Mrs. J. E. Panton makes reference to Skittles, the courtesan, and uses the word "sex" to mean sexual intercourse (Mrs. J. E. Panton on her 1850s childhood in *Leaves from a Life*, 1908. http://www. victorianlondon.org).

This is why in *The Dark Victorian: Risen*, I have both Art and Jim, two very frank individuals, use the word "sex" to mean "sexual intercourse". Here in *Bones*, Delphia perfectly understands what Jim means when he refers to it ("But really, sex is *sex*. I hope I don't have to explain what I mean by the use of the word. Such are the matters of those with a body."). "Sex" for sexual intercourse may not be very commonly used to mean such in the year 1880, but in this alternate history I'm writing, it renders certain subjects more transparent to discuss, and to give us an understanding of the character of the person using the word.

Slang terms and euphemisms aside, the term "sexual intercourse" meant what it meant since 1798 (via http://www.etymonline.com). The word "sexual", as used by Manon, could also mean pertaining to copulation (1766, also http://www.etymonline.com). She also uses the euphemism "pleasure" to refer to sexual intercourse.

Vivisection:

Here are two sources you may read to get the visuals and historical understanding that I was too wimpy to write about.

Scientific American, "Charles Darwin and the Vivisection Outrage",

By Eric Michael Johnson, October 6, 2011. (http://blogs.scientificamerican.com/primate-diaries/2011/10/06/vivisection-outrage/)

"A History of Antivivisection from the 1800s to the Present: Part I (mid-1800s to 1914)", published in *Veterinary Heritage*, the bulletin of the American Veterinary Medical History Society, May 2008. (http://brebisnoire.wordpress.com/a-history-of-antivivisection-from-the-1800s-to-the-present-part-i-mid-1800s-to-1914/).

❈

SUNDARK

An Elle Black Penny Dread
(Unedited rough cut excerpt)
Chapter One

On a humble street of Camden Town, among the tiny cottages of worker families and their green vegetable gardens, a small row of red brick villas sat, facing one of the few paved streets. Modest in size and only two stories, edged with low iron fences protecting strips of trimmed flower bushes, pensioners and lowly clerks might be found dwelling within. In the small walled gardens in back, herbs, fruit, and vegetables grew, wet laundry swayed in the breeze, and on one plot a chicken coop stood, belonging to retired navy Sergeant Elmer Montague.

Next to Sergeant Montague's home and in the middle of the row, a villa's entryway could be distinguished from the rest by the presence of a marble statue of a seated lady sphinx. Her hair in curls, a shawl draped over her shoulders and leonine back, she smiled with her great paws laid out before her and didn't seem to mind that the top of her bosom peeked above her lace trimmed bodice. Behind her the red front door shone in the afternoon sunlight and its polished black iron doorknocker gleamed.

Mrs. Haggins, an older woman with silvered hair, walked down the sidewalk and turned for the gate leading to the red door. She carried a basket filled with sundries; soap for the dishes and laundry, a bottle of aspirin, a tin of black pepper, a paper bag of peppermints, a ball of white string, a sponge, a box of matches, and a copy of the magazine, *An Englishwoman's Friend*. She opened the door and laid the magazine on the foyer's console. She removed her bonnet and shawl and passed the parlour entrance for the kitchen, where she retrieved an apron and disappeared within.

The parlour was bright with sunlight that shone on the red throw rugs and stuffed chairs. A low fire in the fireplace crackled and warmed the room. Several framed daguerreotypes and tintypes dotted the mantle. One tintype showed a man in a pith helmet, sitting astride a camel before an Egyptian pyramid. In the family portrait by the tintype, the same man stood with a woman, a dark-haired girl, and smaller blond boy.

Next to the portrait was another of a young, proud blond man. A daguerreotype of a dark-haired gentleman with lidded eyes and pencil moustache lay hidden behind a terra-cotta Egyptian sphinx and a sandstone cat sculpture of Bastet. And laid between Bastet and a mantle clock covered in red velvet with gold metal castings was a framed cabinet card. In the photograph, a smiling blonde woman in a light-coloured dress stood arm in arm with a smaller dark-haired woman in black whose eyes were darkened with kohl. The card's bottom border bore, along with the photography studio's name imprinted in gold, the inscribed word: MARRIED

As the mantle clock ticked, a paper rustled in the room. Mrs. Elle Black, aged twenty-four, sat by the windows facing the street and read *The Times*.

Clad in a grey-trimmed black housedress with three-quarter sleeves, white lace cuffs, a white bodice front, black buttons, and white cravat, Elle looked the picture of a proper middle-class English wife except for certain peculiarities. Her hair, perhaps originally auburn, was dyed with henna to a shade of deep red and smelled of cloves, which she had added to the colouring to achieve the red's darkness. Her hazel eyes were lined with kohl and her lips had the light paint of rouge. Whenever deliverymen or postmen came to the house and caught sight of Mrs. Black, they could not help but wonder what manner of man or men such an exotic kept company with.

She had just finished bottling ginger beer she'd been brewing in the basement, dusted all the shelves, spot-cleaned the hallway carpeting, swept all rooms, and run her mechanical carpet sweeper over the rest of the rugs. Though there was always more household maintenance needing attendance, it was that time of afternoon where she liked to take off her apron, apply rouge to her lips, and wait by the parlour window for her spouse, Mrs. Faedra

White-Black.

She turned a page of her paper and read about the latest murder case reported by her favourite journalist, Helia Skycourt, and which involved the Secret Commission agents Artifice, the artificial ghost, and Jim Dastard, the animated skull. Elle had read of their first celebrated case where the duo had rid London of a dangerous re-animationist. The present article affirmed that the pair had also defeated the murderous black arts surgeon known as the Bone Stealer. Elle found Artifice being both Quakeress and a strongwoman a queer and exciting combination.

"And she's an artificial ghost," Elle said aloud, delighting in the description.

She studied the illustration of Artifice fighting zombi men in a hospital room and wondered if she and Artifice would ever meet. Faedra said the agent was staying at the Vesta, an exclusive club discreetly located in Whitechapel and which catered to those who favoured the company of their own sex. Faedra passed the club during her work as a buildings rent collector, her tenants located in the same warren. Though it was a club she and Faedra would love to patronise (as long as it wasn't terribly deviant), a membership seemed extravagant. But the club held occasional ticketed events that they could afford and thus attend. Elle would like, if she'd courage enough, to then ask Artifice for her autograph.

Elle clipped the Bone Stealer case out of the paper and arranged it in her scrapbook.

She heard Faedra and Mrs. Haggins speaking in the foyer and realised that her spouse had passed by the window while she had been busy pasting. She set her scrapbook aside and rose to greet Faedra at the parlour's entrance.

"You are the sweetest!" Faedra said after Elle's kiss in greeting. Being partly American, her British accent had an inflection. Her blue eyes sparkled as Elle retrieved her handkerchief from her sleeve to wipe Faedra's mouth of the rouge her own lips had left there. "Now what have I done to merit such affection?"

"By looking beautiful, Faedy," Elle said.

She loved when Faedra returned from work. Though Faedra

laboured among the poor, resolving their tenant squabbles and investigating those who needed housing, she liked to dress prettily and did not seek to diminish colours or style like fellow female philanthropists did in order to look charitable and demure. Right then she was in a splendid blue dress that was darker than her own blue eyes. The outfit was burgundy-striped with black velvet lapels and collar and with woven burgundy buttons running down the bodice front. Atop her blonde hair, she wore a cavalier hat that was black with a silver round medallion in the hatband's front and a fluffy arcing plume at the side. Faedra laid the magazine *The Englishwoman's Friend* on the side table, removed the long silver hatpin from her hat, and set it and her chapeau beside the magazine.

"Yet I look beautiful everyday," Faedra pouted as she pulled off her kid gloves. "Perhaps you are placating me in advance for something you've a notion for, Elle."

"Perhaps I am," Elle said with a smile, and returned to her seat by the window. She picked up a letter. "A matter has been brought to my attention which you may agree I should apply my talents to, Faedy. Due to the urgency of the request, we should expect our letter-writer, a Miss Josefina Dufish, to visit today."

"And what matter is this?" Faedra said, approaching Elle. "How odd that she should come so quickly without an acknowledgement first from us."

"Well, though I take no fee for my services, it is still a service. No different from the demands of the tenants who've need of your attentions, whether you've time to listen to them or not. First, tell me how your week will be, dear? I know much is going on."

Faedra sat in the armchair across from the window and leaned back with a sigh.

"Such a day, Elle! I have not one but three women accusing their husbands of physical abuse! I also have two families behind on payment and two more to investigate before I allow them rooms in the buildings. There's a plumbing matter, and a roof matter, as an artist is complaining of leaks into his garret. When it has not even rained, of course. And I've a woman accusing another of stealing a chicken."

"Oh, dearest! It sounds like a very busy week for you. I am so glad these workwomen respect you. The other rent collectors are spinsters who don't understand the troubles of these married women and therefore give little value to their opinions."

"Well I try to listen," Faedra said. "As father was poor himself before he became rich with his importing business. I wish my brothers had his passion. But the women do like it that I'm married. Had we children, Elle, they would respect me even more! Now. What of this letter, darling? And when you tell it to me, sit on my lap."

"You are a silly goose," Elle said, rising to oblige Faedra's request.

After she was seated on Faedra's lap, she read the letter aloud.

"Dear Mrs. Black and Mrs. White-Black,

"It is with great urgency that I write you, for there is no one else or any authority I can turn to. My name is Josefina Dufish and I work as secretary to Mr. Hardwick, the owner of Sundark Hotel, located in Chiselhurst. The hotel is the reason why I need your help.

"If you are unfamiliar with the Sundark, I will explain. Forty years ago, an illusionist built Sundark as a gift to his wife, a powerful spiritualist. The house has mechanical abilities. It can rotate and change to fit astronomical and solar predictions. It's said it can rearrange itself to work with the magnetic properties of the earth. But it has a dark history, for houseguests disappeared in it, the illusionist's wife was driven mad somehow, and then the illusionist disappeared.

"I feel that Sundark's dark history has returned. Hotel guests are now vanishing, and they are doing so, faster than before."

"Faster than—well, their disappearance is easy to explain, Elle, they didn't want to pay the bill!" Faedra said.

"It appears so, doesn't it?" Elle said. "Yet she goes on to say that the house has an old reputation for queer happenings, that here and there a guest might vanish. She believes that history was concocted just to make the Sundark more notorious.

However, the more recent disappearances seem different, perhaps caused by malevolent spirits, and she fears for herself and the guests. Thus, she must visit us immediately."

"I see. She has invited you to stay at this Sundark, hasn't she?" Faedra said, taking the letter to look at it. "No wonder you welcomed me with a kiss."

"But I kiss you when you come home everyday, Faedy."

"Today you were such an eager puppy," Faedra said, smiling. "Oh! Up with you! My leg's asleep."

Elle rose and Faedra did as well. Elle returned to her seat and picked up her scrapbook as Faedra paced, pondering the letter.

"With all my responsibilities this week, I can't accompany you," she said. "But you're not off to this queer hotel, just yet. After we hear more about this business, we shall see. Sundark! I can't say I've heard or read of it, but I've not lived here that many years. What about you, Elle?"

"I haven't, Faedy. But then I grew up mostly in the country and abroad."

"Well. It is Chiselhurst. It would be good for you to go, you've been an utter hermit, dear."

"It is a worthy reason to leave the house, I suppose," Elle said, smiling.

Faedra huffed. Elle looked at her curiously as Faedra dropped the letter near her and turned for the fireplace.

"Seeing your dead husband walking about Regent St. last week has driven you into hiding," she said. "I know you'd rather avoid another experience of his phantom, but if he really were that, wouldn't he have appeared to you in our home, by now?"

"I suppose," Elle murmured, looking down at her scrapbook. "And I understand that you're cross because I haven't accompanied you out since my encounter."

"Oh, Elle! I don't mean to make light of your experience, dear."

Elle watched Faedra pick up the daguerreotype of the dark-haired man. He was elegantly dressed, slim, tall, broad of shoulders, with black wavy hair. His complexion was dark, like one deeply tanned, and his lidded eyes beneath his arched dark brows had a slight slant, lending his gaze a feline air.

"I've just never been more annoyed at your first spouse than now," she said.

"Oh, Faedy," Elle said.

"Are you certain what you saw was him?" Faedra demanded. "Because I must wonder how he raised himself from the dead!"

"It was no other, Faedy, he was a singular man. That is why I'm certain he was a phantom. Only His Royal Highness' Secret Commission may resurrect the dead, so it can't be an easy feat. And really, why raise Valentin? He was a mere rake, though I loved him."

"Whether ghost or man, he is still a failure!" Faedra said. "For he had no recollection to come for you."

Elle rose and quickly joined Faedra by the mantle. She hugged her.

"Please don't fret," Elle said.

"It can't be helped. Had he lived I would have been life-friend to you only, and not have all of you, as I do now."

Elle held Faedra's face and kissed her.

When their lips parted, Faedra was smiling. Elle dabbed Faedra's mouth with her handkerchief. She looked at the daguerreotype in Faedra's hands.

"In this supernatural work we do," Elle said pensively. "We've encountered too many people who see what they wish to see."

"Yes. Those manifestations, originating from our fervent minds or some lingering energy, which you call phantoms and the Society for Psychical Research calls 'crisis apparitions'. But Elle, after all these years, now you need to see Valentin again?"

Elle took the daguerreotype and placed it back on the mantle.

"I don't believe I do," she said. "But my eyes have spoken otherwise."

"Mrs. Black, Mrs. White-Black," Mrs. Haggins called from the parlour door.

"Yes, Mrs. Haggins?" Elle and Faedra answered in unison.

"There's a visitor here to see you, a Miss Josefina Dufish, ma'ams," Mrs. Haggins said, stepping into the parlour to hand

Faedra a card.

"'Du*fish*'!" a female voice with a Caribbean accent called behind her.

"Doo-*feesh*," Mrs. Haggins said sourly.

A petite African-Jamaican woman entered, curvaceous of figure and wearing a black and white striped dress and a sloped, silver-buckled black hat with white feathers. She carried a small, black and white striped parasol and declined Mrs. Haggins' offer to take it from her. Elle thought Josefina quite young, but as Elle was a young woman herself, she knew she might be mistaken about her potential client's youth. Josefina firmly shook both Faedra and Elle's hands and at their invitation sat in a chair with its back to the fireplace.

Elle moved her scrapbook and supplies out of the way, set her chair to face the room and sat. Faedra took the armchair across from Josefina and Elle. In this way, they formed a triangle around the parlour's turtle top table. With Josefina clearly lit by the window, Elle could contemplate Josefina's figure should anything uncanny occur.

"Mrs. Black, Mrs. White-Black, thank you for receiving me," Josefina said.

End excerpt.

About The Author

Elizabeth Watasin is the acclaimed author of the Gothic steampunk novel *The Dark Victorian: RISEN* and the creator/artist of the indie comics series *Charm School*. She has worked as an animation artist on thirteen Disney feature films, including *Beauty and the Beast*, *Aladdin*, *The Lion King*, and *The Princess and the Frog*, and has written for *Disney Adventures* magazine. She lives in Los Angeles with her black cat named Draw, busy bringing readers uncanny heroines in shilling shockers and adventuress tales.

Follow the news of her latest projects at A-Girl Studio.
www.a-girlstudio.com
www.facebook.com/ElizabethWatasinX
twitter.com/ewatasin
http://www.goodreads.com/author/show/202881.Elizabeth_Watasin

Look for Elizabeth's third gothic tale in The Dark Victorian series:
EVERLIFE.
And get ready for her Elle Black penny dread, SUNDARK.

KEEP CALM

GHOST
AND
SKULL

ARE
HERE

Made in the USA
Charleston, SC
03 March 2013